GAMES MASTER'S GUIDE

501

UNIQUE NON-PLAYER CHARACTERS

FROM BARDS TO BARMAIDS, MAGES, MERCHANTS AND MORE

*"Adventurer bold, if you're impressed,
Please leave a five-star review, no less!
On Amazon's page, your praise will soar,
To help this bard craft stories more!"*
– Finn Dustwhistle, Bard of the Open Road

Copyright © [2025] by [S J Arcane]
All rights reserved.
No portion of this book may be reproduced in any form without written permission from the publisher or author, except as permitted by U.S. copyright law.

Greetings and Salutations, Intrepid Games Master!

Within these hallowed pages rests a tome unlike any other, a book forged in the fires of creativity and imagination—the Book of 501 Non-Playable Characters.

We extend our deepest gratitude for choosing this indispensable companion, a guide that will lead you, the Games Master, through the shadowed corners of countless realms and into encounters yet untold.

This book is not a mere compilation of names and faces—it is a wellspring of inspiration, a key to the myriad stories that await discovery within your campaign. Each character, from acolyte to wizard, breathes life into the world you weave, poised to become an ally, a foe, or an enigma in your players' journey.

How to Use this Tome:
When the time comes to summon a new figure into your tale, do not simply turn the pages—let the dice be your guide.

1. **Choose Your Path:** Decide what manner of NPC your story requires. Be it a humble acolyte or a powerful wizard, the choice lies with you.
2. **Call Upon the Fates:** Cast your die and trust the roll to decide which soul shall step forth. For sections of 10 characters, the d10 shall serve you well. For those with 20, the d20 holds sway. Let the number revealed by the die guide you to the chosen one's place in these pages.
3. **Unveil the Character:** Once the die has spoken, turn to the character whose number aligns with your roll. They stand ready to be shaped by your voice and brought to life within the tale you spin.

Example of Fortune's Favor: Should your quest call for a wizard, let the d15 clatter across your table. A roll of 10 will summon forth the Tenth wizard from the depths of this tome. Their story, their motivations, now rest in your hands, awaiting the moment of their fateful introduction.

But do not be bound by these words alone. Each NPC, though written, remains unfinished—an empty vessel awaiting your hand to fill them with purpose and meaning. Twist their backstories, mold their destinies, until they fit seamlessly into the world you have crafted. Use these characters not just as bystanders but as vibrant threads in the tapestry of your campaign. Allies, foes, strangers, or guides—let them shape the fate of your adventurers, sparking joy, conflict, or intrigue wherever the story takes them.

Final Words of Wisdom: Remember, Games Master, the true magic lies not within these pages or even within the dice you roll—but in your boundless imagination. This book merely opens the door to possibility. Step through it, and let the adventure unfold.
Your world awaits, teeming with life, mystery, and wonder. Embrace the unknown, summon these characters when the moment is right, and may your stories echo through the ages.
Happy gaming, and may your legends be immortal!

> "Heed this: not all who smile are friends, and not all shadows hide foes. Trust your instincts, for they are often wiser than you know."
>
> – Kael Stormrider, Songsmith of the Tempest

Now Bring your NPC's to Life with Traits & Roles

Ah, adventurer! Gather 'round and let me explain the mystical art of creating memorable characters for your tales. With but a simple roll of the dice, the very essence of a non-player character can spring forth, fully formed and brimming with life. Here's how to harness this powerful tool:

Step 1: Discover the NPC's Defining Trait

First, take your trusty twenty-sided die (d20) and roll it. The result reveals a quirk, fear, motivation, or flaw that shapes the NPC's very soul. It may be as simple as a love for shiny trinkets… or as dark as guilt over a terrible mistake.

Step 2: Determine Their Role in the Story

Now, roll the d20 again to unveil how this character interacts with the heroes of your tale. Are they a steadfast ally, a reluctant informant, or perhaps even a hidden threat? Fate decides their purpose—or, if it suits your tale better, choose the role that will weave most naturally into your story.

An Example in Action

You roll a 7 for the NPC's defining trait: They carry a grudge against a specific organization.
Next, you roll a 13 for their role: Quest-Giver.

The NPC: A surly blacksmith whose shop was ruined by a guild of thieves. They offer the adventurers a quest to track down these brigands and retrieve stolen goods—but is revenge their true goal?

With just two rolls of the dice, you breathe life into an ordinary townsperson, transforming them into a character brimming with potential! Whether they aid the party, hinder them, or simply observe, your tale will be richer for it.

Now, adventurer, go forth and let the dice guide your hand!

NPC Traits & Roles

Step 1: NPC Traits Table

Roll a d20 to determine the NPC's defining quirk, fear, motivation, or flaw.

D20	Quirks/Fears/Motivations/Flaws	D20	Quirks/Fears/Motivations/Flaws
1	Compulsively collects small, shiny objects.	11	Chronic liar, even when it serves no purpose.
2	Afraid of the dark, always carries a lantern.	12	Hopes to leave a lasting legacy, no matter the cost.
3	Desperately seeks approval from authority figures.	13	Fears being alone, always seeks companionship.
4	Refuses to eat or drink in front of others.	14	Believes they are destined for greatness, despite evidence to the contrary.
5	Obsessively cleans their surroundings.	15	Secretly yearns for a peaceful life far from their current troubles.
6	Has recurring dreams of a forgotten past.	16	Overly cautious, prepares for every possible outcome.
7	Carries a grudge against a specific organisation.	17	Obsessed with learning a forbidden or lost piece of knowledge.
8	Is an incurable gambler, deeply in debt.	18	Always speaks in riddles or cryptic phrases.
9	Fearful of magic, avoids spellcasters.	19	Haunted by guilt over a past mistake.
10	Motivated by revenge against a specific person or creature.	20	Terrified of a specific creature (e.g., Spiders, Dragons, Wolves).

Step 2: Roll For A Dynamic Interaction

Roll a d20 to decide how the NPC might initially interact with the players

D20	Dynamic Interaction Role
1-4	Ally: Willing to help the party, either for a cause or personal gain.
5-8	Bystander: Neutral and uninvolved unless persuaded or coerced.
9-12	Enemy: Actively opposes the players, either openly or covertly.
13-14	Quest-Giver: Has a task or mission for the players.
15-16	Victim: Needs the players' protection or assistance.
17-18	Informant: Knows useful information but may require persuasion.
19	Hidden threat: Appears friendly but has secret motives.
20	Wildcard: Their role shifts based on the players' actions (roll again or choose).

CONTENTS

Acolytes.................................1
Adventurers..........................7
Assassins.............................13
Bards....................................20
Barmaids.............................27
Beastmasters.....................31
Beggars................................37
Bounty Hunters.................41
Clerics..................................47
Conjurers............................51
Druids..................................55
Enchanters.........................60
Explorers.............................66
Fighters...............................70
Gladiators...........................74
Guards.................................80
Healers................................86
Hunters................................90
Innkeepers.........................94
Knights.................................98
Mage...................................104
Mercenaries.....................110
Merchants........................114

Monks.................................118
Mystics...............................122
Necromancers.................126
Nobles................................132
Paladins.............................136
Pirates................................141
Random City Dwellers........147
Random Slum Dwellers......154
Random Villager Dwellers.161
Rangers..............................168
Rogues................................174
Scouts.................................180
Shaman..............................184
Smiths................................188
Sorcerer.............................192
Spy......................................198
Thief...................................204
Town Crier........................210
Warrior..............................214
Witch..................................218
Witch Hunter...................224
Wizard...............................228

Acolytes

Exploring the concept of an Acolyte reveals a tapestry of mystical and devout possibilities in fantasy realms. The role of an acolyte depends on the prominence of religion, the organization of faith, and the relationship between deities and mortals. In some lands, acolytes may be revered as divine conduits, their prayers and rituals essential to community wellbeing. In others, they might be seen as humble servants, tending to the needs of temples and their followers.

Picture a world where acolytes are more than mere attendants to priests. Some might serve powerful religious orders, practicing rare and potent miracles. Others might wander, spreading their faith, offering blessings, or seeking enlightenment. During times of crisis, acolytes could become key figures, their divine intervention swaying the tides of fate through healing or holy fury.

Arcana
- DC 10: Acolytes trained in the sacred arts are likely to wield a variety of divine spells, capable of healing, protecting, and purifying. Their rituals can mend the wounded, banish curses, and guide the lost, making them invaluable companions in both peace and conflict.
- DC 20: Advanced acolytes may channel even more powerful divine energies, performing miracles that can alter the very fabric of reality. Their prayers can seek visions, call upon divine retribution, or even raise the dead, bending the will of their deity to their needs through devoted service.

History
- DC 10: Throughout history, acolytes have often been the keepers of sacred knowledge and tradition. Their texts and lore preserve the teachings of their faith, chronicling divine intervention and worldly struggles alike. However, interpretations may vary, colored by doctrine and mysticism.
- DC 15: Acolytes have long served as intermediaries between the divine and the mortal. Understanding their past allegiances, the extent of their faith, and the influence of their religious leaders can reveal much about their motivations and potential actions.

Bribery and Influence
An acolyte's willingness to accept favors or perform deeds hinges on a myriad of spiritual and worldly considerations:
- Devotion: The depth of their faith and religious duty
- Goals: Aspirations for spiritual enlightenment or religious ascendancy
- Allegiances: Loyalty to their deity, temple, or religious order
- Local Norms: Cultural attitudes towards faith and clerical influence
- Personal Connections: Bonds with fellow acolytes, priests, and congregants
- Opportunity: The significance of the task to their religious mission
- Safety: The risk involved in deviating from or adhering to their faith
- Witnesses: The presence of other devout followers or possible detractors
- Consequences: The divine and social outcomes of their actions
- Punishments: The repercussions for betrayal, heresy, or misuse of divine power

Acolytes

Armor Class: 12 (Robes)
Hit Points: 27 (5d8)
Speed: 30ft.

STR: 10 (+0) **DEX:** 12 (+1) **CON:** 14 (+2) **INT:** 11 (+0) **WIS:** 16 (+3) **CHAR:** 14 (+2)

Saving Throws: Wisdom +5, Charisma +4

Skills: Insight +5, Religion +2, Medicine +5, Persuasion +4
Senses: passive Perception 13
Languages: Common, Celestial, and one other language of choice
Proficiency Bonus: +2
Challenge: 1/4 (50 xp)

Class Features
- **Spellcasting:** The Acolyte is a spellcaster. Its spellcasting ability is Wisdom (spell save DC 13, +5 to hit with spell attacks).
  - Cantrips: Guidance, Sacred Flame
  - 1st Level Spells (2 slots): Cure Wounds, Bless, Shield of Faith
  - 2nd Level Spells (2 slots): Prayer of Healing, Hold Person
- **Channel Divinity (1/short rest):** The Acolyte can use its Channel Divinity to invoke a powerful ability for support, such as Turn Undead or to restore hit points to a fallen ally.

Actions
- Multi-attack: The Acolyte can make one melee attack and cast a spell in the same turn.
- Mace: Melee Weapon Attack: +2 to hit, reach 5 ft., one target. Hit: 5 (1d6+2) bludgeoning damage.
- Guiding Bolt: Ranged Spell Attack: +5 to hit, range 120 ft., one target. Hit: 13 (3d6) radiant damage, and the next attack roll against the target has advantage.

Bonus Actions
- Healing Word: The Acolyte can cast Healing Word as a bonus action, restoring 1d4 + Wisdom modifier hit points to one creature within 60 feet.

Reactions
- Shield of Faith: The Acolyte can cast the Shield of Faith spell in reaction to an attack against them, granting a +2 bonus to their Armor Class for the duration.

Thalidan Blackrose

"Darkness is the ultimate truth." 1

A devoted acolyte of a shadowy cult, worshiping an ancient and malevolent god of darkness. Cloaked in ceremonial robes etched with ominous runes, he preaches fear and despair, wielding his charisma to manipulate the weak into servitude. Beneath his calm demeanor lies a relentless ambition to unleash his deity's power upon the world, his actions leaving terror in their wake.

For the Insightful

Thalidan has an uncanny ability to instill fear in others and manipulate it to his advantage, bending even the bravest to his will.

Description

A ruggedly handsome man with pale, angular features that radiate both menace and allure. His piercing silver eyes seem to bore into one's soul, and his perpetually calm sneer exudes an air of superiority. He moves with a deliberate grace, each step echoing his calculated intent. When he speaks, his deep, velvety voice carries a hypnotic undertone, entrancing listeners as it chills them.

Wants & Needs

- **Want:** Seeks to bring his dark god into the physical realm, believing it to be the ultimate path to power and enlightenment.
- **Need:** To gather rare and powerful artifacts for his forbidden rituals to fulfill his destiny.

Secret or Obstacle

His soul is eternally bound to his god, and failure to complete his mission condemns him to unending torment in the abyss.

Carrying (Total CP: 32):

- **Shadowfang Dagger (10 points):** A wickedly curved blade that fills its wielder with unholy resolve.
- **Codex of Night's Grasp (15 points):** A tome of forbidden rituals and dark invocations.
- **Vial of Abyssal Ichor (7 points):** A volatile substance used to empower dark rites and curses.

Acolyte Tactics

Acolytes employ their abilities with piety and purpose, using divine spells not only for worship but as tools of influence and protection. In conflict, they may bolster allies through blessings and healing magic, or invoke divine wrath upon their enemies. Their rituals are capable of turning the tide in dire situations, both on the battlefield and within communities. In times of peace, their guidance and blessings can foster unity and bring solace, acting as a spiritual anchor for the faithful.

Acolyte Of Shadows

Nari "Nimble" Nocturne
"Feel the rhythm of the stars." **2**

Brief: Nari is a graceful dancer and an acolyte of a moon deity, her movements reflecting the celestial rhythms of dreams and secrets. Her silver tattoos shimmer like starlight as she protects the vulnerable through her enchanting performances.
Acolyte Type: Acolyte of the Moon
For the Insightful: Nari's connection to the moon grants her a natural ability to detect hidden truths and vulnerabilities in others, revealing what lies beneath their masks.
Description: Nari moves with a fluidity that seems almost otherworldly, her silver tattoos glowing softly under the moonlight. Her dark skin contrasts beautifully with her luminous robes, and her eyes hold the mysteries of the night sky. Her performances, often seen in the quiet hours of the city, carry a calming, protective aura that draws in the lost and downtrodden.
Wants & Needs: Nari dreams of organizing a grand midnight festival to honor her deity, but she needs decorations, performers, and community support to bring it to life.
Secret or Obstacle: A secretive group pursues her, believing her dances unlock forbidden knowledge they wish to exploit.
Carrying (Total CP: 18):
- Silvery moon staff (8 points): A staff that channels the moon's divine energy.
- Book of lunar rituals (5 points): Contains prayers and ceremonial rites.
- Bag of mystical herbs (3 points): Used for purification and enchantment.
- Small silver flute (2 points): Produces melodies that soothe and protect.

Elara Brightwood
"Light guides us all." **3**

Brief: Elara is a beacon of hope, an acolyte of a benevolent deity of healing and light. Her radiant smile and gentle nature inspire others even amidst despair.
Acolyte Type: Acolyte of Light
For the Perceptive: Elara's sharp intuition allows her to detect even the faintest traces of hope or despair in others, guiding her in offering aid where it is most needed.
Description: Elara's flowing white robes reflect her devotion to her deity, and her radiant smile seems to brighten any space she enters. She moves with calm determination, tending to the sick and offering solace to those who have lost hope. Despite her serene demeanor, her own struggles are hidden beneath her unwavering faith.
Wants & Needs: Elara seeks healing supplies and community support to alleviate the suffering of those in the city's slums.
Secret or Obstacle: Elara hides her own chronic illness, fearing it would diminish her ability to help others.
Carrying (Total CP: 20):
- Healing herbs (8 points): Restores vitality to the wounded.
- Holy symbol of light (5 points): A talisman that channels her deity's energy.
- Prayer beads (4 points): Used for rituals and meditation.
- Small vial of blessed water (3 points): Purifies and heals ailments.

Borsk Ironwill
"Strength through faith." **4**

Brief: Borsk is a stalwart champion of a deity of valor, embodying both spiritual and physical strength. His iron resolve makes him a revered leader and an intimidating defender of justice.
Acolyte Type: Acolyte of Strength
For the Athletic: Borsk's formidable physique and disciplined training grant him endurance and strength far beyond most mortals.
Description: Clad in heavy armor adorned with his god's sigils, Borsk stands as a wall of unyielding faith. His steel gaze and booming voice command respect, while his bulging muscles make him a fearsome warrior. Borsk often leads prayers in the temple but never hesitates to defend his flock with mace and shield. Despite his stern exterior, he struggles with self-doubt, fearing failure in the eyes of his deity.
Wants & Needs: Borsk seeks sturdy armor and loyal followers to help him purge the city's slums of corruption.
Secret or Obstacle: Borsk is haunted by a deep fear of failing his god and those who depend on him.
Carrying (Total CP: 30):
- Heavy mace (10 points): A weapon blessed with divine strength.
- Steel shield (8 points): Engraved with protective runes.
- Armor emblazoned with holy symbols (10 points): Provides both defense and divine inspiration.
- Amulet of strength (2 points): Boosts his physical endurance.

Seraphina Dreamweaver *"Embrace the magic within."* 5

Brief: Seraphina is a whimsical acolyte of dreams and magic, her presence as otherworldly as the fantastical tales she weaves. She is both enchanting and enigmatic, a living embodiment of wonder.
Acolyte Type: Acolyte of Dreams
For the Magical: Seraphina can sense and manipulate the magical energies around her, creating subtle, dreamlike effects to beguile or protect.
Description: Seraphina's colorful robes shimmer faintly, like an aurora in motion. Her flowing hair catches the light in ways that seem almost supernatural, and her dreamy gaze often feels like it's fixed on a far-off realm. She speaks in riddles and metaphors, leaving those around her enchanted but puzzled. Her ability to reveal glimpses of unseen magic has earned her admirers and skeptics alike, as her connection to dreams sometimes leaves her detached from reality.
Wants & Needs: Seraphina seeks magical artifacts and a sanctuary where she can safely perform her rituals.
Secret or Obstacle: She struggles to distinguish dreams from reality, which complicates her efforts to interact with the waking world.
Carrying (Total CP: 18):
- Wand of dreams (8 points): Channels illusions and calming magic.
- Book of enchanted stories (5 points): Contains tales imbued with subtle magical power.
- Pouch of stardust (3 points): Used to amplify her dreamlike spells.
- Crystal ball (2 points): Reveals fragmented visions of possible futures.

Felix "Fox" Foxglove *"Luck favors the bold."* 6

Brief: Felix is a sly and quick-witted acolyte of a trickster god of luck and mischief. With his flamboyant charm and cunning, he lives for excitement and daring escapades.
Acolyte Type: Acolyte of Luck
For the Perceptive: Felix's sharp instincts allow him to read subtle changes in demeanor or expression, using this to outwit opponents and exploit opportunities.
Description: Felix is a wiry man with sharp features and a perpetual mischievous grin. His colorful attire is flamboyant, designed to draw attention, while his quick hands are just as adept at swiping valuables as they are at rolling loaded dice. Felix's charm and confidence make him a crowd favorite in the slums, but those who know him better regard him with suspicion. Despite his carefree demeanor, Felix is constantly chasing his next gamble, driven by a need to prove himself.
Wants & Needs: Felix craves the thrill of gambling and needs funds and accomplices to fuel his schemes.
Secret or Obstacle: Felix is acutely aware of his precarious position—his luck is finite, and failure is just one misstep away.
Carrying (Total CP: 16):
- Set of loaded dice (4 points): Ensures the odds are always in his favor.
- Lockpicking kit (5 points): A professional set for breaking into even the most secure places.
- Deck of marked cards (4 points): Ideal for rigging games of chance.
- Lucky rabbit's foot (3 points): A charm said to boost his luck.

Morgana Nightshade *"Knowledge is the real power."* 7

Brief: Morgana is a stern acolyte of a god of knowledge, whose pursuit of ancient secrets has made her both feared and respected.
Acolyte Type: Acolyte of Knowledge
For the Insightful: Morgana's deep understanding of arcane laws enables her to foresee events, giving her a strategic edge.
Description: Tall and imposing, Morgana wears flowing black robes etched with arcane symbols. Her piercing eyes seem to scrutinize everyone she meets, as if weighing their worth. A no-nonsense demeanor surrounds her like a shroud, and her words carry the weight of intellect and authority. Morgana spends her days pouring over ancient texts and uncovering forgotten truths, but her relentless pursuit of knowledge has led her down dangerous paths. Her willingness to dabble in forbidden magic has strained her relationship with her own order, though she views it as a necessary risk.
Wants & Needs: Morgana seeks rare tomes and scrolls to aid her research into an ancient relic of great power.
Secret or Obstacle: Her fascination with forbidden knowledge has put her at odds with her temple and could lead to her exile.
Carrying (Total CP: 22):
- Ancient tome of secrets (10 points): Contains powerful spells and forgotten lore.
- Arcane focus (5 points): A tool that channels magical energy.
- Pouch of rare herbs (4 points): Used for spell components and rituals.
- Quill and ink (3 points): Essential for recording her discoveries.

Jasper "Jolly" Green
"Laughter is the best spell." **8**

Brief: Jasper is a rotund and jovial acolyte of a god of mirth and celebration, spreading joy and laughter wherever he goes.
Acolyte Type: Acolyte of Mirth
For the Insightful: Jasper's ability to uplift spirits borders on magical, allowing him to turn despair into hope with a well-timed joke or song.
Description: Jasper's colorful jester-like attire reflects his lighthearted nature. His booming laughter echoes through crowded streets, and his infectious humor can disarm even the most serious of individuals. He wields humor and cheer as weapons against despair, believing that joy is the greatest gift he can offer.
However, Jasper's jovial facade hides a deep sadness from a tragedy in his past. He channels his pain into bringing happiness to others, but his grief occasionally breaks through the surface, leaving him vulnerable.
Wants & Needs: Jasper seeks comedic props and a larger venue to spread his god's message of joy to a wider audience.
Secret or Obstacle: Jasper's inner sorrow often threatens to overwhelm him, challenging his ability to remain a beacon of happiness.
Carrying (Total CP: 15):
- Set of juggling balls (3 points): Used in his comedic performances.
- Tattered joke book (4 points): Filled with his best material.
- Brightly colored lute (6 points): Produces magical melodies that inspire joy.
- Flask of ale (2 points): A personal indulgence for difficult days.

Liora Suncrest
"With faith comes strength." **9**

Brief: Liora is a radiant acolyte of a solar deity, embodying light and perseverance. Her serene presence inspires hope in even the darkest times.
Acolyte Type: Acolyte of the Sun
For the Devout: Liora's unwavering faith allows her to inspire and uplift those around her, instilling courage and determination.
Description: Liora's golden hair shines like sunlight, and her calm, compassionate demeanor makes her a beacon of hope in the city's slums. Her simple robes reflect her humility, while her radiant smile brings comfort to those who have suffered.
Despite her outward strength, Liora is haunted by visions of darkness encroaching upon the city. These premonitions fuel her dedication to her deity but also weigh heavily on her mind.
Wants & Needs: Liora dreams of building a grand temple in the slums to offer sanctuary to the downtrodden. She needs community support and donations to achieve her goal.
Secret or Obstacle: Liora's visions of impending darkness fill her with fear that she may not be able to prevent the catastrophe.
Carrying (Total CP: 18):
- Golden holy symbol (5 points): Channels the healing and protective power of her deity.
- Potion of healing (5 points): Restores vitality to the wounded.
- Pouch of blessed seeds (4 points): Used for rituals of renewal and growth.
- Small prayer book (4 points): Contains her daily devotions and blessings.

Darius "Doom" Voss
"Embrace the inevitable." **10**

Brief: Darius is a somber acolyte of a god of death and decay, helping others come to terms with the end of life. His eerie calm makes him strangely compelling.
Acolyte Type: Acolyte of Death
For the Insightful: Darius's grim understanding of mortality gives him a unique ability to predict future events with unsettling accuracy.
Description: Darius is a gaunt, brooding figure with hollow cheeks and doleful eyes that seem to pierce into the soul. His black cloak hangs heavily on his bony frame, and his whispered words carry a strange, soothing power.
Though his presence is unnerving, Darius brings peace to those nearing the end of their journey, offering solace and acceptance. However, he is haunted by the spirits of those he failed to save, their tormented whispers echoing in his dreams.
Wants & Needs: Darius seeks ancient texts and artifacts to deepen his understanding of the afterlife and the mysteries of death.
Secret or Obstacle: He is haunted nightly by the spirits of the dead, who remind him of his failures.
Carrying (Total CP: 21):
- Obsidian ceremonial dagger (7 points): Used in death rituals.
- Scrolls of death rituals (8 points): Contain prayers and incantations for guiding souls.
- Vial of graveyard soil (4 points): Amplifies necromantic magic.
- Worn black cloak (2 points): A symbol of his devotion to his deity.

Adventurers

The role of an adventurer depends on the world's dangers, the allure of the unknown, and the socioeconomic demands. In certain lands, adventurers may be seen as heroes and champions, their exploits celebrated in song and story. Whereas, in others, they might be viewed as reckless mercenaries or treasure-seeking rogues, living on the edge of society.

Imagine a world where adventurers are more than mere warriors or mages. Some might serve noble causes, protecting the realm from ancient evils. Others might pursue personal quests, seeking glory, riches, or vengeance. During turbulent times, adventurers could become pivotal players, their actions influencing the fate of nations and the balance of power.

Arcana
- **DC 10:** Any seasoned adventurer is likely to have encountered and utilized a variety of arcane and divine spells. From elemental magic to healing rituals, their versatility in spellcraft allows them to tackle diverse challenges, whether in battle or exploration.
- **DC 20:** Experienced adventurers often possess powerful enchantments and rare artifacts, lending them abilities that border on the legendary. Understanding the intricate lore of such items and spells can reveal hidden strengths and vulnerabilities.

History
- **DC 10:** Adventurers have historically been trailblazers and legends, their deeds chronicled in tales and histories. Their battles against monsters, forays into ancient ruins, and discoveries of lost secrets form the backbone of many a bard's repertoire.

- **DC 15:** The true motivations of adventurers are as varied as their number. What drives them, be it personal vendetta, unquenchable curiosity, or a sense of justice, can often be gleaned through studying their past exploits and alliances.

Bribery and Influence
An adventurer's response to offers of favor, alliance, or bribery is shaped by a web of personal and situational factors:
- **Motivation:** Their primary drive, whether gold, glory, or altruism
- **Compensation:** The riches or rewards promised
- **Goals:** Long-term aspirations or immediate needs
- **Allegiances:** Loyalty to their party, patrons, or personal code
- **Local Norms:** The cultural attitude towards adventurers and mercenaries
- **Personal Connections:** Bonds with fellow adventurers and NPCs
- **Opportunity:** The strategic value of the offer in relation to their current mission
- **Safety:** The risk involved in accepting or declining the offer
- **Witnesses:** The presence of party members or other influential figures
- **Consequences:** The potential impact on their reputation and future prospects
- **Punishments:** Possible repercussions from failure, betrayal, or honor-bound oaths

Adventurers

Armor Class: 15 (Leather Armor)
Hit Points: 45 (6d10)
Speed: 30ft.

STR: 14 (+2) **DEX:** 16 (+3) **CON:** 14 (+2) **INT:** 10 (+0) **WIS:** 12 (+1) **CHAR:** 13 (+1)

Saving Throws: Strength +4, Dexterity +5

Skills: Acrobatics +5, Athletics +4, Survival +3, Persuasion +3
Senses: passive Perception 11
Languages: Common, Elvish, and one other language of choice
Proficiency Bonus: +2
Challenge: 1 (200 xp)

Class Features
- **Versatile Fighter:** The Adventurer can choose between using melee weapons, ranged weapons, or a mix, enhancing their adaptability in various combat situations.
- **Second Wind (1/short rest):** As a bonus action, the Adventurer can regain 1d10 + class level hit points.
- **Expertise:** Choose one skill; double the proficiency bonus for that skill.

Actions
- **Multi-attack:** The Adventurer can make two attacks with their chosen weapon or make one attack and cast a single spell (if applicable).
- **Shortsword:** Melee Weapon Attack: +5 to hit, reach 5 ft., one target. Hit: 7 (1d6+3) piercing damage.
- **Longbow:** Ranged Weapon Attack: +5 to hit, range 150/600 ft., one target. Hit: 8 (1d8+3) piercing damage.

Bonus Actions
- **Cunning Action:** The Adventurer can use a bonus action to Dash, Disengage, or Hide.

Reactions
- **Uncanny Dodge:** When the Adventurer is hit with an attack, they can use their reaction to halve the damage taken.

Kaelan Ashford

"Every shadow hides a story; I just want to write mine."

A strikingly handsome human rogue with an air of mystery, Kaelan navigates treacherous world between bounty hunters and hidden secrets.

For the Insightful: Possesses a keen understanding of human nature, allowing him to manipulate situations to his advantage and predict others' actions.

Brief: Kaelan stands tall at 6 feet with tousled raven-black hair that frames his chiseled face. His piercing blue eyes hold a depth of experience, hinting at both charm and concealed pain. He dresses in fitted dark clothing that allows for fluid movement, with a subtle flair that showcases his style. An easy smile often graces his lips, but the occasional shadow of doubt flickers across his expression.

Wants & Needs: To locate a legendary artifact rumored to have a substantial payout, sufficient to settle his debts and secure his freedom from relentless pursuers.

Secret Or Obstacle: Kaelan's past includes a botched heist involving a powerful crime lord, leaving him with a bounty on his head. He struggles with his reputation and fears the consequences of returning to the life of crime.

Carrying: ((Total CP: 30)
Stiletto Dagger (10 points)
Map of Hidden Treasures (8 points)
Cloak of Invisibility (7 points)
Portion of Healing Elixirs (5 points)

Adventurer Tactics

Adventurers employ a blend of strategy and skill, using their diverse abilities to overcome obstacles and enemies. In combat, they may form tactical groups, each member contributing their unique expertise—be it as a frontline fighter, a spellcasting support, or a stealthy scout. Their adaptability and resourcefulness often mean they can turn even the direst situations to their advantage. Outside of combat, their skills in negotiation, trap detection, and survival strategies make them invaluable in any quest.

Treasure seeker & Rogue

Roran Stonebreaker
"Strength is forged in the fires of adversity." **2**

Brief: A resolute dwarf fighter with a heart as unyielding as stone, Roran fights for glory and honor, driven by the desire to restore his family's name.
Vocation: Mercenary & Bounty Hunter
For the Athletic: Roran's unparalleled resilience enables him to endure both physical and emotional challenges that would break most warriors.
Description: Standing at a solid 4'8", with a thick braided beard and deep-set brown eyes, Roran embodies the unwavering strength of his clan. His heavy armor, adorned with the crest of his ancestors, exudes authority. Roran speaks with a deep, commanding voice, carrying an aura of honor and duty.
Wants & Needs: Roran seeks a legendary artifact lost in battle to restore his family's honor.
Secret or Obstacle: He harbors guilt over a failed mission that cost his brother's life, a burden he silently bears.
Carrying (Total CP: 32):
- Battle Axe (15 points): Forged from the finest steel, balanced for devastating strikes.
- Shield of the Ancients (10 points): A relic imbued with protective enchantments.
- Healing Potions (5 points): Provides quick recovery in combat.
- Dwarven Warhammer (2 points): A backup weapon for close encounters.

Sylas Nightshade
"Shadows can be your ally or your enemy. Choose wisely." **3**

Brief: Sylas is a stealthy half-elf rogue whose charm and quick wit make him a valuable ally—or a dangerous adversary—in the shadows.
Vocation: Thief & Information Broker
For the Perceptive: Sylas reads body language with uncanny precision, allowing him to anticipate intentions and movements before they happen.
Description: Sylas's tousled black hair and piercing green eyes give him an air of mystery. Clad in dark leathers, he blends seamlessly into the shadows, striking a balance between stealth and agility. Though aloof, his sharp tongue and charm make him difficult to resist.
Wants & Needs: He seeks to reclaim a stolen family heirloom while struggling to balance honor with his rogue lifestyle.
Secret or Obstacle: Sylas is hunted by debt collectors after a failed heist left him in their crosshairs.
Carrying (Total CP: 29):
- Dagger of Invisibility (12 points): A blade that grants brief invisibility to its wielder.
- Lockpicking Set (6 points): Essential for disabling traps and opening doors.
- Cloak of Shadows (8 points): Conceals the wearer in low light.
- Thieves' Tools (3 points): A compact kit for bypassing locks and mechanisms.

Elara Sunwhisper
"With every dawn comes a new story to be told." **4**

Brief: A compassionate and wise human cleric, Elara spreads kindness and healing, serving as a beacon of hope to the downtrodden.
Vocation: Healer & Spiritual Guide
For the Insightful: Elara possesses an innate ability to sense others' emotional and physical pain, offering guidance and solace where it is needed most.
Description: Elara's flowing blonde hair and gentle blue eyes radiate peace. Draped in light robes adorned with holy symbols, she brings calm to those in turmoil. Her soothing voice and healing touch make her indispensable to those suffering in the wake of chaos.
Wants & Needs: She seeks to cure a spreading plague threatening her village, requiring supplies and allies to assist her mission.
Secret or Obstacle: Elara conceals a past as a member of a forbidden sect, fearing ostracization if her history is revealed.
Carrying (Total CP: 31):
- Divine Focus (10 points): Amplifies her healing magic.
- Healing Herbs (8 points): Used in potent restorative remedies.
- Holy Symbol (6 points): Channels divine energy during rituals.
- Grimoire of Forgotten Prayers (7 points): Contains rare and powerful invocations.

Thalia Quickfoot *"Life is a dance; I just need the right rhythm."* 5

Brief: Thalia, a charming bard, travels the world collecting tales and songs, using her quick wit and talent to navigate even the stickiest of situations.
Vocation: Adventurer & Entertainer
For the Perceptive: Thalia's charisma allows her to read the mood of any crowd, adapting her approach to charm and diffuse tension effortlessly.
Description: Petite and lively, with curly auburn hair and hazel eyes, Thalia's cheerful laugh and colorful outfits brighten any room. Her enchanted lute and knack for storytelling have earned her a beloved reputation, though she harbors insecurities about her talent.
Wants & Needs:
Thalia dreams of fame as a legendary bard, seeking stories and songs from every corner of the land.
Secret or Obstacle: Her outgoing nature hides a deep fear of failure and self-doubt about her abilities.
Carrying (Total CP: 27):
- Enchanted Lute (10 points): Produces music that inspires and enchants.
- Journal of Stories (8 points): A collection of tales from her travels.
- Fiddle of Joy (6 points): Brings laughter and lightheartedness to any group.
- Collection of Trinkets (3 points): Keepsakes gathered from her adventures.

Galvin Ironfist *"Let the enemy break against my shield; I will hold my ground."* 6

Brief: A steadfast paladin, Galvin defends the innocent and upholds justice, embodying the righteousness of his order.
Vocation: Protector of the Innocent
For the Perceptive: Galvin's presence inspires courage in his allies while intimidating enemies into submission.
Description: Galvin's broad shoulders and gleaming plate armor exude authority. His neatly trimmed beard and piercing blue eyes add to his commanding presence. His holy sword and shield stand as symbols of his unwavering devotion to protecting the weak.
Wants & Needs: Galvin seeks to restore his shattered order's honor by defeating an encroaching evil.
Secret or Obstacle: He struggles with betrayal by his former comrades, leaving him mistrustful and wary.
Carrying (Total CP: 34):
- Divine Sword (15 points): A blade imbued with divine energy.
- Shield of Valor (10 points): Bears the crest of his order, providing unmatched defense.
- Holy Tome (5 points): Contains scriptures of his deity.
- Healing Potions (4 points): Restores vitality in times of need.

Kaelara Mistblade *"The truth is like the fog; it conceals until the sun rises."* 7

Brief: A mysterious elven ranger, Kaelara thrives in the wilderness, safeguarding the natural world from encroaching dangers.
Vocation: Explorer & Protector of Nature
For the Insightful: Kaelara has acute instincts for survival and navigation, making her a trusted guide through uncharted lands.
Description: Tall and graceful, Kaelara's silver hair flows like moonlight, and her piercing violet eyes hold a calm wisdom. She dresses in subtle hues that blend seamlessly with the forest, her movements quiet yet deliberate. Her ethereal presence earns admiration from adventurers and creatures alike, though she carries the weight of protecting her homeland after witnessing its devastation.
Wants & Needs: Kaelara seeks to find the lost grove of her ancestors while working to safeguard her homeland from threats.
Secret or Obstacle: Kaelara fears she may fail to protect her homeland from future devastation, a fear that drives her tireless efforts.
Carrying (Total CP: 28):
- Longbow of the Wilds (12 points): Crafted from enchanted wood, perfect for long-range precision.
- Elven Dagger (5 points): A finely honed blade for close encounters.
- Cloak of the Forest (6 points): Provides stealth and camouflage in natural settings.
- Herbalism Kit (5 points): Essential for creating salves and healing remedies.

Dorian Runehand   *"Wisdom is the greatest weapon; knowledge, the sharpest blade."* 8

Brief: Dorian is a sagacious wizard driven by an insatiable thirst for uncovering ancient secrets and unlocking the mysteries of the arcane.
Vocation: Researcher & Spellcaster
For the Insightful: Dorian can decipher ancient texts and runes faster than most scholars, making him a valuable asset in tactical planning.
Description: Middle-aged with thinning hair and round glasses perched on his nose, Dorian exudes an air of authority. His robes, adorned with glowing arcane symbols, reflect his deep commitment to mastering magic. Despite his composed exterior, he is burdened by the consequences of a spellcasting mishap that nearly destroyed him.
Wants & Needs: Dorian seeks to unlock the secrets of ancient magic while resisting the temptation to let his knowledge consume him.
Secret or Obstacle: Dorian hides his fear of failure stemming from a catastrophic experiment that shook his confidence.
Carrying (Total CP: 31):
- Arcane Staff (12 points): Channels immense magical power.
- Grimoire of Old Magic (10 points): Contains spells of ancient origin.
- Crystal Focus (4 points): Amplifies his magical abilities.
- Scrolls of Wisdom (5 points): Provide valuable insights and tactical guidance.

Jaxine Wildbane   *"No foe is too great; no challenge too daunting."* 9

Brief: Jaxine is a fierce and skilled barbarian whose indomitable spirit and combat prowess inspire fear and respect among her allies and enemies.
Vocation: Wanderer & Champion
For the Perceptive: Jaxine's relentless drive and fearlessness push her companions to overcome their own limits in battle.
Description: A towering figure with wild, braided hair and fierce blue eyes, Jaxine's presence is as commanding as her battle cries. Scars crisscross her muscular frame, each one a testament to her victories. She wears armor adorned with trophies of past conquests, and her booming voice rallies those around her. Beneath her warrior's bravado, she struggles with feelings of isolation, fearing emotional connections in a world of constant conflict.
Wants & Needs: Jaxine dreams of uniting rival clans under her banner, seeking allies and challenges to prove her worth.
Secret or Obstacle: Her fear of forming emotional attachments leaves her isolated, though she craves camaraderie.
Carrying (Total CP: 30):
- Great Axe of Fury (15 points): A massive weapon capable of devastating blows.
- Battle Standard (7 points): A banner symbolizing her strength and leadership.
- Healing Salve (5 points): Used for quick recovery during battle.
- Trophy Necklace (3 points): A personal collection of her most significant victories.

Fennor Shadowfang   *"In the shadows, I find my strength."* 10

Brief: Fennor is a cunning and resourceful tabaxi rogue who thrives on stealth and mischief, constantly seeking the thrill of his next score.
Vocation: Adventurer & Treasure Hunter
For the Insightful:
Fennor is an expert at reading paths and routes, making him an exceptional escape artist in tight situations.
Description: With sleek black and gold fur that shimmers in the moonlight, Fennor moves like a whisper in the night. His playful demeanor and quick footwork make him both charming and elusive, often masking the cunning mind beneath. Though he delights in the thrill of the hunt, Fennor hides from a past littered with debts and rivalries, constantly looking over his shoulder.
Wants & Needs: Fennor seeks lost treasures and ancient artifacts while chasing the rush of his next big heist.
Secret or Obstacle: Fennor is pursued by a rival gang demanding repayment for debts accrued during a failed heist.
Carrying (Total CP: 26):
- Twin Daggers (10 points): Light and deadly, perfect for quick strikes.
- Thieves' Kit (7 points): Tools for bypassing traps and locks.
- Cloak of Elusiveness (6 points): Enhances stealth and evasion.
- Lockpicks (3 points): A backup for his intricate toolkit.

Assassins

Assassins are the shadows lurking within the darkness, masters of stealth and deception, whose very presence sends shivers down the spines of their targets. In the realms of fantasy worlds, these enigmatic figures are highly trained in the arts of silence and subterfuge, often employed by powerful factions to carry out clandestine missions. Skilled in the use of poisons, traps, and a variety of weaponry, assassins blend lethal efficiency with an unyielding resolve. Some may work alone, navigating the treacherous underbelly of society, while others operate within a tightly-knit guild, sharing secrets and techniques that can eliminate foes without a trace. With their ability to infiltrate heavily guarded locations and vanish without a sound, assassins are the ultimate tacticians, often walking the fine line between hero and villain.

Despite their deadly expertise, one must approach the subject of assassins with caution. Their reputation precedes them, and many are driven by a strict code that can sometimes be unyieldingly ruthless. Trust is a precious commodity in their world; betrayal can lead to swift repercussions and a life lived in constant paranoia. It's wise to remember that crossing paths with an assassin can lead to dangerous entanglements, as their allegiances are often as changeable as the wind. Engaging them for assistance in a delicate matter may come with unexpected costs, not to mention the possibility of becoming a target yourself if their intentions shift. In the realm of shadows, the light of trust is dim—making negotiations with these masters of the night a gamble best approached with both caution and respect.

Arcana
- **DC 10:** Skilled assassins are likely to use a variety of subterfuge and stealth techniques, employing poison, traps, and magical artifacts to achieve their aims. Their repertoire might include spells that enhance their lethal capabilities or obscure their presence entirely, making them whispers in the night.
- **DC 20:** Master assassins may command powerful illusions or shadow-based magic, allowing them to vanish in plain sight or create diversions that sow confusion. Their ability to manipulate the environment to entrap their targets demonstrates a mastery of dark arts and keen strategic thinking.

History
- **DC 10:** Throughout history, assassins have played pivotal roles in shaping the world's power dynamics. Their deeds are often cloaked in myth and rumor, with tales of great coups and betrayals finding their way into bardic songs and cautionary tales.
- **DC 15:** The motivations of assassins can be as complex as their skills. Understanding their background, the codes they adhere to, and their personal quests often sheds light on their methods and targets.

Assassins

Armor Class: 17 (Studded Leather)
Hit Points: 78 (12d8+24)
Speed: 30ft., 30ft. climb

STR: 12 (+1) **DEX:** 20 (+5) **CON:** 14 (+2) **INT:** 14 (+2) **WIS:** 12 (+1) **CHAR:** 16 (+3)

Saving Throws: Dexterity +9, Intelligence +6, Wisdom +5

Skills: Acrobatics +9, Deception +10, Sleight of Hand +9, Stealth +13, Perception +5
Senses: passive Perception 15
Languages: Common and two other languages of choice
Proficiency Bonus: +4
Challenge: 9 (5,000 xp)

Class Features
- **Evasion:** When the assassin fails a Dexterity saving throw, they take half damage. On a successful save, they take no damage.
- **First Strike:** The assassin has advantage on initiative rolls. When they hit a surprised creature, the target must make a DC 16 Constitution saving throw. On failure, the damage dealt is doubled.

Actions
- Multi attack: The assassin can make two attacks with their short sword.
- Short Sword: Melee Weapon Attack: +9 to hit, reach 5 ft., one target. Hit: 8 (1d6+5) piercing damage.
- Hand Crossbow: Ranged Weapon Attack: +9 to hit, range 30/120 ft., one target. Hit: 10 (1d8+5) piercing damage.

Bonus Actions
- Cunning Action: The assassin can use a bonus action to Dash, Disengage, or Hide.

Reactions
- Uncanny Dodge: When the assassin is hit with an attack, they can use their reaction to halve the damage taken.

Riven Blackthorn *"Silence is the deadliest of weapons."*

Bribery and Influence

An assassin's willingness to engage in bribery or manipulation is contingent upon a network of strategic considerations:

- **Motivation:** Their driving force—be it profit, revenge, or ideological loyalty
- **Compensation:** The monetary or material rewards offered for their allegiance or services
- **Goals:** Long-term objectives that might align with the offer
- **Allegiances:** Loyalty to guilds, patrons, or personal oaths
- **Local Norms:** The cultural perception of assassins and their effectiveness
- **Personal Connections:** Ties with other players in the game, including allies and rivals
- **Opportunity:** The potential gain or loss from accepting the bribe or deal
- **Safety:** The risks of exposure or betrayal involved in the arrangement
- **Witnesses:** The presence of parties who could jeopardize the assassin's anonymity
- **Consequences:** The possible fallout from their actions and how it might affect their standing
- **Punishments:** The repercussions for failing to honor an agreement or for betrayal within their ranks

Assassin Tactics

Assassins employ a lethal blend of strategy and guile, expertly maneuvering through their surroundings to achieve their objectives. They might infiltrate locations unnoticed, using stealth and intelligence to gather information before making their move. In combat, they favor quick, decisive strikes, aiming to incapacitate or eliminate targets before they can react. Their ability to blend in with shadows, create diversions, and vanish after a kill makes them masters of their dark trade.

Riven Blackthorn

"Silence is the deadliest of weapons." **1**

Brief: A calculating half-elf assassin known for eliminating targets with precision, Riven serves a shadowy guild, his motives as enigmatic as his methods.
Vocation: Contract Killer for a Shadowy Guild
For the Perceptive: Riven blends seamlessly into shadows, becoming nearly invisible, and has an uncanny ability to spot vulnerabilities in his surroundings.
Description: Riven stands at 5'10", with sharp features, piercing green eyes, and long black hair tied loosely at the back. His dark leather armor, etched with the symbols of his guild, speaks to his deadly profession. A cold pragmatist, he rarely displays emotion, focusing entirely on his assignments.
Wants & Needs: Riven seeks to rise through the ranks of his guild and earn a powerful magical artifact while exacting vengeance for his family's murder.
Secret or Obstacle: Riven hides his past as a noble, fearing discovery and retaliation from his former life.
Carrying (Total CP: 29):
- Shadow Dagger (10 points): A blade that absorbs light, leaving no trace.
- Cloak of Shadows (7 points): Grants enhanced stealth and movement.
- Lockpicking Tools (5 points): Essential for bypassing barriers.
- Poison Vials (7 points): Potent toxins for silent eliminations.

Zara Nighthawk

"Nightfall carries my name; darkness grants my freedom." **2**

Brief: A cunning tiefling assassin whose fiery charm and silver tongue make her as dangerous in conversation as in combat.
Vocation: Freelance Assassin
For the Insightful: Zara uses her charisma and persuasion to manipulate enemies into becoming unwitting pawns.
Description: With fiery red skin, an athletic build, and long curling horns, Zara cuts a striking figure. She dresses in sleek garments designed for movement, her playful smirk often masking lethal intent. Her vibrant eyes are mesmerizing, concealing her sharp and calculating nature.
Wants & Needs: Zara aims to build her own empire of intrigue and deceit, carving a place for herself among the elite assassins of the underworld.
Secret or Obstacle: Zara struggles to escape her family's infamous criminal reputation while forging her own identity.
Carrying (Total CP: 30):
- Twin Shortswords (12 points): Perfectly balanced for swift strikes.
- Charm Amulet (8 points): Enhances her natural charisma.
- Grappling Hook (5 points): Allows swift escapes.
- Assorted Poison Darts (5 points): Coated with paralyzing toxins.

Korin Quickstrike

"The quicker the blade, the less time for remorse." **3**

Brief: A nimble halfling assassin with unmatched agility, Korin's speed makes him a deadly adversary in close quarters.
Vocation: Street Assassin & Burglar
For the Athletic: Korin boasts extraordinary reflexes, able to dart in and out of danger effortlessly.
Description: Short and wiry, Korin's mischievous hazel eyes and curly brown hair disguise his deadly skillset. He wears light armor that allows for swift movement, his wide grin belying his lethal precision.
Wants & Needs: Korin seeks to establish a reputation in the underworld, earning respect among the larger races.
Secret or Obstacle: Korin was forced into assassination by thugs who kidnapped his twin sister, a fact he hides to protect her.
Carrying (Total CP: 24):
- Dagger of Venom (10 points): Coated in deadly toxin.
- Thieves' Tools (5 points): Essential for bypassing locks.
- Intelligence Scrolls (4 points): Provide tactical insights for missions.
- Set of Smoke Bombs (5 points): Enables quick escapes.

Arathil Silentstep   *"The stillness of the night is the lullaby of death."* 4

Brief: An enigmatic elven assassin who strikes swiftly and silently, Arathil's connection to nature enhances his deadly precision.
Vocation: Protector of Nature, Assassin of Corrupt Nobles
For the Insightful: Arathil's deep understanding of nature allows him to track targets with unmatched efficiency and stealth.
Description: Ethereally beautiful, Arathil's flowing silver hair and sharp cheekbones give him an almost otherworldly presence. He wears intricately crafted leather armor adorned with foliage, blending seamlessly into the wilderness. His calm, deadly focus belies a storm of inner conflict.
Wants & Needs: Arathil seeks to purge corruption from the ruling classes while balancing his morality with his lethal methods.
Secret or Obstacle: He struggles with the morality of using deadly force against those who harm the forest, questioning his path.
Carrying (Total CP: 28):
- Elven Longbow (12 points): Exceptionally accurate at long range.
- Dagger of Silence (8 points): Muffles sound upon contact.
- Herbalism Kit (4 points): Used for crafting healing remedies.
- Camouflage Cloak (4 points): Enhances his stealth in natural environments.

Jarek Bloodthorn   *"Pain is merely the payment for silence.* 5

Brief: A ruthless human assassin, Jarek's brute strength and ferocity make him a terrifying presence in the underworld.
Vocation: Professional Hitman for Hire
For the Athletic: Jarek excels in hand-to-hand combat, with deadly precision even when unarmed.
Description: With a muscular build and scars crisscrossing his body, Jarek's hardened features and piercing grey eyes tell of a violent life. His leather armor is simple but intimidating, adorned with spikes and tools of his trade. Despite his reputation, memories of his kills haunt him in quieter moments.
Wants & Needs: Jarek seeks wealth and power to take control of the local underworld.
Secret or Obstacle: He battles guilt and regret over those he has killed, questioning the morality of his actions.
Carrying (Total CP: 31):
- Bloodstained Blade (15 points): Wielded in countless brutal assassinations.
- Set of Throat-Cutting Daggers (8 points): Lightweight and razor-sharp.
- Grappling Hook (4 points): For swift movement and ambushes.
- Smoke Bombs (4 points): Creates cover for escape or surprise attacks.

Liora Moonshadow   *"The moon is my witness; the night, my ally."* 6

Brief: A graceful half-drow assassin, Liora's agility and stealth make her a phantom of the shadows, feared and revered alike.
Vocation: Drow Underworld Operative
For the Athletic: Liora's exceptional acrobatics allow her to traverse rooftops and ledges with effortless ease.
Description: With striking silver hair and deep purple skin, Liora's piercing violet eyes mesmerize and intimidate. Her form-fitting clothing allows her to melt into the darkness, giving her the advantage of surprise. Despite her prowess, she struggles to reconcile her identity as a half-drow.
Wants & Needs: Liora seeks to establish herself among elite assassins while navigating prejudice from both drow and surface society.
Secret or Obstacle: Liora struggles with her identity as a half-drow, often feeling alienated from both halves of her heritage.
Carrying (Total CP: 27):
- Moonlit Dagger (12 points): Shines faintly, delivering fatal precision.
- Cloak of Invisibility (8 points): Provides unparalleled stealth.
- Thieves' Kit (5 points): Essential for disarming traps.
- Assorted Poison Vials (2 points): A collection of deadly concoctions.

Borin Grimblade   *"Concealed death comes for us all, yet it is I who select the moment."*   7

Brief: A brooding dwarf assassin with a dark past, Borin uses stealth and precision to eliminate his targets without hesitation.
Vocation: Former Soldier Turned Loner Assassin
For the Perceptive: Borin can detect hidden traps and ambushes with unparalleled accuracy, making him an invaluable operative.
Description: With rugged features and a wild beard streaked with iron-gray, Borin's cold, calculating eyes betray years of battle-hardened experience. His muted clothing enhances his stealth, while his grim demeanor makes him an intimidating figure. Borin's guilt over his violent past drives his quest for redemption, though his methods remain brutal.
Wants & Needs: Borin seeks to expose corrupt officials while redeeming himself for past misdeeds.
Secret or Obstacle: He struggles with his violent instincts, questioning whether he truly seeks justice or simply more bloodshed.
Carrying (Total CP: 30):
- Hand Axe of Precision (10 points): A weapon designed for deadly accuracy.
- Hidden Throwing Darts (7 points): Used for silent ranged eliminations.
- Dwarven Lockpicks (5 points): Crafted to bypass even the toughest locks.
- Grappling Hook (8 points): Allows for swift ascents and escapes.

Selene Darkwhisper   *"When death approaches, let your heart be your guide."*   8

Brief: A mysterious gnome assassin with a talent for illusion magic, Selene manipulates perception to mislead and eliminate her foes.
Vocation: Freelance Illusionist & Assassin
For the Insightful: Selene uses illusions to create distractions, misdirecting her enemies before striking from the shadows.
Description: Selene's vibrant blue hair and sparkling green eyes make her appear unassuming, but her playful demeanor hides a lethal edge. Her colorful garments are embroidered with arcane symbols, helping her blend into any crowd while preparing her magical traps. Despite her skill, she hides a fear of being misunderstood in a world that doubts gnome assassins.
Wants & Needs: Selene dreams of crafting a legacy as the most skilled illusionist assassin in her society, showcasing her artistry on a grand stage.
Secret or Obstacle: Selene fears her talents will be exploited or misunderstood, making her reluctant to trust others.
Carrying (Total CP: 26):
- Illusionary Blade (10 points): Creates an illusionary aura, confusing enemies.
- Smoke Bombs (5 points): Perfect for quick escapes.
- Trickster's Toolkit (7 points): Contains items to enhance her illusions.
- Cloak of Disguise (4 points): Allows her to blend seamlessly into her surroundings.

Lyra Rivenheart   *"Trust is a weapon; I rarely wield it."*   9

Brief: A charismatic dragonborn assassin, Lyra commands respect while executing her deadly assignments with precision.
Vocation: Leader of a Rogue Band of Assassins
For the Perceptive: Lyra's commanding presence allows her to manipulate situations, using her charisma to intimidate or inspire.
Description: Tall and imposing, Lyra's emerald green scales shimmer like gemstones, and her piercing yellow eyes hold an unyielding determination. She wears sleek black armor designed for agile combat, enhancing her deadly elegance. Lyra's voice carries authority, but beneath her fearsome exterior lies a burning desire for vengeance against those who betrayed her.
Wants & Needs: Lyra seeks to maintain control of her band of assassins while forging a legendary pact with ancient dragons to elevate her status.
Secret or Obstacle: She is hunted by both former allies and law enforcement after betraying a crime lord.
Carrying (Total CP: 32):
- Serpent's Fang Dagger (12 points): Infused with venom for lethal efficiency.
- Regalia of Command (10 points): Enhances her leadership abilities.
- Dragon Scale Shield (5 points): Provides lightweight yet formidable protection.
- Elixirs of Shadow (5 points): Boost her stealth and agility.

Finnian "Finn" Stormcrow — *"Chaos is a dance; I lead with the sharpest edge."* 10

Brief: A free-spirited half-orc bard and assassin, Finn charms his targets with humor and charm before eliminating them with precision.
Vocation: Bard & Assassin for Hire
For the Insightful: Finn's exceptional skill in manipulation and deception makes him capable of disarming even the most wary opponents.
Description: With sun-kissed skin, a roguish smile, and long hair tied back in a braid, Finn combines charisma with deadly efficiency. His flamboyant attire distracts from his lethal capabilities, allowing him to lure targets into a false sense of security. Finn dreams of blending music and assassination into a single deadly art, though he fears rejection from both worlds.
Wants & Needs: Finn seeks to perfect his dual craft, finding a performance that combines deadly art with captivating music.
Secret or Obstacle: Finn struggles with revealing his dual identity, fearing rejection from both his assassin peers and artistic circles.
Carrying (Total CP: 28):
- Enchanted Rapier (12 points): A weapon that hums with magical energy.
- Lute of Illusions (8 points): Creates hypnotic effects to disorient foes.
- Vials of Lethal Brew (5 points): A potent poison for quick eliminations.
- Mask of Shadow (3 points): Enhances his stealth during missions.

Eldin "The Whisper" Sable — *"Words are powerless; only silence holds real meaning."* 11

Brief: A suave drow assassin whose talent for strategy and stealth makes him a sought-after killer in the underworld.
Vocation: Renowned Assassin Operating in the Drow Underworld
For the Insightful: Eldin plans his assassinations with meticulous precision, executing them flawlessly and leaving no trace behind.
Description: Eldin's pale skin, striking white hair, and piercing red eyes give him an intimidating allure. He moves gracefully in his form-fitting black armor, exuding confidence and menace. Eldin hides a dark family secret that drives his relentless ambition to rise as the most feared assassin in the drow world.
Wants & Needs: Eldin seeks to claim the title of the greatest assassin while unseating the reigning master.
Secret or Obstacle: Eldin's family's past haunts him, fueling his ambition but isolating him from others.
Carrying (Total CP: 29):
- Shadowblade (13 points): A silent weapon with a deadly edge.
- Cloak of Darkness (8 points): Shrouds the wearer in impenetrable shadow.
- Enchanted Bolts (4 points): Deliver precise, magical strikes.
- Smoke Bombs (4 points): Useful for sudden disappearances.

Rokul Firefist — *"Flames cleanse the weak; I wield them to dominate."* 12

Brief: A fire genasi assassin, Rokul wields both fire magic and physical prowess with unmatched ferocity, leaving destruction in his wake.
Vocation: Assassin for a Fiery Cult
For the Perceptive: Rokul uses his precise control over fire to both terrify and incapacitate his enemies, wielding it as both a weapon and an escape tool.
Description: Rokul's molten lava-like skin glows faintly, and his fiery red hair seems to dance like flames. His presence radiates heat, while his enchanted black cloak cools him and amplifies his power. A fierce and imposing figure, Rokul commands respect and fear alike, though his volatile anger often leads him astray.
Wants & Needs: Rokul seeks to eliminate rival factions and unlock the secrets of immortal fire-based magic to dominate the city.
Secret or Obstacle: Rokul struggles with his fiery temper, which alienates allies and drives him into self-destructive rage.
Carrying (Total CP: 35):
- Flame Tongue Dagger (15 points): Ignites with magical fire on command.
- Alchemical Fire Bombs (10 points): Explosive devices for mass destruction.
- Amulet of Flame Control (6 points): Enhances his fire magic precision.
- Infernal Hook (4 points): A brutal weapon for grappling foes.

Bards

Bards are the charming minstrels of the realm, captivating audiences with their vibrant stories, enchanting melodies, and mischievous antics. They thrive in lively taverns and bustling marketplaces, where a foot-tapping tune or a wittily spun tale can turn a dull evening into an unforgettable night. With a lute slung over their shoulder and a quick quip always at the ready, bards have the remarkable ability to lift spirits and sway hearts. Whether they're reciting epic ballads of heroism or retelling the latest gossip with exaggerated flair, these artists blend humor and inspiration, often leaving their listeners in fits of laughter or tears—sometimes both!

One such bard once turned up late to a royal banquet, claiming he had been held up by a "dragon" that turned out to be just a very irate goat! The court erupted in laughter, and from then on, the bard was known as the "Goat Whisperer," a title he wore with pride.

Yet, tread carefully when engaging with a bard, for while they bring joy and merriment, their penchant for mischief can lead to unforeseen consequences! A well-placed jest can easily stir a noble's ire or spark a spontaneous dance-off among their audience—never a good idea if your rival just happens to be a flamboyant orc with a penchant for breakdancing. Moreover, bards often collect stories and secrets like souvenirs, weaving them into their performances. As delightful as their tales may be, remember: do not share private matters with a bard, for the last thing you want is your most embarrassing moment immortalized in a catchy tune that circulates through the tavern circuit! Approach these witty wanderers with caution and be prepared for a lifetime of unforgettable (and possibly embarrassing) ballads sung in your name!

Arcana
- **DC 10:** Any bard learned in the arcane arts will likely have a repertoire of spells that can charm, inspire, and deceive. Their magical performances can mask true intentions, hide information, or sway an audience to their perspective, making them versatile players in any gambit.
- **DC 20:** Advanced bardic magic can unravel the secrets hidden by others. With lore-rich songs and empowered rituals, they can discern truths or enhance their own mystique. The secrets of others, veiled in melodies, can be paramount to those who listen closely and understand the harmonics of ancient magic.

History
- **DC 10:** In many societies, bards are the keepers of history. Their tales carry the weight of ages, preserving the exploits of heroes and the lessons of failures. However, a bard's account may vary; truth is often flavored by the biases and creativity of the teller.
- **DC 15:** Bards have historically been patrons' favorites, rewarded handsomely by nobles or commoners for their art. Understanding a bard's benefactors and past allegiances can reveal much about their motivations and vulnerabilities. Their loyalty is often to the highest bidder or the most compelling cause.

Bards

Armor Class: 15 (Leather Armor)
Hit Points: 40 (8d8)
Speed: 30ft.

STR: 10 (+0) **DEX:** 14 (+2) **CON:** 12 (+1) **INT:** 13 (+1) **WIS:** 12 (+1) **CHAR:** 18 (+4)

Saving Throws: Dexterity +4, Charisma +7

Skills: Acrobatics +4, Performance +7, Persuasion +7, History +4, Insight +4
Senses: passive Perception 14
Languages: Common, Elvish, and two other languages of choice
Proficiency Bonus: +3
Challenge: 5 (1,800 xp)

Class Features
- **Spellcasting:** The Bard is a spellcaster. Its spellcasting ability is Charisma (spell save DC 15, +7 to hit with spell attacks).
  - Cantrips: Vicious Mockery, Minor Illusion
  - 1st Level Spells (4 slots): Cure Wounds, Dissonant Whispers, Faerie Fire, Healing Word
  - 2nd Level Spells (3 slots): Invisibility, Suggestion
  - 3rd Level Spells (3 slots): Hypnotic Pattern, Leomund's Tiny Hut
- **Bardic Inspiration (5/long rest):** As a bonus action, the bard can grant an ally within 60 feet an inspiration die (1d8). The ally can add this die to one ability check, attack roll, or saving throw.

Actions
- Multiattack: The bard can make one weapon attack and cast a spell in the same turn.
- Rapier: Melee Weapon Attack: +6 to hit, reach 5 ft., one target. Hit: 8 (1d8+4) piercing damage.
- Shortbow: Ranged Weapon Attack: +6 to hit, range 80/320 ft., one target. Hit: 7 (1d6+4) piercing damage.

Bonus Actions
- Bardic Inspiration: The bard can use a bonus action to inspire an ally within range, granting them an inspiration die.

Reactions
- Counterspell: The bard can use their reaction to interrupt a spell being cast within 60 feet and potentially negate it, using their spell slots as needed.

Merrick Tunewalker

"The road is my stage; every step unfolds a new rhythm."

Bribery and Influenc

A bard's acceptance of patronage or favor depends on a symphony of factors:

- **Compensation:** Riches, fame, or other forms of payment
- **Goals:** Personal ambitions or quest for knowledge
- **Allegiances:** Loyalties to patrons or causes
- **Local Norms:** The tradition of patronage or patron-client relationships
- **Personal Connections:** Friendships and rivalries within their circles
- **Opportunity:** The importance of the task to their art or reputation
- **Safety:** Risk involved in fulfilling the favor
- **Witnesses:** The visibility of their actions and potential consequences
- **Consequences:** Possible benefits or setbacks from their involvement
- **Punishments:** Cultural repercussions for betrayal or misuse of their talents

Bardic Tactics

Bards deploy their skills with cunning and flair, using performances not merely for entertainment but as strategic tools. In a conflict, they may bolster allies with inspiring anthems or dishearten foes with biting satire. Their use of magical songs can create illusions or compel actions, all while maintaining the guise of a harmless minstrel. In times of peace, a bard's tales can sway public opinion or secure alliances, their influence creeping beyond the notes of their lyre.

Merrick Tunewalker

"The road is my stage; every step unfolds a new rhythm." **1**

Brief: A wanderer with a spirit of adventure, Merrick travels far and wide, weaving the stories of his journeys into his music.
Vocation: Traveler & Chronicler
For the Insightful: Merrick observes the cultures and people he encounters, drawing inspiration for his songs and tales.
Description: Merrick's tousled brown hair and weathered expression give him the look of a well-traveled bard. His patched clothing is adorned with symbols of pathways and songs, and his eyes shine with a lifetime of stories yet to be told.
Wants & Needs: Merrick hopes to create an epic travelogue through song and story, finding solace in the open road.
Secret or Obstacle: He carries the guilt of losing a close friend on a previous journey, a regret that haunts his travels.
Carrying (Total CP: 28):
- Traveler's Lute (12 points): Crafted to endure the rigors of travel while producing sweet melodies.
- Compass of Inspiration (6 points): A magical compass that points toward the next great story.
- Collection of Postcards from Friends (4 points): Sentimental keepsakes from his companions.
- Map of Legendary Routes (6 points): Charts paths known only to seasoned adventurers.

Thorne Trickster

"Life's a game—keep your cards close and your laughter closer." **2**

Brief: A mischievous gnome bard who delights in tricks and clever performances, spreading chaos and joy wherever he goes.
Vocation: Trickster & Entertainer
For the Insightful: Thorne's mastery of sleight of hand and clever jokes make him a social wildcard.
Description: Thorne's untamed hair is adorned with trinkets and charms, and his flamboyant outfit reflects his playful nature. His layered clothing is designed to hide an array of tricks, ready to dazzle or deceive.
Wants & Needs: Thorne dreams of pulling off a legendary prank that will be remembered for generations.
Secret or Obstacle: He secretly fears being exposed as a fraud, a thought that keeps him from trusting others.
Carrying (Total CP: 27):
- Trickster's Deck of Cards (10 points): A magical deck capable of producing illusions.
- Bag of Jokes (5 points): Contains a collection of enchanted quips and gags.
- Musical Wand (6 points): Plays tunes that lighten moods or confuse enemies.
- Gnome's Magical Marbles (6 points): Creates minor explosions or distractions.

Ragnar Stoneheart

"Through music and strength, we shall forge our destiny." **3**

Brief: A stout dwarf bard whose rousing songs and unwavering courage inspire his allies in the direst of battles.
Vocation: Battle Bard & Morale Officer
For the Insightful: Ragnar's strong sense of camaraderie makes him a rallying force in times of need.
Description: Ragnar's braided beard is adorned with metal rings, and he wears heavy leather armor with battle-worn marks. His booming voice can lift even the weariest soldiers, while his resolute demeanor commands respect.
Wants & Needs: Ragnar seeks to protect his clan, lead them to glory, and write an epic that honors their history.
Secret or Obstacle: He struggles with doubts about his leadership abilities amid growing tensions in his clan.
Carrying (Total CP: 32):
- Battle Drum of Rallying (15 points): Produces rhythms that inspire courage and focus.
- War Song Scrolls (8 points): Contains chants of ancient victories.
- Dwarven Heirloom Lute (5 points): A family artifact passed down through generations.
- Blessed Tankard (4 points): Fills with morale-boosting ale.

Fiddle Diddle
"Why be serious when you can laugh over a pint?" **4**

Brief: A jovial half-elf bard who uses humor to connect with his audience, spreading joy wherever he performs.
Vocation: Traveling Entertainer
For the Perceptive: Fiddle has an uncanny ability to find the funny side of even the gravest situations.
Description: Fiddle's bright green eyes sparkle with mischief, and his mismatched clothing jingles with every step. His infectious laughter lights up a room, though his tendency to disappear during tense moments leaves others puzzled.
Wants & Needs: Fiddle wishes to make people laugh and forget their worries, all while secretly searching for his long-lost father.
Secret or Obstacle: He hides his noble lineage, fearing rejection from those who mock his past.
Carrying (Total CP: 25):
- Lute of Laughter (10 points): Produces sounds that force even the grimmest to chuckle.
- Comedic Scrolls (5 points): A collection of funny verses and jokes.
- Mysterious Family Crest (5 points): A reminder of his hidden heritage.
- Jester's Hat (5 points): Symbolizes his lighthearted approach to life.

Lyra Silverstrings
"Life is but a song; let it flow with every note." **5**

Brief: A graceful tiefling bard with melodies so enchanting they soothe hearts and calm chaos.
Vocation: Court Performer & Advisor
For the Perceptive: Lyra's deep emotional awareness allows her to tailor performances to the mood of her audience.
Description: With flowing silver hair and deep blue skin, Lyra often wears robes that shimmer as if caught in a perpetual breeze. Her soft, haunting voice captures even the most resistant listener, offering them a moment of peace.
Wants & Needs: Lyra longs to inspire others through music and dreams of finding the love of a fellow bard she has yet to meet.
Secret or Obstacle: Lyra hides a paralyzing fear of performing in front of large audiences, despite her apparent confidence.
Carrying (Total CP: 22):
- Enchanted Lute (15 points): Produces harmonies that influence emotions.
- Crystal Ampoule for Voice Enhancement (5 points): Amplifies her enchanting voice.
- Silver Hairpin (2 points): A keepsake from her first performance.

Blaze Embernote
"Every fire can be turned into a masterpiece." **6**

Brief: A flamboyant dragonborn bard who captivates audiences with fiery performances, blending music and pyrotechnics.
Vocation: Fire-Dancer & Performer
For the Perceptive: Blaze's mastery of fire displays keeps his audience on the edge of their seats, seamlessly weaving flames into his acts.
Description: Blaze's shimmering red scales and glowing golden eyes are paired with a patched leather jacket lined with flame motifs. His confident grin and dramatic flair have made him a crowd favorite, though his fiery temper often complicates his relationships.
Wants & Needs: Blaze dreams of creating the ultimate fire performance, earning recognition and respect from his guild.
Secret or Obstacle: He struggles to control his fire-breathing talent during moments of heightened emotion, risking disaster.
Carrying (Total CP: 28):
- Fireproof Mandolin (10 points): Built to withstand extreme heat.
- Pack of Flame Charcoal (5 points): Fuel for his fiery displays.
- Pyrotechnics Kit (8 points): A collection of fireworks and flame effects.
- Journal of Past Performances (5 points): Chronicles his evolving acts.

Seraphina Brightheart   *"The heart shines brightest when shared with others."* 7

Brief: An uplifting aarakocra bard, Seraphina's music and empathy bring light and joy to everyone she encounters.
Vocation: Traveler & Healer
For the Insightful: Seraphina has a remarkable ability to sense and lift the emotions of those around her, offering solace and strength.
Description: Seraphina's golden feathers shimmer in the sunlight, and her emerald-green plumage adds a striking contrast. Her melodious voice harmonizes perfectly with her graceful movements, creating a performance that is as much a visual wonder as an auditory delight. Despite her outward confidence, she harbors a deep fear of losing her newfound connections.
Wants & Needs: Seraphina hopes to find a place she can call home while spreading joy and peace through her music.
Secret or Obstacle: She fears abandonment and struggles to let herself fully trust her companions.
Carrying (Total CP: 29):
- Healing Lyre (14 points): Plays melodies that restore health and hope.
- Aarakocra Feather Cloak (7 points): Provides warmth and protection.
- Book of Songs of the Skies (4 points): Contains celestial compositions.
- Wish Stone (4 points): Said to grant small but meaningful wishes.

Caelum Whisperwind   *"Whispers carry power; every note weaves the fabric of fate."* 8

Brief: A mysterious human bard who uses soft melodies and subtle spells to captivate and manipulate his audience.
Vocation: Shadow Bard & Political Advisor
For the Perceptive: Caelum's mastery of persuasion allows him to bend the will of even the most stubborn minds, influencing events from behind the scenes.
Description: Draped in dark, flowing robes that blend into the shadows, Caelum's piercing blue eyes seem to hold a wealth of untold stories. His presence is calm yet commanding, and his soft-spoken words have an almost hypnotic quality. Caelum's secretive past keeps him constantly looking over his shoulder.
Wants & Needs: Caelum seeks validation of his abilities and hopes to uncover secrets that could alter the course of history.
Secret or Obstacle: He fled from a shadowy organization that still hunts him, and he fears being found.
Carrying (Total CP: 26):
- Enchanted Whisper Flute (12 points): Plays melodies that sow confusion or compliance.
- Cloak of Camouflage (8 points): Helps him blend seamlessly into any environment.
- Mysterious Rune Stone (3 points): An artifact with unknown properties.
- Journal of Spells (3 points): Contains subtle enchantments and hidden magic.

Jasmin Moonshadow   *"The night holds secrets; let them sing."* 9

Brief: An enigmatic elf bard, Jasmin's celestial songs transport listeners to realms of wonder and mystery.
Vocation: Mystic Performer & Dreamweaver
For the Insightful: Jasmin's connection to the energies of the moon and stars allows her to unlock hidden emotions and truths through her music.
Description: With alabaster skin and silver-blue hair that shimmers like moonlight, Jasmin is the picture of ethereal beauty. Her robes are adorned with celestial patterns, and her dreamy gaze often seems lost in thought. Despite her talent, she is troubled by the knowledge that her music can influence dreams in ways she does not fully understand.
Wants & Needs: Jasmin seeks to uncover the mysteries of the universe and find the legendary "Song of the Stars."
Secret or Obstacle: She fears the power of her songs, which can manipulate dreams, leading her to question her own gift.
Carrying (Total CP: 27):
- Celestial Lyre (14 points): Produces melodies infused with starlight magic.
- Dreamcatcher (4 points): Captures fragments of dreams to inspire her compositions.
- Book of Night Songs (5 points): Chronicles ancient celestial hymns.
- Pendant of Moonlight (4 points): Glows faintly, amplifying her connection to the night sky.

Tobias "Toby" Nolander "When all else fails, sing!" 10

Brief: A quirky halfling bard, Toby's infectious optimism and humor brighten even the darkest of days.
Vocation: Street Performer & Hopeful Adventurer
For the Perceptive: Toby's talent for improvisation allows him to tailor songs and skits to suit any audience or situation.
Description: Short and stocky, Toby's curly brown hair bounces as he moves, and his waistcoats are as colorful as his personality. His eyes twinkle with mischief, and his jokes and tunes draw people in effortlessly. Despite his cheerfulness, Toby doubts his abilities and fears he may never reach his full potential.
Wants & Needs: Toby hopes to spread joy and gather stories from his travels, eventually writing a legendary musical.
Secret or Obstacle: He fears his lack of adventuring skills will prevent him from achieving his dreams.
Carrying (Total CP: 23):
- Pan Flute (10 points): Creates calming and uplifting melodies.
- Notebook of Original Songs (5 points): Contains his growing repertoire.
- Cleverly Designed Instruments (4 points): Compact and multifunctional.
- Collection of Faces (4 points): Masks and props for comedic effect.

Kara Silverfire "May my voice ignite the fire within." 11

Brief: An inspiring human bard, Kara's fiery passion transforms her performances into powerful calls for change.
Vocation: Champion of the People & Activist
For the Insightful: Kara's ability to stir emotions makes her a rallying force for the oppressed, galvanizing action through her art.
Description: Kara's wild red hair seems to shimmer like flames, and her leather armor bears intricate designs that reflect her fiery spirit. Her fierce determination shines in her performances, which leave her audience inspired to fight for justice.
Wants & Needs: Kara seeks a legendary artifact to rally the people in their fight for equality and justice.
Secret or Obstacle: She hides her noble background, fearing it could undermine her cause as a champion for the downtrodden.
Carrying (Total CP: 30):
- Song of the Hearthstone (12 points): A ballad that strengthens resolve.
- Flame Ring of Freedom (10 points): A magical ring that amplifies her charisma.
- Charisma-Boosting Potion (3 points): A temporary aid for inspiring speeches.
- Social Movement Leaflets (5 points): A collection of her campaign materials.

Varin the Bold "Courage is the melody that drives the heart." 12

Brief: A legendary bard known for his valiant ballads, Varin rallies warriors with songs of heroism and unity.
Vocation: War Bard & Hero of Legends
For the Perceptive: Varin's rousing anthems inspire bravery, motivating even the most hesitant allies to act.
Description: Clad in intricate armor decorated with symbols of valor, Varin's imposing figure and confident demeanor command respect. His booming voice carries over battlefields, lifting spirits and uniting his allies under a common cause.
Wants & Needs: Varin seeks to create a saga worthy of legends and unite noble houses under one banner.
Secret or Obstacle: The death of his mentor in battle weighs heavily on him, causing him to doubt his own bravery.
Carrying (Total CP: 31):
- Sword of Songs (15 points): Resonates with heroic melodies during combat.
- Tome of Heroic Tales (8 points): Chronicles his greatest deeds and those of his allies.
- Beloved Shield (4 points): A gift from his mentor, symbolizing protection.
- Battle Cry Scroll (4 points): Unleashes a powerful morale-boosting chant.

Barmaids

Barmaids are the heart and soul of every bustling tavern, serving not only food and drink but also the laughter and camaraderie that keep spirits high in a fantasy realm. With their quick wit and even quicker hands, these industrious women navigate the crowded establishment with grace, expertly balancing tankards of ale and plates piled high with hearty fare.

Known for their charm and resourcefulness, barmaids often hear the juiciest gossip from travelers and locals alike, making them valuable sources of information for adventurers seeking insight into the goings-on of the world. Their ability to foster a warm and inviting atmosphere transforms the tavern into a home away from home, where stories of repute and rumor intertwine over shared drinks and hearty laughter.

However, crossing a barmaid can lead to humorous—and sometimes chaotic—consequences! One enterprising barmaid, known for her no-nonsense attitude, once had a rowdy patron who thought it amusing to start a food fight during the peak of a busy evening. With a swift flick of her wrist, she famously retaliated by tossing an entire pie—mysteriously filled with day-old fish stew—right back at him!

The pie not only hit its mark but also sent the poor fellow flying backward, landing squarely into a barrel of ale. The entire tavern erupted in laughter as the barmaid, unfazed, declared, "Well, at least he'll have a new fragrance!" From then on, patrons knew better than to mess with her; after all, a barmaid with a piquant sense of justice can turn a night of revelry into a comedy show that no one would soon forget.

So, while they are dedicated to serving up joy and hospitality, tread lightly around these formidable women—forgetting your manners could lead to being the punchline of a very memorable joke!

Mira Tumblebrew

"Every pint deserves a smile." 1

Brief: A cheerful barmaid working in a bustling slum tavern, Mira is known for her infectious laughter and ability to handle rowdy customers.
Vocation: Barmaid at "The Laughing Mug."
For the Athletic: Mira navigates crowded spaces with ease, deftly avoiding spills while keeping order among unruly patrons.
Description: Mira is a stout human with curly auburn hair and bright green eyes. She wears a simple, slightly worn dress with a stained apron, a testament to her years of service. Her warm smile and friendly demeanor make her beloved among the regulars.
Wants & Needs: Mira dreams of saving enough money to open her own tavern and create a peaceful home away from the chaos of the city.
Secret or Obstacle: She hides her past as an orphan, fearing judgment from those who might learn of her origins.
Carrying (Total CP: 17):
- Serving Tray (1 point): Durable and ever-ready for quick service.
- Sturdy Tankard (2 points): A personal favorite for handling rowdy patrons.
- Special Brew Recipe Book (3 points): Contains unique drink recipes.
- Simple Charm Bracelet (1 point): A keepsake from her childhood.

Lana Greenbottle   *"Service with a smile, and don't forget the tip!"* 2

Brief: A savvy halfling barmaid at an inn frequented by adventurers, Lana captivates guests with her quick wit and mischievous charm.
Vocation: Barmaid at "The Wandering Halfling Inn."
For the Perceptive: Lana has a knack for reading people's moods and serving their needs before they even ask.
Description: Petite and vibrant, Lana's curly brown hair is tied in a neat bun, and her hazel eyes sparkle with mischief. Her well-fitted attire is designed for comfort and flair as she glides gracefully through the tavern.
Wants & Needs: Lana dreams of writing her own book of adventurer stories, secretly longing to go on an adventure herself.
Secret or Obstacle: She hides a talent for poetry, fearing that sharing it would lead to ridicule or rejection.
Carrying (Total CP: 18):
- Magical Serving Wand (5 points): Keeps drinks cool or warm as needed.
- Journal of Adventurer Tales (7 points): Filled with overheard stories and sketches.
- Set of Fine Glassware (3 points): Adds elegance to her service.
- Personal Charm (3 points): A lucky charm gifted by a regular patron.

Freya Silverhands   *"A drink shared is a life celebrated."* 3

Brief: An elegant human barmaid at an upscale establishment, Freya's poise and gracious demeanor draw the attention of high-profile patrons.
Vocation: Barmaid at "The Gilded Chalice."
For the Insightful: Freya excels at diplomacy, using her charm and tact to navigate delicate conversations.
Description: Freya is tall and graceful, with flowing blond hair and striking blue eyes. She wears finely tailored dresses adorned with silver accents, exuding an air of sophistication that matches the upscale clientele she serves.
Wants & Needs: Freya aspires to become a business partner at the tavern, providing stability for her family.
Secret or Obstacle: Freya hides her working-class origins, often feeling unworthy among the nobles and elite patrons she serves.
Carrying (Total CP: 21):
- Elegant Serving Tray (3 points): Adds a touch of refinement to her service.
- Fine Wine Pourer (8 points): Enhances the flavor of luxury beverages.
- Binder of House Recipes (5 points): Contains exclusive cocktail recipes.
- Family Locket (5 points): A treasured heirloom reminding her of her roots.

Poppy Brightbloom   *"Cheer up, darling! There's ale to be had!"* 4

Brief: A spirited gnome barmaid with a flair for music, Poppy's vibrant personality brings life to every tavern she graces.
Vocation: Barmaid & Part-Time Performer at "The Merry Minstrel."
For the Insightful: Poppy's natural musical talent enhances the tavern's atmosphere, drawing patrons into her lively performances.
Description: With bright pink hair styled in braided ribbons, Poppy wears a colorful dress and cheerful apron. Her infectious laughter and energy make her the star of the tavern, though she secretly fears performing solo.
Wants & Needs: Poppy dreams of becoming a famous bard, traveling the world, and gathering enough tips to fund her adventures.
Secret or Obstacle: She hides anxiety about performing in front of large audiences, relying on friends for support.
Carrying (Total CP: 19):
- Small Instrument (5 points): A cheerful accompaniment for her songs.
- Book of Song Lyrics (5 points): Contains melodies and rhymes to entertain patrons.
- Two Small Trinkets (4 points): Lucky charms given by customers.
- Special Spice Mix (5 points): Adds a unique touch to drinks and dishes.

Isolde Ironfoot   *"Good ale and good company, that's all I need."* 5

Brief: A resilient dwarven barmaid from a family of brewers, Isolde is renowned for her strength and hearty laughter.
Vocation: Barmaid at "The Stout Tankard Brewery."
For the Athletic: Isolde can effortlessly lift heavy kegs and barrels, handling the most demanding physical tasks in the tavern.
Description: Stout and sturdy, Isolde has a thick braid of dark hair and deep-set brown eyes. She wears rugged clothing adorned with brewery logos, and her boisterous laugh is as comforting as a freshly poured pint. Though strong and capable, Isolde quietly fears that her strength overshadows her femininity.
Wants & Needs: Isolde hopes to keep her family's brewery thriving and dreams of hosting the region's largest beer festival.
Secret or Obstacle: She struggles with self-identity, worried that her physicality defines her more than her personality.
Carrying (Total CP: 22):
- Heavy Serving Tray (2 points): Built to endure rough tavern conditions.
- Special Barrel Opener (5 points): A tool handed down in her family.
- Handmade Tankard (6 points): A treasured keepsake from her late father.
- Collection of Brewing Secrets (9 points): Contains generations of family recipes.

Eira Snowfall   *"Every drink tells a story; let's make it memorable."* 6

Brief: An elegant barmaid from a northern establishment, Eira's enchanting storytelling makes every drink an experience to remember.
Vocation: Barmaid at "The Frosty Flagon."
For the Perceptive: Eira's sharp memory allows her to recall patron preferences effortlessly, creating a personalized touch for every customer.
Description: Eira's flowing white hair and icy blue eyes give her a striking, ethereal appearance. She wears warm, delicate clothing suited for cold climates, complemented by graceful accessories. Her melodic voice captivates guests, transporting them with tales from the frozen north.
Wants & Needs: Eira dreams of exploring distant lands and writing a book filled with travelers' stories.
Secret or Obstacle: She fears venturing too far from home, held back by her family's protective tendencies.
Carrying (Total CP: 22):
- Warm Cloak (5 points): Provides comfort in the harshest winters.
- Collection of Travelers' Stories (10 points): A book filled with anecdotes and legends.
- Unique Glassware (4 points): Designed to keep drinks icy cold.
- Small Trinket of Good Luck (3 points): A gift from her younger sibling.

Juna Wavecrest   *"Life's a wave—ride it hard and enjoy every drop."* 7

Brief: A spirited barmaid from a seaside tavern, Juna's breezy demeanor and impeccable timing make her a favorite among sailors and travelers.
Vocation: Barmaid at "The Siren's Call Tavern."
For the Insightful: Juna has an extraordinary sense of timing, ensuring drinks and food are served exactly when needed.
Description: With vivid blue hair and sun-kissed skin, Juna embodies the energy of the coast. She wears light, flowing clothing that allows her to move freely, her warm smile brightening the beachside tavern. Despite her sunny demeanor, Juna quietly yearns for adventure beyond the oceanfront.
Wants & Needs: Juna dreams of saving enough money to open her own beach resort, welcoming travelers from all over.
Secret or Obstacle: She feels trapped in her current life, longing for new horizons but unsure how to begin her journey.
Carrying (Total CP: 25):
- Shell-shaped Serving Tray (5 points): Adds a playful nautical touch to her service.
- Map of the Coastline (6 points): Marked with hidden beaches and coves.
- Wind Charm (4 points): Enhances the breeze within the tavern.
- Set of Beach-Inspired Glasses (10 points): Crafted with vibrant sea colors.

Kara Blackbeer *"Here's to strong drinks and stronger friendships!"* 8

Brief: A no-nonsense barmaid at the town's most popular tavern, Kara is known for her sharp tongue and quick wit.
Vocation: Barmaid at "The Rowdy Rooster."
For the Perceptive: Kara has a talent for defusing fights before they escalate, often using humor to maintain peace in the tavern.
Description: Kara has dark brown hair and amber eyes that gleam with authority. She wears rugged attire and an apron bearing the tavern's logo, her straightforward manner endearing her to locals. Despite her confidence, she secretly longs for a more adventurous life beyond the town.
Wants & Needs: Kara hopes to keep the tavern running smoothly while dreaming of brewing her own signature ale.
Secret or Obstacle: She fears being stuck in the same town forever, yearning for new experiences and adventures.
Carrying (Total CP: 20):
- Heavy Serving Tray (4 points): Doubles as a shield in emergencies.
- Special Beer Stein (6 points): Keeps drinks cold longer.
- First Aid Manual (5 points): Used to treat rowdy patrons' injuries.
- Collection of Fun Recipes (5 points): Adds personality to her drink menu.

Selina Swift *"Sass with a side of service!"* 9

Brief: A spunky tiefling barmaid with a fiery personality, Selina is renowned for her sass and ability to handle troublesome patrons.
Vocation: Barmaid at "The Fiery Pint."
For the Insightful: Selina's quick reflexes and sharp tongue diffuse potential conflicts with a mix of charm and intimidation.
Description: With deep red skin, long curved horns, and vibrant purple hair, Selina stands out in any crowd. She wears stylish yet functional clothing that enhances her bold presence, often accessorized with flashy jewelry.
Wants & Needs: Selina dreams of running her own establishment, hosting the best tavern show in the region.
Secret or Obstacle:
Selina fears showing vulnerability, believing it might undermine her authority.
Carrying (Total CP: 23):
- Serving Kit (3 points): Essential tools for her trade.
- Glamorous Serving Tray (6 points): Adds flair to her service.
- Set of Enchanted Dice (5 points): Used for tavern games.
- Collection of Sassy Sayings (9 points): Selina's personal repertoire of comebacks.

Anya Frost *"There's magic in every round, trust me!"* 10

Brief: A mysterious elven barmaid with a talent for mixing magical drinks, Anya's enchanting presence makes her tavern a hotspot for travelers.
Vocation: Barmaid at "The Arcane Elixir."
For the Insightful: Anya uses her magical skills to create drinks with unique effects, captivating her customers with every pour.
Description: With silvery hair and almond-shaped violet eyes, Anya's beauty is ethereal and alluring. She wears elegant robes adorned with arcane symbols, exuding mystery as she expertly mixes potions that double as cocktails.
Wants & Needs: Anya hopes to discover secrets of the old world through her craft and create a drink capable of altering destinies.
Secret or Obstacle: She fears that her magic will fail at a critical moment, disappointing her patrons and herself.
Carrying (Total CP: 30):
- Magic Potion Set (15 points): Contains ingredients for her enchanting recipes.
- Enchanted Serving Tray (8 points): Keeps drinks levitating and pristine.
- Journal of Recipes (4 points): Notes on experimental concoctions.
- Arcane Trinket (3 points): A small charm that enhances her magical abilities.

Beast Masters

The concept of "what even is a beast master?" opens the door to a fascinating interplay between humans and their animal companions in fantasy settings. The role of a beast master is often shaped by cultural respect for nature, the bond between species, and the methods employed to harness the wild. In some realms, beast masters are celebrated as champions of the natural world, revered for their ability to communicate with and command creatures of all kinds. In others, they may be seen as mercenaries, using their beasts for combat and personal gain.

Envision a world where beast masters are more than mere handlers of animals. Some may be part of ancient orders dedicated to preserving harmony between civilization and nature, while others might roam the land seeking to forge bonds with rare and powerful beasts. During times of strife, these individuals can become pivotal allies, their trained companions striking fear into foes and providing vital support in perilous situations.

Arcana
- **DC 10:** Competent beast masters are likely to possess a variety of nature-based spells or abilities, allowing them to enhance their connection with animals. They might use magical charms to communicate, heal, or empower their companions, turning them into formidable allies in battle.
- **DC 20:** Master beast masters have honed their skills to a supernatural degree, able to summon creatures from distant realms or enhance their own physical prowess through their bonds. They might command the loyalty of legendary beasts and draw upon their powers, wielding nature's fury with grace and cunning.

History
- **DC 10:** Throughout history, beast masters have often served as guardians of the wild, their stories intertwined with the myths of their lands. Their adventures in the untamed wilderness and legendary feats of companionship with mythical creatures provide a rich tapestry of lore.
- **DC 15:** The motivations of beast masters can vary widely, from a deep-seated respect for life and the balance of nature to personal quests driven by the desire for revenge against those who threaten the wild. Understanding these motivations can reveal their choices in relationships and conflicts.

Bribery and Influence
A beast master's willingness to engage in negotiations or accepting favors is influenced by a complex web of factors:
- Motivation: Their primary drives, such as protecting their animal companions, preserving nature, or gaining greater power
- Compensation: The resources or rewards promised for their allegiance or assistance
- Personal Connections: Relationships with other adventurers, nature spirits, or animal lords
- Opportunity: The potential for deeper bonds with rare creatures or new challenges
- Safety: Concerns regarding the well-being of their animals and the risks posed by human or creature threats

Beast Masters

Armor Class: 14 (Leather Armor)
Hit Points: 60 (10d10)
Speed: 30ft.

STR: 14 (+2) **DEX:** 16 (+3) **CON:** 14 (+2) **INT:** 10 (+0) **WIS:** 12 (+1) **CHAR:** 11 (+0)

Saving Throws: Strength +5, Dexterity +6

Skills: Animal Handling +4, Athletics +5, Perception +4, Survival +4
Senses: passive Perception 14
Languages: Common, and understands the languages of their beast companion
Proficiency Bonus: +3
Challenge: 6 (2,300 xp)

Class Features
- **Beast Companion:** The Beast Master has a loyal beast companion (such as a wolf, hawk, or bear) that acts on their initiative in combat and can attack or take specific actions based on the Beast Master's commands.
- **Exceptional Training:** The Beast Master has trained their animal companion to perform additional tasks and can share their proficiency bonus with it, enhancing its capabilities.
- **Combat Training:** When the Beast Master uses their action to command their beast to attack, it can make an additional attack.

Actions
- Multi-attack: The Beast Master can make two attacks, one with their weapon and one with their beast companion.
- Longbow: Ranged Weapon Attack: +6 to hit, range 150/600 ft., one target. Hit: 9 (1d8+5) piercing damage.
- Beast Attack (Wolf): Melee Weapon Attack: +5 to hit, reach 5 ft., one target. Hit: 10 (2d6+3) piercing damage. The target must succeed on a DC 13 Strength saving throw or be knocked prone.

Bonus Actions
- Command Beast: The Beast Master can use a bonus action to command their beast companion to take an action, such as Dash, Disengage, or Help.

Reactions
- Protective Instinct: When the Beast Master or their companion is attacked, the Beast Master can use their reaction to impose disadvantage on the attack roll.

Thorn Wildheart

"Through bond and instinct, we find strength in the wild."

A rugged human ranger with an unshakable bond to nature, Thorn roams the wilderness alongside his loyal wolf companion, Shadow.

For the Insightful:
Thorn has an innate ability to communicate with animals, sensing their emotions and needs.

Description:
Thorn's unkempt brown hair and rugged, weathered face reflect his years in the wild. Clad in leather clothing reinforced with animal hides, he blends seamlessly into his forest surroundings. His wolf, Shadow, mirrors his demeanor—alert, intelligent, and fiercely loyal. Thorn carries the weight of past tragedy, though he masks it with quiet resilience.

Wants & Needs: Thorn seeks to protect the wild from encroachment, hoping to uncover ancient druidic knowledge to restore balance.

Secret or Obstacle: He carries the guilt of a hunting accident that claimed his brother's life, a shadow that haunts his every decision.

Carrying (Total CP: 28):
- Bow of Silent Strikes (12 points): A mastercrafted bow that fires soundless arrows.
- Leather Armor of the Wild (8 points): Reinforced for stealth and protection in the forest.
- Herbalism Kit (4 points): Used for crafting salves and natural remedies.
- Wolf Collar of Bonding (4 points): Strengthens the link between Thorn and his wolf companion.

Beastmaster Tactics

Beast masters deploy their instincts and knowledge of the natural world in both combat and exploration. In battle, they work in perfect harmony with their companions, utilizing their beasts to flank foes, scout ahead, or even serve as shields for one another. Their ability to read the emotions and intentions of animals allows them to predict behaviors and respond effectively, creating a seamless blend of strategy and skill. Outside of combat, their expertise in tracking, foraging, and survival ensures they can thrive in even the most challenging environments.

Ranger & Beast master

Elara Skywhisper

"Together, we soar higher than alone." **2**

Brief: An elegant elven beast master who explores the skies alongside her majestic eagle, Talon.
Vocation: Explorer & Protector of the Skies
For the Athletic: Elara exhibits unmatched skill in archery, using Talon to scout and strike with precision.
Description: With flowing silver hair and bright blue eyes, Elara exudes grace and strength. Her light armor is adorned with feathers and symbols of the natural world, allowing ease of movement. Talon, her eagle companion, watches from above, alert and protective, sharing an unspoken bond that fuels her resolve.
Wants & Needs: Elara hopes to uncover artifacts that bring balance to nature, strengthening her bond with Talon.
Secret or Obstacle: She fears a past failure—when she couldn't save a fellow ranger—may threaten her ability to trust herself and Talon.
Carrying (Total CP: 30):
- Longbow of Eagles (15 points): Fires arrows that strike with pinpoint accuracy.
- Feathered Cloak of the Sky (8 points): Enhances her agility and protects from the elements.
- Scout's Binoculars (4 points): Offers a keen view of distant landscapes.
- Potion of Winged Flight (3 points): Temporarily grants limited flight.

Rokthar Ironjaw

"A beast fights for its master; a master fights for his beast." **3**

Brief: A hulking half-orc warrior whose strength and loyalty to his bear companion, Grizzle, define his identity.
Vocation: Warrior & Beast Protector
For the Insightful: Rokthar possesses immense physical strength and an unbreakable bond with his bear companion, acting as one in combat.
Description: Rokthar's imposing frame, long black hair, and prominent tusks exude power. His armor, adorned with trophies of past victories, reflects his storied adventures. Grizzle, a massive and powerful bear, mirrors Rokthar's strength and serves as both guardian and companion.
Wants & Needs: Rokthar seeks recognition as a champion beast master, aiming to defeat a rival beast master to prove his worth.
Secret or Obstacle: Haunted by the memory of a fallen companion, Rokthar wrestles with self-doubt despite his outward confidence.
Carrying (Total CP: 31):
- Great Axe of the Wilds (15 points): A weapon of devastating strength.
- Bear Armor (10 points): Protects Grizzle during intense battles.
- Healing Salves (3 points): Used to treat injuries in the field.
- Toothy Grin Talisman (3 points): An artifact believed to boost courage.

Lyra Moonshadow

"In the shades of night, we find our strength." **4**

Brief: A stealthy drow ranger who prowls the darkness with her loyal panther companions, Onyx and Ember.
Vocation: Assassin & Beast Companion
For the Insightful: Lyra's exceptional skill in stealth and tracking is amplified by her panthers' instincts, making her nearly invisible.
Description: Lyra's silver hair and luminescent violet eyes glow faintly in the shadows. Clad in leather armor dyed deep black, she moves silently through the night, her agile panthers mirroring her every step. Onyx and Ember are fiercely loyal, embodying Lyra's quiet determination and grace.
Wants & Needs: Lyra longs to uncover the secrets of her drow lineage while proving herself as a protector of the surface world.
Secret or Obstacle: She struggles with the stigma of her drow heritage, feeling the need to constantly prove herself to others.
Carrying (Total CP: 29):
- Dual Shortbows (12 points): Allows for rapid, precise shots.
- Cloak of Night (8 points): Enhances her stealth under moonlight.
- Drow Poison Vials (5 points): Paralyzing toxins used in combat.
- Set of Climbing Gear (4 points): Essential for traversing treacherous terrain.

Finn Riverstone
"Flow with the river; let your spirit guide you." **5**

Brief: A contemplative firbolg who bonds deeply with river wildlife, accompanied by his playful otter, Ripple.
Vocation: Guardian of Rivers and Wildlife
For the Perceptive:
Finn's understanding of rivers and streams allows him to navigate and predict natural behaviors perfectly.
Description:
Finn's tall, broad frame is covered in earthy tones, with green skin and hair resembling river grass. His gentle eyes exude wisdom and calm, while his otter companion, Ripple, adds playful energy. Finn's simple attire is decorated with water-inspired patterns, reflecting his connection to aquatic realms.
Wants & Needs: Finn seeks to protect rivers and wildlife from pollution, hoping to uncover forgotten aquatic magic.
Secret or Obstacle: The destruction of local habitats weighs heavily on Finn, making him question his ability to safeguard nature.
Carrying (Total CP: 26):
- Fishing Spear (8 points): A versatile tool for hunting and defense.
- Herbalism Kit (6 points): Used to craft healing balms and remedies.
- Water Elemental Charm (6 points): Grants water-based magical abilities.
- Underwater Breathing Potion (6 points): Allows extended exploration beneath the surface.

Margret Fernshield
"Life is preserved in balance; the beast and I are one." **6**

Brief: A dedicated human druidess bonded to a mighty stag, Margret embodies wisdom and harmony with nature's balance.
Vocation: Druid & Wildlife Protector
For the Perceptive: Margret's deep understanding of the natural world allows her to sense imbalances and take decisive action to restore harmony.
Description: Margret's long, curly brown hair is entwined with leaves and vines, reflecting her bond with the forest. Her hazel eyes glow with calm determination as she moves gracefully through the sacred groves, her robes embroidered with natural symbols. Her stag companion, Thorn, stands tall and majestic, a living emblem of the forest's resilience.
Wants & Needs: Margret dreams of creating a haven to protect the sacred groves from encroaching civilization and preserve their beauty for all species.
Secret or Obstacle: Margret wrestles with guilt over using her powers to harm others, even when the greater good is at stake.
Carrying (Total CP: 27):
- Leaf-blade Dagger (10 points): A sacred weapon crafted to protect the forest.
- Nature's Staff (8 points): Channels her druidic magic to heal or defend.
- Healing Salves (5 points): Herbal remedies for injuries.
- Druidic Tome (4 points): Contains knowledge of natural spells and rituals.

Zarok Thunderscale
"Together, we forge storms that even the bravest fear." **7**

Brief: A fierce dragonborn beast master who inspires allies with his leadership while storming into battle alongside his thunder lizard, Stormfeather.
Vocation: Warrior & Beast Master
For the Insightful: His natural leadership unites creatures and allies alike, turning chaotic battlefields into coordinated victories.
Description: Zarok's bright blue scales shimmer with crackling energy, and his golden eyes burn with a warrior's resolve. Clad in reinforced armor and a billowing storm-themed cape, he strikes an imposing figure. His thunder lizard, Stormfeather, is a massive beast whose presence alone can send enemies fleeing. Together, they are an unstoppable force.
Wants & Needs: Zarok seeks to prove his worth to the dragonborn clans by conquering legendary beasts and recovering a storm artifact of immense power.
Secret or Obstacle: Zarok bears the shame of fleeing from a past battle, a decision that haunts his honor and reputation.
Carrying (Total CP: 32):
- Thunderous Spear (15 points): A weapon imbued with storm energy.
- Heavy Armor of the Storm (10 points): Protects him in the fiercest battles.
- Healing Tonic (4 points): Restores vitality during combat.
- Battle Standard of Thunder (3 points): Inspires allies with a surge of courage.

Tasha Lightpaw   *"Light dances in the darkness; let me and my friend lead the way."*   8

Brief: A playful catfolk beast master with agile reflexes and a knack for acrobatics, Tasha adventures alongside her feline companion, Pounce.
Vocation: Scout & Trickster
For the Athletic: Tasha's agility and acrobatics make her a master of navigating treacherous terrain and evading danger.
Description: With vibrant orange and black stripes, large green eyes, and a mischievous grin, Tasha exudes playful energy. Her colorful leathers are adorned with intricate patterns, blending charm with utility. Her feline companion, Pounce, mirrors her antics—small but fierce, with bright blue eyes and a knack for getting into trouble.
Wants & Needs: Tasha dreams of gathering tales of adventure and sharing her exploits through song and story across the realm.
Secret or Obstacle: She hides her past as a formidable warrior, having chosen a more carefree life after being shunned for her unconventional path.
Carrying (Total CP: 24):
- Twin Daggers (8 points): Razor-sharp blades for quick strikes.
- Adventurer's Musical Instrument (4 points): A lute that adds flair to her tales.
- Thieves' Tools (5 points): Essential for unlocking doors and secrets.
- Feline Companion's Charm (7 points): Strengthens her bond with Pounce.

Greth Thornstrike   *"There is no hunter more skilled than one with a loyal beast."*   9

Brief: A rugged dwarven hunter who relies on his loyal badger companion, Muck, to navigate the wilds and strike down his prey.
Vocation: Hunter & Tracker
For the Perceptive: Greth's sharp instincts allow him to detect danger from afar, using Muck as a guide to avoid ambushes and hazards.
Description: Greth's stout, muscular build is complemented by a wild beard and piercing gray eyes. His hide armor, decorated with badges of past victories, tells the story of a determined hunter. His badger, Muck, is a fierce and clever companion who scouts the terrain ahead, ensuring Greth's survival in the harshest environments.
Wants & Needs: Greth seeks to reclaim his family's ancestral lands from invaders and prove his lineage's worth through his bond with Muck.
Secret or Obstacle: Greth struggles with insecurities about his small stature compared to his kin, fearing he may not measure up.
Carrying (Total CP: 29):
- Dwarven Crossbow (12 points): Fires bolts with deadly precision.
- Sturdy Hunting Gear (7 points): Provides protection and mobility.
- Healing Potions (8 points): Keeps Greth and Muck in fighting condition.
- Badger Collar of Loyalty (2 points): Enhances Muck's abilities in the field.

Nadia Heavensong   *"With grace and spirit, our lives are intertwined as one."*   10

Brief: A celestial aasimar beast master who channels divine energy through her eagle companion, Emberwing, to heal and inspire those around her.
Vocation: Angel of Mercy & Guardian of Nature
For the Insightful: Nadia's aura of celestial energy allows her to heal and uplift her allies, inspiring hope in the darkest moments.
Description: Nadia's golden skin glows faintly with celestial light, and her flowing blonde hair is adorned with feathers and radiant crystals. Her robes, embroidered with celestial symbols, billow gracefully as she moves. Emberwing, her majestic eagle, soars above, a beacon of light and protection.
Wants & Needs: Nadia hopes to purify the lands of dark forces and forge alliances to strengthen her cause.
Secret or Obstacle: She carries the burden of a darker past, having once served a ruthless overlord before turning to the light.
Carrying (Total CP: 31):
- Blessed Bow (12 points): Fires arrows imbued with divine energy.
- Potion of Celestial Healing (8 points): Restores health to allies.
- Crystal Focus (6 points): Channels her celestial magic for protection.
- Talon Pendant of Protection (5 points): Enhances Emberwing's defensive capabilities.

Beggars

Beggars are an integral and often overlooked part of the tapestry in any fantasy world. Found among the cobblestone streets of bustling cities or tucked away in shadowy alleyways, these individuals come from all walks of life, each with their own stories marked by hardship and resilience. While many beggars are indeed struggling for survival, some disguise their true nature as they gather the secrets and tales of those who pass them by.

They may appear unassuming, but their keen eyes and attentive ears make them the unexpected chroniclers of the urban landscape, often privy to happenings that even the noblest of nobles could miss. A song here, a whispered rumor there—beggars weave the fabric of everyday life, turning their plight into an intricate network of information.

However, the world of beggars is not without its perils, as illustrated by the cautionary tale of "Old Sweeney," a once-humble beggar known for his legendary speeches about the "golden opportunity" that solitude and lowliness could provide. Sweeney often spoke of a magical coin he could trade for information that might change one's fate.

Eager adventurers seeking fortune would approach him, desperate to obtain the rumored coin. Yet, unbeknownst to them, Sweeney had crafted the entire story to keep himself entertained and to deter the more aggressive crowd.

One fateful day, two particularly ambitious adventurers attempted to force the truth out of him, convinced that he was hiding some great secret. In the ensuing chaos, Sweeney cleverly slipped away, leaving behind only a pair of flustered would-be heroes surrounded by a now-furious tavern patron demanding his lost pouch of gold!

From that day forward, the tale of the "Golden Coin" and the crafty beggar served as a cautionary reminder: in a world rife with deception, appearances can be misleading. Crossing a beggar may lead to unexpected outcomes, so it's wise to treat them with the respect they deserve.

Old Man Ebron

"Every coin has a story; every story, a coin." 1

Brief: A venerable human beggar with a kind heart, Ebron spins tales of wisdom and mischief to those willing to listen.
Vocation: Storyteller & Beggar
For the Perceptive: Ebron possesses an extraordinary memory, able to recount the city's history and the countless lives that pass through its streets.
Description: Ebron is an elderly man wrapped in layers of tattered clothing, his graying hair and weathered hands speaking of years long past. His gentle, twinkling brown eyes hint at the life of a man who once stood in the spotlight. Despite his humble demeanor, his words weave stories that capture the attention of passersby.
Wants & Needs: Ebron hopes to gather enough coins for a warm meal while secretly dreaming of writing a book to preserve his stories.
Secret or Obstacle: He hides his past life as a successful bard, fearing judgment for the loss of his fame.
Carrying (Total CP: 15):
- Wooden Staff (1 point): A walking stick well-worn from travel.
- Tattered Journal of Stories (5 points): Holds the fragments of tales and legends.
- Small Wooden Trinkets (4 points): Simple carvings given to children in exchange for kindness.
- Found Coins (5 points): A collection of copper coins and odd foreign currency.

Lila the Lost   *"Even the smallest kindness can change a life."* 2

Brief: A soft-spoken half-elf beggar with haunting beauty, Lila hides a noble past and a yearning for connection.
Vocation: Beggars' Assistant & Listener
For the Perceptive: Lila can sense emotions with unsettling clarity, often knowing who struggles long before they admit it.
Description: Lila's tangled dark hair and radiant green eyes betray a noble lineage now lost. Her faded silk dress—once elegant but now tattered—whispers of better days. Her gentle voice soothes the sorrowful, drawing sympathy and coin alike.
Wants & Needs: She hopes to find a path back to her family, longing for belonging and safety.
Secret or Obstacle: Lila hides her true identity as a fallen noble's daughter, terrified of the rejection she might face if discovered.
Carrying (Total CP: 12):
- Faded Scrap of Silk (2 points): A remnant of her former life.
- Small Knick-knacks (3 points): Collected trinkets to barter or gift.
- Journal of Lost Dreams (5 points): Filled with longing letters and sketches.
- Lucky Stone (2 points): A small keepsake she believes holds protection.

Garrick Stonehand   *"A man's worth isn't counted by the coins he carries."* 3

Brief: A gruff dwarf beggar whose wisdom and strength offer guidance to the weary and desperate.
Vocation: Philosopher & Street Mentor
For the Insightful: Garrick's keen understanding of hardship allows him to offer practical advice and aid to those struggling.
Description: Garrick is a stocky dwarf with a thick, dirt-streaked beard and hands scarred by years of labor. His patched-up coat and weary yet stern demeanor often silence bustling crowds. Despite his rough exterior, his words resonate with surprising kindness.
Wants & Needs: Garrick hopes to gather enough donations to survive and dreams of reforming how the city views beggars.
Secret or Obstacle: He hides his past as a skilled blacksmith, ashamed that an accident left him unable to forge.
Carrying (Total CP: 22):
- Dirty Caps (2 points): A collection of worn headgear.
- Collection of Stones (5 points): Small polished stones he finds beautiful.
- Flask of Stale Ale (5 points): A bittersweet reminder of simpler times.
- Tattered Book of Philosophy (10 points): Holds musings and wisdom passed down through his family.

Mira Quickfoot   *"A coin for a smile, and a smile for a coin!"* 4

Brief: A lively halfling beggar known for her quick wit and acrobatics, Mira charms and entertains her way to survival.
Vocation: Street Performer & Beggar
For the Athletic: Mira is highly skilled in acrobatics, drawing crowds with flips and tricks that bring joy and coin.
Description: With a contagious grin, curly blonde hair, and mismatched bright clothes, Mira exudes vibrant energy. Her upbeat personality and playful spirit make her a familiar face in the marketplace, where she dazzles crowds with her street performances.
Wants & Needs: Mira dreams of earning enough buzz to join a traveling circus and escape the city's grime.
Secret or Obstacle: She hides her roots in a family of thieves, desperately seeking to create a better reputation for herself.
Carrying (Total CP: 20):
- Juggling Balls (5 points): Brightly colored and well-used.
- Tattered Hat (2 points): Passed around to collect tips.
- Small Wooden Flute (5 points): Plays jaunty tunes during her performances.
- Collection of Trinkets (8 points): Mementos and gifts from appreciative onlookers.

Olwen Brightspark *"Hope is a flickering flame; let it guide your way."* 5

Brief: A cheerful gnome beggar who sells handmade charms and trinkets, Olwen brightens even the darkest alleys with her optimism.
Vocation: Charm Seller & Beggar
For the Perceptive: Olwen excels at crafting small items imbued with symbolic luck, her keen hands turning scraps into treasures.
Description: Olwen is small and bubbly, with wild orange hair and a patchwork dress filled with loops and pockets. Each stitch seems to hold a story, and her wide, joyful smile charms adults and children alike. Despite her optimism, her sparkling demeanor hides a quiet anxiety about the future.
Wants & Needs: Olwen dreams of saving enough to open a small shop filled with lucky charms and handcrafted trinkets.
Secret or Obstacle: Her trinket business struggles to succeed, and she relies on her positivity to mask her fears about failure.
Carrying (Total CP: 24):
- Collection of Handmade Charms (10 points): Tiny tokens said to bring luck or joy.
- Small Wooden Box of Trinkets (8 points): Holds her completed creations for sale.
- Lucky Rabbit's Foot (3 points): A charm she believes protects her.
- Herbal Bracelet (3 points): A woven band said to ward off misfortune.

Valen Shadowclaw *"All darkness has a glimmer of light."* 6

Brief: A mysterious tabaxi beggar who quietly observes the city's secrets while longing for freedom.
Vocation: Observer & Beggar
For the Perceptive: Valen has a sharp eye for detail, often overhearing whispered secrets in the city's crowded streets.
Description: Valen's sleek black fur and piercing yellow eyes give him an enigmatic aura. Cloaked in tattered robes that shroud his agile form, he moves through the shadows with grace. Though approachable, there's a sense that he's always listening, weighing every word spoken in his presence.
Wants & Needs: Valen gathers knowledge about the city's underbelly, dreaming of escaping the life of servitude to explore freely.
Secret or Obstacle: He hides his past as a spy for a criminal organization, fearing pursuit should his identity be revealed.
Carrying (Total CP: 22):
- Whispering Scrolls (6 points): Cryptic notes containing city secrets.
- Simple Disguise Kit (4 points): Tools to alter his appearance in a pinch.
- Collection of Secrets (8 points): Information traded or gathered over time.
- Tattered Cloak (4 points): Helps him blend into the crowd unnoticed.

Cynthia Rainwater *"Kindness can bloom even in the harshest of storms."* 7

Brief: A soft-spoken half-orc beggar who hands out flowers to bring cheer to those she meets.
Vocation: Flower Vendor & Beggar
For the Insightful: Cynthia possesses an uncanny ability to sense moods, often handing out the perfect flower to lift someone's spirits.
Description: Cynthia's striking green skin and braided hair adorned with flowers give her a gentle, natural beauty. Her flowing, cheerful dress—though worn—reflects her inner warmth. She speaks softly, her calm demeanor providing comfort to the downtrodden, though her own hopes remain fragile.
Wants & Needs: Cynthia wishes to open her own flower shop, growing and selling blooms to brighten the city.
Secret or Obstacle: She was shunned by her family for being different, and her search for acceptance fuels her gentle persistence.
Carrying (Total CP: 20):
- Collection of Wildflowers (8 points): Carefully gathered blooms to give or sell.
- Small Basket for Flowers (6 points): Holds and displays her wares.
- Notes on Flower Care (3 points): Handwritten advice for keeping flowers healthy.
- Simple Wooden Keychain (3 points): A tiny gift given to her long ago.

Harold the Grizzled — 8
"A wise man knows when to speak and when to beg."

Brief: A gruff and weathered beggar who offers practical advice and life lessons drawn from years of hardship.
Vocation: Advisor & Beggar
For the Perceptive: Harold has an innate ability to read others, often knowing when to offer words of wisdom or when to stay silent.
Description: Harold is a scruffy old man with a tangled beard, sunken cheeks, and eyes that have seen both tragedy and joy. Dressed in layered rags that once offered warmth, he carries himself with quiet dignity. Though rough around the edges, his guidance is often sought by those struggling to find their way.
Wants & Needs: Harold dreams of finding a small home where he can write down his life's lessons in peace.
Secret or Obstacle: He battles moments of grief over a lost family, struggling to find meaning in his isolation.
Carrying (Total CP: 18):
- Walking Stick (2 points): A sturdy staff that aids his movements.
- Scrap of Paper (5 points): Notes filled with advice and memories.
- Small Pouch of Coins (10 points): Hard-earned copper coins.
- Old Deck of Cards (1 point): A worn deck used for games or fortune-telling.

Belle Nightingale — 9
"Let the song of hope guide your heart."

Brief: A soft-spoken beggar with a voice as enchanting as the wind, Belle captivates listeners with songs that carry both sorrow and hope.
Vocation: Musical Beggar
For the Insightful: Belle possesses an incredible singing voice that can evoke deep emotions, drawing the attention—and coins—of passersby.
Description: Belle's golden hair flows like sunlight, framing her ethereal features and bright, soulful eyes. Her simple dress, though worn, billows gently as she moves. Her voice echoes through the streets, soothing those who stop to listen. Despite her gift, she hides a crippling fear of judgment, masking it with modest humility.
Wants & Needs: Belle longs to perform on a grand stage, earning enough to leave the streets behind and share her songs with the kingdom.
Secret or Obstacle: She hides her talent for songwriting, fearing rejection from those who might not see her worth.
Carrying (Total CP: 19):
- Simple Lute (6 points): A cherished instrument passed down through her family.
- Collection of Lullabies (6 points): Songs that soothe troubled hearts.
- Small Pouch of Coins (4 points): Donations from grateful listeners.
- Tattered Book of Songs (3 points): Holds verses she dreams of perfecting.

Jonas Winddust — 10
"Life is a storm; we learn to dance in the rain."

Brief: A lively and energetic beggar whose acrobatics and humor bring laughter to even the darkest corners of the city.
Vocation: Acrobat & Beggar
For the Athletic: Jonas's exceptional skill in acrobatics allows him to perform daring tricks that win applause and small coins.
Description: Jonas is wiry and thin, his mismatched clothing reflecting a life of hardship. His brown hair sticks up wildly, giving him a perpetual look of mischief, and his bright blue eyes sparkle with playful charm. Whether juggling or performing flips, Jonas's antics bring joy to the streets, though he fears his light-hearted nature hides his insecurities.
Wants & Needs: Jonas dreams of earning enough to join a traveling circus, spreading joy and laughter across the land.
Secret or Obstacle: He struggles with deep fears of failure, believing that his comedic approach to life makes him less serious in the eyes of others.
Carrying (Total CP: 21):
- Acrobatic Props (5 points): Balls, hoops, and ribbons for his performances.
- Collection of Jokes (6 points): A notebook filled with his best lines and stories.
- Small Pouch of Coins (6 points): Hard-earned tips from his crowd work.
- Brightly Colored Cloak (4 points): A patchwork garment that adds flair to his routines.

Bounty Hunters

The notion of bounty hunters reveals a gritty and captivating role within fantasy realms. The role of a bounty hunter is profoundly influenced by societal rules, the perception of justice, and the nature of the law itself.

In some lands, bounty hunters are seen as honorable enforcers of justice, tracking down wrongdoers for rewards and retribution. In others, they may be viewed as ruthless mercenaries, exploiting loopholes in the law to serve their own agendas.

Imagine a world where bounty hunters are more than mere trackers. Some might belong to elite guilds that uphold strict codes of conduct, while others operate solo, guided by personal vendettas and the promise of wealth. In times of turmoil, these individuals can shift the balance of power, their skills and knowledge of the criminal underworld making them valuable allies, or deadly adversaries.

Arcana
- DC 10: Competent bounty hunters are likely to possess a range of skills, from tracking and stealth to hand-to-hand combat and interrogation. They might rely on local lore or magical artifacts to gain an edge in their pursuits, using spells to enhance their abilities or uncover hidden truths.
- DC 20: Master bounty hunters may draw upon powerful enchantments or unique abilities that allow them to foresee their targets' movements or manipulate the shadows that cloaked their presence. Their expertise could include summoning creatures or wielding ancient relics that aid in their hunts.

History
- DC 10: Throughout history, bounty hunters have often been crucial figures in the tales of old, their exploits woven into the fabric of folklore and legend. Their pursuits of notorious criminals or mythic beasts often result in storied encounters that resonate through time.
- DC 15: The motivations of bounty hunters can be as varied as their methods. Understanding their backgrounds—whether driven by revenge, a desire for justice, or simply the lure of gold—can provide insight into their choices and destinies.

Bribery and Influence
A bounty hunter's response to offers of companionship or bribes hinges on a variety of intricate considerations:
- Motivation: Their driving force for pursuing bounties—be it revenge, justice, or profit
- Compensation: The financial reward or treasures promised for capturing or eliminating a target
- Goals: Long-term aspirations that align with their profession, such as infamy or wealth
- Allegiances: Loyalty to patron organizations, clients, or personal codes of honor
- Personal Connections: Relationships with other bounty hunters, law enforcement, or criminals
- Opportunity: The significance of the offer in relation to their current contract or reputation
- Consequences: The potential fallout affecting their standing within the bounty hunter and criminal communities

Bounty Hunters

Armor Class: 16 (Studded Leather)
Hit Points: 55 (10d8)
Speed: 30ft.

STR: 14 (+2) **DEX:** 18 (+4) **CON:** 14 (+2) **INT:** 12 (+1) **WIS:** 13 (+1) **CHAR:** 10 (+0)

Saving Throws: Dexterity +8, Wisdom +5

Skills: Acrobatics +8, Investigation +5, Stealth +8, Survival +5, Insight +5
Senses: passive Perception 15
Languages: Common and one language of choice
Proficiency Bonus: +3
Challenge: 5 (1,800 xp)

Class Features
- **Tracking Expert:** The Bounty Hunter is skilled in tracking targets and gains advantage on Wisdom (Survival) checks to track creatures.
- **Bounty Hunter's Mark:** The Bounty Hunter can designate a target as their quarry. For the duration of this feature (1 hour), they gain a bonus to damage rolls against the target equal to their proficiency bonus, and they can't be surprised while tracking this creature.
- **Hunter's Reflex:** The Bounty Hunter can add their proficiency bonus to their initiative rolls.

Actions
- **Multi-attack:** The Bounty Hunter can make two attacks with their chosen weapon.
- **Shortsword:** Melee Weapon Attack: +8 to hit, reach 5 ft., one target. Hit: 9 (1d6+4) piercing damage.
- **Heavy Crossbow:** Ranged Weapon Attack: +8 to hit, range 100/400 ft., one target. Hit: 12 (1d10+4) piercing damage.

Bonus Actions
- **Quick Escape:** The Bounty Hunter can use a bonus action to disengage or hide, utilizing their knowledge of stealth tactics.

Reactions
- **Unerring Shot:** When the Bounty Hunter attacks a creature that they have marked as their quarry, they can use their reaction to gain advantage on the attack roll.

Roxan Nightblade

"Silence is my weapon; shadows are my home."

A cunning half-elf bounty hunter with unmatched precision, Roxan navigates shadowy terrain to catch elusive targets.

For the Athletic:
Roxan possesses exceptional agility and acrobatics, allowing her to traverse difficult terrain with deadly grace.

Description:
Roxan's long blonde hair frames a striking face marked by a single scar over her missing eye. Her emerald green eye gleams with determination. She wears sleek black leather armor tailored for stealth and movement, and her aloof demeanor often leaves her motives obscured. Her calm confidence hides the dangerous life she's left behind.

Wants & Needs:
Roxan hunts for a legendary artifact said to grant immense power, dreaming of earning enough gold to retire quietly.

Secret or Obstacle:
Roxan hides her past as a member of a thieves' guild, fearing her former allies will come for her—and take her other eye.

Carrying (Total CP: 29):
- Dual Daggers of Silence (10 points): Lightweight weapons perfect for silent takedowns.
- Cloak of Shadows (8 points): Shrouds her in darkness, granting stealth advantages.
- Grappling Hook (5 points): Assists with vertical climbs and escapes.
- Tracking Gear (6 points): Tools for finding and identifying targets.

Bounty hunter & tracker

Bountyhunter Tactics

Bounty hunters employ a mixture of cunning, patience, and decisive action to fulfill their contracts. They often begin their pursuits with meticulous planning—gathering intelligence, setting traps, and utilizing stealth to close in on their targets. In combat, they may rely on quick, efficient tactics, using their knowledge of terrain and their targets' habits to gain the upper hand. Outside of pursuit, they are adept negotiators, often navigating complex social dynamics to locate and apprehend fugitives, all while remaining one step ahead of rivals.

Griffon Runebringer 2
"Every hunt is a story; it's time to write mine."

Brief: A burly human bounty hunter with a flair for the dramatic, Griffon seeks high-profile targets to build his legend.
Vocation: Bounty Hunter & Mercenary
For the Insightful: Griffon's natural charisma and physical strength make him a dominating presence in both battles and negotiations.
Description: Griffon is stout and muscular, with rugged features and a booming laugh that earns trust—or wariness—wherever he goes. He dons a mix of chainmail and leather armor adorned with hunt symbols, his notepad for bounties always at the ready. His swagger and booming voice are unmistakable, masking the guilt from hunts that went tragically wrong.
Wants & Needs: Griffon is driven to capture the notorious fugitive The Shade and earn fame, fortune, and recognition for his skills.
Secret or Obstacle: He still wrestles with guilt from a hunt gone awry, where he lost a trusted ally.
Carrying (Total CP: 29):
- Broadsword (15 points): A massive, imposing blade for brutal strikes.
- Heavy Armor (10 points): Provides durability and protection in combat.
- Bounty Board Notepad (4 points): Holds contracts, notes, and sketches of fugitives.

Vaelia Silverclaw 3
"Pursuit is my passion; justice is my reward."

Brief: A fierce tiefling bounty hunter who combines charm and ferocity to capture her quarry.
Vocation: Vigilante & Bounty Hunter
For the Insightful: Vaelia's sharp leadership skills and keen intuition make her a force both in negotiations and combat.
Description: Vaelia's deep crimson skin and sleek black hair contrast with her piercing gold eyes, which seem to see through lies. She wears dark leather armor fitted with numerous pockets and straps for her tools. Though she moves with confident grace, a hidden sorrow for those she's lost weighs heavily on her.
Wants & Needs: Vaelia seeks to bring to justice the criminal responsible for her family's ruin, hoping to restore her family's honor.
Secret or Obstacle: She carries deep guilt for being unable to protect her loved ones, which sometimes clouds her judgment.
Carrying (Total CP: 28):
- Twin Sabers (12 points): Razor-sharp blades designed for precision.
- Enchanted Cloak (8 points): Grants her enhanced mobility and stealth.
- Set of Bounty Tokens (5 points): Marks of captured fugitives she's tracked.
- Potion of Fury (3 points): Enhances her combat abilities for brief bursts of strength.

Kara Ashenshadow 4
"Step lightly and carry a big stick."

Brief: A resourceful dwarf bounty hunter who uses clever traps and tactical planning to ensnare her targets.
Vocation: Bounty Hunter & Guerrilla Tactician
For the Insightful: Kara's talent for setting traps and ambushes allows her to turn the battlefield against her enemies.
Description: Kara is short and sturdy, her fiery red hair contrasting with her sharp green eyes. She wears reinforced leather armor layered for both utility and comfort, with pockets filled with specialized tools. A former military engineer, she balances a practical demeanor with a surprisingly warm sense of humor.
Wants & Needs: Kara dreams of earning enough gold to fund a trap-making business, crafting the ultimate hunting device.
Secret or Obstacle: She keeps her military past hidden, fearing it will conflict with her current reputation on the streets.
Carrying (Total CP: 27):
- Crossbow (10 points): A versatile ranged weapon for targeting foes.
- Collection of Specialized Traps (10 points): Ingenious devices for capturing or disabling targets.
- Maps of Known Fugitives (4 points): Provides her with detailed information about her quarry.
- Tinker's Kit (3 points): Tools to maintain her gear and traps.

Thrain Bloodwraith
"A hunter must embrace death before it embraces him." 5

Brief: A fearsome half-orc bounty hunter who blends brute strength with dark magic to hunt elusive prey.
Vocation: Bounty Hunter & Dark Mage
For the Athletic: Thrain's remarkable endurance allows him to track targets tirelessly across long distances without rest.
Description: Thrain's tall, muscular frame is adorned with tribal tattoos that glow faintly when his dark magic is invoked. His black hair is tied back, and his worn armor seems to absorb the light. His deep voice and piercing gaze unsettle those who dare cross him, though he fights an inner struggle against the darkness he wields.
Wants & Needs: Thrain seeks to capture a fugitive who wronged his family and reverse the dark curse hanging over his bloodline.
Secret or Obstacle: Thrain fears his connection to dark magic may one day consume him entirely.
Carrying (Total CP: 30):
- Shadow Blade (15 points): A cursed blade that cuts through both flesh and spirit.
- Spell Components (4 points): Essential tools for his dark incantations.
- Tome of Shadows (1 point): Contains forbidden knowledge he hesitates to use.
- Dark Armor of Camouflage (10 points): A set of armor that blends with shadows, concealing him in darkness.

Elysia Dawnwhisper
"Swift as the wind, silent as the moon." 6

Brief: An agile elf bounty hunter with unmatched archery skills, Elysia moves like a shadow through the wilderness to track her prey.
Vocation: Bounty Hunter & Expert Tracker
For the Perceptive: Elysia possesses an innate talent for camouflage and blending into natural environments, becoming nearly invisible in the wild.
Description: Elysia's slender form and flowing silver hair make her appear almost ethereal as she glides through forests and hills. Her piercing aqua eyes miss no detail, while her earthy-toned leather armor allows her to melt into her surroundings. Despite her graceful calm, her heart carries the weight of long hunts and the loneliness of her calling.
Wants & Needs: Elysia seeks to bring down a notorious beast terrorizing her homeland, hoping to win honor and respect among her kin.
Secret or Obstacle: She fears growing too attached to her surroundings and allies, as her hunts often force her to leave them behind.
Carrying (Total CP: 29):
- Elven Longbow (12 points): A mastercrafted weapon designed for precision and power.
- Camouflage Cloak (8 points): A flowing cloak that renders her nearly invisible in nature.
- Antlered Arrows (6 points): Enchanted arrows designed to pierce magical defenses.
- Herbalist Kit (3 points): Tools for creating healing salves or tracking potions.

Bennick Thorne
"Honor is earned; a bounty is just the beginning." 7

Brief: A charming and cunning human bounty hunter who uses silver-tongued persuasion and wit to secure bounties.
Vocation: Bounty Hunter & Con Man
For the Insightful: Bennick excels at deception, gaining trust and extracting information before striking with calculated precision.
Description: Bennick's dashing appearance—tousled dark hair, sharp features, and a devilish smile—makes him a natural in social settings. He wears flamboyant, well-tailored clothing that conceals several hidden daggers. Beneath his charming demeanor lies a man always two steps ahead, constantly juggling the line between bounty hunter and trickster.
Wants & Needs: Bennick seeks a high-profile bounty to establish his reputation while living a life of indulgence and luxury.
Secret or Obstacle: His past as a con artist still haunts him, and he constantly fears exposure that would shatter his carefully built façade.
Carrying (Total CP: 26):
- Elegant Rapier (12 points): A refined, lightweight blade perfect for dueling.
- Disguise Kit (6 points): Essential tools for altering his identity on the fly.
- Set of Lockpicks (4 points): Used for both infiltration and escape.
- Collection of Notes (4 points): Scribbled information on his marks and rivals.

Sabine Frost — *"Cold steel and colder hearts get the job done."* 8

Brief: A icy sorceress-turned-bounty hunter, Sabine combines combat prowess and frost magic to subdue her quarry.
Vocation: Bounty Hunter & Sorceress
For the Perceptive: Sabine wields both mystic insight and magical prowess, capable of subduing targets with precision and control.
Description: Sabine's pale complexion, silver hair, and icy blue eyes give her an otherworldly beauty that unnerves those who cross her. Her frost-etched robes shimmer faintly with residual magic, and her calculating demeanor leaves no room for doubt. Though she hunts with ruthless efficiency, she struggles to reconcile her powers with her own sense of humanity.
Wants & Needs: Sabine seeks vengeance on a fugitive who betrayed her, hoping to restore her family's tarnished legacy.
Secret or Obstacle: She fears her magical abilities may be seen as a curse, and hides her family's tragic history.
Carrying (Total CP: 33):
- Frostbite Staff (15 points): A staff that channels chilling magic with devastating precision.
- Ice-Ejected Throwing Knives (8 points): Enchanted blades that freeze on impact.
- Book of Spells (5 points): Contains frost incantations and mystical knowledge.
- Warding Crystal (5 points): Provides a protective aura against magical attacks.

Kanyn Windrider — *"Let the winds guide my arrows to their mark."* 9

Brief: An adventurous aarakocra bounty hunter who soars through the skies, using aerial perspectives to track his prey.
Vocation: Aerial Bounty Hunter
For the Athletic: Kanyn's aerial agility and unmatched skill with a bow make him a deadly hunter from above.
Description: Kanyn's vibrant feathers in shades of blue and green mark him as a striking figure even in the skies. His keen eyes pierce through the horizon, tracking his targets with pinpoint precision. Dressed in fitted armor designed to allow unrestricted flight, Kanyn is both graceful and deadly, though memories of past failures weigh heavily on him.
Wants & Needs: Kanyn seeks to capture a rare beast for its legendary hide, dreaming of achieving fame as the greatest aerial hunter.
Secret or Obstacle: He fears his past failure to save a friend will haunt him, and strives to prove his worth to the hunting community.
Carrying (Total CP: 31):
- Longbow of the Skies (15 points): A finely crafted bow optimized for aerial combat.
- Feathery Cloak (8 points): Provides protection without hindering his flight.
- Scout's Binoculars (4 points): Enhances long-range vision for tracking.
- Arrows of Precision (4 points): Specialized arrows designed for perfect accuracy.

Rhea the Unseen — *"Invisibility is my ally; shadows, my sanctuary."* 10

Brief: A stealth-focused dwarf bounty hunter who specializes in infiltration and evasion, disappearing without a trace.
Vocation: Stealth Specialist Bounty Hunter
For the Insightful: Rhea is a master of evasion and concealment, skilled in reading her environment and slipping past foes unseen.
Description: Rhea's grizzled appearance—braided grey hair and sharp, reflective eyes—belies her unmatched stealth skills. She wears dark, nondescript clothing that blends perfectly into her surroundings, making her all but invisible when she wishes. A lifetime of evading detection has made her quiet and deliberate, though she yearns for a peaceful life away from the shadows.
Wants & Needs: Rhea is driven to hunt the elusive assassin Nightshade, hoping to claim the reward and buy herself a plot of land to settle down.
Secret or Obstacle: She struggles with her instinct for secrecy and her desire for peace, constantly torn between the two.
Carrying (Total CP: 24):
- Shadow Dagger (10 points): A lightweight blade designed for quick, silent strikes.
- Cloak of Invisibility (8 points): Grants temporary invisibility when activated.
- Tools of Silence (4 points): Equipment for disabling traps and locks without a sound.
- Riverstone for Stealth (2 points): A small enchanted stone that muffles footsteps.

Clerics

Clerics are the devoted servants of the divine, wielding the power of faith to heal, protect, and guide those in need within a fantasy world. Often found in temples or adventuring alongside heroes, these holy figures are a beacon of hope and guidance. With their deep connection to their deities, clerics channel divine magic to perform miraculous feats, whether it's mending a grievous wound in the heat of battle or lifting a town's spirits with a heartfelt prayer. Their unwavering faith not only grants them remarkable abilities but also shapes their personalities, as many clerics embody the teachings and tenets of their chosen god, becoming upstanding moral compasses for their companions and communities alike.

However, it's wise to be cautious around clerics—especially if one finds themselves in a pickle! Take the humorous example of Brother Cedric, a well-meaning cleric who was known for his overly enthusiastic approach to healing. During one particularly raucous tavern night, Cedric decided to demonstrate his divine prowess by offering to bless every drink in the house, believing it would alleviate the hangovers of the revelers. The cheers were loud and enthusiastic as he raised his hands in prayer, but in his haste, he accidentally invoked a minor spell that transformed the ale into—of all things—fruit punch!

In that moment, the mood shifted from merriment to confusion, as patrons found their mugs overflowing with a sugary concoction fit for children's parties rather than hearty adventurers. Laughter erupted at the unexpected twist, and Brother Cedric quickly learned that not every blessing is sought after during a night out.

So, while clerics bring their divine gifts to the world, one should always remember to tread lightly in their presence. A well-intentioned gesture might lead to unexpected—and often comical—outcomes. Respect their power, and perhaps choose your words wisely around them, lest you end up with a bouquet of flowers in hand instead of a healing spell, or worse, a pint of very non-alcoholic fruit punch in the middle of a rowdy tavern!

Maris Brightmoon

"When the light fades, may we be the torchbearers of hope." 1

Brief: A devoted human cleric who worships the goddess of light and healing, Maris is a beacon of compassion and selflessness.

Vocation: Healer & Advisor

For the Perceptive: Maris possesses deep insight into the intricacies of healing spells, often balancing physical restoration with emotional comfort.

Description: Maris radiates warmth in her white and gold robes, each fold etched with symbols of her goddess. Her long chestnut hair and gentle blue eyes reflect her unwavering kindness. She is soft-spoken yet resolute, a trusted confidant who works tirelessly to bring peace and comfort to those in need. However, the shadows of her past—her time as a soldier—leave her haunted by lives she could not save.

Wants & Needs: Maris wishes to spread her goddess's teachings and dreams of creating a sanctuary for the needy.

Secret or Obstacle: She struggles with the trauma of her battlefield days, fearing she lacks the strength to maintain peace.

Carrying (Total CP: 30):
- Holy Symbol of Light (8 points): A sacred artifact that channels her healing magic.
- Healing Potions (12 points): A stock of powerful restorative elixirs.
- Journal of Prayers (5 points): A collection of divine invocations.
- Set of Blessed Herbs (5 points): Healing components blessed by her goddess.

Sareth Ironwill "Strength of spirit can forge a path through the darkest of times." 2

Brief: A steadfast dwarven war cleric devoted to the god of protection, Sareth inspires courage among his allies and shields them in battle.
Vocation: War Cleric & Protector
For the Perceptive: Sareth has an unmatched grasp of battlefield tactics, using his insight to guide allies through perilous conflicts.
Description: Sareth's sturdy frame and auburn braids radiate an aura of unshakable strength. His green eyes burn with determination, and his armor, engraved with divine symbols, carries the weight of his devotion. He is a shield in both name and action, always standing between danger and those he vows to protect. Though his leadership inspires confidence, he harbors a quiet fear of failing his comrades.
Wants & Needs: To hone his skills and lead his allies to victory, striving to become a legendary champion of faith.
Secret or Obstacle: Sareth battles a lingering fear of inadequacy, questioning his ability to lead when it matters most.
Carrying (Total CP: 34):
- Warhammer of the Guardian (15 points): A massive, rune-inscribed weapon symbolizing his faith.
- Shield of Faith (10 points): A divine barrier that deflects even the fiercest blows.
- Tactics Scrolls (4 points): Strategic notes for inspiring allies during battle.
- Potion of Strength (5 points): A powerful brew that bolsters his endurance.

Leira Moonsong "Guided by the stars, we find our paths illuminated." 3

Brief: A serene elven cleric who serves the goddess of the moon, Leira possesses unmatched wisdom and celestial insight.
Vocation: Seer & Spiritual Guide
For the Insightful: Leira channels the mysteries of the night sky, using celestial guidance to reveal hidden truths and pathways.
Description: Leira's silver hair flows like moonlight, and her soft lavender eyes shimmer with otherworldly clarity. She wears ethereal robes adorned with celestial motifs, and her calming voice brings peace to even the most restless souls. Although her wisdom guides many, Leira privately fears misinterpreting the divine signs she so deeply relies upon.
Wants & Needs: To unravel the mysteries of the cosmos and help lost souls find their way in the world.
Secret or Obstacle: She doubts her own divination abilities, terrified that any mistake may lead others astray.
Carrying (Total CP: 28):
- Crystal Orb of Divination (12 points): A shimmering focus that reveals celestial guidance.
- Moonlit Staff (10 points): A weapon imbued with moonlight, both elegant and powerful.
- Book of Celestial Lore (4 points): A tome of star-based rituals and secrets.
- Potion of Clarity (2 points): A brew to sharpen her insight and focus.

Gretchen Willowshade "Nature is our greatest treasure; let us protect her fiercely." 4

Brief: A resilient ranger-cleric who worships the goddess of nature, Gretchen is a fierce defender of the wilds and its creatures.
Vocation: Nature Cleric & Guardian
For the Insightful: Gretchen possesses an exceptional understanding of flora and fauna, using nature's gifts to heal and defend.
Description: Gretchen is tall and rugged, her auburn hair often adorned with twigs and leaves. Her deep green eyes reflect the quiet wisdom of the forests she protects. Wearing earth-toned cloaks that allow her to blend seamlessly into the wilderness, she patrols her sacred groves with vigilance. Her nurturing demeanor conceals an unyielding ferocity when faced with threats to nature's balance.
Wants & Needs: To defend her forests and establish harmony between civilization and the natural world, dreaming of creating a wildlife sanctuary.
Secret or Obstacle: Gretchen struggles with her anger toward those who harm nature, fearing the rage may consume her soul.
Carrying (Total CP: 26):
- Wooden Staff (10 points): A sturdy, rune-inscribed weapon crafted from an ancient tree.
- Healing Salves (6 points): Natural remedies for treating wounds and poisons.
- Herbalism Kit (4 points): Tools for crafting potions and salves from wild herbs.
- Nature's Tome (6 points): A book of rituals and protective spells dedicated to the wilds.

Valen Trueheart *"Justice prevails through compassion and strength."* 5

Brief: A resolute human cleric devoted to the god of justice, Valen fights tirelessly for the oppressed, balancing his iron will with compassion.
Vocation: Cleric of Justice
For the Insightful: Valen possesses extraordinary negotiation skills, often acting as a mediator to resolve conflicts before they escalate.
Description: Valen stands tall, a shining symbol of righteousness. His brown hair is neatly tied back, and his bright blue eyes reflect unwavering determination. His polished armor gleams with symbols of balance and justice, inspiring allies and striking fear in wrongdoers. Calm and composed, Valen's words are as powerful as his sword, though he carries lingering guilt over past failures that weigh heavily on his sense of purpose.
Wants & Needs: Valen seeks to champion causes for the downtrodden and oppressed, aiming to create a fair world through divine intervention.
Secret or Obstacle: He hides deep feelings of guilt for failing to save a family from injustice, which fuels his fear of inadequacy.
Carrying (Total CP: 30):
- Divine Symbol of Justice (8 points): A sacred emblem that channels his divine authority.
- Shield of the Just (10 points): A sturdy shield marked with symbols of balance and protection.
- Book of Laws (5 points): A tome outlining the doctrines of justice and order.
- Healing Elixir (7 points): A potent potion to mend wounds and restore vitality.

Thalos Emberforge *"Through fire, we forge our destinies."* 6

Brief: A passionate tiefling cleric who channels the god of fire, Thalos inspires his allies with unyielding spirit and burning resolve.
Vocation: Cleric of Fire & Inspiration
For the Perceptive: Thalos possesses a fierce independence that ignites action in those around him, rallying allies to face any challenge.
Description: Thalos's wild red hair and fiery amber eyes match his unrelenting passion for life. His dark robes are adorned with flame-like embroidery that flickers faintly with divine energy. Thalos is bold and fearless, often leading with booming laughter that matches the crackling of his fire magic. However, the power he wields also fuels a simmering temper that he struggles to keep in check.
Wants & Needs: To ignite courage in the hearts of the fearful and craft a legendary weapon infused with divine flames.
Secret or Obstacle: Thalos fears losing control of his fiery powers, worried they may harm those he seeks to protect.
Carrying (Total CP: 29):
- Flame-Forged Mace (15 points): A weapon infused with divine fire, capable of burning enemies on contact.
- Ember Crystal (8 points): A glowing gem that amplifies his flame-based magic.
- Journal of Fire Spells (4 points): A collection of powerful flame incantations.
- Healing Flames (2 points): Magic that restores allies while scorching nearby foes.

Althea Highstar *"In unity, we rise; in faith, we stand."* 7

Brief: A celestial aasimar cleric dedicated to bringing communities together, Althea serves as a beacon of light and unity.
Vocation: Cleric of Community & Light
For the Insightful: Althea possesses a natural ability to inspire and unify people, shining a light of hope in the darkest times.
Description: Althea's luminescent golden skin and radiant hair make her presence feel almost otherworldly. Dressed in flowing robes embroidered with celestial patterns, she moves with a graceful serenity that calms even the most troubled souls. Her voice carries a divine resonance, soothing tensions and fostering understanding. Despite her confidence, she struggles with the weight of bringing together conflicting views.
Wants & Needs: To heal divisions within her community and establish a foundation where all can thrive together.
Secret or Obstacle: Althea fears she may not have the strength or influence to bring unity to her divided people.
Carrying (Total CP: 21):
- Holy Symbol of Community (8 points): A divine focus that amplifies her unifying magic.
- Healing Staff (6 points): A versatile weapon capable of both healing and defense.
- Journal of Teachings (4 points): A record of wisdom and communal rituals.
- Set of Blessed Stones (5 points): Sacred stones used to consecrate spaces and bolster allies.

Holly Greenvale   "Earth's bounty feeds the body; faith feeds the soul."   8

Brief: A gentle druidic cleric devoted to the goddess of harvest, Holly protects the balance of nature while providing for her community.
Vocation: Agricultural Cleric
For the Perceptive: Holly possesses deep knowledge of agriculture and nature, using it to sustain crops and ensure bountiful harvests.
Description: Holly's chestnut hair is interwoven with wildflowers, and her bright green eyes sparkle with the warmth of life. She wears flowing, earth-toned robes that reflect her close connection to nature. Her gentle demeanor nurtures hope in those she aids, but the creeping encroachment of civilization on her sacred lands leaves her anxious for the future.
Wants & Needs: To ensure bountiful harvests for her community and restore balance to lands ruined by overdevelopment.
Secret or Obstacle: She fears losing her connection to nature, burdened by the rapid spread of civilization into the wilds.
Carrying (Total CP: 26):
- Staff of Growth (10 points): A wooden staff that encourages plants to flourish at her touch.
- Healing Herb Satchel (6 points): A collection of restorative herbs for treating ailments.
- Seed Collection (5 points): Rare and sacred seeds used to replant barren lands.
- Tome of Nature's Secrets (5 points): A guide to ancient flora-based rituals and remedies.

Cyrus Stormwatcher   "Weather the storm; heal the soul."   9

Brief: A brooding human cleric devoted to the god of tempest, Cyrus channels the power of storms to heal, protect, and restore balance.
Vocation: Cleric & Emotional Healer
For the Insightful: Cyrus possesses an exceptional ability to read emotional wounds, providing comfort and clarity to those lost in turmoil.
Description: Cyrus cuts a striking figure in his storm-grey robes, their edges embroidered with symbols of thunder and rain. His tousled black hair and stormy grey eyes seem to reflect the very storms he channels. Calm in demeanor yet prone to intense, unpredictable bursts of energy, Cyrus walks a fine line between controlled serenity and tempestuous fury. While his magic comforts others, he struggles with his own inner storms, often hiding his emotional turmoil beneath a stoic exterior.
Wants & Needs: To find balance between his divine power and his emotions, while guiding others through their struggles.
Secret or Obstacle: Cyrus fears his emotional struggles might hinder his ability to lead and heal others in critical moments.
Carrying (Total CP: 29):
- Wand of Storms (10 points): A divine wand capable of summoning lightning and tempests.
- Healing Potions (6 points): A series of vials that mend wounds during battle.
- Journal of Emotions (4 points): A personal record used to help others identify and address their struggles.
- Amulet of Tranquility (9 points): A relic that calms turbulent energy within the wielder.

Eldrin Starshroud   "Magic is the light that guides us through the darkest night."   10

Brief: A wise elven cleric of celestial magic, Eldrin wields starlight to heal, protect, and reveal hidden truths, guiding others through the darkest of times.
Vocation: Celestial Cleric & Arcane Healer
For the Insightful: Eldrin senses the unseen, uncovering hidden magic and unraveling truths that others might overlook.
Description: Eldrin's silvery hair flows like moonlight, and his glowing blue eyes reflect the starlight he channels. His constellation-embroidered robes shimmer faintly, mirroring his calm and composed presence. Speaking with quiet wisdom, Eldrin offers clarity and comfort, yet he carries the burden of unsettling visions that leave him questioning his own fallibility.
Wants & Needs: To unlock celestial mysteries and prevent the calamities foretold in his visions while guiding others to safety.
Secret or Obstacle: Eldrin fears his visions may be flawed, leading those who trust him into danger.
Carrying (Total CP: 32):
- Staff of Starfire (12 points): Channels celestial energy for healing and bursts of radiant power.
- Celestial Codex (8 points): A tome of starlit spells and divine wisdom.
- Starlight Potion (6 points): Restores vitality and enhances focus in critical moments.
- Moonstone Pendant (6 points): Amplifies magic while shielding the wearer from harm.

Conjurers

Conjurers are masters of summoning, weaving spells to bring forth creatures, objects, and forces from realms beyond mortal comprehension. They walk a fine line between the material and the arcane, drawing upon planes both wondrous and perilous. To witness a skilled conjurer at work is to glimpse the infinite: a glittering portal to another world, a creature born of pure starlight, or a sword forged in the fires of an elemental abyss. Yet, with such power comes grave responsibility—and equally grave risks. Conjurers do not merely bend the fabric of reality; they bargain with it, often at a price unseen by the untrained eye.

Those who underestimate a conjurer's art do so at their peril, for their magic is not bound by mortal laws. Consider the grim tale of Aldren Vyse, a conjurer of considerable renown, whose temper was as fiery as his command over the planes. Aldren was once called to a small village to mediate a land dispute between two rival families. One elder, seeking to intimidate Aldren into favoring his claim, insulted the mage publicly, dismissing his craft as mere parlor tricks. Aldren, calm at first, warned the man to reconsider his words. When the insults continued, Aldren raised his staff and uttered a single incantation.

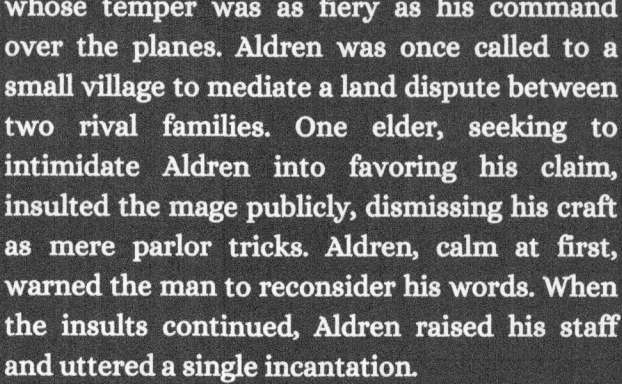

From the ether, a shadow coalesced—a towering figure with blazing eyes and wings of tattered void. The creature, bound to Aldren's will, did not harm the elder directly. Instead, it hovered silently above him for hours, its presence an unrelenting weight upon his soul. The elder's confidence crumbled; his boasts turned to pleas for mercy. When the creature finally vanished at Aldren's command, the elder was left a husk of his former self, aged beyond his years. The message was clear: to provoke a conjurer is to invite forces beyond mortal reckoning, forces that care little for the laws of man or mercy.

Conjurers are not to be trifled with. Treat these wielders of the arcane with respect, for even the smallest misstep could summon consequences far more dire than intended.

Fendril Mossweaver

"With each thread, I shape reality to my desires." 1

Brief: A meticulous half-elf conjurer who channels elemental forces to summon beings of nature.
Vocation: Conjurer & Elemental Summoner
For the Perceptive: Fendril's deep connection to the elements allows him to control powerful natural summons in battle.
Description: Wearing an elaborately embroidered robe covered in symbols of nature, Fendril wields a gnarled staff entwined with vines. His sharp green eyes and calm demeanor conceal the weight of his past—a dangerous failure that fuels his cautious mastery of conjuring.
Wants & Needs: Seeks to create the ultimate elemental familiar, dreaming of earning recognition among nature's guardians.
Secret or Obstacle: Haunted by a past incident where he lost control of a summoned creature.
Carrying (Total CP: 28):
- Staff of Elemental Command (12 points): Wields command over earth, wind, and water.
- Spell Components Pouch (6 points): Stores rare herbs and crystals.
- Tome of Elemental Lore (5 points): Ancient texts detailing summoning rituals.
- Collection of Crystals (5 points): Focuses magic for precise control.

Eirik Firestorm

"Every spark is the beginning of a grand inferno." **2**

Brief: A passionate human conjurer who specializes in summoning fiery entities to unleash destruction.
Vocation: Fire Conjurer & Elemental Architect
For the Insightful: Eirik's natural charm allows him to tame even the most volatile fire elementals.
Description: Adorned in flame-patterned robes and magical fire charms, Eirik's bright orange eyes glow like embers. His exuberant personality masks a simmering fear of losing control, as his power grows dangerously close to consuming him.
Wants & Needs: Dreams of summoning the ultimate fire elemental and crafting a legendary artifact to harness its strength.
Secret or Obstacle: Worries that his fire magic will one day spiral out of control, burning everything he holds dear.
Carrying (Total CP: 30):
- Flame Wand (15 points): Channels searing flames.
- Fire Spells (8 points): A collection of destructive incantations.
- Ember Container (4 points): Holds sparks from legendary fire creatures.
- Fire Crystals (3 points): Boosts fire magic's intensity.

Galdor Mistshroud

"In the veils of fog, we find potential untapped." **3**

Brief: A whimsical gnome conjurer who manipulates light and illusions to deceive and confound.
Vocation: Illusion Conjurer & Trickster
For the Insightful: Galdor's expertise in illusions allows him to manipulate sight and perception with precision.
Description: Galdor is a short, spry figure clad in robes that shift colors like mist. His blue eyes twinkle with mischief, always hiding a deeper insecurity about his talents. Despite his playful nature, his illusions are nothing short of mesmerizing.
Wants & Needs: Aspires to perform the ultimate illusion and earn recognition as the greatest trickster mage.
Secret or Obstacle: Fears being exposed as a fraud, despite his incredible skills.
Carrying (Total CP: 25):
- Wand of Illusions (10 points): Weaves light and shadow into images.
- Set of Illusion Cards (5 points): Used to create distracting displays.
- Crystal Sphere of Light (6 points): Amplifies magical illusions.
- Book of Deceptions (4 points): Notes on advanced illusion spells.

Thorn Blackwhisper

"From shadows, I summon power untold." **4**

Brief: A brooding half-orc conjurer who draws strength from the Shadow Realm, manipulating unseen forces.
Vocation: Shadow Conjurer & Summoner
For the Insightful: Thorn's communion with shadow entities gives him an edge in stealth and combat.
Description: Draped in dark robes etched with shadow runes, Thorn moves with an eerie grace. His green skin and intense gaze unsettle even allies, as he wrestles with the dangerous power he controls.
Wants & Needs: Seeks to form a bond with a legendary shadow creature to protect those he cares about.
Secret or Obstacle: Fears losing himself to the very shadows he commands.
Carrying (Total CP: 29):
- Shadowblade (10 points): A dagger forged in shadow.
- Amulet of the Night (6 points): Grants vision in darkness.
- Shadow Essence Bottle (3 points): Captures ethereal shadows.
- Tome of Dark Conjurations (10 points): Contains forbidden shadow magic.

Riven Stormcaller   *"Nature's fury is both a weapon and an ally."* 5

Brief: A An aged elf conjurer who summons storms and celestial lightning to dominate battles.
Vocation: Storm Conjurer & Weather Shaman
For the Insightful: Riven's mastery of storm magic gives him unparalleled control over weather-based spells.
Description: Riven's storm-patterned robes crackle with latent energy, matching his silver hair and dark blue eyes. Storm familiars swirl near him, signaling the weight of his responsibility to balance power and control.
Wants & Needs: Desires to master celestial storm summoning to protect his homeland from disasters.
Secret or Obstacle: Fears the devastating consequences of unleashing uncontrollable storm magic.
Carrying (Total CP: 28):
- Staff of Storms (15 points): Harnesses lightning's wrath.
- Handbook of Storm Summoning (8 points): Chronicles weather-based spells.
- Healing Waters (2 points): Soothes injuries with rain magic.
- Sparkstone (3 points): Stores raw electrical energy.

Fintan Grovekeeper   *"From the roots, we draw our strength."* 6

Brief: A firbolg conjurer who summons woodland creatures and plant spirits to maintain harmony.
Vocation: Nature Conjurer & Protector
For the Perceptive: Fintan's deep understanding of the forest allows him to summon guardians to aid in defense.
Description: Fintan's bark-like skin and moss-covered robes make him appear as one with the forest. His calm demeanor and protective nature inspire trust, though he harbors fears of encroaching civilization.
Wants & Needs: Dreams of preserving sacred groves and expanding his village's woodland reserves.
Secret or Obstacle: Worries that he may fail to protect his homeland from destruction.
Carrying (Total CP: 27):
- Staff of the Wilds (10 points): Summons plant-based allies.
- Herbalist's Journal (6 points): Notes on healing plants and rituals.
- Collection of Seeds (7 points): Used to summon plant guardians.
- Animal Familiar's Charm (4 points): Strengthens bonds with summoned creatures.

Tobias Ironroot   *"Forging the strength of the earth within our grasp."* 7

Brief: A stalwart dwarf conjurer who draws his power from the earth, summoning stone and rock to shield his allies.
Vocation: Earth Conjurer & Stone Shaper
For the Insightful: Tobias's deep understanding of stone magic allows him to summon constructs of unmatched durability.
Description: Clad in earth-toned armor etched with ancient runes, Tobias radiates unwavering strength. His braided beard and twinkling brown eyes reflect wisdom earned through hardship. Tobias summons towering stone guardians to defend those in need, though he wrestles with his family's demands to embrace traditional stonework. He dreams of creating a golem that will stand the test of time, a legacy carved in stone.
Wants & Needs: Seeks to craft a legendary golem that will protect his community and honor the earth's ancient powers.
Secret or Obstacle: Fears disappointing his family, who believe his magic is a betrayal of their crafting heritage.
Carrying (Total CP: 31):
- Earthshaper's Hammer (12 points): Channels earth magic to shape and control stone.
- Rune-etched Gauntlets (10 points): Enhances his ability to summon sturdy constructs.
- Grimoire of Stone (5 points): Contains rituals for crafting earth guardians.
- Crystals of Preservation (4 points): Focuses energy to maintain summoned creatures.

Astra Nightwhisper

"In shadows, I create wonders unseen." **8**

Brief: A mysterious elven conjurer who channels the depths of the Shadow Realm to summon creatures of darkness.
Vocation: Shadow Conjurer & Dream Weaver
For the Perceptive: Astra's deep understanding of shadow magic allows her to weave both nightmares and protection from the unseen.
Description: Astra's obsidian hair and violet eyes shimmer in the moonlight as if kissed by the stars. Her dark robes ripple like shadows, embroidered with starlight patterns that seem to move. She commands shadow creatures with quiet authority, a power that makes her both revered and feared. Haunted by a failed summoning that brought chaos to her village, Astra treads carefully between mastery and the abyss.
Wants & Needs: Aspires to master shadow conjuring to atone for her mistakes and secure her place as a shadow guardian.
Secret or Obstacle: Lives in fear of losing control again, believing her magic could consume her and those she cares for.
Carrying (Total CP: 26):
- Shadow Scepter (10 points): Channels energy to manifest shadow creatures.
- Moonstone Pendant (5 points): Enhances shadow spells in moonlight.
- Night Vision Potion (3 points): Allows clear sight in darkness.
- Grimoire of Shadow Creatures (8 points): Details summoning rituals for shadow entities.

Selene Starbloom

"With the flicker of starlight, all dreams are born." **9**

Brief: A celestial tiefling conjurer who draws magic from the stars, summoning cosmic beings to guide her path.
Vocation: Celestial Conjurer & Astral Sage
For the Insightful: Selene's mastery of astral magic allows her to create stunning illusions and call forth celestial allies.
Description: Selene's silver skin shimmers faintly under the starlight, and her turquoise hair flows like a river of light. Her celestial staff is adorned with constellations that glow softly in the dark. With calm grace, Selene summons beings of radiant energy, dazzling her allies and foes alike. Yet, the burden of prophecy rests heavy on her shoulders, as she fears her visions may one day foretell calamity.
Wants & Needs: Seeks to uncover the legendary star of prophecy, dreaming of becoming a revered oracle among her people.
Secret or Obstacle: Struggles with the crushing weight of her prophecies, fearing the cost of revealing the truth.
Carrying (Total CP: 28):
- Celestial Staff (12 points): Channels cosmic energy to summon astral beings.
- Book of Celestial Enchantments (8 points): Contains ancient spells tied to the stars.
- Dream Essence Potion (4 points): Calms minds and reveals hidden visions.
- Star Crystals (4 points): Focuses energy for celestial summons.

Kira Emberweaver

"Threading fire's dance to create jewels from ashes." **10**

Brief: A spirited fire conjurer who merges artistry and destruction, mastering flames to create both beauty and devastation.
Vocation: Fire Conjurer & Artisan
For the Insightful: Kira's skill with flame magic allows her to conjure powerful fire elementals while creating breathtaking displays.
Description: Kira's fiery red hair and glowing amber eyes burn with intensity and confidence. Her flame-etched robes ripple with heat, swirling like embers caught in the wind. Kira sees fire as a dance—both destructive and life-giving—and moves with graceful precision. Though her power is unmatched, she hides an underlying fear of losing control, knowing her flames could consume everything if unleashed fully.
Wants & Needs: Seeks to summon the ultimate fire elemental and forge a legacy of artistry within the flames.
Secret or Obstacle: Battles her insecurities about losing control during conjurations, fearing her fire's unpredictable nature.
Carrying (Total CP: 29):
- Flamefire Wand (14 points): Harnesses fire to conjure devastating elementals.
- Journal of Fire Artistry (8 points): A detailed tome of fiery rituals and creations.
- Firestone Amulet (4 points): Stabilizes her conjured flames.
- Ember Essence Vials (3 points): Stores raw elemental fire for controlled use.

Druids

Druids are the guardians of nature in the fantasy realm, deeply connected to the natural world and its myriad life forms. With a profound respect for the balance of ecosystems, these spellcasters harness the powers of the elements, flora, and fauna, using their magic to heal, protect, and transform. Whether they're communing with animals, calling upon the forces of nature to aid in battle, or shape-shifting into fearsome beasts, druids embody the spirit of the wild. Often found in lush forests, meadows, or sacred groves, druids exude an aura of serenity, guiding their companions with wisdom derived from a life spent in harmony with nature. Their unique abilities to manipulate the environment make them invaluable allies on any quest, capable of turning the tide in the most dire of situations. However, it is essential to approach druids with caution, as their deep affinity for the natural world can lead to unsettling outcomes if provoked. A cautionary tale is often told about Rowan, a once-revered druid who lost touch with the harmonious balance he was sworn to protect. In his zeal to avenge his beloved forest being torn down for development, Rowan decided to summon the wrath of nature itself. He called forth a horde of woodland creatures, but instead of acting solely on his will, the magic surged out of control, awakening dark spirits of the forest long forgotten. The once-gentle animals, fueled by Rowan's anger, morphed into terrifying beasts, wreaking havoc on the town that had encroached upon their home.

The villagers barely escaped with their lives, but the haunting memory remained. Rowan vanished into the depths of the forest, forever marked by the consequences of overstepping the balance of nature. Now, a whispered warning circulates among adventurers: disrespect a druid's connection to the wild, and you risk invoking not just their wrath, but unleashing untamed forces that could turn friend into foe. So, when dealing with druids, remember to tread lightly, uphold the sanctity of nature, and never underestimate the consequences of their fierce loyalty to the wild!

Elina Frostglen

"The frost teaches patience, for even winter must yield to the sun." 1

Brief: A serene elven druid who wields the power of ice and snow to protect her homeland.
Vocation: Winter Druid & Guardian of Frost
For the Perceptive: Elina's deep bond with the frozen wilderness allows her to manipulate snow and ice, shielding allies and freezing foes with precision.
Description: Elina's pale, ethereal beauty reflects the landscapes she calls home, with silver-blue hair like frost and piercing azure eyes holding endless calm. Her robes, embroidered with delicate snowflakes, exude a cool serenity even in chaotic battles. Her quiet nature masks deep wisdom, a stillness forged through years of meditating in the coldest wilds. She moves gracefully, like a winter whisper, yet beneath her tranquil surface lies a fierce protector.
Wants & Needs: Elina seeks to preserve the balance of the seasons, fearing the rise of unnatural heat in her homeland; she longs to find an ancient artifact said to restore harmony to the world's frozen places.
Secret or Obstacle: Haunted by visions of a dying, thawed forest, she doubts her power and fears it may not be enough.
Carrying (Total CP: 28):
- Staff of Eternal Winter (12 points): Channels the magic of ice and snow.
- Snowflake Cloak (8 points): Grants resistance to cold and enhances stealth in winter terrain.
- Crystal of Frostbound Spirits (5 points): Allows communication with ancient winter spirits.
- Herbal Bundle of Northern Remedies (3 points): Heals frostbite and enhances resilience.

Druids

Armor Class: 15 (Hide Armor)
Hit Points: 70 (10d8+20)
Speed: 30ft.

STR: 12 (+1) **DEX:** 14 (+2) **CON:** 14 (+2) **INT:** 11 (+0) **WIS:** 18 (+4) **CHAR:** 10 (+0)

Saving Throws: Intelligence +3, Wisdom +8

Skills: Nature +6, Medicine +8, Perception +8, Survival +8
Senses: passive Perception 18
Languages: Common, Druidic, and one language of choice
Proficiency Bonus: +3
Challenge: 6 (2,300 xp)

Class Features

- Wild Shape (2/short rest): The Druid can use their action to polymorph into a beast they have seen before. The Druid retains their intelligence, wisdom, and charisma scores. They can stay in this form for up to 3 hours.
- Spellcasting: The Druid is a spellcaster. Their spellcasting ability is Wisdom (spell save DC 16, +8 to hit with spell attacks).
  - Cantrips: Druidcraft, Thorn Whip
  - 1st Level Spells (4 slots): Goodberry, Healing Word, Entangle
  - 2nd Level Spells (3 slots): Barkskin, Moonbeam
  - 3rd Level Spells (3 slots): Call Lightning, Plant Growth
  - 4th Level Spells (2 slots): Guardian of Nature, Greater Invisibility

Actions

- Multi-attack: The Druid can cast a spell and make two melee attacks with their staff.
- Quarterstaff: Melee Weapon Attack: +5 to hit, reach 5 ft., one target. Hit: 7 (1d8+3) bludgeoning damage. This attack counts as magical for the purpose of overcoming resistance.
- Spell Attack (Thorn Whip): Ranged Spell Attack: +8 to hit, range 30 ft., one target. Hit: 8 (1d6+4) piercing damage, and the target is pulled 10 ft. closer to the Druid.

Reactions

- Animal Companion (if Circle of the Shepherd): The Druid can use their reaction to summon a spirit animal to aid allies, providing temporary hit points or enhancing their attacks.

Bramblethorn Greentoe   *"Even the smallest roots can crack the mightiest stone."* 2

Brief: A whimsical halfling druid who brings the untamed power of plants to life, balancing humor with nature's ferocity.
Vocation: Wild Druid & Plant Whisperer
For the Insightful: Bramblethorn summons vines and roots to entangle his enemies while nurturing allies with herbal remedies.
Description: Bramblethorn's bright green eyes and leafy beard make him look like part of the wild itself. His moss-covered robes are adorned with small blossoms and seeds that sprout wherever he treads. Though his lighthearted wit often amuses his companions, his connection to the wild runs deep. In combat, he summons creeping vines, entangling his enemies with a flick of his staff, while his laughter echoes through the trees like a playful breeze.
Wants & Needs: He dreams of finding the Heartseed, a mythical seed that could restore a long-lost forest, making him a hero to nature.
Secret or Obstacle: He struggles to control his creations, fearing his magic might one day spiral into chaos.
Carrying (Total CP: 26):
- Verdant Staff of Growth (10 points): Commands plants with ease.
- Seed Pouch of Living Chaos (6 points): Sprouts vines or flowers on command.
- Dew of Renewal (5 points): A potent herbal remedy.
- Field Guide of Forgotten Flora (5 points): Provides knowledge of ancient plants.

Rowan Flameheart   *"Let the fires of nature burn away the rot of corruption."* 3

Brief: A fiery genasi druid who channels blazing infernos to cleanse the wilds of decay and rebirth new life.
Vocation: Flame Druid & Nature's Inferno
For the Insightful: Rowan's mastery of fire magic purifies the land, ensuring the balance between destruction and creation remains intact.
Description: Rowan's molten gold eyes burn with intensity, while his ember-tinted skin glows like smoldering coals. His robes, singed at the edges, shift between red and orange hues, mimicking the living fire he commands. Though fierce in battle, Rowan views fire as both a destroyer and nurturer—burning away the corrupt to make room for the new. He walks the line between fury and control, constantly mindful of the power he wields.
Wants & Needs: Rowan seeks the Flame of Renewal, a relic said to cleanse corrupted lands with fire, restoring them to their natural state.
Secret or Obstacle: He fears losing control of his fire, becoming the destroyer he swore to oppose.
Carrying (Total CP: 30):
- Flamebound Staff (12 points): Focuses his fire magic.
- Ashen Mantle (8 points): Protects him from fire damage while amplifying his spells.
- Phoenix Ash Charm (5 points): Briefly reignites Rowan's strength if he falls in battle.
- Scroll of Blazing Rebirth (5 points): Summons flames to purge corruption.

Arlen Moonsway   *"In moonlight, shadows reveal the truth we cannot see."* 4

Brief: A contemplative human druid attuned to the power of the moon, guiding allies and spirits with its serene magic.
Vocation: Lunar Druid & Spirit Guide
For the Perceptive: Arlen uses the moon's light to reveal hidden truths, heal wounds, and banish darkness from the land.
Description: Arlen's silver eyes glow softly in the dark, a reflection of his deep bond with the moon. His robes, woven with shifting lunar patterns, emit a gentle light that calms all who stand near him. Often mistaken for a wandering spirit himself, Arlen moves with dreamlike grace, calling forth moonlit beams to heal his allies or vanquish shadowy threats. Yet his connection to the ethereal realm weighs on him, as spirits cling to him for guidance.
Wants & Needs: Arlen seeks the Moonshard, a relic said to strengthen the boundary between the mortal world and the spirit realm.
Secret or Obstacle: The spirits he guides linger too long, whispering to him and threatening to shatter his mind.
Carrying (Total CP: 27):
- Moonlit Staff (10 points): Channels beams of healing and banishment.
- Lunar Amulet (6 points): Allows Arlen to project moonlight to reveal hidden enemies.
- Spiritbinder Journal (6 points): Contains ancient rites for communicating with the dead.
- Moonflower Petals (5 points): A rare herb that enhances his restorative spells.

Thalos Rootbinder

"The earth's roots hold the secrets to strength unbroken." **5**

Brief: A stoic half-orc druid who commands the ancient power of roots and stone to shield the natural world.
Vocation: Earthwarden & Protector of Groves
For the Insightful: Thalos channels his connection to the earth to fortify allies, entangle enemies, and preserve the balance of the land.
Description: Thalos's broad frame is adorned with bark-like armor etched with druidic runes. His mossy green hair twists into thick braids, and his eyes glow faintly with the wisdom of the earth. Though quiet and solemn, his presence exudes a deep calm, like a mountain that endures the passage of ages. In battle, he calls forth mighty roots to ensnare foes or hardens his allies' defenses with stone-infused magic. Thalos views himself as the shield of the wild, unyielding and immovable.
Wants & Needs: Thalos seeks the Rootstone Relic, an artifact said to awaken the earth's primal defenses against growing threats.
Secret or Obstacle: He fears losing control of his powers, as deep beneath the earth lie forces even he cannot fully tame.
Carrying (Total CP: 28):
- Staff of Rootbound Might (12 points): Summons roots to entangle enemies or form protective barriers.
- Stoneplate Cloak (8 points): Enhances his durability and allows him to absorb damage.
- Earthheart Gem (5 points): Grants him brief control over terrain in battle.
- Roots of Healing Balm (3 points): A rare salve that rejuvenates and strengthens allies.

Mira Windbloom

"Where flowers bloom, life and hope follow." **6**

Brief: A kind-hearted gnome druid who weaves the gentle magic of blossoms to heal the land and its people.
Vocation: Bloom Druid & Nature's Caretaker
For the Perceptive: Mira's mastery of floral magic enables her to restore life, cleanse corruption, and protect her allies in times of need.
Description: Mira's petite frame is crowned with wildflowers that seem to bloom naturally in her soft pink hair. Her clothing is a patchwork of vibrant greens and yellows, reflecting the springtime magic she carries. Her bright, curious eyes reveal her unshakable optimism, even in the darkest forests. Mira's spells bloom with vivid color as she conjures flowers to heal wounds, spread calming scents, or ensnare her foes in thorny vines.
Wants & Needs: Mira dreams of finding the Everbloom Seed, a mythical flower said to restore entire ecosystems with a single bloom.
Secret or Obstacle: Her gentle nature masks a fear of confrontation; she worries that when danger strikes, she won't have the courage to stand her ground.
Carrying (Total CP: 26):
- Bloomstaff of Renewal (10 points): Summons healing flowers and vines.
- Pollen Satchel of Serenity (6 points): Releases calming scents to ease tension in battle.
- Thorny Bramble Gloves (6 points): Enhances her ability to protect allies with defensive flora.
- Vial of Nectar Essence (4 points): Accelerates the growth of plants to restore damaged land.

Kael Thornsong

"The wild's song carries both beauty and fury." **7**

Brief: A passionate elven druid who commands the symphony of nature, using sound to inspire allies and confound foes.
Vocation: Nature Bard & Forest Harmonist
For the Insightful: Kael's ability to manipulate sound and nature allows him to weave melodies that bolster allies or disorient enemies.
Description: Kael's lithe figure moves with the grace of a forest breeze, his silver hair braided with small leaves and feathers that hum softly as he walks. His attire, a tunic of woven greens and browns, shimmers faintly when he speaks his spells. Kael's melodies resonate with the wild, calling creatures to his aid or soothing the weary hearts of his companions. In combat, his voice becomes a weapon, commanding the winds or unleashing earthen tremors with powerful refrains.
Wants & Needs: Kael searches for the Harmonic Crystal, a legendary relic that amplifies nature's song to heal entire forests.
Secret or Obstacle: He struggles with his role as a guide, haunted by moments when his songs failed to protect those he loved.
Carrying (Total CP: 27):
- Lyrastaff of Nature's Chord (10 points): Amplifies his spellcasting through harmonious melodies.
- Windcaller Pendant (7 points): Allows him to summon gusts of wind with his voice.
- Echoing Gloves of Resonance (6 points): Enhances his ability to disrupt enemies with sound magic.
- Songbook of Verdant Hymns (4 points): Contains forgotten melodies tied to nature's magic.

Thara Deepvale *"The shadows are not to be feared—they are part of the balance."* 8

Brief: A mysterious human druid who walks the boundary between light and shadow, guarding the secrets of the hidden wilds.
Vocation: Shadow Druid & Warden of the Dark
For the Perceptive: Thara bends shadows to her will, cloaking her movements and striking her enemies with whispers of darkness.
Description: Thara's long black cloak seems to merge with the shadows, while her amber eyes pierce the dark with unsettling clarity. Her voice is a soft murmur, calming yet tinged with mystery, as if she holds the answers to forgotten secrets. While her allies trust her guidance, others fear her shadowy magic, which she uses to conceal, protect, or strike unseen foes. Thara views the balance of light and dark as sacred, walking a path few dare tread.
Wants & Needs: Thara seeks the Shadebinder Relic, an artifact that can solidify her bond with the realm of shadows.
Secret or Obstacle: The shadows call to her constantly, tempting her toward a darkness she struggles to resist.
Carrying (Total CP: 28):
- Shadowmeld Staff (12 points): Manipulates and shapes shadows in combat.
- Umbral Cloak (8 points): Renders her invisible in dim light.
- Eclipsed Amulet (5 points): Grants her protection against light-based magic.
- Tome of Shadow Whispers (3 points): Contains hidden knowledge of shadow spells.

Ferris Rootwhisper *"The forest speaks to those who take the time to listen."* 9

Brief: A patient firbolg druid who communes with the oldest trees, using their strength and wisdom to protect the land.
Vocation: Treewarden & Guardian of the Ancient Wilds
For the Insightful: Ferris's bond with the ancient trees allows him to manipulate wood and channel their strength into powerful spells.
Description: Ferris towers over most, his bark-like skin etched with patterns resembling tree rings. His deep voice rumbles like distant thunder, carrying the quiet authority of the wilds. His mossy cloak and wooden staff are adorned with leaves that seem to grow anew each day. Ferris can summon towering roots to defend his allies or call upon the wisdom of elder trees to guide his path.
Wants & Needs: Ferris seeks the Elderheart Acorn, a relic said to awaken the spirits of the oldest trees.
Secret or Obstacle: He fears the ancient forests are dying, and his connection to the wild may fade with them.
Carrying (Total CP: 30):
- Staff of Ancient Bark (12 points): Manipulates wood and roots to defend allies.
- Heartwood Amulet (8 points): Strengthens his bond with ancient trees.
- Vial of Sap Essence (6 points): Temporarily grants allies increased durability.
- Carved Totem of Forest Spirits (4 points): Channels protective energy from the wild.

Faelor Thornshroud *"The wild's fury is a whisper; wield it wisely, or be consumed."* 10

Brief: A mysterious and reclusive half-orc druid, guards ancient forests and channels primal energies to defend nature's balance.
Vocation: Primal Guardian & Wild Shaper
For the Insightful: Faelor shares an instinctual bond with the primal forces of the wild, allowing him to shape-shift into powerful beasts and harness the earth's raw energy.
Description: Tall and imposing, Faelor's lean frame is wrapped in robes of enchanted vines. His ashen-green skin, marked with faintly pulsing druidic tattoos, reflects his connection to nature's power. Beneath his hood, amber eyes watch for any threat to the balance. A solitary figure, he vanishes into forests, emerging only to unleash the wild's wrath on those who desecrate it. Despite his gruff exterior, his bond with the land reveals an old soul devoted to its fragile harmony.
Wants & Needs: Faelor seeks the Thornheart Relic, an ancient staff to restore sacred groves and halt civilization's spread.
Secret or Obstacle: Haunted by losing control of his beast form, Faelor fears his primal side may consume him.
Carrying (Total CP: 29):
- Thornheart Relic (12): A gnarled staff channeling the forests' ancient fury.
- Wildshaper's Cloak (8): Enables seamless transformation into animals.
- Tome of Primal Forms (5): Holds knowledge of legendary beasts.
- Vial of Verdant Essence (4): Restores nature's energy to its wielder.

Enchanters

The role of an enchanter is deeply influenced by societal perceptions of magic, the complexity of spellcraft, and the ethical dilemmas surrounding enchantments. In some realms, enchanters are celebrated as esteemed magicians, masters of transformation and manipulation who bring wonder and intrigue to the world. In others, they may be viewed with suspicion, blamed for bewitching hearts and minds to serve their own ends.

Imagine a world where enchanters are more than mere spellcasters. Some might belong to ancient orders that guard the secrets of arcane knowledge, while others might wander as independent sorcerers, skillfully crafting charms and spells to enthrall or empower. During times of conflict, these masters of illusion and charm can be pivotal, tipping the balance of power with their potent creations.

Arcana
- **DC 10:** Competent enchanters are likely to possess a wide array of spells that manipulate emotions, enhance objects, or create illusions. They might employ charms to bolster allies' abilities or confuse foes with dazzling displays of magic, making them valuable assets in any party.
- **DC 20:** Master enchanters may command powerful enchantments that can alter the very nature of reality. Their capabilities could include creating magical constructs or infusing items with extraordinary powers. Their artistry in spellcraft enables them to weave complex enchantments that reveal hidden truths or bring about monumental transformations.

History
- **DC 10:** Throughout history, enchanters have played crucial roles in shaping cultures, their spells memorialized in legends and tales. Their craft often intersects with the fabric of society, influencing everything from politics to art, and their magical creations sometimes become the stuff of myth.
- **DC 15:** The motivations of enchanters can be as diverse as their spells. Understanding their backgrounds—be they scholars searching for knowledge, artists pursuing beauty, or schemers hungry for power—can provide deep insight into their behavior and choices.

Bribery and Influence
An enchanter's willingness to engage in deals or accept bribes is shaped by numerous enchanting factors:
- Motivation: Their primary drivers, such as the pursuit of knowledge, wealth, or artistic expression
- Compensation: The magical artifacts, gold, or knowledge promised in exchange for their services or secrets
- Allegiances: Loyalty to specific guilds, schools of magic, or personal philosophie
- Consequences: The possible ramifications for their actions, especially if they exploit their magical talents unethically
- Punishments: Expected repercussions from breaching magical laws, the codes of guilds, or societal norms

Enchanters

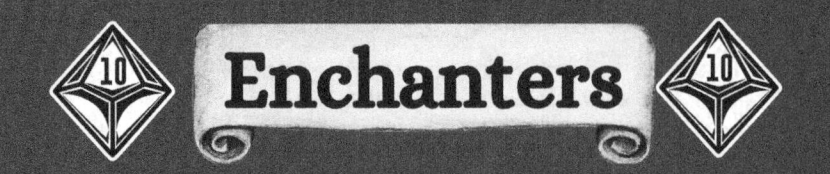

Armor Class: 13 (Mage Armor)
Hit Points: 50 (8d8+8)
Speed: 30ft.

STR: 10 (+0) **DEX:** 14 (+2) **CON:** 12 (+1) **INT:** 18 (+4) **WIS:** 12 (+1) **CHAR:** 14 (+2)

Saving Throws: Intelligence +8, Charisma +6

Skills: Arcana +8, Deception +6, Persuasion +6, Insight +5
Senses: passive Perception 15
Languages: Common, Elvish, and two other languages of choice
Proficiency Bonus: +3
Challenge: 5 (1,800 xp)

Class Features
- Spellcasting: The Enchanter is a spellcaster. Their spellcasting ability is Intelligence (spell save DC 16, +8 to hit with spell attacks).
  - Cantrips: Minor Illusion, Prestidigitation, Vicious Mockery
  - 1st Level Spells (4 slots): Charm Person, Disguise Self, Sleep
  - 2nd Level Spells (3 slots): Suggestion, Enthrall
  - 3rd Level Spells (3 slots): Hypnotic Pattern, Fear
  - 4th Level Spells (2 slots): Dominate Person, Greater Invisibility
- Enchantment Specialist: The Enchanter gains advantage on saving throws against being charmed, and they can cast spells that charm or compel others with enhanced effectiveness.

Actions
- Multi-attack: The Enchanter can cast a spell and make a weapon attack in the same turn.
- Dagger: Melee Weapon Attack: +6 to hit, reach 5 ft., one target. Hit: 5 (1d4+2) piercing damage.
- Charm Spell (Charm Person): A target must succeed on a DC 16 Wisdom saving throw or be charmed by the Enchanter for 1 hour. While charmed, the target regards the Enchanter as a trusted friend.

Reactions
- Counterspell: The Enchanter can use their reaction to attempt to nullify a spell of equal or lower level being cast within 60 feet.

Ysara Dreamcaster

"From dreams, we fashion reality; let us weave magic through the night."

A graceful elven enchanter, Ysara specializes in dream magic and illusions, using her artistry to soothe minds and inspire wonder.

For the Insightful: Ysara can enter dreams, weaving enchantments that calm the restless or harness nightmares for protection.

Description: Ysara's flowing silver hair and lavender eyes hold the brilliance of distant stars. She wears twilight silk robes adorned with arcane charms that shimmer softly in darkness. Her calming voice and poised demeanor draw others close, offering both peace and insight.
Her dream magic has left a mark—her aura, though soothing, carries a faintly haunting quality.

Wants & Needs:
- Wants: To uncover deeper mysteries of the dream realm and heal emotional wounds.
- Needs: Forbidden dream lore to protect others from creeping nightmares.

Secret or Obstacle:
Ysara fears her own nightmares might manifest, threatening those she seeks to help.

Carrying: (Total Carry Points: 28)
- Dreamweaver Wand (12 points): A wand etched with moonlight runes, guiding dreams and illusions.
- Tome of Dream Patterns (8 points): Maps and symbols for navigating the dreamscape.
- Dreamcatcher Pendant (4 points): Captures nightmares to protect the wearer.
- Essence of Sleep Potion (4 points): Induces deep slumber, enhancing dream magic.

Enchanter Tactics

Enchanters employ a blend of creativity and strategic thinking to achieve their ends, often using their knowledge of psychology and magic to outmaneuver opponents. In combat, they may cast spells that disrupt foes or bolster allies, turning the tide through cunning and innovation. Their expertise allows them to create illusions that can blind or confuse enemies, providing critical openings for attack. Outside of combat, enchanters are skilled negotiators, using their abilities to charm or manipulate others to achieve their goals.

Dream enchanter & Illusionist

Alaric Silverwind — 2
"Enchantments are the art of turning the ordinary into the extraordinary."

Brief: A suave human enchanter, Alaric turns mundane items into legendary artifacts with charm and precision.
Vocation: Master Enchanter & Item Creator
For the Insightful: Alaric's skill at reading desires allows him to craft magical items that resonate deeply with their owners.
Description: Alaric's dark, shoulder-length hair and piercing blue eyes exude refinement. He wears finely embroidered robes with silver detailing, while enchanted trinkets jingle softly at his waist. His wit and magnetic presence make him both admired and envied.
Though confident, he hides insecurities about meeting his family's lofty expectations.
Wants & Needs:
- Wants: To craft a legendary artifact that lasts for generations.
- Needs: A workshop to showcase and perfect his enchanting skills.

Secret or Obstacle: Alaric fears falling short of his family's legendary legacy, pushing himself to perfection.
Carrying: (Total Carry Points: 30)
- Enchanter's Toolkit (10 points): Precision tools for crafting magical objects.
- Amulet of Charisma (6 points): Enhances his charm and presence subtly.
- Collection of Rare Gems (6 points): Energy-rich gems for enchantments.
- Tome of Enchantment Recipes (8 points): Instructions for crafting magical artifacts.

Thaddeus Nightshade — 3
"True power lies in subtlety and finesse."

Brief: A brooding half-elf illusionist, Thaddeus crafts intricate illusions that unsettle and deceive.
Vocation: Illusion Enchanter & Mischief-Maker
For the Insightful: Thaddeus masters sensory illusions, obscuring reality with tricks that confound even sharp minds.
Description: With dark hair, piercing emerald eyes, and silver-filigreed robes, Thaddeus thrives in mystery. His quiet words, often laced with double meanings, unsettle listeners. His illusions are flawless, but his grip on reality wavers, leaving him in a constant battle with his mind.
Wants & Needs:
- Wants: To perfect illusions that inspire awe and fear.
- Needs: A mentor to help him distinguish illusion from reality.

Secret or Obstacle: Thaddeus fears becoming lost in his illusions, unable to tell them from reality.
Carrying: (Total Carry Points: 28)
- Illusionist's Wand (12 points): A black wand for shadowy illusions.
- Grimoire of Shadows (10 points): Contains forbidden illusion spells.
- Essence of Deception (4 points): Enhances illusions with liquid shadow.
- Mirror of Illusions (2 points): Reflects false realities.

Bramwell Emberforge — 4
"With the flick of my wrist, magic ignites the mundane."

Brief: A boisterous dwarven enchanter, Bramwell channels fire magic into dazzling artifacts and potent weapons.
Vocation: Fire Enchanter & Magical Craftsman
For the Insightful: Bramwell's mastery of fire allows him to transform its volatile energy into powerful enchantments.
Description: With a bushy red beard, glowing amber eyes, and flame-stitched armor, Bramwell embodies fiery creativity. His booming laughter echoes through workshops, masking the underlying fear of his magic spiraling out of control.
Wants & Needs:
- Wants: To craft a flame-enchanted weapon of legend.
- Needs: Control over his fire magic to ensure its safety.

Secret or Obstacle: Bramwell fears that his flames, if unchecked, could cause catastrophic harm.
Carrying: (Total Carry Points: 29)
- Flameforge Staff (12 points): Channels raw fire energy.
- Gemstone of Fire (8 points): A ruby imbued with elemental flames.
- Book of Flame Invocations (4 points): Contains advanced fire spells.
- Fireproof Gloves (5 points): Enchanted to resist extreme heat.

Dorian Brightspark
"Every hue of light conceals boundless potential." **5**

Brief: An eccentric gnome enchanter obsessed with light magic, Dorian uses illumination to inspire and dazzle those around him.
Vocation: Light Enchanter & Illusion Artist
For the Perceptive: Dorian's extraordinary understanding of colors and light allows him to craft radiant illusions that captivate and confuse.
Description: Small and sprightly, Dorian's wild multi-colored hair and twinkling hazel eyes are as vibrant as his creations. His robes shimmer under any light, decorated with charms that sparkle with magical energy. Though whimsical and cheerful, his inventive ideas often push the limits of what's considered practical or sane.
Wants & Needs:
- Wants: To illuminate the world with his creations, crafting artifacts that redefine reality.
- Needs: Recognition and understanding to overcome his reputation as a "mad" inventor.

Secret or Obstacle: Dorian fears being misunderstood or dismissed for his eccentricity, which often leaves him isolated.
Carrying: (Total Carry Points: 26)
- Wand of Radiance (10 points): A prism-tipped wand that channels brilliant light.
- Prism of Illumination (6 points): A focus for creating dazzling illusions.
- Codex of Light Spells (5 points): A book of powerful light-based incantations.
- Colorful Charms (5 points): Small trinkets that store and release bursts of light energy.

Kieran Twilightshade
"Enchantments weave life's tapestry, binding us all together." **6**

Brief: A soft-spoken tiefling enchanter, Kieran uses emotional currents to create spells that heal and foster harmony.
Vocation: Emotion Enchanter & Whisperer
For the Perceptive: Kieran's innate ability to sense emotional energy allows him to craft spells that resonate with the hearts of others.
Description: With deep purple skin, curling horns, and flowing white hair, Kieran's ethereal presence soothes those around him. His shimmering robes reflect twilight hues, mirroring his calm and compassionate nature. Despite his serenity, his struggles with inner darkness remain hidden beneath his soft exterior.
Wants & Needs:
- Wants: To use his magic to heal wounds and build understanding among people.
- Needs: Support in managing his emotional burdens so they don't interfere with his work.

Secret or Obstacle: Kieran hides his bouts of depression, fearing that his struggles might undermine his role as a healer.
Carrying: (Total Carry Points: 27)
- Heartstring Staff (12 points): Channels emotional energy into restorative spells.
- Tome of Emotional Charms (7 points): Contains enchantments tied to feelings.
- Crystal Pendant (4 points): Stores and amplifies emotional energy.
- Love Tokens (4 points): Small enchanted charms that promote peace and understanding.

Selene Shadowgaze
"In shadows lies the power to enchant and transform." **7**

Brief: An enigmatic dark elf enchanter, Selene uses shadow magic to weave powerful charms and illusions.
Vocation: Shadow Enchanter & Illusionist
For the Insightful: Selene possesses an unparalleled mastery of shadows, using them to enthrall, conceal, or bewilder her targets.
Description: Selene's deep obsidian skin and silver hair cascade like liquid moonlight. Her dark, elegant robes blend into shadows, amplifying her mysterious aura. Her piercing gaze and commanding presence both fascinate and unnerve those around her. Yet, she fears the shadows she commands might consume her, erasing her moral compass.
Wants & Needs:
- Wants: To master shadow magic and craft the ultimate enchantment of enthrallment.
- Needs: To maintain her grip on morality as she delves deeper into shadow lore.

Secret or Obstacle: Selene hides her fear that the power of shadows will one day overwhelm her, leaving her lost in darkness.
Carrying: (Total Carry Points: 26)
- Shadowmancer Staff (10 points): Channels shadows into spells of concealment and illusion.
- Cloak of Shadows (6 points): Allows the wearer to vanish into darkness.
- Set of Dark Crystals (2 points): Stores shadow magic for quick use.
- Grimoire of Enchantment (8 points): Contains spells for shadow manipulation and charm crafting.

Liora Starlight 8
"With a flick of the wrist, we can touch the stars."

Brief: A radiant aasimar enchanter, Liora draws celestial energy into her creations to bring hope and light to others.
Vocation: Celestial Enchanter & Alchemist
For the Perceptive: Liora channels celestial energy to craft artifacts that inspire and uplift those around her.
Description: Liora glows softly, her golden hair cascading in waves that reflect her divine heritage. Her celestial-patterned robes shine faintly in darkness, exuding warmth and serenity. While her creations inspire hope, she conceals her struggle with the pressure of living up to celestial expectations.
Wants & Needs:
- Wants: To create artifacts that bring hope and light to dark places.
- Needs: Self-confidence to embrace her own path, free of imposed expectations.

Secret or Obstacle: Liora fears failing to meet the lofty standards of her celestial lineage.
Carrying: (Total Carry Points: 28)
- Stellar Wand (10 points): Channels celestial energy into radiant spells.
- Codex of Celestial Lore (8 points): Ancient celestial knowledge.
- Flasks of Light Elixirs (6 points): Potions that restore vitality and dispel darkness.
- Pendant of Hope (4 points): Inspires courage and resolve.

Ivy Hardleaf 9
"Nature's whispers become woven enchantments."

Brief: A vibrant druidic enchanter, Ivy channels the natural world to craft spells that nurture and protect.
Vocation: Nature Enchanter
For the Perceptive: Ivy draws power from plants and earth, enhancing her enchantments with life-giving energy.
Description: With lively green hair, bright eyes, and dresses woven from leaves, Ivy embodies the essence of the wild. Her connection to nature inspires her creations, though she quietly struggles to find her own path, separate from her mother's legacy.
Wants & Needs:
- Wants: To create spells that restore and nurture the natural world.
- Needs: The confidence to step out of her mother's shadow and embrace her unique gifts.

Secret or Obstacle: Ivy fears failing to meet her family's expectations as a renowned druid enchanter.
Carrying: (Total Carry Points: 27)
- Leafy Staff (10 points): Channels the energy of plants into spells.
- Herbal Spellbook (8 points): Contains plant-based incantations.
- Tonic of Natural Growth (4 points): Accelerates plant growth and restores vitality.
- Collection of Seeds (5 points): Rare seeds with magical properties.

Maya Flamewhisper 10
"With every spark, new magic ignites."

Brief: A passionate fire sorceress, Maya channels flame into stunning spells and enchantments that awe and inspire.
Vocation: Fire Enchanter & Creator
For the Insightful: Maya's natural affinity for flame allows her to wield fire as both art and destruction.
Description: Maya's fiery-red hair and glowing golden eyes match her vibrant personality. Her flame-patterned robes shimmer with hues of red and orange, reflecting her dynamic and impulsive nature. Though her magic inspires awe, she fears her passion might lead to unintended harm.
Wants & Needs:
- Wants: To craft fire enchantments that redefine magical combat.
- Needs: Balance and control to temper her impulsive tendencies.

Secret or Obstacle: Maya fears losing control of her fiery magic, causing unintended devastation.
Carrying: (Total Carry Points: 29)
- Firebrand Wand (12 points): Channels intense fire spells.
- Spellbook of Flames (8 points): Contains advanced fire-based incantations.
- Potion of Fire Resistance (3 points): Protects against extreme heat.
- Fiery Elixir Ingredients (6 points): Rare components for fire enchantments.

Explorers

Explorers are the bold wanderers who brave the uncharted corners of the realm, driven by insatiable curiosity and a yearning for discovery. Known for their cunning and adaptability, these intrepid souls traverse perilous mountains, tangled jungles, and boundless seas in search of forgotten relics, lost civilizations, and untold horrors. With maps in hand, compasses at their side, and an unquenchable thirst for knowledge, explorers walk a thin line between triumph and doom. Their tales of perilous journeys and grand discoveries inspire others to chart their own paths, but they are also riddled with blood, madness, and regret—a reminder that the world's darkest secrets do not yield themselves lightly. Aspiring adventurers must take heed: not all that glitters holds glory, and some treasures are better left entombed.

Take, for example, the grim fate of Alden, a reckless explorer whose ambition drowned out all wisdom. Lured by whispered legends of an ancient ruin that held a relic of unspeakable power, he dismissed the warnings of wary tribes who spoke of the place as cursed ground, haunted by a nameless force. For days, Alden crawled through labyrinthine tunnels, enduring unspeakable traps and horrors. Finally, he found it—a pulsing, blackened crystal that drank the very light around it.

In claiming it, Alden sealed his doom. The ruin trembled as the thing awakened—a monstrous entity of shadow and hate, clawing its way back into the world. It hunted him through the crumbling halls, its guttural roars filling the void as his mind shattered. Alden's final cries were lost to the darkness, and though his body was never found, the locals tell of a shadow that now stalks those ruins, endlessly searching for its next foolhardy prey.

Let Alden's tale serve as a warning: Discovery is no gentle pursuit; it is a descent into the unknown, where madness and death wait for those who tread too boldly. So, adventurers, set forth with steel and caution, for the hidden paths you walk may lead not to riches, but to ruin—and some doors, once opened, can never be closed.

Lirael Windwalker

"The wind carries my spirit; every journey is a tale waiting to be told."

Brief: A lively half-elf explorer who soars across endless skies, Lirael masters aerial navigation and weather patterns, driven by an insatiable curiosity to chart uncharted heights.
Vocation: Sky Explorer & Cartographer
For the Perceptive: Lirael's exceptional sense of direction and uncanny ability to predict shifting winds ensure her glider's graceful flight, even through the roughest skies.
Description: With flowing brown hair adorned with feathers and teal eyes like open skies, Lirael embodies wanderlust. She wears a leather vest and breezy trousers, ideal for aerial acrobatics, and her enchanted, feather-carved glider never leaves her side. Despite her daring nature, she conceals a crippling fear of heights, trusting the winds to carry her safely.
Wants & Needs: To chart undiscovered lands and uncover lost sources of ancient magic hidden in the skies.
Secret or Obstacle: Though she soars high, Lirael hides a paralyzing fear of falling, a secret that gnaws at her every flight.
Carrying (Total Carry Points: 27):
- Enchanted Glider (15 points): A magically reinforced glider with feathered patterns for extended, controlled aerial travel.
- Map of the Skies (5 points): A magically inscribed map charting winds and hidden landmarks above the clouds.
- Feathered Compass (4 points): An enchanted compass aligning to favorable air currents.
- Exploration Journal (3 points): A journal brimming with sketches, notes, and secrets of her adventures.

Bromir Ironfist
"Every rock holds a tale; every cave a treasure." **2**

Brief: A sturdy and relentless dwarf explorer, Bromir ventures deep into caverns in search of ancient relics and hidden treasures, driven by his love of the earth's secrets.
Vocation: Cave Explorer & Treasure Hunter
For the Insightful: Bromir's unmatched knowledge of geology helps him uncover valuable minerals, hidden relics, and secret paths in even the darkest depths.
Description: With a thick brown beard, weathered skin, and sharp eyes, Bromir embodies dwarven resilience. He wears rugged leather armor and a miner's helmet with an enchanted lantern to pierce the shadows. His booming laugh keeps spirits high, though he quietly fears the crushing silence and endless dark of the deep earth.
Wants & Needs:
- Wants: To uncover legendary treasures and secure a lasting legacy for his clan.
- Needs: To overcome his fear of getting lost in the vast, winding caverns he explores.

Secret or Obstacle: Bromir hides a creeping fear of the oppressive darkness, often gripping ropes or walls to reassure himself.
Carrying: (Total Carry Points: 29)
- Pickaxe of the Bedrock (10 points): An enchanted tool that breaks through even the hardest stone.
- Shovel of Unearthing (5 points): Magically reveals buried artifacts and relics.
- Explorer's Pack (8 points): Includes climbing gear, torches, and survival tools for underground exploration.
- Gemstone Collector's Kit (6 points): Tools and lenses for safely extracting and identifying precious gems.

Iris Thistledown
"With nature as my guide, I wander where few dare to tread." **3**

Brief: A curious and observant gnome explorer, Iris ventures through forests, mountains, and ruins to uncover the secrets of flora, fauna, and forgotten places.
Vocation: Nature Explorer & Botanist
For the Perceptive: Iris's keen eye allows her to spot hidden plants, animal trails, and environmental details that others often overlook.
Description: With wild, curly green hair and bright, inquisitive eyes, Iris looks every bit the wandering botanist. She wears practical, durable clothes suited for travel, her satchel always stocked with tools and notes. Though endlessly curious, she quietly doubts her abilities when surrounded by more seasoned adventurers.
Wants & Needs:
- Wants: To catalog rare plants and animals, dreaming of discovering a legendary healing herb.
- Needs: To overcome her timid nature and trust her knowledge and instincts.

Secret or Obstacle: Iris fears being underestimated and often second-guesses herself when facing the unknown.
Carrying: (Total Carry Points: 26)
- Field Journal (6 points): Filled with sketches and notes on plants, animals, and discoveries.
- Herbalism Satchel (8 points): Contains tools for identifying and preserving rare herbs.
- Nature's Compass (5 points): A magical compass that always points toward areas of rich natural energy.
- Gnome-sized Climbing Gear (7 points): Lightweight equipment tailored for climbing trees, cliffs, and ruins.

Kael Stormchaser
"Every storm holds the promise of discovery." **4**

Brief: A bold and charismatic explorer, chasing storms and turbulent skies to uncover their secrets and chart anomalies.
Vocation: Storm Explorer & Meteorologist
For the Insightful: Kael's sharp instincts help him predict sudden weather shifts, navigating treacherous landscapes and fierce storms with confidence.
Description: With windswept blond hair and storm-gray eyes, Kael thrives where others falter. He wears a weather-resistant cloak and sturdy gear built to endure nature's fury. His infectious enthusiasm masks a lingering anxiety—he fears being caught unprepared by the very storms he pursues.
Wants & Needs:
- Wants: To uncover weather anomalies and unlock the magical secrets hidden in tempests.

Secret or Obstacle: Kael secretly battles anxiety when storms rage out of control, relying on meditation to steady his nerves.
Carrying: (Total Carry Points: 25)
- Weather-Tracking Wand (10 points): Detects and predicts changes in weather patterns.
- Storm Journal (5 points): Maps, observations, and theories on storms and their magical properties.
- Adventurer's Gear (6 points): Includes durable clothing, climbing ropes, and survival tools.
- Flare for Signal (4 points): A magical flare to call for aid or mark safe paths in a tempest.

Tamsin Glimmertail   *"The glimmer of lost treasures is only a step away."* 5

Brief: A stealthy and astute elven explorer, Tamsin navigates ancient ruins and forgotten places, uncovering hidden relics and deciphering lost histories.
Vocation: Ruins Explorer & Archaeologist
For the Insightful: Tamsin's sharp intuition allows her to decode ancient symbols and clues, revealing pathways and treasures others miss.
Description: With silver hair cascading like moonlight and piercing amber eyes, Tamsin blends seamlessly into the shadows. She wears dark, flexible gear designed for silent movement through ruins, her quiver of enchanted arrows always at the ready. Though fearless in her pursuits, she harbors unease about the truths her explorations may reveal about her lineage.
Wants & Needs: Wants: To uncover a legendary artifact and piece together the forgotten history of her people.
- Needs: The courage to face the darker truths that her discoveries may unveil.

Secret or Obstacle: Tamsin fears that what she uncovers may reveal unsettling truths about her family's past, shaking her identity.
Carrying: (Total Carry Points: 31)
- Bow of the Hidden (12 points): A silent, enchanted bow that strikes true even in darkness.
- Map of Ruins (10 points): A magically detailed map that reveals hidden chambers and traps.
- Archaeological Kit (6 points): Tools for safely uncovering and preserving ancient artifacts.
- Enchanted Lantern (3 points): A dim, shadow-casting light that illuminates only what she needs to see.

Sorin Riverstone   *"Follow the currents; they lead to untold wonders."* 6

Brief: A seasoned human explorer with an unshakable connection to rivers and waterways, Sorin guides others through treacherous waters in search of forgotten secrets.
Vocation: River Explorer & Guide
For the Perceptive: Sorin's exceptional boating skills and natural sense of direction allow him to navigate whirlpools, hidden waterways, and dangerous river routes with ease.
Description: With wavy brown hair and twinkling blue eyes, Sorin radiates calm and confidence. He wears water-resistant clothing and carries tools salvaged from his many journeys. His hearty laughter often echoes over rushing waters, but he harbors a quiet fear of the dark, unseen depths below the surface.
Wants & Needs: Wants: To chart the safest and most mysterious river routes, uncovering hidden whirlpools and their secrets.
- Needs: To overcome his hesitation when facing murky, unpredictable waters.

Secret or Obstacle: Sorin fears what lies in the shadowy depths of unknown waters, often second-guessing his instincts when danger looms unseen.
Carrying: (Total Carry Points: 28)
- Compact River Raft (10 points): A lightweight, magically reinforced raft ideal for navigating turbulent waters.
- Fishing Gear (5 points): Tools for gathering food and detecting river disturbances.
- Watersource Map (6 points): A detailed map revealing hidden currents and secret waterways.
- River Charm (7 points): A magical amulet that grants brief control over small water currents.

Lucius Nightforge   *"With each step into the dark, we uncover the light within."* 7

Brief: A resilient and determined tiefling explorer, Lucius delves into shadowy caves seeking ancient secrets and lost knowledge.
Vocation: Cave Explorer & Dark Historian
For the Insightful: Lucius's adaptability and endurance allow him to navigate treacherous terrain and uncover hidden paths where others dare not tread.
Description: With deep red skin, curling horns, and a mane of dark hair, Lucius cuts a striking figure. He wears practical, rugged gear suited for exploration, including a hooded cloak that blends into darkness. Though confident, he fears being judged solely by his infernal heritage and tirelessly strives to prove his worth through his discoveries.
Wants & Needs: Wants: To document ancient caves and uncover lore that will earn him recognition as a legendary historian.
- Needs: To overcome the prejudice surrounding his origins and prove his worth through his findings.

Secret or Obstacle: Fears that his infernal bloodline will overshadow his achievements, keeping him from the respect he seeks.
Carrying: (Total Carry Points: 32)
- Pickaxe of Insight (10 points): An enchanted pickaxe that reveals hidden pathways when striking stone.
- Dark Lantern (8 points): A magical lantern that illuminates unseen details in complete darkness.
- Journal of Lore (8 points): A detailed record of ancient symbols, findings, and discoveries.
- Rare Stone Collecting Kit (6 points): Tools for preserving and studying rare stones and minerals.

Thessia Dawnfire — 8
"Explore fearlessly, for every dawn brings new horizons."

Brief: A luminous elven explorer driven by an insatiable curiosity, Thessia traverses uncharted lands and skies, uncovering new paths and hidden wonders.
Vocation: Pathfinder & Cartographer
For the Athletic: Thessia's endurance and sharp navigation skills allow her to safely traverse dangerous landscapes and chart accurate maps for those who follow.
Description: With silvery hair that catches the light of dawn and brilliant, sky-blue eyes, Thessia is a beacon of adventure. Her flowing, lightweight clothing allows for swift movement, blending with her surroundings. While outwardly confident, she harbors a quiet fear of failure—of returning home without discoveries to share.
Wants & Needs:
- Wants: To chart uncharted territories and uncover the secrets of ancient civilizations.
- Needs: To overcome her fear of returning empty-handed and embrace the journey as its own reward.

Secret or Obstacle: Thessia fears the pressure of unfulfilled expectations, pushing herself to the brink in her pursuit of discovery.
Carrying: (Total Carry Points: 30)
- Mapmaking Kit (10 points): Tools enchanted to create accurate maps as she travels.
- Compass of Destiny (8 points): A magical compass that guides her toward her next great discovery.
- Exploration Journal (5 points): Filled with notes, maps, and sketches of her findings.
- Rare Plant Seeds (7 points): Unique seeds collected during her journeys, carrying the potential for magical growth.

Orin Flowsky — 9
"Adventure flows like a river; we must not resist its currents."

Brief: A cheerful and whimsical halfling explorer, Orin wanders across the lands, sharing stories of his adventures and bringing joy to those he meets.
Vocation: Traveling Storyteller & Explorer
For the Insightful: Orin's natural charm and keen social instincts allow him to befriend strangers, gathering lore and fostering camaraderie wherever his travels take him.
Description: Round and rosy-cheeked, with curly brown hair and bright, twinkling eyes, Orin's presence is as warm as a campfire. He wears patched, colorful clothes and carries a small pack full of maps, snacks, and instruments. His infectious laughter masks a quiet fear of solitude, which drives him to seek friendships and shared tales.
Wants & Needs:
- Wants: To compile his adventures into a grand book of tales that will inspire others to explore.
- Needs: To overcome his fear of being alone and find purpose beyond the stories he tells.

Secret or Obstacle: Orin fears isolation, relying on companionship to navigate the emotional challenges of life on the road.
Carrying: (Total Carry Points: 24)
- Collection of Maps (10 points): Hand-drawn maps marking hidden trails and unique landmarks.
- Story Compendium (5 points): A book filled with songs, fables, and legends gathered on his journeys.
- Music Flute (4 points): A simple enchanted flute that soothes hearts and lifts spirits.
- Halfling-Sized Camping Gear (5 points): Lightweight tools for setting up cozy campsites on the road.

Anais Sunshadow — 10
"The twilight reveals beauty that daylight conceals."

Brief: A thoughtful and enigmatic elven explorer, Anais seeks the mysteries of twilight realms, where nature and magic intertwine in hidden harmony.
Vocation: Twilight Explorer & Researcher
For the Insightful: Her sharp instincts allow her to uncover hidden paths and mystical creatures that remain unseen.
Description: With dark silver hair and glowing amber eyes, Anais seems to carry the twilight itself. Her muted, twilight-hued clothing blends seamlessly with shadows, allowing her to move unnoticed. Calm and observant, her quiet demeanor invites curiosity, though she quietly fears that the deeper secrets she seeks might sever her connection to nature.
Wants & Needs: Wants: To catalog the mystical creatures and plants of the twilight and unlock their forgotten secrets.
- Needs: To preserve her bond with nature as she delves deeper into the arcane mysteries of the twilight realm.

Secret or Obstacle: Anais fears that uncovering the twilight's deepest knowledge may corrupt her spirit, pulling her away from the harmony she holds dear.
Carrying: (Total Carry Points: 26)
- Twilight Staff (10 points): A staff that glows faintly in twilight, guiding her path, enhancing her connection to dark realms.
- Nature's Compass (4 points): A magical tool that reveals hidden paths and twilight sanctuaries.
- Cloak of Shadows (4 points): Grants temporary invisibility under twilight skies.
- Journal of Mystical Beings (8 points): A carefully kept record of creatures, plants, and arcane secrets discovered on her journeys.

Fighters

Fighters are the champions of battle in the fantasy realm, renowned for their strength, skill, and resolve. Armed with diverse weapons and often clad in protective armor, these warriors stand as the frontline defenders against all manner of foes, from marauding beasts to dark sorcerers. Masters of martial combat, they excel in various fighting styles, whether wielding a sword with precision, executing powerful unarmed strikes, or charging into battle as towering juggernauts. Fighters inspire admiration, serving as role models for aspiring warriors, and their bravery often earns respect from both allies and enemies. Whether honing their craft in training rings or engaging in large-scale battles, fighters exemplify courage and steadfastness.

However, aspiring fighters should beware the pitfalls of their path. A cautionary tale speaks of Garrick the Bold, a renowned fighter famed for unmatched prowess. In a fit of bravado, Garrick declared he could take on five challengers at once, chasing fame and glory. Ignoring warnings from comrades about overconfidence, he stepped into the ring with more foes than he could handle. As the bell rang and the crowd cheered, Garrick was quickly overwhelmed—too many fists, swords, and elbows coming at him. What began as a show of strength turned into chaos, with Garrick accidentally knocking himself unconscious against a wooden post of the arena.

Garrick's tale reminds fighters that while strength and bravery are admirable, overconfidence can lead to costly mistakes. In battle, it's not just about hitting the hardest but also about strategy, teamwork, and knowing limits. So, as you don your armor and prepare for combat, respect the challenges ahead. Train diligently, heed allies' wisdom, and fight with humility—lest you find yourself learning firsthand just how unpredictable the art of fighting can be.

Garric Ironshield

"Strength is forged in struggle; we are steel." 1

Brief: A stalwart and unyielding dwarven fighter, Garric stands as a shield for his people, known for his unmatched resilience and unshakable will on the battlefield.

Vocation: Defender & Champion of His People

For the Perceptive: Garric's mastery of defense and tactical combat allows him to hold the line, protecting allies and turning the tide of even the fiercest battles.

Description: With a thick, braided beard and piercing blue eyes, Garric embodies dwarven determination. His heavy plate armor bears his clan's ancient sigil, and his massive shield inspires both allies and enemies. Though his presence is intimidating, the scars he carries—both seen and unseen—remind him of the cost of vengeance and war.

Wants & Needs: Wants: To defend his homeland from invading forces and earn a legacy as a legendary shield-bearer.

Secret or Obstacle: Haunted by the scars of a brutal past duel with a rival, Garric's desire for redemption risks becoming a quest for vengeance.

Carrying: (Total Carry Points: 32)
- Dwarven Warhammer (15 points): A heavy, rune-etched weapon that strikes with crushing force.
- Shield of Resilience (10 points): A massive shield enchanted to withstand even the most devastating blows.
- Battle Standard (4 points): A clan banner that inspires allies to fight harder when raised.
- Healing Potion (3 points): A vial of restorative brew to mend wounds in the heat of battle.

Kellan Strongheart   *"A true warrior fights not for glory, but for those who cannot."* 2

Brief: A noble and steadfast human fighter, Kellan dedicates himself to protecting the innocent and upholding justice in a fractured world.
Vocation: Knight & Protector
For the Insightful: Kellan possesses a keen sense of justice, often lifting the spirits of those around him with his unwavering confidence and leadership.
Description: Broad-shouldered and resolute, Kellan's cropped blond hair and bright green eyes reflect his unyielding resolve. He wears polished chainmail beneath a flowing tabard emblazoned with his house emblem, his calm demeanor balancing his fierce presence. Despite his noble heritage, he quietly questions his worthiness to lead.
Wants & Needs: Wants: To unite the divided factions of his kingdom and restore peace through his actions.
- Needs: To overcome the doubts that weigh heavily on his shoulders, proving himself as a true leader.

Secret or Obstacle: Burdened by the expectations of his lineage, Kellan wrestles with feelings of inadequacy in his quest to lead with honor.
Carrying: (Total Carry Points: 28)
- Sword of Justice (12 points): A shining blade imbued with an aura of righteousness.
- Knights' Shield (8 points): A sturdy shield emblazoned with his family crest, offering superior defense.
- Journal of Battles (4 points): A personal record of strategies and lessons learned on the battlefield.
- Healing Ointments (4 points): Remedies to treat wounds and keep him fighting in prolonged battles.

Torin Stonebreaker   *"Every strike brings us closer to victory."* 3

Brief: A hardy and fearless half-orc fighter, Torin thrives in the chaos of combat, channeling his strength and endurance to overcome any foe.
Vocation: Warrior & Adventurer
For the Athletic: Torin's exceptional endurance and raw power allow him to dominate opponents in long, grueling battles, often outlasting even the fiercest adversaries.
Description: Torin's muscular frame, olive skin, and long black hair mark him as both a warrior and a survivor. His studded leather armor bears the scars of countless battles, a testament to his experience. Behind his booming laughter and bravado, he quietly struggles with a fear of being underestimated because of his heritage.
Wants & Needs: Wants: To carve his name into legend through heroic deeds, earning the respect of warriors across the land.
- Needs: To overcome his insecurities and prove his worth through his unyielding spirit.

Secret or Obstacle: Torin hides his sensitivity beneath a bold exterior, often masking his struggles with bravado to avoid showing vulnerability.
Carrying: (Total Carry Points: 29)
- Battleaxe of Power (15 points): A massive, rune-etched weapon that cleaves through armor and shields.
- Leather Armor of Resilience (8 points): Reinforced armor that provides durability without restricting movement.
- Potion of Might (4 points): Temporarily enhances his already formidable strength.
- Talisman of Protection (2 points): A small charm that wards off minor blows in battle.

Fenwick Sharpblade   *"Speed and precision are my allies in battle."* 4

Brief: A quick-witted halfling rogue fighter, relying on agility and cunning to outmaneuver foes and strike where it hurts.
Vocation: Rogue Fighter & Agile Defender
For the Insightful: Fenwick's sharp reflexes and strategic mind allow him to anticipate enemy moves, turning the tide of battle with speed and precision.
Description: Small and wiry, Fenwick's tousled brown hair and sharp, bright eyes reflect his playful, mischievous nature. He wears lightweight leather armor for swift movement and carries twin daggers always within reach. Though his humor lightens the mood, it masks his fear of failure, driving him to constantly prove himself on the battlefield.
Wants & Needs: Wants: To gain the respect of seasoned warriors and make a name for himself as a hero of legend.
- Needs: To overcome his self-doubt and believe in his abilities, rather than compensating with bravado.

Secret or Obstacle: Fears that he may never live up to his potential, using humor to hide his insecurities in the face of danger.
Carrying: (Total Carry Points: 25)
- Twin Daggers of Speed (10 points): Razor-sharp blades enchanted for quick, lethal strikes.
- Leather Armor (6 points): Light and flexible armor that provides protection without sacrificing mobility.
- Grappling Hook (3 points): A tool for climbing, escaping, or creating tactical advantages.
- Smoke Bombs (6 points): Small bombs that create cover, allowing Fenwick to disappear or outflank his enemies.

Oren Coldsteel *"Honor and strength guide my blade."* 5

Brief: A disciplined and stoic human fighter, Oren dedicates himself to mastering the sword and upholding a code of honor and justice.
Vocation: Swordmaster & Honorable Defender
For the Insightful: Oren's profound understanding of swordplay tactics allows him to counter opponents with precision, turning defense into victory.
Description: Tall and lean, with sharp features and short-cropped black hair, Oren's presence commands respect. His polished armor gleams with intricate etchings, and his longsword carries an aura of unwavering discipline. Though his demeanor is serious and resolute, he hides the scars of a dishonorable defeat that still haunt his dreams.
Wants & Needs: Wants: To uphold the code of honor and train a new generation of disciplined warriors.
- Needs: To overcome the lingering shame of his past defeat and trust in his abilities as a teacher.

Secret or Obstacle: Oren fears that his past failure may cast doubt on his methods, tarnishing the legacy he seeks to build.
Carrying: (Total Carry Points: 30)
- Longsword of Honor (15 points): A master-crafted blade etched with runes of precision and justice.
- Enchanted Shield (10 points): A shield that absorbs impact, turning strikes into opportunities for counterattacks.
- Training Manual (3 points): A guide to his personal techniques and disciplined fighting style.
- Healing Bandages (2 points): Enchanted wraps that swiftly mend minor wounds.

Dorian Blackwood *"Strength lies in the bond between man and nature."* 6

Brief: A rugged and seasoned ranger fighter, Dorian roams the wilderness to protect the lands from marauders and restore nature's fragile balance.
Vocation: Ranger & Wilderness Protector
For the Perceptive: Dorian's natural instincts and knowledge of the wild allow him to navigate untamed lands with ease, spotting dangers and hidden paths that others miss.
Description: Dorian's muscular build and earthy-toned armor, layered with furs, help him blend seamlessly with his surroundings. His sharp gaze, framed by a well-trimmed beard and windswept hair, constantly scans for threats. While stoic and capable, he quietly bears the emotional weight of witnessing the land's slow devastation.
Wants & Needs: Wants: To protect nature from those who seek to exploit it and restore lost lands to their natural beauty.
- Needs: To find peace with the burden of protecting a world he fears may never fully recover.

Secret or Obstacle: Dorian struggles with the emotional toll of witnessing nature's destruction, questioning whether his efforts are enough.
Carrying: (Total Carry Points: 28)
- Bow of the Wilds (10 points): An expertly crafted bow enchanted to strike with precision in any terrain.
- Twin Dagger Set (6 points): Balanced blades for close combat and swift strikes.
- Herbalism Supplies (5 points): Tools for crafting remedies and poisons from natural ingredients.
- Tracker's Perk Charm (7 points): A magical charm that heightens his senses, aiding in tracking and survival.

Finnian Stonebreaker *"Every obstacle is merely a stepping stone."* 7

Brief: A optimistic and determined fighter, using his strength and unwavering spirit to overcome challenges and inspire hope.
Vocation: Brawler & Assailant for Justice
For the Athletic: Finnian's incredible endurance allows him to weather hardships and face opponents head-on, outlasting those who would falter.
Description: With sandy blond hair, warm brown eyes, and a broad, powerful build, Finnian exudes a friendly confidence that draws others to him. Dressed in reinforced, durable gear, he combines strength and determination to shield those in need. Behind his ever-present grin lies a lingering doubt that his unyielding optimism could one day lead others into danger.
Wants & Needs: Wants: To protect the helpless and unite people under a banner of hope.
- Needs: To trust himself fully, recognizing that his leadership can inspire rather than endanger.

Secret or Obstacle: Fears that his relentless optimism could fail him in dire moments, leading others into harm.
Carrying: (Total Carry Points: 26)
- Battle Axe (10 points): A heavy weapon, its strikes delivering crushing force on the battlefield.
- Protective Gear (6 points): Reinforced armor designed to endure prolonged combat.
- Healing Stone (6 points): A magical stone that emits restorative energy to mend wounds.
- Set of Survival Tools (4 points): Tools for navigating and enduring harsh environments.

Lyra Windrider
"The winds of fate favor those who fight fiercely." **8**

Brief: A nimble and determined elven warrior, Lyra uses her unmatched speed and dexterity to master dual-wielding combat and protect her homeland from dark forces.
Vocation: Agile Warrior & Protector
For the Athletic: Lyra's remarkable flexibility and speed make her a formidable opponent, allowing her to outmaneuver and overwhelm foes with precision.
Description: With flowing golden hair and bright green eyes that shine with determination, Lyra strikes a balance of grace and ferocity. She wears lightweight armor adorned with intricate elven designs, allowing swift movement without sacrificing protection. Despite her confidence, she often challenges herself to prove her worth on the battlefield.
Wants & Needs: Wants: To master the art of dual-weapon fighting and protect her homeland from ever-looming threats.
- Needs: To overcome her self-doubt and trust in her ability to lead others in combat.

Secret or Obstacle: Lyra's insecurities about her battlefield effectiveness push her to extremes, testing her limits to prove her strength.
Carrying: (Total Carry Points: 27)
- Twin Elven Swords (12 points): Razor-sharp, balanced blades designed for swift, fluid strikes.
- Leather Armor of Agility (8 points): Lightweight armor that enhances flexibility and speed.
- Combat Handbook (3 points): A guide detailing advanced dual-wielding techniques.
- Healing Potion (4 points): A restorative potion for swift recovery in battle.

Maelis Ravenshadow
"In the dance of shadows lies the heart of the warrior." **9**

Brief: A cunning and stealthy tiefling fighter, Maelis uses her agility and deadly precision to dismantle foes while blending seamlessly into the shadows.
Vocation: Shadow Fighter & Huntress
For the Insightful: Maelis possesses an uncanny ability to blend into her surroundings, surprising foes and striking with lethal efficiency before slipping back into concealment.
Description: With vibrant crimson skin, sharp horns, and flowing dark hair, Maelis moves like a whisper in the dark. Her flexible armor allows for silent movement, and her piercing gaze seems to always anticipate the enemy's next step. Beneath her stoic exterior, she fears her infernal bloodline might make her a target, pushing her to rely on herself rather than accept help.
Wants & Needs: Wants: To reclaim her community's honor and empower her people through strength and resilience.
- Needs: To overcome her fear of vulnerability and learn to trust others on the battlefield.

Secret or Obstacle: Maelis fears that her infernal heritage will bring harm to those she cares for, leading her to distance herself emotionally.
Carrying: (Total Carry Points: 29)
- Shadowblade (12 points): A dark, enchanted blade that strikes silently and vanishes into shadow.
- Lightweight Armor (6 points): Flexible armor that enables swift and silent movement.
- Collection of Specialized Daggers (5 points): Balanced blades for close combat or throwing.
- Smoke Bombs (6 points): Tools for creating cover, perfect for escape or ambushes.

Anara Stormcall
"Thunder guides my blade, and lightning dances at my feet." **10**

Brief: A fierce and commanding human warrior, Anara channels the power of storms to strike with overwhelming strength and lead her allies to victory.
Vocation: Storm Warrior & Tactical Fighter
For the Athletic: Anara's physical prowess, combined with her affinity for storm magic, allows her to dominate the battlefield while amplifying the abilities of those around her.
Description: With short-cropped dark hair streaked with silver and storm-gray eyes, Anara exudes strength and confidence. Her robust armor is adorned with lightning motifs, crackling faintly with energy. Her sharp reflexes and booming voice make her a force to be reckoned with, though she secretly fears failure when leading others into battle.
Wants & Needs: Wants: To master the tempest within her and unite storm mages and warriors into an unstoppable force.
- Needs: To overcome her self-doubt and trust in her ability to lead, even when the stakes are high.

Secret or Obstacle: Anara hides a deep fear of failing those she leads, questioning whether her powers are enough to inspire true unity on the battlefield.
Carrying: (Total Carry Points: 27)
- Stormbreaker Warhammer (15 points): A weapon that crackles with thunderous energy, striking with the power of a storm.
- Lightning Cloak (8 points): A cloak enchanted to unleash bursts of lightning when Anara is attacked.
- Thunderstone (4 points): A magical stone that unleashes a deafening shockwave to disrupt enemies.

Gladiators

The concept of a gladiator conjures images of bravery and spectacle in fantasy settings. The role of a gladiator is shaped by the cultural values surrounding combat, honor, and entertainment. In some realms, gladiators are celebrated as champions of the arena, revered for their strength, skill, and bloodshed, while in others, they may be seen as mere pawns in a brutal game of survival and amusement.

Imagine a world where gladiators are more than just fighters. Some may emerge from the ranks of noble warriors, seeking glory and fame in the blood-soaked sand of the arena, while others might be former slaves, forced into combat to secure their freedom. In times of conflict, these warriors can become powerful symbols of rebellion or champions of the oppressed, their feats inspiring the masses to rise against tyranny.

Arcana
- DC 10: Competent gladiators are often skilled combatants, trained in various weapons and styles. While their focus is generally on physical prowess, some may utilize magical enhancements, such as enchanted weapons or protective spells, to gain an edge in the arena.
- DC 20: Master gladiators may command powerful magical artifacts or have access to rare combat spells that enhance their abilities dramatically. They can invoke magical feats that turn them into near-invulnerable forces on the battlefield, leaving a trail of awe and admiration in their wake.

History
- DC 10: Throughout history, gladiators have been immortalized in stories and songs, their battles echoing in the halls of power and among the common folk. Their triumphs and defeats become the stuff of legend, offering both entertainment and moral commentary on society.
- DC 15: The motivations of gladiators often run deep, ranging from a thirst for glory, revenge against oppressors, or the pursuit of freedom. Understanding their individual journeys can provide potent insights into their character and drive.

Bribery and Influence
A gladiator's response to offers of alliances or bribes is shaped by a complex set of factors:
- Motivation: Their primary drivers, such as the pursuit of fame, freedom, or personal honor
- Compensation: The riches, influence, or opportunities for glory promised in exchange for their loyalty or skills
- Allegiances: Loyalty to other gladiators, factions within the arena, or influential figures who support them
- Personal Connections: Partnerships with fellow fighters, sponsors, and mentors within the arena
- Opportunity: The significance of the offer in relation to their current standing or upcoming matches
- Consequences: The potential fallout from their involvement in alliances, particularly if they offend sponsors or fans
- Punishments: Possible repercussions from violating the honor of the arena or challenging prevailing power dynamics.

Gladiators

Armor Class: 16 (Chain Mail)
Hit Points: 85 (10d10+30)
Speed: 30ft.

STR: 18 (+4) **DEX:** 14 (+2) **CON:** 16 (+3) **INT:** 10 (+0) **WIS:** 12 (+1) **CHAR:** 14 (+2)

Saving Throws: Strength +8, Constitution +7

Skills: Athletics +8, Intimidation +6, Performance +6, Survival +5
Senses: passive Perception 11
Languages: Common and one additional language of choice
Proficiency Bonus: +4
Challenge: 7 (2,900 xp)

Class Features
- Arena Fighter: The Gladiator has proficiency in all martial weapons and can use their Dexterity modifier for the attack and damage rolls of finesse weapons.
- Combat Superiority: The Gladiator can gain a superiority die (1d8) to enhance their attacks, adding it to their damage rolls or using it to perform combat maneuvers.
- Legendary Resilience: Once per long rest, the Gladiator can choose to succeed on a failed saving throw, reflecting their grit and experience in life-or-death situations.

Actions
- Multi-attack: The Gladiator can make three attacks with their chosen weapon on their turn.
- Gladius: Melee Weapon Attack: +8 to hit, reach 5 ft., one target. Hit: 10 (1d8+4) slashing damage.
- Trident: Melee Weapon Attack: +8 to hit, reach 5 ft. or ranged 20/60 ft., one target. Hit: 9 (1d6+4) piercing damage. This weapon can grapple the target if used within melee range.

Bonus Actions
- Second Wind (1/short rest): As a bonus action, the Gladiator can regain 1d10 + their level in hit points.

Reactions
- Deflect Blow: When hit by an attack, the Gladiator can use their reaction to reduce the damage taken by 1d10 + their Dexterity modifier.

Darius The Unyielding

"Pain is temporary, but victory is eternal."

A towering and battle-hardened gladiator, Darius wields unmatched strength and tactical brilliance, earning him an undefeated reputation in the arena.

For the Insightful:
Darius's blend of raw physical power and strategic thinking allows him to outlast and outmaneuver his opponents, turning every fight into a calculated victory.

Description:
With a chiseled jawline, piercing blue eyes, and tousled dark hair, Darius commands attention wherever he goes. His imposing physique, marked by scars of hard-fought battles, tells a story of conquest. Clad in gleaming, reinforced armor, he wields a mighty broadsword with effortless confidence, embodying the spirit of an unstoppable warrior.

Wants & Needs:
- **Wants:** To cement his legacy as the greatest gladiator of all time and retire to train the next generation of warriors.
- **Needs:** To overcome his fear of failure, understanding that one loss cannot erase his triumphs.

Secret or Obstacle: Darius harbors a deep-seated fear that his undefeated streak is all that defines him, and a single defeat could tarnish his legacy forever.

Carrying: (Total Carry Points: 34)
- Heavy Broadsword of Might (15 points): A massive, rune-etched sword capable of cleaving through the toughest armor.
- Reinforced Battle Armor (10 points): Imposing armor that absorbs devastating blows while maintaining mobility.
- Gladiatorial Champion's Ring (4 points): A symbol of his status, granting minor resistance to exhaustion.
- Healing Potions (5 points): Restorative draughts for swift recovery after grueling battles.

Gladiator Tactics

Gladiators employ a mixture of brute force, agility, and tactical acumen to achieve victory in the arena. In combat, they may engage in fierce melee, utilizing their agility to dodge attacks while delivering powerful strikes. They often work to understand their opponents' styles and weaknesses, adapting their tactics on the fly. Outside the arena, their experience in conflict allows them to navigate political intrigue and social dynamics effectively, as alliances forged and rivalries created in blood and sweat play a crucial role in their survival.

Champion Gladiator & Undefeated Warrior

Korrin Steelbreaker
"Steel bends, but the spirit never breaks." **2**

Brief: A hulking half-orc gladiator, Korrin channels his indomitable spirit and raw strength into dominating the arena, fueled by a desire for freedom and vengeance.
Vocation: Gladiator & Champion of the Arena
For the Athletic: Korrin's immense stamina and resilience allow him to endure grueling fights, outlasting opponents in physically exhausting battles.
Description: With a powerful, muscular frame, deep green skin, and a thick mane braided down his back, Korrin's fierce presence is unmistakable. His gray eyes burn with determination, and his heavy armor, scarred from countless battles, reflects his tumultuous journey. Behind his stoic exterior lies the pain of losing his family to the very games he fights to survive.
Wants & Needs: Wants: To gain freedom for himself and others trapped in servitude within the coliseum.
- Needs: To channel his rage into focused strength and outwit the deceitful politics of the arena.

Secret or Obstacle: Korrin carries the haunting memory of losing his family to the arena's brutal games, fueling his thirst for justice and vengeance.
Carrying: (Total Carry Points: 32)
- Massive Greatsword (15 points): A brutal weapon capable of cleaving through armor with ease.
- Reinforced Armor (10 points): Heavy protection that absorbs devastating blows.
- Battle Standard (3 points): A symbol of defiance, inspiring hope among his allies.
- Healing Potions (4 points): Vital for recovering after punishing battles.

Vespera Bloodthorn
"The night conceals my favor; the arena will witness my rise." **3**

Brief: A cunning and agile tiefling gladiator, Vespera uses her speed and precision to outmaneuver opponents, dazzling the crowd with her unpredictable and deadly maneuvers.
Vocation: Gladiator & Trickster
For the Insightful: Vespera's exceptional reflexes and quick thinking allow her to dodge and counterattack with precision, turning the tide of any battle.
Description: With red skin, elegantly curled horns, and smoldering amber eyes, Vespera is both captivating and dangerous. Her lightweight armor, designed for swift movement, complements her agile fighting style. Though her sharp wit and charm mask her confidence in the arena, she secretly wrestles with fears of losing control and being consumed by her dark past.
Wants & Needs: Wants: To prove her worth beyond the prejudices tied to her infernal heritage and become the arena's most skilled gladiator.
- Needs: To overcome her self-doubt and trust her instincts under pressure.

Secret or Obstacle: Fears that her control will slip in moments of intense pressure, a weakness she strives to cunningly mask.
Carrying: (Total Carry Points: 27)
- Dual Daggers of Shadows (12 points): Enchanted blades that strike swiftly and silently.
- Lightweight Armor (8 points): Allows for maximum mobility and agility.
- Smoke Bombs (5 points): Tools for creating chaos and cover during combat.
- Enchanted Ring of Agility (2 points): Enhances her speed and reflexes.

Thalius Ironfist
"Honor and might shape the victor's path." **4**

Brief: A stalwart dwarven gladiator, combining unshakable valor and tactical skill to stand as a proud champion of his heritage and clan.
Vocation: Gladiator & Defender of His Heritage
For the Insightful: Thalius's tactical mind enables him to anticipate his opponents' moves, countering effectively and turning their strategies against them.
Description: With a thick, braided beard adorned with metal rings and a stern, battle-worn expression, Thalius commands respect in the arena. He dons heavy armor engraved with his clan's crest, and his massive warhammer speaks to his formidable strength. Though his resolve is ironclad, he quietly struggles with the weight of living up to his clan's expectations.
Wants & Needs: Wants: To honor his clan by becoming a legendary champion and symbol of dwarven pride.
- Needs: To overcome his self-doubt and trust in his ability to carry his clan's legacy forward.

Secret or Obstacle: Thalius fears falling short of his family's high standards, doubting if he can truly live up to their legacy.
Carrying: (Total Carry Points: 30)
- Warhammer of Might (14 points): A massive, rune-etched hammer that delivers devastating blows.
- Heavy Plate Armor (10 points): Imposing armor that offers unmatched protection in the arena.
- Healing Salves (1 point): Quick remedies to mend minor injuries during combat.
- Shield with Clan Crest (5 points): A sturdy shield bearing his family's emblem, symbolizing his dedication to his heritage.

Jorak the Swift
"Speed is the blade's greatest ally." **5**

Brief: A nimble human gladiator, Jorak wields unmatched agility and quick footwork to outmaneuver enemies with stylish, decisive strikes.
Vocation: Gladiator & Acrobat
For the Perceptive: Jorak's athletic prowess allows him to evade incoming attacks and counter with ferocity, turning his opponents' strength against them.
Description: Lean and agile, with sandy hair and piercing blue eyes, Jorak radiates confidence. His lightweight armor is both fitted for mobility and adorned with the markings of a seasoned fighter. An infectious smile complements his charm, but he hides a deep-seated fear of failure that drives him to perform increasingly dangerous stunts.
Wants & Needs: Wants: To win the favor of the crowd and one day become a celebrated hero of the arena.
- Needs: To overcome his fear of falling, which often leads him to reckless acts in pursuit of glory.

Secret or Obstacle: Jorak's fear of failure pushes him to take unnecessary risks, which could one day cost him dearly.
Carrying: (Total Carry Points: 28)
- Twin Shortswords (10 points): Balanced for swift, precise strikes.
- Lightweight Armor (6 points): Designed to enhance agility without sacrificing protection.
- Grappling Hook (4 points): A tool for quick escapes or tactical maneuvering.
- Potion of Agility (8 points): Temporarily enhances his speed and reflexes during critical moments.

Neris Stormblade
"In every drop of rain, the promise of my victory lies." **6**

Brief: A fierce elven gladiator, Neris commands the elemental power of storms, combining precision swordplay with crackling energy to overwhelm her foes.
Vocation: Gladiator & Storm Mage
For the Perceptive: Neris's innate ability to control the weather gives her a unique advantage in combat, channeling storm energy to augment her strikes.
Description: With long silvery hair and piercing turquoise eyes that shimmer with energy, Neris cuts a commanding figure in the arena. Her form-fitting armor, accented with storm motifs, reflects her elemental affinity. Beneath her hypnotic presence lies a quiet fear of losing control over her powers, which could turn her strengths into a dangerous liability.
Wants & Needs: Wants: To harness the full potential of her storm magic and become a champion who defends her homeland.
- Needs: To master her emotions and control her elemental power, ensuring it doesn't endanger herself or others.

Secret or Obstacle: Neris fears the chaos her storm magic could unleash if she loses focus, pushing her to tread carefully in battle.
Carrying: (Total Carry Points: 29)
- Elemental Blade (10 points): A sword infused with storm energy, crackling with lightning on every strike.
- Stormcaller Pendant (7 points): Enhances her connection to the storm, amplifying her magical abilities.
- Lightweight Armor (9 points): Provides protection while allowing for swift, graceful movements.
- Healing Elixir (3 points): A restorative potion for recovery after taxing battles.

Fennick Swiftwind
"With finesse and skill, I carve my path to greatness." **7**

Brief: An agile and charismatic halfling gladiator, dazzling the arena with his flamboyant fighting style and unmatched speed.
Vocation: Gladiator & Performer
For the Insightful: Fennick's agility and charm allow him to disarm opponents—both physically and emotionally—leaving them off-balance and vulnerable.
Description: Short and wiry, with chestnut hair and bright hazel eyes, Fennick's vibrant personality lights up the arena. He wears light, colorful armor designed for maximum flexibility, and his playful antics keep spectators entertained. Beneath his confident exterior, he hides insecurities about his size, constantly striving to prove himself against larger foes.
Wants & Needs: Wants: To win the crowd's affection and earn his place as the arena's most beloved fighter.
- Needs: To overcome his fear of being underestimated due to his stature and trust in his unique abilities.

Secret or Obstacle: Fennick masks his insecurities with humor, struggling internally to believe in his worth beyond his entertaining style.
Carrying: (Total Carry Points: 24)
- Finesse Rapier (10 points): A light, elegant blade designed for swift and precise strikes.
- Light Armor of Charisma (6 points): Enhances his agility while adding flair to his appearance.
- Collection of Props (3 points): Tools for performance, including smoke bombs and harmless tricks to captivate the audience.
- Healing Kit (5 points): Essential supplies for treating wounds between matches.

Zarek Bloodmoon
"In the heat of battle, blood reveals strength." **8**

Brief: A ravenous and ferocious dragonborn gladiator, Zarek channels his unmatched brute strength to dominate the arena and earn the respect of his clan.
Vocation: Gladiator & Champion of His Kind
For the Perceptive: Zarek's immense physical power allows him to overpower foes with raw force, making him a fearsome presence in any battle.
Description: With crimson scales and piercing yellow eyes, Zarek towers over his opponents. His heavy armor, adorned with dragon motifs, reflects his proud heritage, while his booming voice commands attention. Beneath his imposing exterior, Zarek struggles to control his anger, fearing it might push him to unnecessary violence.
Wants & Needs: Wants: To reclaim his family's honor through triumph in the arena and unify his clan under his strength.
- Needs: To master his emotions and channel his fury into focused determination.

Secret or Obstacle: Zarek's temper threatens to undermine his goals, risking chaos and dishonor in the heat of battle.
Carrying: (Total Carry Points: 30)
- Colossal Greataxe (15 points): A massive weapon capable of cleaving through even the toughest armor.
- Heavy Armor (10 points): Provides immense protection, decorated with symbols of his draconic lineage.
- Dragon Emblem Shield (4 points): A shield bearing his clan's crest, inspiring allies and intimidating foes.
- Healing Aids (1 point): Essential for swift recovery after intense combat.

Sylara Dawnshard
"My blade sparkles with the brightness of a thousand suns." **9**

Brief: A fierce and radiant fighter, Sylara wields a longsword imbued with divine energy, standing as a beacon of hope and justice in the arena.
Vocation: Gladiator & Defender of the Faithful
For the Perceptive: Sylara's divine focus allows her to channel radiant energy into her strikes, making her an adversary feared by both darkness and chaos.
Description: With flowing blonde hair and striking blue eyes, Sylara exudes an aura of light and determination. Her gleaming plate armor, adorned with symbols of light, reflects her unwavering dedication to justice. Though she inspires those around her, she privately battles feelings of inadequacy, questioning her worthiness of the powers she wields.
Wants & Needs: Wants: To uphold justice against evil in the arena and leave a lasting legacy as a revered champion.
- Needs: To overcome her self-doubt and fully embrace her role as a defender of the light.

Secret or Obstacle: Sylara fears her own insecurities will hold her back from realizing her true potential as a champion of justice.
Carrying: (Total Carry Points: 30)
- Radiant Longsword (12 points): A blade that shines with divine light, searing enemies with radiant energy.
- Heavy Plate Armor (10 points): Protects her while reinforcing her presence as a symbol of strength.
- Shield of Light (5 points): An enchanted shield that reflects light to blind or disorient foes.
- Healing Salves (3 points): Restorative ointments to recover from injuries during or after combat.

Mira Nightshade
"Dance like the shadows, strike like a serpent." **10**

Brief: A cunning and agile elven fighter, Mira uses her stealth and sharp instincts to outmaneuver her foes and surprise them with precise, devastating strikes.
Vocation: Stealth Fighter & Trickster
For the Insightful: Mira's mastery of stealth and quick strikes allows her to approach battles with clever tactics.
Description: With sleek black hair and deep green eyes that glimmer with mischief, Mira glides effortlessly through the shadows. Her tight-fitting leather armor enhances her agility, and her movements are fluid and mesmerizing. Beneath her confidence lies a fierce determination to break free from the prejudices she faces as a woman in a male-dominated arena.
Wants & Needs: Wants: To prove that cunning and agility can triumph over brute strength, earning her rightful place among the arena's greatest warriors.
- Needs: To rise above the biases and pressures placed upon her, trusting her abilities to carve her path.

Secret or Obstacle: Fears being underestimated, constantly battling her peers sexist attitudes while striving to prove her worth.
Carrying: (Total Carry Points: 26)
- Serpent's Fang Daggers (10 points): Lethal, curved blades designed for swift and precise strikes.
- Lightweight Stealth Armor (6 points): Enhances her mobility and ability to vanish into the shadows.
- Smoke Bombs (5 points): Creates diversions and cover for quick escapes or ambushes.
- Assorted Gadgets (5 points): Tools and traps designed to give her the edge in unpredictable situations.

Guards

The notion of guards unveils a multifaceted role within the fabric of fantasy realms. The position of a guard is deeply shaped by local politics, societal norms regarding law and order, and the nature of crime in their surroundings. In some societies, guards are upheld as the defenders of peace and justice, secure in the trust of the people they protect. In others, they may be viewed as enforcers of oppressive regimes, feared and resented by the very citizens they are sworn to shield.

Imagine a world where guards are more than mere sentinels standing watch. Some may be part of organized city watch groups that serve the local government, while others could belong to private militias catering to influential families or guilds. During times of unrest or war, these individuals may find themselves torn between duty and moral dilemmas, their choices impacting the lives of many.

Arcana
- DC 10: Competent guards are often trained in basic combat techniques and familiar with the use of common weapons. While they primarily focus on maintaining order, some may have access to basic protective spells or magical items that enhance their abilities and effectiveness on the job.
- DC 20: Elite guards, particularly in larger cities or those that face frequent magical threats, may include spellcasters among their ranks. These proficient guards might wield powerful enchantments to detect magic, bolster their defensive capabilities, or even incapacitate foes with non-lethal spells.

History
- DC 10: Throughout the ages, guards have been integral to the narrative of countless societies. Their presence can reflect a city's stability or turmoil, and their actions often become the basis for stories of valor or betrayal, echoing through time as cautionary tales or heroic sagas.
- DC 15: The motivations of guards can vary significantly. Understanding their backstories—whether driven by a sense of duty, loyalty to corrupt leaders, or personal ambition—provides valuable insight into their decisions and interactions with the world.

Bribery and Influence
A guard's willingness to engage in bribery or corrupt dealings is heavily influenced by a network of interpersonal dynamics and situational factors:
- Motivation: Their primary drives, whether for wealth, reputation, or a genuine desire for community safety
- Compensation: The allure of riches or favors offered in exchange for neglecting their duties
- Goals: Long-term aspirations that may include rising through the ranks or gaining favor with influential figures
- Allegiances: Loyalty to their superiors, the community, or their fellow guards
- Personal Connections: Relationships with citizens, criminals, and other power players in the city
- Consequences: The potential repercussions or disciplinary actions for corruption or dereliction of duty in a law enforcement setting of accepting bribes on their reputation and standing within the guard or punishment dealt out.

Guards

Armor Class: 16 (Chain Mail)
Hit Points: 45 (6d10+12)
Speed: 30ft.

STR: 16 (+3) **DEX:** 12 (+1) **CON:** 14 (+2) **INT:** 10 (+0) **WIS:** 12 (+1) **CHAR:** 10 (+0)

Saving Throws: Strength +5, Constitution +4

Skills: Athletics +5, Perception +3, Insight +3, Intimidation +2
Senses: passive Perception 13
Languages: Common and one additional language of choice
Proficiency Bonus: +2
Challenge: 2 (450 xp)

Class Features
- Indomitable Will: The Guard has advantage on saving throws against being frightened and charmed.
- Martial Training: The Guard is proficient with all simple and martial weapons, as well as light and medium armor.
- Shield Block: When a creature within 5 feet of the Guard is hit by an attack, the Guard can use their reaction to impose disadvantage on the attack roll by interposing their shield.

Actions
- Multi-attack: The Guard can make two attacks with their weapon.
- Spear: Melee Weapon Attack: +5 to hit, reach 5 ft., one target. Hit: 7 (1d6+3) piercing damage.
- Crossbow: Ranged Weapon Attack: +5 to hit, range 80/320 ft., one target. Hit: 6 (1d8+2) piercing damage.

Bonus Actions
- Prepare Defense: The Guard can use a bonus action to take the Defensive Action, gaining +2 AC until the start of their next turn.

Reactions
- Commanding Presence: When an ally within 30 feet is attacked, the Guard can use their reaction to give that ally a bonus to their AC equal to their proficiency bonus until the end of the attack.

Ronan Shieldsong

"In all things, balance is the path to peace."

A disciplined and thoughtful human guard, Ronan dedicates himself to preserving peace in a bustling district, mediating conflicts before they escalate.

For the Insightful:
Ronan's exceptional negotiation skills allow him to resolve disputes and defuse tense situations with poise and authority.

Description: With greying brown hair and calm hazel eyes, Ronan's measured demeanor inspires trust among those he protects. His blend of leather and heavy armor provides both mobility and resilience, symbolizing his balance between diplomacy and defense. Despite his outward calm, Ronan struggles to reconcile his personal ideals with the rigid demands of authority.

Wants & Needs: Wants: To bring harmony to his community by fostering cooperation and establishing a council to amplify all voices.
- Needs: To resolve his inner conflict over balancing justice with the law, ensuring his actions align with his principles.

Secret or Obstacle:
Ronan's conflicting view of authority leaves him questioning whether his adherence to the law compromises his moral compass.

Carrying: (Total Carry Points: 36)
- Heavy Broad Sword (15 points): A well-crafted blade, capable of defense and intimidation alike.
- Military Issue Armor (10 points): Durable armor designed to protect without hindering movement.
- Mediation Scrolls (6 points): Enchanted documents used to soothe tension and promote understanding.
- Healing Potions (5 points): Restorative draughts to aid himself or others in the aftermath of conflict.

Peacekeeper

Guard Tactics

Guards employ a blend of vigilance, strategy, and teamwork to uphold the law. They often use established patrol routes, set up checkpoints, and maintain a constant watch on potential trouble spots. In the face of threats, guards will often call for reinforcements, constructing a defensive line against intruders. Outside of direct confrontations, they rely on their knowledge of the community to maintain order, defusing conflicts before they escalate and gathering intelligence on suspicious activities.

Garron Stonebrow *"Law and order demand respect; chaos deserves none."* 2

Brief: A heavily-built dwarf guard, Garron is known for his unwavering adherence to the law and his firm, no-nonsense approach to maintaining order.
Vocation: City Gate Guard
For the Insightful: Garron's expertise in weaponry and tactics shines during training drills, often inspiring younger recruits with his skill and discipline.
Description: With a thick, braided beard and piercing gray eyes, Garron's imposing stature commands respect. His sturdy armor, adorned with the city guard's insignia, complements his muscular frame and stern demeanor. Though his exterior is tough, Garron harbors a soft spot for citizens he grew up with, sometimes bending the rules to protect them.
Wants & Needs: Wants: To lead the city guard and ensure justice is upheld in his city.
- Needs: To reconcile his occasional favoritism with his strict adherence to the law.

Secret or Obstacle: Garron's protective instincts toward certain citizens could compromise his duty, leaving him vulnerable to accusations of bias.
Carrying: (Total Carry Points: 30)
- Battle Axe of Justice (12 points): A weapon imbued with runes symbolizing authority and resolve.
- Standard Issue Shield (8 points): A sturdy shield that displays the city's crest.
- Guard's Manual (5 points): A guide to city law and regulations.
- Healing Salves (5 points): Essential for treating wounds sustained in defense of the gate.

Falkar Deepstrike *"Money talks louder than the law."* 3

Brief: A corrupt human guard, Falkar thrives in the shadows of the city, turning a blind eye to crime in exchange for personal gain.
Vocation: Corrupt Guard & Enforcer for the Highest Bidder
For the Insightful: Falkar's street savvy gives him an intimate knowledge of the city's underground, allowing him to navigate illicit dealings with ease.
Description: Tall and wiry, with unkempt hair and a scruffy beard, Falkar's sly grin hints at his true nature. His lightweight armor shows signs of wear, reflecting his apathy toward official duties. While he excels at feigning loyalty to the law, Falkar fears his connections to the city's crime lords could turn on him at any moment.
Wants & Needs: Wants: To amass wealth and power through corruption, eventually owning his own tavern far from the watchful eyes of the law.
- Needs: To navigate the dangerous web of underground crime without betraying himself to rival factions.

Secret or Obstacle: Fears his double dealings could expose him to betrayal or vengeance from the very criminals he enables.
Carrying: (Total Carry Points: 26)
- Dagger of Deceit (5 points): A concealed blade perfect for quick, silent takedowns.
- Standard Issue Armor (6 points): Functional yet unimpressive armor that blends him into the guard.
- Money Pouch (5 points): Filled with bribes and ill-gotten gains.
- Informant's Ledger (10 points): A record of illicit transactions and secrets, ensuring leverage against enemies.

Tarek Farsight *"The eyes of the guard miss nothing."* 4

Brief: A vigilant elven palace guard, Tarek is renowned for his keen perception and unwavering loyalty to the royal family.
Vocation: Palace Guard & Protector of the King
For the Perceptive: Tarek's exceptional eyesight and acute awareness allow him to detect threats from great distances, giving him a critical edge in protecting the crown.
Description: Tall and slender, with long silver hair and sharp green eyes, Tarek's refined demeanor exudes confidence and precision. His elegant armor allows for freedom of movement while proudly displaying the royal insignia. Despite his loyalty, Tarek harbors a growing unease over the king's decisions, fearing they may lead the kingdom toward unrest.
Wants & Needs: Wants: To safeguard the royal family and ascend the ranks to become a trusted advisor.
- Needs: To reconcile his doubts about the king's leadership and find a way to raise his concerns without betraying his duty.

Secret or Obstacle: Tarek's quiet disapproval of the king's decisions weighs heavily on him, threatening his unwavering loyalty to the throne.
Carrying: (Total Carry Points: 24)
- Longbow of Watchfulness (12 points): An enchanted bow capable of striking distant targets with deadly precision.
- Elegant Armor (8 points): Lightweight yet protective, designed for palace guards.
- Guardsman's Ledger (4 points): A record of daily patrols and security insights.

Brannock Thornvein *"The more you bribe, the less I'll see."* 5

Brief: A brutish half-orc tavern guard, Brannock uses his intimidating presence and willingness to accept bribes to maintain a semblance of order while looking the other way.
Vocation: Tavern Guard
For the Perceptive: Brannock's raw strength allows him to control unruly patrons through intimidation rather than relying on official authority.
Description: Large and muscular, with a shaved head and numerous tattoos chronicling his brawling history, Brannock is an imposing figure. His heavy armor, displaying the tavern's colors, contrasts with the mischievous glint in his eye. Beneath his gruff demeanor lies a surprisingly gentle heart, yearning to protect those who cannot defend themselves.
Wants & Needs: Wants: To secure a steady income through bribes and tips, with dreams of opening his own tavern.
- Needs: To balance his opportunistic tendencies with his hidden desire to champion the downtrodden.

Secret or Obstacle: Brannock's gentle heart often conflicts with his corrupt practices, leaving him torn between profit and his sense of justice.
Carrying: (Total Carry Points: 24)
- Heavy Club (8 points): A simple yet effective weapon for quelling fights.
- Scrappy Armor (6 points): Pieced-together gear that offers decent protection without hindering movement.
- Bribery Ledger (5 points): A record of illicit transactions, ensuring leverage if needed.
- Healing Elixirs (5 points): Quick remedies for patching up after bar brawls.

Elias Warbringer *"Strength is only as good as the heart behind it."* 6

Brief: A steadfast tiefling guard, Elias channels his immense strength and compassion into protecting the vulnerable and challenging societal prejudices against his kind.
Vocation: Guard of the People & Protector of the Innocent
For the Perceptive: Elias's strong sense of justice compels him to use his power to shield the weak and stand against bullies, regardless of personal risk.
Description: With deep maroon skin, striking white hair, and ornate horns curling back from his forehead, Elias is an awe-inspiring figure. His sturdy armor, adorned with hopeful symbols, reflects his unwavering commitment to justice. While his appearance intimidates many, Elias hides a deep inner struggle with societal judgment and the duality of his identity.
Wants & Needs: Wants: To create a safer world where all people, regardless of status, can live without fear.
- Needs: To overcome his own doubts and embrace the strength of his convictions, proving his worth as a protector.

Secret or Obstacle: Elias struggles with the societal stigma tied to his tiefling heritage, feeling the weight of expectations placed upon him.
Carrying: (Total Carry Points: 28)
- Forceful Longsword (12 points): A weapon crafted for powerful, decisive strikes.
- Sturdy Armor (8 points): Reinforced to withstand heavy attacks, embodying his strength and resolve.
- Principles of Justice Book (4 points): A tome of moral teachings that guides his decisions.
- Healing Kits (4 points): Essential for tending to allies or victims after conflicts.

Jared Blackdawn *"Fear is a whisper; power is a shout."* 7

Brief: A ruthless and cunning human guard, enforcing the law as he sees fit, leveraging his underhanded tactics to climb the ranks of a corrupt system.
Vocation: Corrupt Guard & Enforcer
For the Insightful: Jared's sharp intellect and ability to exploit the weaknesses of others make him a formidable manipulator, capable of bending situations to his favor.
Description: Tall with short-cropped black hair and piercing gray eyes, Jared cuts a commanding figure. His battered armor, adorned with faded insignia from a questionable past, hints at his long and dubious career. Jared's sly smirk reveals a wealth of secrets, though his alliances in the criminal underworld leave him constantly watching his back.
Wants & Needs: Wants: To amass power & wealth through cunning & deceit, ultimately dominating the city's corrupt hierarchy.
- Needs: To guard against betrayal from both allies and enemies, ensuring his survival in a treacherous world.

Secret or Obstacle: Jared's tenuous relationships with the criminal underworld could turn against him, leaving him vulnerable to retribution or exposure.
Carrying: (Total Carry Points: 23)
- Short Sword (10 points): A versatile weapon suited for quick, calculated strikes.
- Standard Issue Armor (8 points): A practical choice for blending in while maintaining mobility.
- Bribery Tokens (5 points): Coins and trinkets used to grease palms and secure favors.

Aldrin Moonscar *"Shadows hide strength; strength conquers darkness."* 8

Brief: A brooding and enigmatic half-elf guard, Aldrin relies on his cunning and intimidation to outwit adversaries and keep the shadowy outpost he defends secure.
Vocation: Shadow Guard & Stealth Operative
For the Perceptive: Aldrin's deep understanding of stealth and combat enables him to outmaneuver enemies and uncover hidden threats.
Description: With dark hair tied back into a ponytail and piercing blue eyes, Aldrin's presence is both sharp and intimidating. His black leather armor, adorned with the insignias of his watch, reflects his role as a silent protector. Though his demeanor is cold and secretive, he hides a desire to protect those he cares about, struggling with trust due to his dark past.
Wants & Needs: Wants: To uncover a conspiracy against his outpost and rise to a higher rank in the guard.
- Needs: To overcome his reluctance to share his past, forging deeper trust with allies.

Secret or Obstacle: Aldrin's mistrust of others isolates him, hindering his ability to collaborate well in dangerous situations.
Carrying: (Total Carry Points: 28)
- Dual Daggers (10 points): Balanced for silent, lethal precision.
- Leather Armor (8 points): Offers protection while maintaining stealth.
- Lockpicks (4 points): Tools for accessing restricted areas or disarming traps.
- Note of Suspected Plans (6 points): A dossier containing leads on potential threats to his outpost.

Thorn Elmsworth *"Stand tall against the storm; all glory favors the brave."* 9

Brief: A noble and courageous gnome guard, Thorn dedicates his unwavering loyalty and sharp observational skills to protecting the realm and his family's honor.
Vocation: Gallant Guard & Noble Protector
For the Perceptive: Thorn's keen observational abilities allow him to notice critical details others might miss, even in the chaos of conflict.
Description: Stocky with curly sandy hair and kind, bright eyes, Thorn's light armor proudly displays vibrant insignias representing his house. His optimistic demeanor and dedication to duty inspire trust and admiration, though his petite stature often compels him to prove his worth among larger warriors.
Wants & Needs: Wants: To uphold his family's honor and ensure the safety of citizens under his care, aspiring to lead an elite guard unit.
- Needs: To gain confidence in himself, embracing his capabilities rather than overcompensating for his size.

Secret or Obstacle: Struggles with feelings of inadequacy due to his size, pushing himself harder than necessary to earn respect.
Carrying: (Total Carry Points: 26)
- Sturdy Short Sword (10 points): A finely crafted blade for precision and defense.
- Leather Armor (5 points): Offers flexibility and reliable protection during patrols.
- Scroll of Tactics (4 points): A guide to battle strategies and formations.
- Healing Potions (7 points): Vital for treating wounds sustained in the line of duty.

Branwen Steelbreeze *"Grace and strength make the perfect guardian."* 10

Brief: A graceful and skilled elven fighter, Branwen combines her agility and precision to protect her city and inspire others through her actions.
Vocation: City Guard & Swordmaster
For the Insightful: Branwen's remarkable speed and tactical awareness enable her to outmaneuver opponents, striking swiftly before they can react.
Description: With long, flowing auburn hair and striking green eyes, Branwen exudes elegance and determination. Her fitted armor is designed for maximum mobility, complementing her confident smile and measured movements. Despite her poise, Branwen harbors concerns that her pride might lead her into recklessness, causing her to hesitate at critical moments.
Wants & Needs: Wants: To maintain peace and defend her community, becoming a symbol of strength for future generations.
- Needs: To temper her pride and trust in her instincts without second-guessing her actions.

Secret or Obstacle: Fears her pride could lead to costly mistakes, leaving her hesitant in moments requiring decisive action.
Carrying: (Total Carry Points: 29)
- Elegant Rapier (12 points): A finely crafted weapon, ideal for swift and precise combat.
- Lightweight Armor (8 points): Protects without compromising her speed or agility.
- Combat Strategy Manuscript (5 points): A detailed guide on advanced fencing techniques.
- Healing Salves (4 points): Essential for quick recovery after battles.

Healers

Healers are the compassionate guardians of life in a fantasy realm, wielding their powers to mend wounds, cure ailments, and restore hope to those in need. Whether they are clerics, druids, or skilled herbalists, healers possess a profound understanding of both magic and medicine, combining mystical abilities with practical knowledge of the human body and the natural world. Often found in bustling villages or on the frontlines of battle, they pour their energy into bringing people back from the brink, ensuring that their companions can continue their quest. With a gentle touch and unwavering dedication, healers inspire not just through their miraculous abilities, but also through their kindness and empathy, reminding all that there is strength in nurturing and preserving life.

However, aspiring healers must not underestimate the challenges of their path. A cautionary tale illustrates this through Mira, a talented healer known for her powerful potions and spells. During a fierce battle against a marauding horde, Mira darted onto the field to aid fallen comrades. Amid the chaos, she found a gravely wounded, intimidating creature—a ferocious wyvern. Hoping to make a difference, she used a rare elixir said to calm even the fiercest beings. Unfortunately, the wyvern had other ideas. Roaring back to life, it unfurled its wings and took off into the sky with Mira clinging to its claw!

Mira's airborne adventure became a village legend, reminding would-be healers of their craft's unpredictability. While the desire to heal is noble, not all beings welcome assistance, especially those driven by pain or instinct. Aspiring healers must approach each situation with caution, respect, and an awareness of potential consequences. Healing can save lives but may also bring unexpected challenges. Equip yourself not only with healing spells but also wisdom, for the healer's path is as perilous as it is hopeful.

Elowen Brightvale

"In every petal lies a spark of healing." 1

Brief: A gentle and skilled elven healer, Elowen uses her profound knowledge of plants and herbs to mend wounds and soothe the suffering, bringing nature's comfort to those in need.
Vocation: Herbalist & Healer
For the Perceptive: Elowen's deep understanding of herbal remedies allows her to craft potent salves and healing potions from natural ingredients.
Description: With long, wavy golden hair and soft green eyes, Elowen radiates kindness. Her flowing robes, embroidered with patterns of leaves and flowers, mirror her nurturing spirit. Though her calm demeanor inspires trust, she harbors a hidden past as a warrior, struggling to reconcile it with her current path of healing.
Wants & Needs: Wants: To discover rare herbs that amplify her healing abilities and establish a sanctuary for the injured.
- Needs: To come to terms with her warrior past and find peace in her role as a healer.

Secret or Obstacle: Elowen's past as a warrior leaves her questioning whether her earlier choices conflict with her current path of compassion and healing.
Carrying: (Total Carry Points: 27)
- Herbalism Kit (8 points): Tools and materials for crafting restorative remedies.
- Healing Salves (6 points): Pre-made ointments for immediate treatment of wounds.
- Tome of Healing Flora (5 points): A guide to identifying and using rare medicinal plants.
- Collection of Rare Seeds (8 points): A trove of magical seeds for cultivating potent herbs.

Balthazar Whitestone
"Every breath deserves a chance for life." **2**

Brief: A wise and compassionate human cleric, Balthazar wields divine energy to heal the wounded and provide solace to troubled souls, serving as a pillar of hope in dark times.
Vocation: Cleric & Healer
For the Insightful: Balthazar's unparalleled understanding of pain and suffering allows him to offer profound emotional and physical support to those in need.
Description: Robust with a neatly trimmed beard and deep brown eyes radiating warmth, Balthazar dons elegant white and gold robes that glow softly with divine power. His calm, reassuring presence comforts the afflicted, though memories of those he couldn't save weigh heavily on his heart.
Wants & Needs: Wants: To alleviate suffering while promoting faith and hope, dreaming of establishing healing sanctuaries across the land.
- Needs: To overcome his feelings of inadequacy and focus on the lives he can save.

Secret or Obstacle: Balthazar struggles with guilt over past failures, questioning his ability to meet the expectations placed upon him.
Carrying: (Total Carry Points: 24)
- Holy Symbol (8 points): Channels divine energy for healing and protection.
- Healing Potion Bundle (10 points): A set of elixirs designed for quick recovery in emergencies.
- Prayer Beads (6 points): Used to focus his divine connection and maintain inner peace.

Gwen Stonemender
"Sometimes, healing a wound is more than just stitching." **3**

Brief: A resilient dwarven healer, Gwen combines her deep connection to the earth with master craftsmanship, creating remedies infused with minerals to mend both body and spirit.
Vocation: Healer & Stone Guardian
For the Perceptive: Gwen's exceptional craftsmanship allows her to blend minerals into her healing practices, enhancing recovery through her unique earth-based techniques.
Description: With long chestnut hair braided with gemstones and warm brown eyes, Gwen radiates determination and compassion. Her leather and stone-enhanced armor bears symbols of healing, reflecting her protective nature. Though her demeanor inspires confidence, she wrestles with the burden of responsibility, fearing that a single mistake could cost a life.
Wants & Needs: Wants: To master the art of earth-infused healing and uncover ancient techniques to save lives.
- Needs: To find faith in her abilities, trusting her skill to guide her through even the direst situations.

Secret or Obstacle: Gwen fears the weight of her responsibilities, doubting her capacity to meet the high stakes of her craft.
Carrying: (Total Carry Points: 29)
- Earthstone Scepter (12 points): A staff that channels earth energy into restorative magic.
- Pouch of Healing Crystals (8 points): Infused with minerals that accelerate physical recovery.
- Book of Ancient Remedies (6 points): A guide to long-lost healing methods.
- Artisan's Tools (3 points): Essential for crafting salves, poultices, and other remedies.

Milo Fernwhisper
"Listen to nature; it speaks the language of healing." **4**

Brief: A whimsical halfling healer, Milo's profound connection to nature and his cheerful demeanor make him a beloved figure among those in need of care and comfort.
Vocation: Natural Healer & Herbalist
For the Insightful: Milo's intuitive understanding of flora and fauna enables him to craft potent remedies, often inspired by the harmony of the natural world.
Description: With curly auburn hair and sparkling blue eyes, Milo's colorful robes are adorned with patterns of leaves and vines. His childlike joy is infectious, yet he hides insecurities about his ability to handle the most dire situations. Despite this, his warmth and positivity create a calming presence wherever he goes.
Wants & Needs: Wants: To establish a network of nature healers, united in their mission to bring comfort to the wounded and discover powerful plant magic.
- Needs: To confront his fear of inadequacy and develop confidence in his ability to tackle life-and-death challenges.

Secret or Obstacle: Milo avoids complex cases, doubting his skills, which sometimes leads him to hesitate in critical moments.
Carrying: (Total Carry Points: 20)
- Herbal Satchel (6 points): A bag filled with essential herbs for crafting quick remedies.
- Small Potions (8 points): Pre-made concoctions for minor wounds and ailments.
- Field Guide to Nature (6 points): A book of plant lore to expand his knowledge.

Irvin Claygale *"Every battle leaves a mark; I help mend what remains."* 5

Brief: A battle-hardened human healer, Irvin combines his medical expertise with practical knowledge of combat wounds to deliver life-saving care under fire.
Vocation: Field Medic & Healer
For the Insightful: Irvin's deep understanding of battlefield injuries enables him to swiftly diagnose and treat wounds with precision and efficiency.
Description: Rugged with short tousled hair and a weathered face, Irvin wears sturdy leather armor designed for mobility in combat zones. His satchel, packed with medical supplies, is always at the ready. Calm and commanding, Irvin provides reassurance to those in pain, though he is haunted by memories of comrades he couldn't save.
Wants & Needs: Wants: To create a dedicated battlefield healing troupe and write a comprehensive manual on field medicine.
- Needs: To confront his guilt over past losses and focus on the lives he can still save.

Secret or Obstacle: Irvin carries the emotional scars of extensive battlefield loss, struggling to accept what he couldn't prevent.
Carrying: (Total Carry Points: 28)
- Medic's Satchel (10 points): Packed with essential supplies for emergency care.
- Healing Kit (6 points): Tools for treating severe injuries.
- Worn Manual of Remedies (5 points): A personal guide to effective battlefield treatments.
- Bandages and Poultices (7 points): Prepared for quick application in critical situations.

Fina Windflower *"Let the winds of life guide you to healing."* 6

Brief: An ethereal air genasi healer, Fina channels the power of air currents to soothe, mend, and inspire, creating an aura of calm wherever she goes.
Vocation: Air Healer & Spiritual Guide
For the Perceptive: Fina's unique ability to manipulate air currents allows her to deliver healing in ways that calm the body and spirit alike.
Description: With flowing blue hair and shimmering skin that reflects natural light, Fina embodies grace and serenity. Her robes, billowing gently as if touched by an unseen breeze, radiate tranquility. Though her presence is comforting, she quietly struggles with doubts about fully living up to her ancestral legacy.
Wants & Needs: Wants: To expand her knowledge of air-based healing techniques and unite healers in creating a safe haven for the afflicted.
- Needs: To overcome her self-doubt and embrace her full potential as a healer.

Secret or Obstacle: Fina fears her heritage might limit her, leaving her uncertain of her ability to reach her full potential.
Carrying: (Total Carry Points: 27)
- Healing Wind Pendant (10 points): Channels air magic to accelerate recovery.
- Herbal Healing Vials (6 points): Potions infused with soothing properties.
- Tomes of Wind Spells (5 points): Guides to harnessing air currents in healing practices.
- Feathered Quill (6 points): Enchanted to draft intricate sigils and healing incantations.

Ronan Shadowbloom *"From shadows, I draw forth the light of healing."* 7

Brief: A mysterious tiefling healer, wielding shadow magic to provide solace and healing, blending his enigmatic powers with compassion.
Vocation: Shadow Healer & Mystic
For the Insightful: Ronan's mastery of shadow magic allows him to transform dark energies into restorative forces, offering healing in unconventional ways.
Description: With deep red skin, curling horns, and captivating dark eyes, Ronan strikes a commanding yet serene figure. His flowing dark robes seem to absorb the light around him, adding to his mystique. Despite his calm demeanor, Ronan grapples with a fear that his shadow magic may be inherently corrupt, threatening his intentions to heal.
Wants & Needs: Wants: Unravel the mysteries of shadow magic and create a form of healing that fosters acceptance for his kind.
- Needs: To overcome his self-doubt and prove that his magic can be a force for good.

Secret or Obstacle: Ronan fears that his magic may carry a taint, risking harm to those he seeks to help.
Carrying: (Total Carry Points: 29)
- Shadow Staff (12 points): Channels dark energy into restorative spells.
- Healing Shadow Crystals (8 points): Contain concentrated shadow energy for precise healing.
- Grimoire of Dark Healing (5 points): A tome of spells blending shadow magic with restorative arts.
- Mystic Amulet (4 points): Enhances his connection to shadow energies while maintaining balance.

Aric Thunderscale   *"Let the storms cleanse and heal all wounds."* 8

Brief: A fierce and commanding dragonborn healer, Aric channels the raw energy of storms to enhance his healing abilities and inspire awe among allies and foes alike.
Vocation: Elemental Healer & Storm Priest
For the Insightful: Aric's unique connection to elemental forces allows him to summon thunderstorms to aid in the healing process, blending destruction with restoration.
Description: With shimmering scales in hues of blue and gold and eyes that swirl with electric energy, Aric exudes an aura of power and intensity. His lightweight armor, etched with intricate storm motifs, complements his commanding presence. Beneath his bold exterior, Aric harbors doubts stemming from a past incident where his storm magic caused unintended harm.
Wants & Needs: Wants: To master the balance between healing magic and elemental powers, aspiring to guide the next generation of elemental healers.
- Needs: To come to terms with his tumultuous past, regaining full confidence in his abilities.

Secret or Obstacle: Aric struggles with memories of a tragic mistake, fearing his powers may do more harm than good.
Carrying: (Total Carry Points: 31)
- Stormcaller Staff (12 points): Harnesses storm energy for both destruction and restoration.
- Elemental Healing Crystals (8 points): Amplify healing magic with the essence of storms.
- Codex of Storm Spells (7 points): Contains spells for blending elemental forces with healing magic.
- Potion of Healing (4 points): A restorative brew for emergencies.

Zardith Moonshadow   *"With every moonlit song, healing can take flight."* 9

Brief: A serene and enchanting bardic healer, Zardith uses her musical talents to mend wounds, soothe hearts, and inspire hope with her melodic magic.
Vocation: Bard & Healer
For the Insightful: Zardith's exceptional ear for music allows her to craft songs that weave healing magic and manipulate emotions, bringing harmony to those in pain.
Description: With flowing silver hair, luminous blue eyes, and a celestial-themed gown, Zardith carries an aura of ethereal grace. Her enchanted lute, intricately carved and imbued with magical resonance, brings warmth and comfort to her performances. Despite her serene demeanor, Zardith fears her music may fail to reach those who truly need it, doubting her ability to make a lasting impact.
Wants & Needs: Wants: To blend her passion for music with healing, leaving a legacy that touches hearts and builds hope.
- Needs: To overcome her fear of inadequacy, finding confidence in her unique approach to healing.

Secret or Obstacle: Worries her music may fall short of its intended purpose, leading her to question her effectiveness as a healer.
Carrying: (Total Carry Points: 26)
- Enchanted Lute (10 points): A magical instrument that enhances the healing power of her melodies.
- Healing Chants Manual (6 points): Contains songs infused with restorative magic.
- Elixirs of Harmony (5 points): Potions that calm emotions and enhance recovery.
- Melody Stones (5 points): Small enchanted gems that amplify her musical spells.

Finnian Farsight   *"With an open heart, I mend what is broken."* 10

Brief: A compassionate human healer, Finnian embodies empathy and dedication, striving to mend both the physical and emotional wounds of those in need.
Vocation: Compassionate Healer & Mentor
For the Insightful: Finnian's innate ability to sense emotional pain allows him to provide holistic healing, addressing both the body and spirit with equal care.
Description: With sandy blond hair, warm brown eyes, and robes adorned with symbols of healing, Finnian exudes an aura of calm and reassurance. His gentle demeanor inspires trust, though the toll of absorbing others' pain often weighs heavily on his spirit. Despite this, his unwavering commitment to his craft drives him to establish a refuge for those seeking solace.
Wants & Needs: Wants: To create a network of healers and to build a sanctuary for the wounded.
- Needs: To maintain his own well-being while offering support to others, balancing his self-care with his dedication to healing.

Secret or Obstacle: Struggles to shield himself from the emotional weight of his work, fearing it may one day overwhelm him.
Carrying: (Total Carry Points: 24)
- Healing Staff (10 points): Enhances his healing magic, providing strength and stability.
- Bag of Healing Supplies (8 points): Filled with remedies and tools for various injuries.
- Journal of Compassionate Practices (6 points): A personal guide to holistic and emotional healing methods.

Hunters

Hunters are skilled trackers and vigilant stalkers of the wilds in a fantasy realm, adept at navigating untamed landscapes and understanding the creatures that inhabit them. With keen senses and extensive knowledge of nature, hunters excel in tracking quarry, whether for food, resources, or sport. Armed with bows, crossbows, or specialized traps, they often use stealth and strategy to outsmart prey, making them invaluable to any adventuring party. Beyond their prowess in the hunt, hunters are often solitary figures or trusted companions to those who seek the thrill of the wild, embodying a bond with nature that extends beyond mere survival. Their tales of adventure resonate with the bravery and cunning required to survive in harsh environments and an ever-changing world. However, aspiring hunters in a Dungeons & Dragons world must heed the dangers that come with the territory. A cautionary tale is shared among seasoned hunters about Jarek, a young, overzealous marksman who sought to prove himself by hunting the legendary Shadowfang, a massive dire wolf known for its cunning and ferocity. Ignoring the warnings of experienced hunters who advised patience and preparation, Jarek embarked on a solo quest to track the creature deep into the heart of the forest. After days of tracking, he confronted Shadowfang, ready to strike. In a moment of rash decision-making, he loosed his arrow without a clear shot. The wolf, rather than being cornered, outmaneuvered him with ease, leading Jarek on a dizzying chase that ended in a muddy bog, leaving him drenched and embarrassed but grateful to escape with his life. This humorous yet sobering account serves as a reminder to all would-be hunters: skill and ambition are essential, but so is respect for the wilderness and its denizens. The wild is filled with unpredictable challenges, and what may seem like an easy target could lead to unforeseen traps—both literal and figurative. As you prepare for the hunt, remember to arm yourself not just with weapons, but also with patience, insight, and respect for nature's balance. After all, the thrill of the hunt is as much about understanding your prey as it is about capturing it!

Korrin Ironhorn

"The mighty fall before the prepared." 1

Brief: A formidable minotaur hunter, Korrin is renowned for his prowess in tracking and taking down large game, including some of the wild's most dangerous beasts.
Vocation: Big Game Hunter & Tracker
For the Perceptive: Korrin's exceptional tracking skills and brute strength allow him to take on massive foes like bears and trolls, using his instincts and sheer determination.
Description: Towering and muscular, with curved horns and a commanding presence, Korrin is the embodiment of raw power. His heavy leather armor, reinforced with metal plates, ensures protection during intense hunts. Though confident, he quietly fears losing his edge with age, pushing himself to match the vigor of younger hunters.
Wants & Needs: Wants: To slay a legendary beast and mount its pelt as a trophy in his homeland.
- Needs: To overcome his fear of waning abilities, embracing the wisdom that comes with experience.

Secret or Obstacle: Haunted by the idea of losing his prowess, constantly wants to prove he's a force to be reckoned with.
Carrying: (Total Carry Points: 31)
- Greataxe of the Hunter (15 points): A weapon designed to take down the largest prey.
- Heavy Leather Armor (10 points): Reinforced gear for durability and protection.
- Beast Tracking Kit (4 points): Essential tools for following trails and identifying tracks.
- Trophies from Recent Hunts (2 points): Keepsakes that symbolize his victories in the wild.

Thalia Quickfoot

"Every quiet footstep is a guarantee of survival." 2

Brief: An agile halfling hunter, Thalia excels in trapping and stealth, specializing in tracking small game with sharp instincts and precision.
Vocation: Small Game Hunter & Trapper
For the Insightful: Thalia's keen instincts for spotting animal tracks and crafting traps make her an expert in navigating and thriving in the wilderness.
Description: With curly chestnut hair tied back with a leather cord and sparkling green eyes full of mischief, Thalia blends seamlessly into her surroundings. Dressed in camouflage clothing made from natural materials, she moves with quiet precision. Despite her skills, she struggles with self-doubt, often feeling underestimated due to her size.
Wants & Needs: Wants: To sell unique pelts and crafts made from her catches, fulfilling her dream of opening a specialty shop for hunting supplies.
- Needs: To overcome her self-doubt and recognize the strength her size and agility afford her.

Secret or Obstacle: Thalia often feels undervalued, her small stature leading her to overcompensate in dangerous situations.
Carrying: (Total Carry Points: 25)
- Set of Traps (10 points): Essential for catching small game with efficiency.
- Lightweight Leather Armor (6 points): Offers protection without sacrificing mobility.
- Hunting Knives (4 points): Tools for both survival and crafting.
- Collection of Furs (5 points): Keepsakes from her successful hunts.

Bram Ironhide

"Only the worthiest of opponents deserve my aim." 3

Brief: A cunning dragonborn hunter, Bram specializes in tracking and taking down dangerous beasts, including the legendary dragons that haunt his homeland.
Vocation: Dragon & Dangerous Beast Hunter
For the Perceptive: Bram's expertise in monster behavior and ambush tactics makes him a formidable opponent to even the most fearsome creatures.
Description: With emerald green scales, fierce red eyes, and a proud stance, Bram exudes a commanding presence. His reinforced armor, adorned with trophies of his greatest hunts, serves as both protection and a testament to his achievements. However, Bram hides a deep fear of confronting another dragon, haunted by the loss of a comrade in a past encounter.
Wants & Needs: Wants: To claim the title of "Dragon Slayer" among his people, bringing honor to his clan.
- Needs: To overcome his lingering doubts and rediscover confidence in his skills.

Secret or Obstacle: Bram is tormented by the memory of losing a close ally to a dragon, questioning his own abilities in the face of such a foe.
Carrying: (Total Carry Points: 30)
- Longbow of Precision (10 points): Designed for accuracy in long-range confrontations.
- Monster Tracking Journal (6 points): Notes and strategies for hunting formidable creatures.
- Special Dragonbane Arrows (8 points): Infused with magic to pierce dragon scales.
- Reinforced Armor (6 points): Protects him in battles against monstrous foes.

Lorik the Shadowstalker

"Silence is my ally; the shadows are my domain." 4

Brief: A stealthy elven hunter, who thrives in the art of ambush, specializing in tracking rare and elusive creatures.
Vocation: Elusive Creature Hunter
For the Insightful: Lorik's extraordinary stealth and agility allow him to approach even the most wary of beasts unnoticed, making him invaluable in capturing or studying rare creatures.
Description: With long silver hair hidden beneath a dark hood and piercing azure eyes, Lorik is a shadowy figure in the wild. His form-fitting armor allows him to blend seamlessly into the environment, while his silent movements reflect a practiced discipline. Lorik harbors a soft spot for the creatures he hunts, often grappling with the morality of killing versus conserving.
Wants & Needs: Wants: To capture and study rare creatures and establish himself as a protector of endangered species.
- Needs: To reconcile his compassion for animals with the demands of his vocation.

Secret or Obstacle: His empathy for the creatures he hunts hinders his effectiveness, leaving him hesitant in critical moments.
Carrying: (Total Carry Points: 28)
- Silent Longbow (12 points): A finely crafted bow designed for precision and quiet operation.
- Lightweight Stealth Armor (6 points): Enhances his ability to move unnoticed.
- Notebook of Creatures (5 points): Contains sketches and notes on rare beasts.
- Trapping and Snaring Kit (5 points): Essential tools for safely capturing elusive prey.

Garrick Coldstream *"Nature's chill sharpens my instincts."* 5

Brief: A rugged human hunter, Garrick specializes in tracking and hunting across icy terrains, mastering the art of survival in the harshest of environments.
Vocation: Winter Hunter & Tracker
For the Insightful: Garrick's remarkable resilience against freezing conditions and ability to read faint tracks in the snow make him a formidable adversary of winter's challenges.
Description: With windburned skin, shaggy dark hair, and piercing blue eyes, Garrick carries a commanding yet weathered presence. His heavy fur-lined armor and sturdy Frostbite Bow are designed for survival in unforgiving climates. Beneath his stoic exterior, he quietly wrestles with the weight of his family's expectations, fearing he may not meet their storied legacy.
Wants & Needs: Wants: To hunt legendary winter game and secure his family's livelihood through the bounty of the frozen wilds.
- Needs: To prove to himself that he is worthy of his family's reputation as great hunters.

Secret or Obstacle: Garrick struggles with the pressure of living up to his family's name, fearing failure more than the hunt itself.
Carrying: (Total Carry Points: 30)
- Frostbite Bow (10 points): Designed for precision in extreme cold.
- Winter Armor (10 points): Heavy furs for warmth and protection.
- Ice Fishing Kit (5 points): Essential for sustenance in the wild.
- Collection of Furs (5 points): Trophies of his skill and survival.

Casimir Stormrider *"Chase the storm, and nature's bounty will follow."* 6

Brief: A charismatic and daring sea elf hunter, Casimir ventures into the depths of the ocean to track elusive prey and uncover the secrets of the underwater world.
Vocation: Marine Hunter & Explorer
For the Perceptive: Casimir's exceptional swimming ability and navigational instincts allow him to track aquatic creatures in even the most treacherous waters.
Description: With vibrant sea-green hair and piercing azure eyes, Casimir moves through water as naturally as air. His lightweight ocean-themed armor enhances his agility while his Trident of the Tides marks him as a master of underwater hunting. Though confident, he secretly battles a fear of the deep sea, haunted by its unseen dangers.
Wants & Needs: Wants: To catch a legendary sea creature and earn the respect of his peers and tribe.
- Needs: To confront his fear of the deep and embrace the mysteries lurking below.

Secret or Obstacle: Casimir's fear of the unknown dangers beneath the waves sometimes undermines his confidence, pushing him to overcompensate with boldness.
Carrying: (Total Carry Points: 28)
- Trident of the Tides (10 points): A weapon crafted for underwater combat and navigation.
- Lightweight Armor (6 points): Designed for fluid movement in aquatic environments.
- Collection of Fishing Gear (5 points): Tools for capturing underwater prey.
- Nautical Map (7 points): Charts secret routes and underwater hunting grounds.

Shoren Skullcrusher *"Strength and cunning are the paths to victory."* 7

Brief: An intimidating ogre hunter, Shoren's raw power and unyielding determination make him a force to be reckoned with, especially when facing the fiercest of predators.
Vocation: Giant & Beast Hunter
For the Insightful: Shoren's overwhelming physical strength allows him to take on the largest and most dangerous predators with relative ease, his keen instincts complementing his brute force.
Description: Massive and imposing, Shoren's muscular frame and crude, makeshift armor of animal hides make him a fearsome sight. He wields a colossal club with ease, showcasing his unmatched strength.
Wants & Needs: Wants: To gain respect within his clan and form the strongest hunting party in the region.
- Needs: To master his temper and ensure his power is wielded responsibly.

Secret or Obstacle: Shoren hides his fear that his unchecked aggression during hunts could lead to unnecessary harm, tarnishing his reputation as a protector.
Carrying: (Total Carry Points: 31)
- Colossal Club (15 points): A massive weapon designed to crush even the strongest foes.
- Heavy Armor of Hides (10 points): Durable protection crafted from the hides of past hunts.
- Tracking Tools (4 points): Essential for following the trails of large beasts.
- Beast Spices (2 points): Used to lure and calm dangerous creatures.

Orin Twilightfoot

"In darkness, I hunt; in shadows, I excel." **8**

Brief: A stealthy and resourceful gnome hunter, Orin thrives in nocturnal settings, mastering the art of hunting under the cover of night.
Vocation: Night Hunter & Master Tracker
For the Insightful: Orin's exceptional stealth skills and sharp instincts allow him to approach even the most cautious prey unnoticed in the veil of darkness.
Description: Small and wiry, with curly white hair and sharp green eyes, Orin moves with practiced ease. He wears dark, practical clothing that enhances his ability to blend into shadows. His enigmatic smirk hints at his cunning traps and resourceful tracking techniques. Despite his confidence, Orin struggles with feelings of inadequacy when compared to larger hunters.
Wants & Needs: Wants: To expand his collection of rare nocturnal pelts and develop new tools that amplify the advantages of darkness.
- Needs: To believe in his abilities and overcome the pressure he feels from comparisons to larger, more traditional hunters.

Secret or Obstacle: Orin harbors self-doubt, fearing he'll always be overshadowed by more imposing hunters.
Carrying: (Total Carry Points: 24)
- Silent Blowgun (8 points): Perfect for quiet, precise strikes.
- Dark Camouflage Armor (6 points): Helps him vanish into the night.
- Night Tracker Kit (5 points): Specialized tools for nighttime tracking.
- Collection of Animal Pelts (5 points): A testament to his skill in hunting rare creatures.

Kade Firewalker

"Only where the fire burns, do the fiercest creatures dwell." **9**

Brief: A bold fire genasi hunter, Kade specializes in hunting heat-dwelling beasts and thrives in extreme environments where others dare not tread.
Vocation: Elemental Creature Hunter
For the Insightful: Kade's natural affinity for elemental fire allows him to adapt quickly to searing climates, enhancing his effectiveness when tracking fiery prey.
Description: With molten skin that glows faintly like embers and bright orange hair that flows like flames, Kade exudes an aura of confidence and energy. His leather armor is adorned with fiery patterns that shift with the heat, while his Flame-forged Bow is a testament to his prowess. Beneath his bold demeanor lies a deep fear of water, a remnant of a childhood incident that continues to haunt him.
Wants & Needs: Wants: To track and capture a legendary fire-dwelling beast, solidifying his place among the great elemental hunters.
- Needs: To overcome his fear of water and reclaim control over his past.

Secret or Obstacle: His fear of water limits his ability to explore territories where fire and water converge, creating inner conflict.
Carrying: (Total Carry Points: 30)
- Flame-forged Bow (12 points): A weapon imbued with fire magic, capable of withstanding extreme heat.
- Heat-Resistant Armor (8 points): Provides protection and comfort in scorching conditions.
- Fire Elemental Tracking Kit (6 points): Essential tools for pursuing fire-dwelling creatures.
- Healing Fire Salves (4 points): Remedies crafted for burns and heat-induced wounds.

Torran Blackstalker

"On the hunt, silence is my greatest weapon." **10**

Brief: A stoic ranger with unmatched tracking skills, Torran specializes in stalking elusive and mystical prey, blending into his surroundings like a ghost.
Vocation: Stealth Hunter & Tracker
For the Perceptive: Torran's exceptional ability to read animal behavior and follow nearly invisible trails makes him a master of the hunt, even in the most challenging terrains.
Description: Tall and lean, with long dark hair and piercing green eyes, Torran is a shadow in the wild. His muted, earth-toned garments and Silent Longbow make him almost invisible in his environment. His calm demeanor hides an enigmatic past and a tendency to keep secrets, leaving those around him unsure of his true motivations.
Wants & Needs: Wants: To track and capture rare and mystical creatures, seeking recognition for his precision and skill.
- Needs: To reconcile with his hidden past and let go of the burdens he carries in silence.

Secret or Obstacle: Torran harbors a troubled past filled with secrets, which often isolate him from those who offer trust.
Carrying: (Total Carry Points: 28)
- Silent Longbow (10 points): A weapon of unparalleled stealth and precision.
- Camouflage Leather Armor (6 points): Designed for silent movement and concealment.
- Beast Tracking Gear (4 points): Tools for tracing elusive prey.
- Enchanted Healing Tinctures (8 points): Potions to aid him in recovering from injuries sustained during the hunt.

Inn Keepers

Innkeepers are the warm-hearted hosts of a fantasy realm, the welcoming faces at bustling lodges and cozy taverns where adventurers and travelers find respite after long journeys. With a deep understanding of hospitality, they provide hearty meals, comfortable beds, and lively conversation, often becoming the heart of local culture. Their establishments brim with the aroma of hearty stew, fresh-baked bread, and the sound of laughter, offering an inviting haven for weary souls. Beyond serving food and drink, innkeepers are revered as keepers of local lore and secrets, sharing tales of heroism or whispers of danger with adventurers.

However, aspiring innkeepers should prepare for the unexpected mayhem that unfolds in the realm's busy taverns.

A beloved comedic tale tells of Old Bess, a respected innkeeper known for her legendary pies and unmatched hospitality. One particularly busy evening, with a tavern full of rowdy adventurers, Bess hosted a "Pie Contest" to showcase her culinary skills. Proud and spirited, she offered a prize for the most creative pie, igniting fierce competition. In the frenzy, Bess mistakenly mixed her prized berry filling with her cat's pungent herbal salve, a concoction used for minor ailments. The resulting pie, a clash of flavors, was both hilarious and nauseating!

When contestants began tasting the pies, the tavern erupted with wild reactions. One adventurer turned bright green, shouting, "I've never tasted anything so... unique!" while another bolted for the door. Bess, eventually swept up in the laughter, turned the disaster into a night of joy that echoed long after. This humorous tale reminds would-be innkeepers: hospitality is rooted in warmth, but surprises and mishaps are inevitable. Creating a welcoming atmosphere requires humor and adaptability. Should you run an inn, embrace the chaos, guard your recipes, and be ready to laugh through the unexpected—because your greatest challenges might create the fondest memories for your guests!

Thorin Emberbrew
"Warm fires and strong ale heal the weary soul." 1

Brief: A jovial and hearty dwarf innkeeper, Thorin runs "The Iron Tankard" in the heart of a mining town, offering a welcoming hearth and lively tales to travelers and locals alike.

Vocation: Innkeeper & Storyteller

For the Perceptive: Thorin's deep knowledge of local gossip and miner affairs allows him to charm his clientele and adapt to their needs seamlessly.

Description: With a bushy brown beard, braided with metal rings, Thorin exudes the warmth of a seasoned host. His bright blue eyes twinkle with humor, and his stained work clothes and apron reflect his hard-working nature. His boisterous laugh can often be heard echoing through the inn, drawing patrons in with his infectious spirit. Beneath his cheer, Thorin quietly worries about the growing competition from larger taverns.

Wants & Needs: Wants: To keep his tavern thriving and expand by starting his own brewery.
- Needs: Strategies to keep up with rising competition and maintain his loyal customer base.

Secret or Obstacle: Secretly fears that larger taverns will overshadow his beloved establishment, pushing him to innovate.

Carrying: (Total Carry Points: 28)
- Fine Ale Selection (10 points): Carefully crafted brews that keep patrons returning.
- Large Hearth Cooking Equipment (8 points): For preparing hearty meals and stews.
- Collection of Folk Tales (5 points): A book of local stories to entertain and inspire guests.
- Map of Local Mines (5 points): A treasure trove of knowledge for miners and adventurers alike.

Ilara Vinemist
"Good wine and warm hearts make this a home." **2**

Brief: An elegant elven innkeeper of "Elysian Sips," Ilara curates an exquisite selection of wines and offers a serene atmosphere, making her establishment a haven for nobles and travelers alike.
Vocation: Innkeeper & Wine Connoisseur
For the Insightful: Ilara's refined palate and extensive viticulture knowledge make her a trusted advisor on pairing wines with meals for even the most discerning guests.
Description: Ilara's long, flowing silver hair and enchanting green eyes radiate grace. Her flowing dresses, adorned with floral patterns, mirror the vibrant colors of her lush vineyard. Her calm demeanor creates a welcoming charm, inviting all who seek solace within her tavern's ivy-laced walls.
Wants & Needs: Wants: To elevate the reputation of her vineyard and host grand noble gatherings.
- Needs: A solution to her summer of low production, which risks tarnishing her establishment's name.

Secret or Obstacle: Ilara harbors anxiety about maintaining her inn's prestige amidst unexpected challenges, fearing it might undermine her life's work.
Carrying: (Total Carry Points: 32)
- Vintage Recipe Book (2 points): A tome of ancient wine-blending secrets.
- Serving Kit (8 points): Exquisite tools for hosting fine dining experiences.
- Fine Wines (22 points): A selection of rare vintages treasured by connoisseurs.

Gregor Ashborn
"In this dump, at least the ale is good." **3**

Brief: A grizzled human innkeeper running "The Shabby Rest," Gregor offers a safe haven for the downtrodden, welcoming those in need of shelter and a hearty drink.
Vocation: Innkeeper at "The Shabby Rest"
For the Perceptive: Gregor's street-hardened wisdom allows him to navigate conflicts with ease and cater to his guests' unique struggles.
Description: Gregor's weathered face and graying hair tell a story of a life filled with hardship, yet his kind brown eyes reveal his compassion. His rough, patched clothing reflects his simple lifestyle, and his inn is a testament to his resourcefulness, cobbled together with makeshift furnishings but brimming with warmth.
Wants & Needs: Wants: To keep his inn running while secretly saving for a better future for his community.
- Needs: Resources to improve his inn's conditions and expand his offerings to better support his patrons.

Secret or Obstacle: Gregor hides his past as a renowned adventurer, fearing the attention it might draw to his quiet new life.
Carrying: (Total Carry Points: 20)
- Basic Ale Selection (5 points): A simple yet satisfying brew selection.
- Makeshift Furnishings (5 points): Repaired and repurposed items used to furnish the inn.
- Healing Supplies (10 points): Basic bandages and tonics for travelers in need.

Fenwick Featherfoot
"Rest is best when shared with good tales." **4**

Brief: A cheerful gnome innkeeper of "The Cozy Nook," Fenwick brings joy and laughter to all who visit his snug forest inn.
Vocation: Innkeeper at "The Cozy Nook"
For the Insightful: Fenwick's remarkable memory for names and stories ensures every guest feels seen and appreciated.
Description: Fenwick's curly golden hair and bright blue eyes exude mischief and charm. His colorful attire reflects the cheerful atmosphere of his inn. His constant smile and lively demeanor make every traveler feel like family.
Wants & Needs: Wants: To expand "The Cozy Nook" while preserving its intimate charm.
- Needs: A steady flow of resources to maintain his high-quality service for an increasing number of visitors.

Secret or Obstacle: Fenwick fears that as his inn grows, the pressures of expansion might dilute the warmth and hospitality he's known for.
Carrying: (Total Carry Points: 29)
- Collection of Guest Tales (10 points): Stories and legends recorded from travelers.
- Gnome-Sized Cutlery (6 points): Perfectly crafted for gnome-sized meals.
- Stock of Comfort Foods (7 points): Familiar dishes that make guests feel at home.
- Healing Herbal Teas (6 points): Soothing brews for weary travelers.

Ragnar Wolfheart — *"Welcome to battle; may the fires warm your spirits."* 5

Brief: A rugged half-orc innkeeper at "The Howling Wolf," Ragnar caters to adventurers and mercenaries, offering hearty ales and a welcoming hearth after long quests.
Vocation: Innkeeper at "The Howling Wolf"
For the Insightful: Ragnar's sharp instincts allow him to anticipate his patrons' needs, making him a beloved figure among the battle-hardened clientele.
Description: With a well-kept dark beard and fierce brown eyes, Ragnar cuts an imposing figure. His simple yet sturdy attire includes a leather apron, and his commanding presence lends gravitas to his bustling tavern. Despite the liveliness of his inn, he carries an air of quiet reflection.
Wants & Needs: Wants: To maintain "The Howling Wolf" as a hub for adventurers, forging camaraderie among warriors.
- Needs: Steady supplies of quality ales and hearty food to meet his patrons' expectations.

Secret or Obstacle: Ragnar hides a deep longing for connection, often feeling isolated despite the lively atmosphere he has cultivated.
Carrying: (Total Carry Points: 30)
- Selection of Robust Ales (12 points): A varied stock of ales that appeal to all tastes.
- Rustic Serving Equipment (5 points): Practical and durable tools for serving.
- Battle Tactics Handbook (6 points): A resource to share strategies with his patrons.
- Healing Draughts (7 points): Restorative drinks for the wounded.

Elyra Sandwalker — *"A good bed makes for a good traveler."* 6

Brief: A refined tiefling innkeeper at "The Sand Dune Lodge," Elyra caters to high-society clientele in a lavish desert inn, blending luxury with comfort.
Vocation: Innkeeper at "The Sand Dune Lodge"
For the Perceptive: Elyra's deep understanding of elite guests allows her to predict their desires, ensuring every need is met before it is expressed.
Description: Elyra's violet eyes and elegantly braided hair adorned with gems complement her sophisticated demeanor. Her flowing garments exude wealth and elegance, drawing travelers into her luxurious oasis.
Wants & Needs: Wants: To host prominent figures and elevate her inn's reputation.
- Needs: Exquisite supplies and rare ingredients to maintain her elite offerings.

Secret or Obstacle: Elyra fears the resurfacing of her past as an outcast, a truth she carefully conceals from her high-society patrons.
Carrying: (Total Carry Points: 32)
- Fine Dining Equipment (12 points): High-quality utensils and serving wares.
- Exotic Drinks (10 points): Rare and unique beverages sourced globally.
- Social Etiquette Handbook (5 points): A guide to impressing high-class guests.
- Lavish Room Furnishings (5 points): Luxurious and inviting interiors.

Cormac Frostforge — *"A warm hearth can mend the coldest of hearts."* 7

Brief: A towering giant innkeeper at "The Icebreaker Lodge," Cormac provides a refuge for travelers braving harsh mountain climates, offering warmth and camaraderie.
Vocation: Innkeeper at "The Icebreaker Lodge"
For the Insightful: Cormac's sheer physical presence and hearty demeanor provide safety and solace to weary travelers navigating the treacherous mountain paths.
Description: With ice-blue eyes and a thick white beard, Cormac exudes a sense of protection and comfort. His rugged attire is suited for the cold, and his booming laugh can melt even the iciest tensions.
Wants & Needs: Wants: To foster a thriving mountain community centered around his lodge.
- Needs: Reliable sources for winter provisions and safety equipment to ensure his patrons' survival.

Secret or Obstacle: Cormac carries the weight of losing friends to avalanches, driving his resolve to keep others safe.
Carrying: (Total Carry Points: 20)
- Collection of Winter Warmers (8 points): Hot drinks and meals for cold nights.
- Survival Guide for Mountaineering (6 points): A guide for safely navigating the mountains.
- Healing Winter Brews (6 points): Herbal mixtures to ward off frostbite and illness.

Orric Dawnwhistle "At 'The Lantern's Glow,' every traveler's story brightens my night." 8

Brief: A warm and inviting gnome innkeeper at "The Lantern's Glow," Orric takes pride in creating a cozy haven for weary travelers in the bustling market town.
Vocation: Innkeeper at "The Lantern's Glow"
For the Insightful: Orric's exceptional knack for remembering every guest's story ensures that all feel valued and important in his inn.
Description: Short and plump, Orric is a lively gnome with a cheerful face framed by wild red hair. His colorful attire, complete with a waistcoat adorned with bright patterns, reflects the lively atmosphere of his inn.
Wants & Needs: Wants: To foster a greater sense of community and host larger gatherings.
- Needs: Steady resources to improve his inn's atmosphere and expand its appeal.

Secret or Obstacle: Orric harbors anxieties over financial insecurity, constantly fearing for his inn's sustainability during slow seasons.
Carrying: (Total Carry Points: 25)
- Collection of Guest Tales (8 points): Stories shared by past guests, a treasured source of inspiration.
- Wooden Lanterns (6 points): Beautifully crafted lanterns that add a magical glow.
- Board Games and Books (5 points): Entertainment for guests to encourage relaxation.
- Healing Herbal Teas (6 points): A favorite among travelers to soothe their weariness.

Gideon Cinderforge "From humble beginnings, great stories emerge." 9

Brief: A rugged fire genasi innkeeper of "The Ember Stone," Gideon is celebrated for his rich culinary creations and fiery ambiance near the base of a volcano.
Vocation: Innkeeper and Chef at "The Ember Stone"
For the Insightful: Gideon's mastery of spices and his understanding of culinary traditions from around the world draw patrons seeking an unforgettable meal.
Description: Striking with fiery hair and a stocky build, Gideon's presence is accentuated by his practical attire in colors reminiscent of his volcanic heritage. His warm smile beckons travelers to his inn's hearth.
Wants & Needs: Wants: To gain renown as a master chef while ensuring his inn thrives.
- Needs: Rare and exotic ingredients to keep innovating his menu.

Secret or Obstacle: Gideon struggles with self-doubt about his cooking, fearing negative feedback might shake his confidence.
Carrying: (Total Carry Points: 28)
- Cooking Implements (10 points): High-quality tools to create exceptional dishes.
- Unique Spice Collection (7 points): Exotic spices sourced from distant lands.
- Gourmet Recipe Book (6 points): Recipes refined over years of practice.
- Assorted Beverages (5 points): A variety of drinks to pair perfectly with meals.

Rufus Mudhollow "Home is where the heart can rest; I've got plenty of space." 10

Brief: A jolly hobgoblin innkeeper at "The Mixed Tankard," Rufus prides himself on creating an inclusive environment for guests of all backgrounds in the city's vibrant district.
Vocation: Innkeeper at "The Mixed Tankard"
For the Perceptive: Rufus's extensive knowledge of his diverse clientele ensures that everyone feels welcomed and catered to.
Description: With a broad face, pointed ears, and a big smile, Rufus is dressed in bright, comfortable clothing. His welcoming nature and jovial spirit make him a favorite among adventurers.
Wants & Needs: Wants: To promote mutual respect by celebrating the diversity of his patrons.
- Needs: Resources to expand his inn and introduce an open kitchen.

Secret or Obstacle: Rufus faces prejudice due to his hobgoblin heritage, often battling assumptions that contradict his warm demeanor.
Carrying: (Total Carry Points: 26)
- Barut's Recipe Collection (8 points): Unique recipes reflecting the cultural tapestry of his guests.
- Worn Craft Supplies (6 points): Tools for crafting decorations and repairs.
- Beverages from Various Regions (6 points): A selection of drinks catering to his diverse patrons.

Knights

The role of a knight is profoundly shaped by the cultural values surrounding honor, loyalty, and the responsibilities of nobility. In some realms, knights are upheld as paragons of virtue, embodying the highest ideals of bravery and honor in the service of their lords and the greater good. In others, they may be criticized as self-serving nobles, caught in the web of politics and power struggles.

Imagine a world where knights are more than mere warriors. Some may belong to esteemed orders dedicated to protecting the realm, while others could serve as personal champions for powerful kings and queens. During times of conflict, these stalwart fighters become critical defenders of their homelands, leading troops into battle and inspiring others with their courage.

Arcana
- DC 10: Competent knights often possess a robust array of combat skills, trained in the usage of swords, lances, and heavy armor. While primarily martial in nature, many may also carry enchanted items or blessings from their patrons that enhance their martial capabilities or protect them in battle.
- DC 20: Elite knights might command powerful magical abilities, allowing them to invoke divine powers or wield legendary weapons with unique enchantments. Their mastery could include spells that heal allies, shield themselves from harm, or even call upon celestial beings to aid them in battle.

History
- DC 10: Throughout history, knights have played pivotal roles in shaping the fate of kingdoms and cultures. Their legendary deeds are often immortalized in epic tales, celebrated in song, and used as moral exemplars in the tales of their valor and sacrifice.
- DC 15: The motivations of knights are often deeply rooted in their upbringing and code of conduct. Understanding their backgrounds—whether driven by a sense of duty, honor, vengeance, or personal ambition—can provide essential insight into their actions and decisions.

Bribery and Influence
knight's response to offers of favors or bribes is influenced by a myriad of deeply held principles and practical considerations:
- Motivation: Their primary drives, including loyalty to their lord, pursuit of glory, or commitment to their code of honor
- Compensation: The riches, titles, or political power promised in exchange for their allegiance or services
- Goals: Long-term aspirations tied to their status, reputation, or quest for justice
- Allegiances: Loyalty to their order, lord, or fellow knights
- Consequences: The repercussions of their actions on their reputation, standing, and the well-being of those they protect.

Knights

Armor Class: 18 (Plate Armor)
Hit Points: 85 (10d10+30)
Speed: 30ft.

STR: 18 (+4) **DEX:** 12 (+1) **CON:** 16 (+3) **INT:** 10 (+0) **WIS:** 14 (+2) **CHAR:** 16 (+3)

Saving Throws: Strength +8, Constitution +7

Skills: Athletics +8, Intimidation +7, History +4, Insight +6
Senses: passive Perception 16
Languages: Common, and one additional language of choice
Proficiency Bonus: +4
Challenge: 7 (2,900 xp)

Class Features
- Combat Expertise: The Knight can choose to take a -5 penalty to their attack roll to gain a +10 bonus to damage dealt on a successful hit.
- Authority of the Battlefield: Allies within 10 feet of the Knight have advantage on saving throws against being frightened.
- Second Wind (1/short rest): As a bonus action, the Knight can regain 1d10 + their level in hit points.

Actions
- Multi-attack: The Knight can make two attacks with their weapon.
- Longsword: Melee Weapon Attack: +8 to hit, reach 5 ft., one target. Hit: 10 (1d8+4) slashing damage.
- Javelin: Ranged Weapon Attack: +8 to hit, range 30/120 ft., one target. Hit: 9 (1d6+4) piercing damage.

Bonus Actions
- Shield Bash: The Knight can use a bonus action to shove a creature within reach, pushing them 5 feet back if they fail a Strength saving throw (DC 16).

Reactions
- Parry: When the Knight is hit by an attack, they can use their reaction to reduce the damage taken by 1d10 + their Dexterity modifier.

Sir Cedric Dawnstar

"Honor guides my blade; justice will prevail."

A noble human knight known for his steadfast commitment to chivalry and justice, Sir Cedric is admired for his valor in battle and leadership on the field.

For the Insightful:
Possesses great tactical acumen, often leading his fellows into battle with exceptional planning and skill.

Description:
Sir Cedric has short, cropped blond hair and piercing blue eyes filled with determination. He wears polished plate armor adorned with the radiant sun emblem of his noble house. His noble demeanor inspires confidence, and his resolute presence reassures those who follow him into the fray.

Wants & Needs:
- **Wants:** To uphold justice and protect the innocent; dreams of being recognized as a legendary hero throughout the land.
- **Needs:** To balance his noble heritage's expectations with his personal sense of duty.

Secret or Obstacle:
Hides insecurities about his occasional indecision in battle, feeling the pressure of living up to his family's storied legacy.

Carrying: (Total CP: 30)
- **Longsword of Justice (12 points):** A finely-crafted blade symbolizing unwavering justice.
- **Ornate Plate Armor (10 points):** Heavy armor engraved with symbols of his house, offering unmatched protection.
- **Tactical Battle Manual (4 points):** A guide to advanced battlefield strategies.
- **Healing Potions (4 points):** Restorative potions for emergencies.

Knight Tactics

Knights employ a combination of martial prowess, strategic planning, and noble conduct in their endeavors. In combat, they often lead charges, rally allies around them, and engage in skirmishes with a blend of heavy armor and fierce weaponry. Their training enables them to act as defenders of the weak and champions of the oppressed, and they often execute tactical maneuvers that take advantage of terrain and formations. Outside of battle, knights must navigate the complexities of court politics and social dynamics, leveraging their reputations and alliances to further their goals.

Protector of the Realm

Dorian Nightshade
"Every shadow hides a truth; find it and wield it." **2**

Brief: A cunning and morally ambiguous knight, Dorian walks the fine line between honor and self-interest, mastering manipulation and shadowy tactics to achieve his goals.
Vocation: Knight & Mercenary
For the Insightful: Possesses keen intelligence and perception, enabling him to manipulate situations to his advantage.
Description: Dorian has dark hair and piercing gray eyes that radiate an air of charm and cunning. His dark, decorative armor features intricate engravings, and he carries a broadsword encrusted with gem-like embellishments. Despite his suave demeanor, his motives remain enigmatic, often masking a more calculating nature.
Wants & Needs: Wants: To amass wealth and influence; dreams of becoming a power broker in noble circles.
- Needs: To secure his place in a treacherous world, avoiding exposure of his darker alliances.

Secret or Obstacle: Hides his involvement with unsavory contacts, living in constant fear of being discovered by those who uphold true honor.
Carrying: (Total CP: 27)
- Broadsword (12 points): A weapon of deadly precision, its gem-like adornments conceal its ominous power.
- Dark Cloak of Charisma (6 points): A shadowy mantle enhancing his charm and stealth.
- Morally Ambiguous Oath (6 points): A symbolic vow sworn in secrecy.
- Assorted Bribery Tokens (3 points): Tools of manipulation for negotiations.

Grimwald Ironaxe
"In battle, only the strong survive." **3**

Brief: A fierce and battle-hardened half-orc knight known for his indomitable strength and unwavering loyalty to his comrades.
Vocation: Knight & Protector of the Realm's Borders
For the Insightful: Displays exceptional combat strength and endurance, thriving in the heat of battle and overpowering the fiercest opponents.
Description: Grimwald is a towering figure with green skin and a muscular build, his short black beard framing a face hardened by countless battles. He dons reinforced armor scarred by the clashes of war, wielding a massive battle axe that symbolizes his ferocity. His presence commands respect, and his battle cries inspire courage in his allies.
Wants & Needs: Wants: To gain glory through battle and establish a legacy of strength and valor for his clan.
- Needs: To prove his worth to those who doubt him due to his heritage.

Secret or Obstacle: Harbors a deep-seated resentment toward those who underestimate his abilities, struggling to let go of past grievances.
Carrying: (Total CP: 29)
- Massive Battle Axe (15 points): A brutal weapon designed for powerful, crushing strikes.
- Reinforced Armor (10 points): Heavy plating that provides unmatched defense.
- War Banner (2 points): A symbol of his loyalty and dedication to his comrades.
- Healing Salves (2 points): Aiding recovery during and after fierce battles.

Roderick Coldsteel
"Justice is but a tool; wield it wisely." **4**

Brief: A stoic knight from a family with a dark past, Roderick seeks redemption and justice while navigating the conflicts of his moral compass.
Vocation: Knight & Enforcer of the Law
For the Insightful: Possesses exceptional analytical skills, dissecting dilemmas with clarity to chart the best course of action.
Description: Roderick stands tall and broad-shouldered, his icy blue eyes reflecting his calm and calculated demeanor. His long black hair flows under a helmet adorned with protective runes, and his heavy armor bears the scars of his relentless pursuit of justice. A greatsword strapped across his back represents both his burden and resolve.
Wants & Needs: Wants: To cleanse his family's name through his actions; dreams of being a beacon of hope in a dark world.
- Needs: To balance his ruthless pursuit of justice with his ideals, avoiding the same mistakes as his forebears.

Secret or Obstacle: Carries the justice-seeking ruthlessness inherited from his family, questioning whether he can uphold his lofty ideals.
Carrying: (Total CP: 32)
- Greatsword (15 points): A massive blade imbued with both symbolic and practical weight.
- Enchanted Armor (10 points): Protective plating infused with defensive enchantments.
- Journal of Family Duty (4 points): Chronicling his family's fall and path toward redemption.
- Healing Crystals (3 points): For tending to injuries sustained in the line of duty.

Jareth Windstrider   *"Elegance in motion is the key to victory."*   5

Brief: A graceful elven knight specializing in swift strikes and agile maneuvers, Jareth believes balance and beauty elevate combat, making him a mesmerizing presence on the battlefield.

Vocation: Knight & Combat Artist

For the Insightful: Possesses incredible agility and finesse, often appearing as a whirlwind of motion during combat, striking with precision and grace.

Description: Jareth has flowing silver hair and bright emerald eyes that glimmer with determination. He dons elegantly crafted lightweight armor designed for fluid movement, blending defense with aesthetic appeal. His demeanor exudes confidence, captivating allies and foes alike.

Wants & Needs: Wants: To master the art of combat and elevate the reputation of elven knights, introducing new techniques to the martial world.
- Needs: To overcome his self-doubt and prove that strength comes in many forms, not just brute force.

Secret or Obstacle: Hides feelings of inadequacy when compared to more brutish warriors, often striving to validate his unique approach to combat.

Carrying: (Total CP: 29)
- Rapier of Swiftness (10 points): A finely balanced weapon that complements his agile fighting style.
- Lightweight Armor (6 points): Crafted for mobility, offering light protection without hindering movement.
- Martial Arts Manual (5 points): A tome detailing advanced techniques for speed and precision in battle.
- Healing Potions (8 points): Potent remedies to sustain him in prolonged engagements.

Urik Blackthorn   *"Loyalty is power; power demands respect."*   6

Brief: A cunning and morally ambiguous knight, Urik serves his own ambitions through a mastery of political intrigue and manipulation.

Vocation: Knight & Political Manipulator

For the Insightful: Possesses sharp wit and a deep understanding of courtly politics, allowing him to navigate treacherous alliances with ease.

Description:
Urik has slick black hair, sharp features, and intense brown eyes that radiate ambition. He wears polished armor adorned with luxurious fabrics, reflecting his noble aspirations. His confident demeanor often commands respect and fear.

Wants & Needs: Wants: To climb the ranks of nobility by securing alliances and leveraging influence.
- Needs: To establish a fortified position that solidifies his control over the realm.

Secret or Obstacle: Hides his questionable alliances, fearing exposure that could lead to betrayal from both enemies and allies.

Carrying: (Total CP: 28)
- Elegant Sword (10 points): A finely crafted blade symbolizing his noble ambitions.
- Decorative Armor (8 points): Opulent yet functional, reflecting his dual focus on aesthetics and protection.
- Political Influence Ledger (5 points): Records of debts and favors owed to him.
- Healing Elixirs (5 points): Restoratives to maintain his strength in dire moments.

Keldor Stoneguard   *"Strength is forged in loyalty and unity."*   7

Brief: A stalwart and loyal dwarf knight, Keldor stands as a shield for his kin, protecting his city with unshakable resolve.

Vocation: Knight & City Defender

For the Insightful: Possesses profound tactical knowledge, enabling him to provide strategic support in times of crisis.

Description:
Keldor is burly and imposing, with a thick beard and strong, weathered features. He wears ornate armor bearing his clan's sigil, carrying a sturdy warhammer as a symbol of his strength. His presence radiates determination and reliability.

Wants & Needs: Wants: To restore honor to his family name by overcoming the greatest threats to his city.
- Needs: To protect his kin and prove himself capable of standing strong in their darkest hours.

Secret or Obstacle: Hides his fear that he might not be strong enough when it truly matters, yearning for a chance to prove his worth.

Carrying: (Total CP: 32)
- Warhammer of the Guardian (15 points): A massive, indomitable weapon designed for defense and offense.
- Heavy Steel Armor (10 points): Durable and unyielding, crafted to endure the harshest of battles.
- Clan Sigil Shield (5 points): A sturdy shield marked with his family crest.
- Basic Healing Kit (2 points): A small collection of remedies for minor wounds.

Malik Darkheart *"Chaos is a tool; I am its master."* 8

Brief: A morally ambiguous knight who thrives in the chaos of battle, Malik sees honor in cunning and the clever use of treachery to outwit his foes.
Vocation: Knight & Agent of Chaos
For the Insightful: Possesses a sharp understanding of combat tactics, using strategies to outmaneuver stronger foes with ease.
Description: Malik is tall and lean, with an athletic build and long, flowing dark hair. His dark armor reflects his shadowy affiliations, and his glowing eyes radiate mischief and ambition.
Wants & Needs:
- Wants: To seize power through clever tactics and strategic uprisings, dreaming of establishing a shadow empire.
- Needs: To overcome his fear of abandonment by his comrades, which fuels his potentially treacherous actions.

Secret or Obstacle:
Malik hides his underlying fear of being deserted, which drives his loyalty to dangerous extremes.
Carrying (Total CP: 30):
- Cunning Blade (10 points): A weapon forged for stealth and swift strikes.
- Lightweight Armor (8 points): Designed for mobility and evasion.
- Tactics Notebook (6 points): Filled with insights and strategies.
- Healing Potions (6 points): For emergencies during battle.

Teren Lightstrider *"Hope and courage are the best shields."* 9

Brief: A noble and valorous knight who dedicates himself to defending the helpless and inspiring courage in those around him.
Vocation: Knight & Champion of the Downtrodden
For the Insightful: Possesses a deep understanding of morale, skillfully supporting allies during the direst moments.
Description: Teren is a beacon of faith with wavy blonde hair and hazel eyes radiating warmth. His shining armor bears inscriptions of hope and justice, inspiring those who follow his lead.
Wants & Needs:
- Wants: To build a brotherhood of justice, spreading hope and protecting the weak.
- Needs: To overcome his fear of falling short of the ideals he preaches, especially in moments of self-doubt.

Secret or Obstacle:
Hides a deep fear of failing to live up to his values, often doubting himself when faced with challenges.
Carrying (Total CP: 31):
- Holy Sword of Valor (15 points): A radiant blade representing justice.
- Shining Armor (10 points): Offers both protection and a symbol of hope.
- Book of Chivalry (4 points): Guides his actions with noble principles.
- Healing Salves (2 points): Essential for aiding allies in the field.

Kaelan Brightblade *"Every dawn brings a new battle; rise to the challenge."* 10

Brief: A spirited knight known for his upbeat attitude and resilience, Kaelan brings joy even to the darkest of situations, inspiring hope in his comrades.
Vocation: Knight & Morale Booster
For the Insightful: Possesses extraordinary bravery and the ability to foster camaraderie, ensuring his allies fight at their best during critical moments.
Description: Kaelan has tousled brown hair and bright blue eyes that radiate enthusiasm. He wears gleaming armor adorned with personal tokens from his adventures. His infectious smile can lighten even the gravest of occasions.
Wants & Needs:
- Wants: To ensure that every fighter feels valued and strong; dreams of fostering a fellowship to tackle the greatest evils.
- Needs: To maintain his positive outlook despite overwhelming challenges.

Secret or Obstacle: Hides a fear of despair, often struggling to maintain his upbeat disposition in the face of loss.
Carrying (Corrected Total CP: 25):
- Scepter of Resilience (12 points): A radiant staff that embodies fortitude and inspires courage.
- Glittering Armor (10 points): Protective armor that shines with hope, symbolizing his unyielding optimism.
- Healing Mixtures (3 points): Potent remedies for minor injuries to keep his companions fighting.

Mages

A Mage conjures images of arcane mastery, profound knowledge, and mystical power in fantasy settings. The role of a mage is shaped by cultural perceptions of magic, the complexity of spellcasting, and the ethical implications of wielding such power. In some realms, mages are revered as scholars and wise advisors, their abilities sought after by kings and commoners alike. In others, they may be viewed with suspicion or fear, deemed dangerous for their capacity to alter reality and bend the laws of nature.

Imagine a world where mages are more than mere spellcasters. Some may belong to prestigious schools of magic, dedicated to the pursuit of knowledge and mastery over the arcane arts. Others could exist as wanderers or hermits, honing their craft in solitude or seeking ancient secrets lost to time. During times of turmoil, these masters of the arcane can become pivotal figures, their magical prowess influencing battles and altering the course of history.

Arcana
- DC 10: Competent mages possess a vast array of spells, from elemental manipulation and illusions to healing and divination. Their knowledge allows them to craft potions, enchant objects, and unravel the mysteries of the world around them, making them versatile allies in both combat and exploration.
- DC 20: Master mages may wield legendary spells that can reshape reality, summon powerful entities, or wield devastating forces. Their deep understanding of magic enables them to overcome complex spell challenges and create unique arcane effects that astound and confound all who witness them.

History
- DC 10: Throughout history, mages have been formidable influences, shaping the destinies of kingdoms and the fates of individuals. Their legacies are often chronicled in tomes of lore and song, with tales of their discoveries and battles becoming interwoven into the fabric of culture and myth.
- DC 15: The motivations of mages can be as diverse as their spellbooks. Understanding their backgrounds—whether driven by curiosity, the thirst for power, or the desire to protect—provides essential insight into their actions and relationships with the world.

Bribery and Influence
A mage's response to offers of favors or gold is influenced by a complex interplay of principles and pragmatic concerns:
- Motivation: Their primary drives, such as the pursuit of knowledge, power, or the well-being of others
- Compensation: The valuable artifacts, spells, or information promised in exchange for their expertise or allegiance
- Consequences: The potential ramifications for their decisions on their reputation and the delicate balance of power or any possible repercussions from breaching ethical codes or violating the laws governing magical practice/

Mages

Armor Class: 12 (Mage Armor)
Hit Points: 40 (8d8)
Speed: 30ft.

STR: 8 (-1) **DEX:** 14 (+2) **CON:** 12 (+1) **INT:** 18 (+4) **WIS:** 10 (+0) **CHAR:** 10 (+0)

Saving Throws: Intelligence +8, Wisdom +4

Skills: Arcana +8, History +8, Investigation +8, Insight +4
Senses: passive Perception 12
Languages: Common, Draconic, Elvish, and one other language of choice
Proficiency Bonus: +3
Challenge: 5 (1,800 xp)

Class Features
- **Spellcasting:** The Mage is a spellcaster. Their spellcasting ability is Intelligence (spell save DC 16, +8 to hit with spell attacks).
  - Cantrips: Fire Bolt, Mage Hand, Prestidigitation
  - 1st Level Spells (4 slots): Magic Missile, Shield, Detect Magic
  - 2nd Level Spells (3 slots): Misty Step, Hold Person
  - 3rd Level Spells (3 slots): Fireball, Counterspell
  - 4th Level Spells (2 slots): Dimension Door, Ice Storm
- **Arcane Recovery:** Once per day during a short rest, the Mage can recover a number of spell slots equal to half their level (rounded up).
- **Spell Mastery:** The Mage has mastered specific spells, allowing them to cast certain spells without expending a spell slot a limited number of times.

Actions
- **Multiattack:** The Mage can cast one spell and make a melee attack using a dagger.
- **Dagger:** Melee Weapon Attack: +6 to hit, reach 5 ft., one target. Hit: 5 (1d4+2) piercing damage.
- **Fireball:** A target must make a DC 16 Dexterity saving throw. On a failed save, the target takes 28 (6d6) fire damage, or half as much on a successful save.

Reactions
- **Counterspell:** The Mage can use their reaction to attempt to interrupt the casting of a spell and nullify it, using a spell slot as necessary.

Tharion Blackthorn

"Within the shadows lies true power."

A mysterious human mage specializing in shadow and illusion magic, Tharion uses his powers to manipulate perceptions and gain control on the battlefield.

For the Insightful:
Possesses an uncanny ability to read emotions and intentions, tailoring his illusions to exploit weaknesses.

Description:
Tharion has a deceptive, youthful appearance with long, untidy hair. His eyes glimmer mysteriously in the dark, hinting at the arcane secrets he wields. Draped in a flowing cloak of shadows, his presence is both captivating and unnerving, drawing attention from allies and foes alike.

Wants & Needs:
- **Wants:** To gather knowledge from ancient tomes about lingering shadows and spirit magic; dreams of achieving mastery in crafting illusion spells.
- **Needs:** To confront his fear of losing himself in his illusions, ensuring he does not succumb to the dark realms he conjures.

Secret or Obstacle:
Hides a deep fear of being lost in his own illusions, worried that he may never escape the shadowy realms of his creation.

Carrying (Total CP: 29):
- **Cloak of Shadows (10 points):** A flowing, magical cloak that enhances his stealth and presence.
- **Illusion Casting Wand (8 points):** A finely-crafted wand, attuned to conjuring vivid illusions.
- **Book of Illusion Spells (6 points):** An ancient tome containing potent illusion magic.
- **Shadow Essence (5 points):** A mystical vial containing raw shadow energy

Mage Tactics

Mages employ a blend of cunning, strategic foresight, and precise spellcasting to achieve their goals. In combat, they often rely on positioning and crowd control, using barriers and illusions to manipulate the battlefield while dealing devastating damage with powerful spells. Adept at recognizing opportunities, they take advantage of weaknesses and exploit the environment to gain the upper hand. Outside of battle, their knowledge allows them to engage in deep conversations, gather intelligence, and decipher arcane mysteries, often serving as advisors or strategists.

Shadow Mage & Illusion

Galadren Leafstride
"Nature's magic flows in harmony with the world." **2**

Brief: A wise and serene druidic mage specializing in nature magic, Galadren is known for his deep connection to flora and fauna, blending his wisdom with gentle power.
Vocation: Nature Mage & Healer
For the Perceptive: Possesses detailed knowledge of herbalism and nature, allowing him to heal and commune with animals with extraordinary effectiveness.
Description: Galadren has long, flowing green hair intertwined with leaves and flowers, wise brown eyes, and a calming presence. He wears robes made from natural fibers, and his staff is adorned with living vines. His gentle demeanor soothes those around him, reflecting his deep bond with nature.
Wants & Needs: Wants: To protect the balance of nature while expanding his knowledge of magical fauna; dreams of creating a sanctuary for endangered species.
- Needs: To overcome frustration with civilization's neglect of nature, yearning for the world to recognize its importance.

Secret or Obstacle: Hides frustration at nature's neglect by civilization, yearning for more people to realize its importance.
Carrying (Total CP: 27):
- Staff of Nature's Wrath (10 points): A sturdy staff entwined with living vines, resonating with nature's magic.
- Herbalist's Kit (7 points): Tools and ingredients for crafting potent remedies.
- Tome of Nature Magic (6 points): A guide to summoning natural forces and healing magic.
- Healing Potions (4 points): Vital restoratives for emergencies.

Niklas Duskmantle
"Knowledge is a weapon; wield it wisely." **3**

Brief: An inquisitive human mage specializing in arcane knowledge, Niklas seeks to uncover forgotten spells and ancient secrets, blending his intellect with powerful magic.
Vocation: Arcane Mage & Scholar
For the Perceptive: Possesses a sharp intellect and exceptional spellcasting skills, often outmaneuvering opponents with clever tactics.
Description: Niklas has short, light brown hair and thoughtful hazel eyes. He wears elegant robes adorned with symbols of arcane power, carrying an assortment of tomes and scrolls. His presence suggests a keen mind, focused on the intricacies of magic.
Wants & Needs: Wants: To discover long-lost magical texts and enhance his knowledge; dreams of achieving the status of a legendary archmage.
- Needs: To overcome the fear of failure in his research, resisting the burden of becoming consumed by the pursuit of knowledge.

Secret or Obstacle: Hides the fear of failing his research and the burden of finding himself consumed by the pursuit of knowledge.
Carrying (Total CP: 29):
- Wand of Arcane Power (10 points): A sleek wand imbued with raw magical energy.
- Ancient Tomes (8 points): Books filled with forgotten incantations and secrets.
- Spell Scrolls (6 points): A collection of versatile spells for combat and study.
- Potion of Insight (5 points): Grants temporary clarity and focus in critical moments.

Varion Shadowglen
"Enlightenment through shadows; the unknown holds great power." **4**

Brief: A mysterious half-elf mage with a penchant for dark magic, Varion walks the line between light and shadow, seeking to harness its mysteries.
Vocation: Dark Mage & Illusionist
For the Insightful: Possesses the ability to manipulate dark energies, enabling him to forge unique spells and illusions.
Description: Varion has silver hair and somber violet eyes, wearing dark robes that flow like smoke. His aura is enigmatic, often drawing curiosity and fear. He tends to keep his true thoughts hidden behind a calm facade.
Wants & Needs: Wants: To master the art of shadow magic and transcend traditional spellcasting; dreams of creating a powerful item amplifying his abilities.
- Needs: To resist the temptation to delve deeper into darker magics, wrestling with his morality and the risks of corruption.

Secret or Obstacle: Hides his struggle with temptation to cross deeper into darker magics, often wrestling with his morality.
Carrying (Total CP: 28):
- Shadow Staff (10 points): A staff that channels shadows into spells of destruction or illusion.
- Book of Dark Spells (8 points): Contains forbidden incantations and powerful curses.
- Cloak of Shadows (6 points): Envelops the wearer in darkness, aiding in stealth and evasion.
- Enchanted Essence (4 points): A rare substance that fuels his dark magic.

Jareth Windstrider
"Elegance in motion is the key to victory." 5

Brief: A graceful elven knight specializing in swift strikes and agile maneuvers, Jareth believes balance and beauty elevate combat, making him a mesmerizing presence on the battlefield.
Vocation: Knight & Combat Artist
For the Insightful: Possesses incredible agility and finesse, often appearing as a whirlwind of motion during combat, striking with precision and grace.
Description: Jareth has flowing silver hair and bright emerald eyes that glimmer with determination. He dons elegantly crafted lightweight armor designed for fluid movement, blending defense with aesthetic appeal. His demeanor exudes confidence, captivating allies and foes alike.
Wants & Needs: Wants: To master the art of combat and elevate the reputation of elven knights, introducing new techniques to the martial world.
- Needs: To overcome his self-doubt and prove that strength comes in many forms, not just brute force.

Secret or Obstacle: Hides feelings of inadequacy when compared to more brutish warriors, often striving to validate his unique approach to combat.
Carrying: (Total CP: 29)
- Rapier of Swiftness (10 points): A finely balanced weapon that complements his agile fighting style.
- Lightweight Armor (6 points): Crafted for mobility, offering light protection without hindering movement.
- Martial Arts Manual (5 points): A tome detailing advanced techniques for speed and precision in battle.
- Healing Potions (8 points): Potent remedies to sustain him in prolonged engagements.

Urik Blackthorn
"Loyalty is power; power demands respect." 6

Brief: A cunning and morally ambiguous knight, Urik serves his own ambitions through a mastery of political intrigue and manipulation.
Vocation: Knight & Political Manipulator
For the Insightful: Possesses sharp wit and a deep understanding of courtly politics, allowing him to navigate treacherous alliances with ease.
Description:
Urik has slick black hair, sharp features, and intense brown eyes that radiate ambition. He wears polished armor adorned with luxurious fabrics, reflecting his noble aspirations. His confident demeanor often commands respect and fear.
Wants & Needs: Wants: To climb the ranks of nobility by securing alliances and leveraging influence.
- Needs: To establish a fortified position that solidifies his control over the realm.

Secret or Obstacle: Hides his questionable alliances, fearing exposure that could lead to betrayal from both enemies and allies.
Carrying: (Total CP: 28)
- Elegant Sword (10 points): A finely crafted blade symbolizing his noble ambitions.
- Decorative Armor (8 points): Opulent yet functional, reflecting his dual focus on aesthetics and protection.
- Political Influence Ledger (5 points): Records of debts and favors owed to him.
- Healing Elixirs (5 points): Restoratives to maintain his strength in dire moments.

Keldor Stoneguard
"Strength is forged in loyalty and unity." 7

Brief: A stalwart and loyal dwarf knight, Keldor stands as a shield for his kin, protecting his city with unshakable resolve.
Vocation: Knight & City Defender
For the Insightful: Possesses profound tactical knowledge, enabling him to provide strategic support in times of crisis.
Description:
Keldor is burly and imposing, with a thick beard and strong, weathered features. He wears ornate armor bearing his clan's sigil, carrying a sturdy warhammer as a symbol of his strength. His presence radiates determination and reliability.
Wants & Needs: Wants: To restore honor to his family name by overcoming the greatest threats to his city.
- Needs: To protect his kin and prove himself capable of standing strong in their darkest hours.

Secret or Obstacle: Hides his fear that he might not be strong enough when it truly matters, yearning for a chance to prove his worth.
Carrying: (Total CP: 32)
- Warhammer of the Guardian (15 points): A massive, indomitable weapon designed for defense and offense.
- Heavy Steel Armor (10 points): Durable and unyielding, crafted to endure the harshest of battles.
- Clan Sigil Shield (5 points): A sturdy shield marked with his family crest.
- Basic Healing Kit (2 points): A small collection of remedies for minor wounds.

Thurgar Ironfist *"Power lies in the heart of the forge."* 8

Brief: A burly dwarven mage known for his affinity with fire and metal, Thurgar combines magic with smithing, creating powerful enchanted weapons.
Vocation: Smithing Mage & Armorer
For the Perceptive: Possesses exceptional crafting skills, often melding items with magical properties through the heat of his forge.
Description: Thurgar has a thick, braided beard of fire-red and striking blue eyes. He wears heavy smithing gear, often stained with soot. His robust frame showcases the strength of his craft and enhances his fiery presence.
Wants & Needs: Wants: To create legendary weapons that might achieve fame; dreams of reopening the ancient dwarven forge to create masterpieces.
- Needs: To overcome his fear of failing to innovate in his craft, worrying that he might be left behind by faster-growing magic users.

Secret or Obstacle: Hides his struggle with staying ahead of advancing magical techniques, fearing his craft might become obsolete.
Carrying: (Total CP: 31)
- Forgemaster's Hammer (12 points): A tool imbued with runes to shape powerful weapons.
- Enchanted Anvil (8 points): A mystical surface for imbuing creations with magical enchantments.
- Tome of Smithing Magic (6 points): An ancient book detailing the art of melding fire and metal.
- Rare Metals (5 points): Precious alloys for crafting extraordinary weapons.

Sylas Lightweaver *"Light has the power to heal, but it can also burn."* 9

Brief: An amiable and optimistic bardic mage, Sylas specializes in light magic and uses his talents to uplift and inspire those around him.
Vocation: Bard & Light Mage
For the Perceptive: Possesses an innate gift for inspiring allies with spells that can empower their abilities.
Description: Sylas has tousled blond hair and bright blue eyes that radiate warmth. He dresses in vibrant robes that glow faintly, complemented by a lute strapped to his back. His cheerful demeanor brings smiles to those he encounters.
Wants & Needs: Wants: To spread joy and hope through music and magic; dreams of performing for a great audience that brings together all races.
- Needs: To overcome self-doubt, fearing that his light magic may not be enough when faced with dark forces.

Secret or Obstacle: Hides struggles with self-doubt, questioning if his light magic is sufficient to fend off encroaching darkness.
Carrying: (Total CP: 26)
- Lute of Radiance (10 points): A magical instrument that amplifies light magic through melody.
- Tome of Light Spells (6 points): A compendium of radiant incantations.
- Elixirs of Courage (5 points): Potions to embolden allies during times of peril.
- Enchanted Dance Flyer (5 points): A mystical script used to inspire gatherings through its light-infused choreography.

Ryu Tanaka *"The way of the elements reveals the truth of all paths."* 10

Brief: A disciplined monk and elemental mage, Ryu specializes in harnessing the power of all four elements to enhance his capabilities in battle.
Vocation: Elemental Monk & Mage
For the Insightful: Possesses an extraordinary connection to the elements, often using them to augment his martial arts skills.
Description: Ryu has cropped black hair and piercing brown eyes. Clad in simple yet elegantly designed robes that flow with his movements, he appears a harmonious blend of combat and magic. His presence is calm but commanding.
Wants & Needs: Wants: To achieve ultimate balance between mind, body, and earth; dreams of teaching others about the ways of elemental harmony.
- Needs: To address his feelings of isolation due to his unique blend of abilities, wrestles with finding his place in mage and monk societies.

Secret or Obstacle: Hides feelings of isolation caused by his unique abilities, yearning for acceptance among his peers.
Carrying: (Total CP: 24)
- Elemental Staff (12 points): A powerful conduit for channeling the forces of fire, water, earth, and air.
- Simple Robes (6 points): Lightweight garments designed for ease of movement.
- Scrolls of Elemental Techniques (6 points): Written guides on mastering elemental harmony.

Mercenaries

Mercenaries are skilled warriors and cunning strategists in a fantasy realm, offering their blades and expertise to the highest bidder. With formidable combat skills and a reputation for results, they serve clients ranging from nobles seeking protection to towns fending off marauders or adventurers bolstering their ranks. Operating in morally grey areas, they are bound by contracts rather than ideals, often forming eclectic bands that thrive on camaraderie, loyalty, and gold. Their tales of battles and victories, shared in taverns, paint them as heroes or rogues, depending on perspective.

However, aspiring mercenaries must beware of the unpredictable life of a sellsword. A popular cautionary tale recounts the exploits of "The Golden Blades," a famed group known for their prowess and reputation. One day, while guarding a valuable shipment, their leader, Grath, grew overconfident. Bragging about their unmatched skill, he devised a plan to ambush the supposed thieves by leaving the shipment unguarded and lying in wait.

But Grath hadn't done his homework. The "thieves" were a band of hyperactive squirrels, drawn by the scent of nuts in the shipment.

When the mercenaries charged out for a grand battle, they found themselves under a nut bombardment from a miniature squirrel army. Chaos ensued as Grath and his team scrambled to fend off the furry invaders, grappling with critters instead of glory.

This comical mishap reminds would-be mercenaries that confidence is crucial, but overestimation can turn plans into disasters. The mercenary life is unpredictable, requiring vigilance and clear thinking as much as combat skill. Before taking a contract, ensure the enemy isn't a horde of squirrels—adventures often take hilariously unexpected turns, leaving you chasing both glory and nuts!

Raelith Shadowblade "In the dark, I find my strength; in the shadows, I thrive." 1

Brief: A mysterious elven rogue known for his stealth and deadly precision, Raelith specializes in infiltration and assassination missions, making him an invaluable asset to those who can afford his price.
Vocation: Assassin & Infiltrator
For the Athletic: Possesses exceptional agility and keen senses, allowing him to evade traps and detect hidden foes.
Description: Raelith has long, jet-black hair and sharp green eyes that seem to see everything around him. He wears dark leather armor that allows for free movement and is equipped with a variety of daggers strapped to his belt. His quiet demeanor often leaves others intrigued.
Wants & Needs: Wants: To gain enough wealth to retire from mercenary work and establish a safe haven for those in need; dreams of a life without conflict.
- Needs: To reconcile his moral code with the nature of his assignments, finding peace with the life he has chosen.

Secret or Obstacle: Hides a moral code that conflicts with his assignments, causing him emotional turmoil during missions.
Carrying: (Total CP: 29)
- Twin Daggers (10 points): Razor-sharp blades designed for swift and silent takedowns.
- Shadow Cloak (6 points): A light, enchanted cloak that aids in blending with the darkness.
- Infiltration Tools (7 points): Lockpicks, grappling hooks, and other devices for covert entry.
- Potion of Agility (6 points): Enhances reflexes and movement for a limited time.

Garrick Steeljaw
"Steel is my companion; it never betrays me." **2**

Brief: A grizzled human fighter and seasoned mercenary, Garrick is a master of melee combat known for taking on difficult tasks with brute strength and battlefield cunning.
Vocation: Melee Combat Mercenary
For the Insightful: Possesses extensive battlefield experience, allowing him to adapt strategies based on the flow of combat.
Description: Garrick has a rugged build with salt-and-pepper hair and a scar across his cheek. He wears heavy armor that has seen many battles, proving his worth through scars of combat. His commanding presence makes him a natural leader.
Wants & Needs:
- Wants: To provide for his family and secure their safety; dreams of finding a cause worth fighting for.
- Needs: To confront doubts about the morality of his contracts, striving to determine whether he fights for the right reasons.

Secret or Obstacle: Hides his doubts regarding the morality of the contracts he takes, often struggling with whether he fights for the right reasons.
Carrying: (Total CP: 30)
- Greatsword of Might (12 points): A massive blade honed for devastating power in battle.
- Sturdy Plate Armor (10 points): Durable armor that has weathered countless fights.
- Mercenary's Code (4 points): A guidebook of ethics and strategies for surviving in the cutthroat world of mercenaries.
- Healing Bandages (4 points): Essential supplies for tending to injuries after battle.

Zara Emberwind
"Fire is my weapon; my rage fuels the flame." **3**

Brief: A fierce fire genasi mercenary known for wielding fire magic in battle, Zara is both feared and respected for her destructive abilities.
Vocation: Elemental Warrior & Fire Mage
For the Perceptive: Possesses great resilience, often using her flame powers to disorient and overwhelm her enemies.
Description: Zara has flame-colored hair and smoldering orange eyes, wearing armor adorned with fire motifs. Her presence radiates heat, often causing nearby air to shimmer. Her confident smile often masks her intensity.
Wants & Needs:
- Wants: To prove her prowess while seeking revenge against those who wronged her family; aspires to control her fire magic fully.
- Needs: To manage her emotional intensity, ensuring she harnesses her abilities without endangering others.

Secret or Obstacle:
Hides her fear that her emotions may spark uncontrollable flames, worrying that she could harm innocents.
Carrying: (Total CP: 31)
- Flame-Forged Staff (12 points): A powerful conduit for channeling fire magic.
- Fire-Resistant Armor (10 points): Protective gear adorned with flame motifs, resistant to intense heat.
- Spell Components for Fire Magic (5 points): Essential materials for weaving her powerful spells.
- Healing Elixirs (4 points): Potent potions for mending wounds and restoring vitality.

Orin Duskmantle
"Life is but a game; I know how to play it well." **4**

Brief: A jovial and cunning gnome mercenary specializing in espionage and strategic planning, Orin thrives on the thrill of outsmarting opponents.
Vocation: Mercenary & Strategist
For the Insightful: Possesses a knack for quick thinking, often devising elaborate schemes to complete missions.
Description: Orin has wild, curly hair and bright gray eyes full of mischief. He sports a patchwork outfit optimized for flexibility, with pockets full of gadgets and contraptions. His grin is infectious, drawing others into his schemes.
Wants & Needs:
- Wants: To accumulate wealth and use his cunning to ensure his success; dreams of leading a band of legendary mercenaries.
- Needs: To overcome his reckless gambling habits, which often land him in precarious situations.

Secret or Obstacle:
Hides a habit of gambling that often leads him to dangerous debts, causing tension with his clients.
Carrying: (Total CP: 22)
- Set of Tactical Gadgets (10 points): A variety of tools and traps for infiltration and sabotage.
- Lightweight Armor (6 points): A flexible suit that allows for quick movement and quiet operation.
- Smoke Bombs (6 points): Useful for creating diversions or covering a stealthy escape.

Finnian Crowforge   *"Those who underestimate a smith's skill know not the strength of iron."*   5

Brief: A muscular dwarf mercenary skilled in both smithing and combat, Finnian leads a group of mercenaries known as "The Iron Shields."

Vocation: Combat Smith & Battle Leader

For the Insightful: Possesses a thorough understanding of weapon forging, enabling him to craft and repair arms in battle.

Description: Finnian has a robust physique, a long, fiery red beard, and striking green eyes. He wears heavy armor with engraved symbols of forged items, often coated in soot. His presence is commanding, earning respect from other mercenaries.

Wants & Needs:
- Wants: To build a name for his crew and protect them as they take on difficult jobs; dreams of establishing the finest smithy in the land.
- Needs: To overcome his fear of being unable to keep his comrades safe in dangerous situations.

Secret or Obstacle:
Hides a nagging fear that he lacks the ability to keep his comrades safe in dangerous situations.

Carrying: (Total CP: 30)
- Shield (10 points): A sturdy shield bearing the insignia of his mercenary group.
- Smithing Equipment (15 points): Tools and supplies for weapon crafting and repairs.
- Battle Tactics Book (3 points): A manual of strategies for tactical battlefield leadership.
- Healing Potion (2 points): A quick remedy for battlefield injuries.

Cedric Oathkeeper   *"Loyalty binds my actions; my word is my bond."*   6

Brief: A proud but morally ambiguous knight known for taking mercenary contracts that line his pockets while playing both sides to gain advantage.

Vocation: Knight-Mercenary & Tactician

For the Perceptive: Possesses a talent for political maneuvering and diplomacy, often using these skills to secure advantageous contracts.

Description: Cedric has dark hair, a neatly trimmed beard, and piercing blue eyes. He dons ornate armor with an emblem conveying a sense of nobility. His charismatic smile can easily charm most, masking his ulterior motives.

Wants & Needs:
- Wants: To amass wealth and status through expedient means; dreams of a life of luxury and power in high society.
- Needs: To reconcile his conflicting sense of loyalty, often torn between his mercenary contracts and the ideals of chivalry
- he espouses.

Secret or Obstacle: Hides his conflicting sense of loyalty, often torn between his mercenary contracts and the ideals of chivalry he espouses.

Carrying: (Total CP: 30)
- Elegant Longsword (10 points): A finely balanced weapon befitting a noble tactician.
- Ornate Plate Armor (10 points): Intricately designed armor, both protective and commanding in presence.
- Healing Ointments (5 points): Essential salves for battlefield wounds.
- Diplomatic Correspondence (5 points): Documents and letters used to manipulate political outcomes.

Kortan Ironclad   *"Steel and thunder are the harbingers of fate."*   7

Brief: A thunderous half-orc mercenary specializing in heavy arms, Kortan is known for his deafening battle cries as he leads charges into combat.

Vocation: Heavy Armed Mercenary

For the Insightful: Possesses immense physical strength and resilience, allowing him to face multiple opponents at once.

Description: Kortan has a bulky build, with coarse black hair tied back and fierce red eyes. He wears heavy armor adorned with bronze and iron ornaments, each artifact symbolizing battles won. His booming laugh resonates, providing courage to his comrades.

Wants & Needs:
- Wants: To fulfill his ambitious dreams of conquest; aspires to become the most feared mercenary in the land.
- Needs: To resolve the inner conflict between his brutal reputation and his wish to protect the innocent.

Secret or Obstacle: Hides a fondness for children, often struggling with his brutal reputation and wishing to protect the innocent.

Carrying: (Total CP: 27)
- Warhammer (15 points): A colossal weapon capable of crushing armor and foes alike.
- Heavy Armor (10 points): Reinforced armor designed to withstand even the harshest attacks.
- Healing Potions (2 points): Quick remedies for combat injuries.

Toren Firevale 8
"Where there's smoke, there's a job."

Brief: A fire genasi mercenary known for his ability to manipulate flames in battle, Toren combines brute force with elemental magic to devastating effect.
Vocation: Elemental Mercenary & Fire Mage
For the Insightful: Possesses incredible combat energy, allowing him to wield fire magic with devastating efficiency.
Description: Toren has flickering flames for hair, glowing orange eyes, and a fierce demeanor. He wears rugged armor that protects against heat, adorned with fire motifs. His presence commands respect and a certain level of dread.
Wants & Needs:
- Wants: To claim victory through his skillful combination of magic and might; dreams of becoming the most feared
- mercenary in fire-based operations.
- Needs: To harness control over his fire magic, preventing recklessness in dangerous situations.

Secret or Obstacle:
Hides a lingering fear of losing control over his fire magic, causing him to act recklessly in dangerous situations.
Carrying: (Total CP: 30)
- Flame-wrought Sword (12 points): A blade imbued with fiery enchantments.
- Fire-resistant Armor (8 points): Rugged, flame-proof protection for battle.
- Healing Elixirs (4 points): Potions for recovering from injuries.
- Collection of Explosive Potions (6 points): Volatile tools for chaotic combat.

Finnar Greenthorn 9
"Nature's bounty shall never go to waste."

Brief: A stoic wood elf mercenary who specializes in guerrilla tactics and hunting, Finnar is a master tracker adept at jobs requiring stealth and cunning.
Vocation: Tracker & Guerrilla Mercenary
For the Insightful: Possesses a deep understanding of nature and animal behavior, allowing for effective tracking and hunting strategies.
Description: Finnar has long, earthy brown hair and soft golden eyes. He wears lightweight leather armor designed for stealth, adorned with leaves and natural designs. His calm demeanor suggests a person deeply in tune with the environment.
Wants & Needs:
- Wants: To protect nature and rid it of those who threaten it; dreams of sharing his knowledge with future generations.
- Needs: To confront his loneliness and desire for companionship, balancing his connection with nature and others.

Secret or Obstacle:
Hides a desire for companionship, often feeling isolated due to his intense connection with nature.
Carrying: (Total CP: 29)
- Longbow of the Forest (12 points): A bow crafted for precise strikes in the wild.
- Forest Camouflage Armor (7 points): Stealth-enhancing leather gear.
- Hunting Traps (5 points): Tools for capturing prey or enemies.
- Healing Salves (5 points): Natural remedies for swift recovery.

Draken Thornspire 10
"With cunning and strength, I shall carve my destiny."

Brief: A dashing and ambitious tiefling mercenary skilled in both swordplay and subterfuge, Draken navigates the underbelly of society with charm and bravado.
Vocation: Bardic Mercenary & Manipulator
For the Perceptive: Possesses a quick tongue and sharp wit, able to talk his way into or out of trouble with ease.
Description: Draken has deep crimson skin, elegantly curling horns, and short, styled black hair. He wears fashionable leather armor allowing for mobility and is adorned with trinkets displaying his conquests. His charming smile often disarms his foes.
Wants & Needs:
- Wants: To rise to prominence among mercenaries and establish himself as a reputable name; dreams of building a mercenary guild tied to his fame.
- Needs: To overcome his struggles with trust, learning to rely on others despite past betrayals.

Secret or Obstacle: Hides his struggles with trust, wary of allowing anyone close due to previous betrayals.
Carrying: (Total CP: 22)
- Dual Cutlasses (10 points): Twin blades built for agility and close combat.
- Light Armor (6 points): Stylish yet functional gear.
- Traveller's Survival Kit (6 points): Essentials for life on the road.

Merchants

Merchants are the bustling economic lifeblood of a fantasy realm, operating a vibrant tapestry of trade, wealth, and commerce. From humble stalls in local markets to grand emporiums filled with exotic goods, these enterprising individuals possess a keen sense for negotiation and a deep understanding of supply and demand. Merchants offer a wide array of products—ranging from mundane tools and everyday necessities to rare artifacts and magical treasures. Their ability to connect buyers with the goods they seek makes them invaluable, often serving as the glue that holds communities together. With their sharp wits and persuasive tongues, merchants spin tales of their wares, transforming simple transactions into memorable experiences.

Aspiring merchants should tread carefully, as crossing the wrong merchant can lead to comedic—or dire—consequences. A well-known tale circulates in taverns about old Roderick, a shrewd merchant renowned for his prized collection of enchanted trinkets. One day, a rival tried to outdo him by offering better prices for the same trinkets, hoping to woo away Roderick's loyal customers. Unbeknownst to him, Roderick had a knack for both craftsmanship and mischief.

To retaliate, Roderick devised a clever plan. He sold the rival a "magical" amulet promising endless luck in business. In reality, it was a simple piece of glass on a thread. On the next market day, the amulet brought nothing but chaotic "luck." The rival endured falling merchandise, runaway goods, and a goat that mistook his trousers for a snack.

This tale warns would-be merchants: trade is as competitive as it is lucrative, and stepping on the toes of seasoned merchants can backfire. In the fast-paced realm of commerce, knowledge is power, and friendly rivalry often beats bitter competition. Think twice before tarnishing a fellow merchant's reputation, or you may find yourself chasing a rogue goat through the marketplace!

Balthus Gildspur — *"Gold shines brighter when invested wisely."* 1

Brief: A shrewd and calculating human merchant who runs "The Gilded Exchange," a large trading post specializing in rare gems and precious metals.
Vocation: Jewelry Trader & Precious Metal Merchant
For the Perceptive: Possesses exceptional negotiation skills and a keen eye for value, enabling him to assess items quickly and trade effectively.
Description: Balthus is tall and well-dressed, with slicked-back dark hair and sharp brown eyes that seem to gauge the worth of anyone he meets. His attire is adorned with rings and necklaces, showcasing the wealth he deals in. His charismatic yet calculating demeanor allows him to charm customers and suppliers alike.
Wants & Needs:
- Wants: To expand his trading empire and become the leading merchant in the region; dreams of establishing his family as the foremost dynasty in trade.
- Needs: To protect his reputation and stay ahead of competitors in the ever-changing marketplace.

Secret or Obstacle: Hides his fear of losing his reputation due to the cutthroat nature of the trade, worried that rivals might outmaneuver him.
Carrying: (Total CP: 20)
- Assessment Glass (8 points): A tool for appraising the quality of gemstones and precious items.
- Rare Gem Collection (12 points): A selection of valuable and enchanted stones.

Fia Brightleaf *"Nature's gifts should be cherished and shared."* 2

Brief: A cheerful and knowledgeable half-elf herbalist, Fia operates "The Natural Remedy," a cozy shop filled with herbs, potions, and nature-inspired goods.

Vocation: Herbalist & Potion Maker

For the Insightful: Possesses incredible expertise in herbalism and natural remedies, often crafting unique potions to aid her clientele.

Description: Fia has long blond hair adorned with flowers and bright hazel eyes. She wears simple yet elegant clothing that allows her to move freely, and her shop is bursting with greenery. Her infectious enthusiasm makes her shop a warm destination for locals in need of healing.

Wants & Needs: Wants: To share her knowledge of herbal medicine; dreams of opening a larger apothecary that serves the entire region.

- Needs: To address the challenges posed by local authorities who undermine the use of herbs, advocating for better regulations to protect her livelihood.

Secret or Obstacle: Hides her dissatisfaction with local authorities who undervalue her craft, often wishing for better recognition and regulations for herbal medicine.

Carrying: (Total CP: 23)

- Herb Collection (10 points): A diverse array of rare and common herbs.
- Potion Brewing Kit (7 points): Essential tools for crafting potent remedies.
- Natural Remedies Guide (6 points): A book of recipes and techniques passed down through generations.

Gregor Whetstone *"A sharp blade is a trusted friend."* 3

Brief: A boisterous and passionate dwarf who runs "Stoneforge Armory," a bustling shop specializing in weapons and armor crafting.

Vocation: Armorer & Weaponsmith

For the Perceptive: Possesses exceptional craftsmanship skills and an artful understanding of weapon balance, ensuring quality in everything he makes.

Description: Gregor has a thick, braided beard, calloused hands, and a booming voice. He wears a leather apron while working, often stained from his craft. His large frame is imposing but friendly, and customers appreciate his straightforward advice on weapon choices.

Wants & Needs: Wants: To provide skilled craft to local fighters and stand against lesser smiths; dreams of crafting a legendary weapon remembered for generations.

- Needs: To balance his workload and maintain the precision of his craft, avoiding decline in quality due to high demand.

Secret or Obstacle: Hides his struggle with aging hands, concerned that his craft may degrade if he cannot keep up with demand.

Carrying: (Total CP: 32)

- Master's Hammer (12 points): A tool designed for precision crafting.
- Crafted Weapons (10 points): A collection of finely made swords and axes.
- Armor Blueprints (8 points): Detailed schematics for crafting protective gear.
- Whetstone (2 points): Essential for keeping blades sharp and battle-ready.

Aric Starbright *"Illuminate your path with enchantments."* 4

Brief: A whimsical and eccentric gnome merchant running "The Mystical Emporium," known for selling magical trinkets, rare artifacts, and enchanted items.

Vocation: Magic Item Merchant & Enchanter

For the Insightful: Possesses an extensive knowledge of magic, providing excellent customer service and helping patrons find the right magical items.

Description: Aric is short and sprightly, with wild copper hair and sparkling blue eyes. He wears brightly colored robes with pockets stuffed full of oddities. His cheerful demeanor and flair for the dramatic make shopping at his emporium a delightful experience.

Wants & Needs: Wants: To become renowned as the premier source for enchanted items; dreams of creating a magical school to train others in the art of enchanting.

- Needs: To stay ahead of the competition, keeping up with new trends in the magical marketplace.

Secret or Obstacle: Hides fear of failing to keep up with the magical trends, worried he may be left behind by competitors.

Carrying: (Total CP: 21)

- Magic Trinkets (10 points): Small enchanted items with various effects.
- Rare Artifacts (5 points): A collection of rare and unique magical relics.
- Enchanted Supplies (6 points): Essential components for crafting and maintaining enchanted goods.

Kara Blackbriar
"Crafting clothing is an art as timeless as the weavings of fate." **5**

Brief: An elegant and fashionable tiefling tailor, Kara runs "The Tailored Thread," a high-end shop catering to noble clientele with exquisite garments.
Vocation: Tailor & Fashion Designer
For the Insightful: Possesses a keen eye for design and understanding of trends, crafting clothing that fits both function and elegance.
Description: Kara has deep purple skin, elegantly curled horns, and striking attire that reflects her talent in fashion. She wears elaborate dresses and a warm smile, welcoming nobles and commoners alike to browse her creations.
Wants & Needs: Wants: To elevate her shop's reputation to be the elite tailoring destination in the realm; dreams of showcasing her designs at grand events.
- Needs: To overcome her fear of rejection from high-society clients, always striving for perfection in a demanding industry.

Secret or Obstacle: Hides her fear of rejection from high-society clients, pushing herself to meet their ever-changing expectations.
Carrying: (Total CP: 28)
- Selection of Fine Fabrics (10 points): Luxurious materials imported from across the realm.
- Sewing Kit (6 points): Precision tools for tailoring and crafting.
- Fashion Design Portfolio (5 points): Sketches and concepts of her latest designs.
- Magic Thread (7 points): Enchanted threads for unique, spell-infused garments.

Barnabas Thistlebeard
"Here, you'll find the finest brews this side of the mountains." **6**

Brief: A hearty dwarf merchant known for running "Thistlebeer Tavern," a popular establishment that serves house-made ales and hearty meals.
Vocation: Brewmaster & Tavern Owner
For the Perceptive: Possesses an excellent palate for brewing, often experimenting with unique flavors that attract patrons to his tavern.
Description: Barnabas is stout with a long, bushy beard and merry blue eyes. He wears an apron over casual clothing and carries a tankard wherever he goes. His infectious laugh and boisterous storytelling enhance the tavern's lively atmosphere.
Wants & Needs: Wants: To increase his tavern's popularity and reach wider markets; dreams of creating a legendary brew that will achieve fame.
- Needs: To manage the demand of his ever-growing clientele, ensuring his supply never falters.

Secret or Obstacle: Hides his anxiety over dwindling supplies as the tavern becomes more popular, worrying that he cannot keep up with demand.
Carrying: (Total CP: 29)
- Selection of House Brews (12 points): A variety of ales crafted to perfection.
- Brewing Equipment (10 points): Tools and kettles for large-scale brewing.
- Recipe Book (5 points): Generations-old recipes refined for excellence.
- Healing Ale (2 points): A restorative brew for weary travelers.

Kallik Nightshade
"From the shadows come the most unexpected treasures." **7**

Brief: A mysterious and charming halfling merchant, Kallik operates "The Twilight Treasures," a shop featuring rare curiosities, antiques, and magical oddities.
Vocation: Curios Merchant and Collector of Oddities
For the Insightful: Possesses an uncanny ability to find hidden treasures and negotiate for valuable items that intrigue his eclectic clientele.
Description: Kallik has curly brown hair, bright eyes, and a sly grin that can broaden at a moment's notice. He wears fitted, stylish clothing adorned with various charms and trinkets. His shop is filled with wonders, reflecting his whimsical nature.
Wants & Needs: Wants: To expand his collection while gaining notoriety; dreams of hosting exhibitions showcasing rarities from across the realm.
- Needs: To maintain ethical dealings, as his curiosity sometimes pulls him toward less reputable merchants.

Secret or Obstacle: Hides his dealings with less reputable merchants, fearing that his involvement may one day lead to trouble.
Carrying: (Total CP: 27)
- Rare Curiosities (10 points): Unique artifacts with mysterious origins.
- Curator's Journal (7 points): Notes and histories of his collected treasures.
- Magical Artifacts (6 points): Enchanted items with unique properties.
- Bargaining Scrolls (4 points): Documents to seal advantageous deals.

Brax Thunderstone — *"Tools of the trade, forged to conquer."* 8

Brief: A burly and skilled smith who runs "Thunderstone Forge," crafting weapons and armor for mercenaries and adventurers, known for his remarkable craftsmanship.

Vocation: Weaponsmith & Blacksmith

For the Insightful: Possesses remarkable craftsmanship, enabling him to create superior weapons that withstand the test of time.

Description: Brax is tall and broad, with a thick beard and calloused hands. He wears a leather apron over practical work clothes, and his forge is characterized by radiant flames. His demeanor is warm and inviting, encouraging patrons to seek his skills.

Wants & Needs: Wants: To build a reputation as the finest forge in the region; dreams of crafting legendary weapons for nobility.
- Needs: To combat the threat of declining clientele due to new competition in the city.

Secret or Obstacle: Hides a worry over potential decline in clientele due to new competition in the city.

Carrying: (Total CP: 31)
- Quality Weaponry (15 points): Finely crafted swords, axes, and shields.
- Smithing Tools (6 points): Essential tools for forging and repairing.
- Armor Schematics (4 points): Detailed plans for crafting advanced armor.
- Magic-enhanced Coal (6 points): Enchanted fuel that burns hotter for intricate forging.

Ulric Bloodmoon — *"Gems, gold, and secrets are my trade."* 9

Brief: An enigmatic and shrewd merchant who runs "Bloodmoon Jewels," specializing in rare and exotic gemstones, often attracting nobles and collectors alike.

Vocation: Gem Merchant & Collector

For the Insightful: Possesses an exceptional eye for quality and value, allowing him to source and trade in high-demand gemstones.

Description: Ulric has an air of mystery, with long sleek hair and sharp features. He wears elegant finery adorned with the gemstones he sells, and sapphire blue eyes that reflect knowledge and cunning. His persuasive nature often captivates wealthy clientele.

Wants & Needs: Wants: To amass wealth and build a prominent name in high society; dreams of discovering a legendary gem that will elevate his status.
- Needs: To manage his dealings carefully, as rivals might threaten his business if they uncover his connections.

Secret or Obstacle: Hides the depths of his dealings with the underworld, concerned that rivals might threaten his business if they discover his true connections.

Carrying: (Total CP: 30)
- Rare Gemstones (12 points): Priceless jewels sourced from exotic locations.
- Elegant Display Cases (7 points): Ornate cases that enhance the allure of his collection.
- Trading Ledger (5 points): Records of transactions and trade secrets.
- Jewel-Crafting Tools (6 points): Precision instruments for cutting and polishing gemstones.

Eldrin Mossfoot — *"From the earth, we find our nourishment."* 10

Brief: A warm-hearted firbolg merchant known for his organic produce and goods, Eldrin operates "Mossfoot's Market," a vibrant store in a bustling market district.

Vocation: Produce Merchant & Herbalist

For the Perceptive: Possesses innate knowledge of farming and herbalism, offering high-quality produce and insights into nature's bounty.

Description: Eldrin has shaggy green hair and a gentle demeanor, with warm brown eyes that radiate kindness. He wears natural fabrics and often has dirt smudged on his cheek from working in the fields. His presence invites patrons to enjoy their surroundings and supports the local community.

Wants & Needs: Wants: To promote sustainable farming while ensuring his produce thrives; dreams of bolstering community ties through gardening workshops.
- Needs: To overcome increasing rents and financial strain on his family's farming legacy.

Secret or Obstacle: Hides his struggles with increasingly higher rents and the strain it puts on his family's farming legacy.

Carrying: (Total CP: 16)
- Organic Produce Selection (10 points): Fresh fruits, vegetables, and herbs from his farm.
- Farmer's Almanac (6 points): A detailed guide of planting techniques and seasonal forecasts.

Monks

Monks are disciplined warriors of mind and body in a fantasy realm, embodying a blend of physical prowess, spiritual enlightenment, and unwavering focus.

Often residing in secluded monasteries, they dedicate their lives to rigorous training, mastering martial arts, meditation, and the manipulation of ki—the life force within all living things. Monks strive for inner peace and balance, honing their abilities to defend the innocent and uphold justice. Their agility and precision make them formidable, able to defeat fearsome foes without heavy armor or weapons.

Adventurers should approach monks with respect, as crossing paths with one can lead to unexpected consequences. A popular tavern tale tells of Brother Lin, a legendary monk known for his serene demeanor and unparalleled skills. One day, a brash group of adventurers swaggered into Lin's monastery, challenging him to a duel to prove their might. Amused, Lin accepted. The adventurers soon discovered their bravado was misplaced. With fluid movements and a peaceful smile, Lin evaded attacks with ease, redirecting their momentum. The first adventurer, swinging an axe, tripped over his own feet as Lin sidestepped, sending him crashing into rice bags. The others soon followed, causing a ruckus of tumbling bodies and scattered grains, to the other monks' bewilderment.

By the end, the adventurers, left in laughter and embarrassment, realized they had underestimated Lin's mastery of combat and composure. Still smiling, Lin turned their bluster into a life lesson, reminding them that true strength lies in wisdom and humility.

This tale reminds adventurers: while the path of a monk may seem gentle, underestimating their discipline can lead to an entertaining defeat. Respect the quietest warriors, for they often reveal the most unexpected wisdom—and the most amusing mayhem!

Sorin Galeheart

"Flow like the wind; strike like the storm." 1

Brief: A disciplined air genasi monk, Sorin excels in agility and speed, using the power of the wind to master his martial arts.
Vocation: Monk of the Wind & Master of Agility
For the Athletic: Possesses exceptional reflexes and balance, allowing him to evade attacks with precision and strike swiftly.
Description: Sorin's flowing white hair and light blue complexion shimmer like the sky at dawn. He wears simple, breathable robes that ripple with his movements. His calm and composed demeanor embodies the tranquility of a gentle breeze, inspiring those around him.
Wants & Needs: Wants: To unlock the full potential of his elemental abilities; dreams of teaching others the way of the wind.
- Needs: To reconnect with the world and form meaningful ties with those he protects.

Secret or Obstacle: Hides his fear of becoming too detached from humanity, struggling to find ties to the people he strives to safeguard.
Carrying: (Total CP: 23)
- Training Staff (10 points): A sturdy staff imbued with the essence of air, used for precision strikes.
- Breath of Light Potions (5 points): A rejuvenating tonic that restores energy.
- Herbal Healing Oils (8 points): Soothing remedies for wounds and fatigue.

Kaelar Stonefist
"Strength is the foundation; resilience is the path." **2**

Brief: A robust dwarf monk known for his mastery of unarmed combat, Kaelar uses his steadfast nature and rock-solid strikes to defend and inspire those around him.
Vocation: Monk of the Mighty Fist & Stoic Defender
For the Insightful: Possesses great strength and durability, allowing him to withstand blows that would fell lesser warriors.
Description: Kaelar has a thick, braided beard and a strong blue gaze. He wears sturdy, reinforced robes suitable for combat. His broad shoulders and imposing stature reflect his dedication to physical training. Kaelar has a thick, braided beard and a strong blue gaze that radiates confidence. He wears sturdy, reinforced robes suitable for combat. His broad shoulders and imposing stature reflect his dedication to physical training, and his calm yet commanding presence often reassures those who rely on his strength.
Wants & Needs:
- Wants: To defend his clan and promote unity among different races.
- Needs: To train the next generation of warriors.

Secret or Obstacle: Hides his struggle with emotions, often pushing them deep down to maintain an impenetrable facade.
Carrying: (Total CP: 30)
- Sturdy Staff of Might (12 points): A powerful weapon symbolizing his strength.
- Heavy Training Robes (10 points): Reinforced robes ideal for intense combat.
- Techniques of the Stone (5 points): A manual detailing advanced defensive techniques.
- Healing Potions (3 points): Potions for quick recovery during training.

Valeria Moonshadow
"Strike in silence; move in shadows." **3**

Brief: A stealthy half-elf monk who specializes in martial arts and shadow magic, Valeria uses agility and grace to outmaneuver opponents and strike with precision.
Vocation: Monk of the Shadow & Stealth Master
For the Perceptive: Possesses exceptional stealth skills, allowing her to blend into her surroundings seamlessly.
Description: Valeria has long silver hair and sharp lavender eyes that seem to pierce the darkness. She wears dark, form-fitting robes that allow her to move swiftly and silently. Her tranquil demeanor often masks a fierce determination, and her quiet confidence conceals the burdens of her past.
Wants & Needs:
- Wants: To master the techniques of stealth and shadow magic.
- Needs: To establish an order of monks dedicated to preserving the balance of light and darkness.

Secret or Obstacle: Hides her fear of failure after witnessing a previous mission go awry, causing her to doubt her abilities.
Carrying: (Total CP: 27)
- Lightweight Twin Staffs (10 points): Ideal for swift and precise strikes.
- Shadow Cloak (6 points): A magical cloak enhancing stealth.
- Shadow Techniques Manual (5 points): Instructions for mastering shadow combat.
- Healing Salves (6 points): Salves to recover from injuries in silence.

Brenna Firewalker
"Embrace the flame within; it will guide your path." **4**

Brief: A spirited fire genasi monk who incorporates fiery martial arts into her practices, Brenna channels the essence of fire to enhance her attacks and inspire others.
Vocation: Monk of the Flame & Fire Mage
For the Insightful: Possesses fiery energy and intense focus, making her a formidable opponent in battle.
Description: Brenna has vibrant red-orange hair that seems to flicker with flames, and deep amber eyes that glow with intensity. She wears robes that flow like fire, decorated with flame motifs. Her vibrant personality often lights up the room, but a spark of impatience occasionally reveals the passionate storm she tries to control.
Wants & Needs:
- Wants: To master the art of fire techniques while protecting those she cares about.
- Needs: To establish an academy for fire practitioners.

Secret or Obstacle: Hides a fear of losing control of her powers during moments of intense emotion.
Carrying: (Total CP: 29)
- Flame-infused Staff (12 points): A staff imbued with the essence of fire.
- Fire-resistant Robes (8 points): Robes designed to withstand intense heat.
- Book of Fiery Techniques (6 points): Advanced knowledge of fire-based martial arts.
- Healing Elixirs (3 points): Potent elixirs for recovery and focus.

Tenzin Ironhand *"Discipline emerges from struggle; the body is a temple."* 5

Brief: A disciplined monk who follows a strict regimen of martial training and meditation, He is a human master of martial arts.
Vocation: Martial arts master & Spiritual teacher
For the Insightful: Possesses an exceptional ability to stay calm under pressure, allowing him to react with unwavering focus.
Description: Tenzin has a shaven head, a chiseled jawline, and focused brown eyes. He wears simple clothing that allows freedom of movement. His stoic presence commands respect and instills confidence in others. Beneath his composed exterior lies a man striving to balance perfection with the need for connection.
Wants & Needs:
- Wants: To impart wisdom to others while honing his own skills; dreams of establishing a dojo for all races to learn martial art traditions.
- Needs: To maintain balance between his pursuit of perfection and building meaningful human connections.

Secret or Obstacle: Hides a struggle with ensuring he does not become lost in his quest for perfection, yearning for human connections.
Carrying: (Total CP: 28)
- Wooden Training Staff (10 points): A sturdy staff used for practice and discipline.
- Comfortable Training Robes (6 points): Loose robes designed for movement and meditation.
- Meditation Manuscript (6 points): Guides him in focusing his mind and energy.
- Healing Balms (6 points): Restorative salves for both himself and others.

Jarek Sunstrider *"Balance the sun and the earth; harmony creates strength."* 6

Brief: A serene dragonborn monk, Jarek embodies the principles of balance and harmony, blending martial arts with elemental techniques.
Vocation: Elemental monk & Master of balance
For the Perceptive: Possesses a deep understanding of elemental forces, channeling them in combat with deadly precision.
Description: Jarek has gleaming bronze scales and fiery orange eyes. He wears robes of vibrant hues that represent his connection to the elements, and he often carries a quarterstaff adorned with elemental symbols. His dedication to harmony stems from a desire to atone for past mistakes.
Wants & Needs:
- Wants: To protect the natural world from destruction and imbalance; dreams of establishing a sanctuary for all creatures.
- Needs: To reconcile his guilt over past destructive decisions by creating something meaningful and enduring.

Secret or Obstacle: Hides a lingering guilt over past decisions that led to destructive outcomes, often seeking redemption through his actions.
Carrying: (Total CP: 30)
- Elemental Quarterstaff (12 points): A powerful weapon inscribed with elemental runes.
- Lightweight Elemental Robes (8 points): Attuned to elemental energy, allowing for freedom of movement.
- Techniques of Elemental Balance (6 points): Knowledge to master harmony in combat.
- Healing Crystals (4 points): Energized crystals that restore vitality.

Lirael Windrider *"Grace in motion; strength in purpose."* 7

Brief: An elegant aasimar monk known for her fluid fighting style and connection to the winds, Lirael uses agility and mindfulness to overcome challenges.
Vocation: Wind monk & Aerial combat specialist
For the Insightful: Possesses remarkable acrobatic abilities, often employing aerial techniques in combat.
Description: Lirael has flowing golden hair and radiant blue eyes. She adorns herself in robes that catch the wind, with flowing sleeves emphasizing her grace. Her presence evokes feelings of tranquility even in chaotic situations, reflecting her determination to bring calm amidst the storm.
Wants & Needs:
- Wants: To perfect her martial arts while safeguarding her community.
- Needs: To strengthen her waning divine powers to ensure her effectiveness in battle.

Secret or Obstacle: Hides a concern about her divine powers waning, leaving her vulnerable in her fights.
Carrying: (Total CP: 23)
- Wind-infused Staff (10 points): A staff imbued with the essence of the wind, light and swift.
- Lightweight Aerial Robes (7 points): Designed to flow effortlessly, enhancing agility.
- Scrolls of Aerial Techniques (6 points): Teachings that improve airborne combat precision.

ᛕarn Frostforge *"Every blow, every breath must be measured and precise."* 8

Brief: A stoic frost giant monk known for his mastery of icy techniques, Karn believes in the power of patience and precision in combat.
Vocation: Frost Monk & Ice Manipulator
For the Insightful: Possesses great strength and the ability to manipulate ice, enabling him to freeze foes in place.
Description: Karn is massive in stature, with icy blue skin and long white hair. He wears thick robes lined with fur, providing warmth and protection. His calm demeanor and focused gaze reflect his mastery of icy techniques. Behind his serene appearance lies a tumultuous past that constantly challenges his control over his emotions.
Wants & Needs:
- Wants: To promote the values of discipline and precision in martial arts; dreams of preserving the natural balance of ice and snow.
- Needs: To overcome the internal struggles of his tumultuous past and maintain control over his inner rage.

Secret or Obstacle: Hides a tumultuous past filled with rage, constantly battling to maintain control over his emotions.
Carrying: (Total CP: 29)
- Staff of Frost (10 points): A weapon infused with icy power, capable of freezing enemies in place.
- Heavy Icy Robes (8 points): Robes offering warmth and resistance against cold.
- Healing Ice Salves (6 points): Remedies for quick recovery in harsh conditions.
- Tome of Frost Techniques (5 points): A guide to mastering ice-based martial arts.

Alaric Thunderfoot *"Every step echoes through eternity."* 9

Brief: A boisterous and jovial firbolg monk, Alaric emphasizes mindfulness and connection to the earth through his grounded martial arts.
Vocation: Earth Monk & Martial Artist
For the Insightful: Possesses a powerful connection to the earth, using it to enhance his strikes and fortify his defenses.
Description: Alaric has dark green skin, thick hair, and bright, earthy brown eyes. He wears simple, natural clothing that allows ease of movement, coupled with adornments made of vines and stones. His jovial demeanor is infectious, lifting the spirits of those around him. Beneath his cheerful exterior lies a profound sadness over the lost traditions of his people.
Wants & Needs:
- Wants: To promote harmony between nature and civilization; dreams of uniting different cultures through warrior traditions.
- Needs: To reconcile his outward cheerfulness with the deeper grief of his people's fading traditions.

Secret or Obstacle: Hides a fear that his joyful demeanor masks deeper sadness over lost traditions among his people.
Carrying: (Total CP: 26)
- Staff of the Earth (10 points): A weapon imbued with the strength of the land.
- Lightweight Natural Robes (7 points): Clothing designed for agility and protection.
- Techniques of Earth Dancing (5 points): A manual of flowing martial movements.
- Herbal Remedies (4 points): Potions crafted from rare plants for healing.

Ilanara Duskweaver *"Embrace the shadows; let them guide your path."* 10

Brief: A cunning and agile dark elf monk specializing in stealth and shadow manipulation, Ilanara thrives in the night.
Vocation: Shadow Monk & Stealth Expert
For the Perceptive: Possesses sharp reflexes, often using shadows and silence to gain the upper hand against foes.
Description: Ilanara has deep purple skin and silver hair that flows like smoke. She wears fitted dark clothing that enhances her ability to move unnoticed. Her mysterious presence often leaves others intrigued, as if she carries secrets of the night. She seeks both mastery of her craft and a place of acceptance among her kin, despite feeling like an outcast.
Wants & Needs:
- Wants: To hone her craft and uncover the ancient knowledge of shadow arts which blends light and dark.
- Needs: To find acceptance among her kin and overcome her feelings of isolation.

Secret or Obstacle: Hides a longing for acceptance among her kin, often feeling out of place due to her unique abilities.
Carrying: (Total CP: 28)
- Shadow-infused Staff (10 points): A weapon that channels the power of shadows.
- Stealth Robes (6 points): Clothing designed for silent movement.
- Manual of Shadow Techniques (7 points): A book detailing advanced shadow arts.
- Healing Nightshade (5 points): A rare herb with potent healing properties.

Mystics

Mystics are enigmatic seekers of knowledge and truth, delving into the arcane and unknown to uncover the mysteries of existence. Guided by intuition honed through meditation, study, and exploration of ethereal planes, they wield ancient rites, divination, and subtle magic to perceive the threads of fate that shape reality. Mystics provide guidance to adventurers, unravel cosmic secrets, or serve as intermediaries between the material and spirit realms, often leaving others in awe or bewilderment. Yet, adventurers should approach mystics with caution, as misjudging their intentions can lead to comical—and chaotic—outcomes.

One popular tale features Elowen, a quirky mystic famed for cryptic prophecies and eccentric behavior.

One day, a bold band of adventurers interrupted her meditation, demanding the location of a legendary treasure. Annoyed but amused, Elowen decided to play a trick. She delivered a riddle: "To seek the treasure, navigate the path of dancing flames, where shadows play—look not with the eye but the heart, for there lies the key."

Confused, the adventurers spent hours wandering the woods, crawling through brambles, stumbling into puddles, and arguing over her cryptic words. In reality, Elowen had simply referred to the inn's cozy front room, where a hearth crackled and a complimentary pie awaited any adventurer brave enough to ask. Exhausted and pie-less, the adventurers returned, while Elowen chuckled, having entertained herself with a little mystic mischief. This tale reminds adventurers that mystics' insights, while profound, often spark confusion or absurdity. Approach them with respect, an open mind, and a sense of humor, for the path to enlightenment may lead to unexpected turns —or simply a slice of freshly baked pie!

Zypherin Windcaller 1
"In the whispers of the breeze, truth can be found."

Brief: A serene air genasi mystic known for her ability to communicate with elemental spirits and harness the winds to reveal hidden paths.
Vocation: Elemental Mystic & Spirit Communicator
For the Insightful: Possesses the ability to read the subtle signs of nature and the emotions carried on the winds, allowing her to predict events before they unfold.
Description: Zypherin has flowing, ethereal blue hair and soft, translucent skin that seems to shimmer in the light. She wears flowing garments adorned with cloud-like patterns, allowing her to move gracefully.
Wants & Needs: Wants: To uncover ancient elemental secrets and maintain the balance between the elemental planes; dreams of forming a council of elemental guardians.
- Needs: To believe in her own worthiness and fulfill the expectations of the elemental spirits.

Secret or Obstacle: Hides her fear of being unable to fulfill the expectations of the elemental spirits, feeling unworthy of the gifts she possesses.
Carrying: (Total CP: 28)
- Elemental Crystal (10 points): A radiant gem that channels the power of the winds.
- Whispering Feather (7 points): A mystical relic that amplifies her connection to the spirits.
- Healing Wind Potion (5 points): A soothing elixir that rejuvenates both body and mind.
- Tome of Elemental Spirits (6 points): An ancient manuscript detailing the ways of elemental communication.

Maeve Moonshadow
"The night reveals what the day conceals." **2**

Brief: A mysterious tiefling mystic who specializes in divination and moon magic, Maeve uses her powers to glimpse potential futures.
Vocation: Divination Mystic & Seer
For the Insightful: Possesses a keen intuition and can read both the stars and spiritual energies, making her an invaluable guide for those seeking clarity.
Description: Maeve has deep crimson skin, silver horns, and long flowing black hair. She wears dark robes with silver trim that glitters like stars, often wrapped in a veil. Her piercing azure eyes hold a wealth of secrets. Despite her calm demeanor, Maeve struggles with feelings of powerlessness when her visions fail to bring certainty, causing her to wrestle with her limits.
Wants & Needs: Wants: To delve deeper into the mysteries of fate and destiny; dreams of creating a sacred space for others to explore their past and future.
- Needs: To overcome her feelings of powerlessness and trust in the guidance of her visions.

Secret or Obstacle: Hides her struggle with feelings of powerlessness when faced with uncertain outcomes, wrestling with the limits of her visions.
Carrying: (Total CP: 29)
- Crystal Ball of Foresight (12 points): A powerful artifact used to peer into possible futures.
- Rune-etched Robes (8 points): Protective robes that enhance her connection to the arcane.
- Diary of Visions (5 points): A journal where Maeve records her cryptic insights.
- Moonstone (4 points): A magical stone amplifying her lunar magic.

Fenris Thorne
"Nature speaks; we must learn to listen." **3**

Brief: A rugged wood elf mystic, Fenris draws strength from nature and serves as a mediator between the spirit world and the living.
Vocation: Nature Mystic & Spirit Guide
For the Perceptive: Possesses deep intuition about the natural world, allowing him to tap into its rhythms and communicate with animals and nature spirits.
Description: Fenris has long, unkempt green hair and piercing brown eyes that reflect the forest's depths. He wears simple, earth-toned clothing made of natural materials, blending seamlessly with his surroundings. His quiet demeanor often invites contemplation, but beneath it lies a deep-seated sorrow over past failures that weigh heavily on his heart.
Wants & Needs: Wants: To protect sacred groves and restore balance to nature; dreams of fostering a coalition of guardians dedicated to nature's preservation.
- Needs: To release the guilt of his past mistakes and embrace his role as a protector.

Secret or Obstacle: Hides a deep-seated sorrow over a past failure to prevent a deforestation incident, feeling a burden of guilt.
Carrying: (Total CP: 24)
- Walking Staff (10 points): A sturdy staff blessed by nature spirits.
- Herbal Medicine (8 points): Remedies crafted from rare plants to heal injuries.
- Protection Charms (6 points): Magical talismans that safeguard him from harm.

Liora Brightflame
"Light answers the darkness; illumination brings clarity." **4**

Brief: A radiant fire genasi mystic, Liora harnesses the power of light to uncover hidden truths and dispel illusions.
Vocation: Light Mystic & Truthseeker
For the Insightful: Possesses an innate ability to see through lies and deception, illuminating the true nature of people.
Description: Liora has radiant golden skin and bright orange hair that flows like flames. She often dresses in flowing white robes adorned with sun symbols, exuding warmth and brilliance wherever she goes. Despite her glowing presence, Liora secretly battles self-doubt, fearing that her own inner darkness might overshadow her ability to bring light to others.
Wants & Needs: Wants: To bring hope to the world while battling those who thrive in darkness; dreams of establishing a sanctuary where truth can be examined.
- Needs: To conquer her self-doubt and fully embrace her role as a beacon of hope.

Secret or Obstacle: Hides her struggle with self-doubt, fearing that her own darkness might overshadow her ability to illuminate others.
Carrying: (Total CP: 28)
- Staff of Light (10 points): A luminous staff that channels radiant energy.
- Illuminated Robes (8 points): Enchanted robes that amplify her light-based magic.
- Tome of Truth (5 points): A book containing ancient wisdom for discerning truths.
- Light-infused Elixirs (5 points): Potent potions that restore clarity and strength.

Basil Runeweaver
"Runes are the language of the universe; each stroke tells a story." **5**

Brief: An elder gnome mystic who specializes in ancient runes and glyphs, Basil uses his knowledge to unlock powerful spells and create magical wards.
Vocation: Runic Mystic & Scholar
For the Insightful: Possesses a deep understanding of ancient texts and symbols, allowing him to craft powerful runic spells.
Description: Basil has wild white hair, twinkling blue eyes, and an assortment of trinkets and gemstones adorning his robes. He often carries a worn satchel filled with scrolls and inkpots. His energy is endearing, drawing others to seek his wisdom. Despite his enthusiasm, Basil harbors a fear of losing his mental acuity with age, which clouds his confidence in his legacy.
Wants & Needs: Wants: To uncover the lost secrets of ancient civilizations and preserve the knowledge of runic magic; dreams of writing an extensive tome on the subject.
- Needs: To find peace with the inevitable changes of aging and secure his legacy for future generations.

Secret or Obstacle: Hides his fear of losing his mental acuity as he ages, wrestling with uncertainties about his legacy.
Carrying: (Total CP: 31)
- Collection of Runes (10 points): A set of powerful runes used for spellcasting.
- Ancient Texts (8 points): Manuscripts detailing forgotten knowledge.
- Ink and Quills (6 points): Tools for documenting his discoveries.
- Protective Sigils (7 points): Magical talismans for warding and defense.

Dara Nightingale
"Music flows through the soul; let it guide our paths." **6**

Brief: A soft-spoken bardic mystic who channels magic through music, Dara uses melodies to enchant, heal, and inspire others.
Vocation: Mystic Bard & Healer
For the Perceptive: Possesses a deep connection to emotions and energies, allowing her to evoke feelings and memories through her music.
Description: Dara has long, flowing hair the color of raven feathers and expressive gray eyes. She wears elegant dresses that flow with her movements, adorned with musical notes and patterns. Her gentle demeanor often fosters a warm environment. However, Dara struggles with stage fright, preferring intimate gatherings to large public performances despite her talent.
Wants & Needs: Wants: To share her music with the world while spreading peace and understanding; dreams of composing a masterpiece that changes hearts.
- Needs: To overcome her reluctance to perform publicly and embrace her role as a beacon of harmony.

Secret or Obstacle: Hides her reluctance to perform publicly due to stage fright, often preferring intimate gatherings over large crowds.
Carrying: (Total CP: 27)
- Enchanted Lute (10 points): A mystical instrument that amplifies her healing melodies.
- Collection of Healing Melodies (6 points): A compilation of music imbued with restorative magic.
- Journal of Compositions (6 points): Personal writings containing her most inspiring works.
- Charms for Inspiration (5 points): Tokens that boost creativity and focus.

Voren Steelwrought
"Discipline and resilience build a fortified mind." **7**

Brief: A sturdy dwarf mystic specializing in martial arts and mental fortitude, Voren believes in the unity of mind and body in achieving one's potential.
Vocation: Physical Mystic & Fighter
For the Athletic: Possesses exceptional capacity for focus and training his body, achieving impressive feats through his resolve.
Description: Voren has a robust build, a long dark beard, and steely gray eyes that reflect his determination. He wears simple clothing that allows for movement during training and meditation. His presence feels solid and reassuring. Yet, he grapples with the fear of his strength being misused or leading to chaos, challenging his dedication to peace and order.
Wants & Needs: Wants: To teach others about the importance of mental strength in martial practices; dreams of creating a dojo that emphasizes holistic training.
- Needs: To reconcile his strength with his fear of violence, ensuring his power serves peace rather than destruction.

Secret or Obstacle: Hides a fear of violence giving way to chaos, often wrestling with apprehensions about his own strength.
Carrying: (Total CP: 29)
- Training Staff (12 points): A weapon designed for both offense and training.
- Meditation Mat (6 points): A tool for centering the mind and body.
- Manual of Mental Focus (6 points): A guide to mastering discipline and clarity.
- Healing Elixirs (5 points): Potent remedies for physical and mental recovery.

Selene Duskwhisper
"Fate weaves around us; let us learn to bend its threads." **8**

Brief: An enigmatic elf mystic skilled in fate and destiny, Selene uses her powers to guide others toward their potential futures.
Vocation: Destiny Mystic & Fortune-Teller
For the Insightful: Possesses remarkable intuition and foresight, allowing her to make predictions or offer insights about others' paths.
Description: Selene has long, flowing silver hair and piercing azure eyes that seem to reflect countless visions. She wears flowing robes adorned with celestial patterns, often appearing ethereal and otherworldly. Her presence captivates and inspires contemplation. Despite her grace, Selene struggles with frustrations over the limits of her foresight, fearing she may fail those who rely on her.
Wants & Needs: Wants: To understand the threads of fate while assisting others in achieving their true paths; dreams of writing a book on destiny and fate.
- Needs: To reconcile her own limitations and trust that her guidance is enough.

Secret or Obstacle: Hides her frustrations with the limits of her foresight, fearful of being unable to assist those she cares about.
Carrying: (Total CP: 28)
- Crystal Pendulum (10 points): A mystical tool to channel and interpret threads of destiny.
- Life Paths Journal (6 points): A personal log of visions and their outcomes.
- Cards of Fate (6 points): A deck used for divinatory readings.
- Elixirs of Clarity (6 points): Potions to sharpen the mind and focus the spirit.

Garruk Tanglewood
"Roots reach deep; let us find our strength in the earth." **9**

Brief: A grounded firbolg mystic who specializes in earth magic, Garruk finds power in nature and its connection to strength and growth.
Vocation: Earth Mystic & Nurturer
For the Perceptive: Possesses a deep understanding of the connection between the earth and the spirit world, enabling him to draw strength from natural surroundings.
Description: Garruk has deep green skin covered in vines and leaves, with warm amber eyes. He wears robes made from natural materials that help him remain connected to nature. His calm demeanor is inviting and nurturing, providing comfort to those around him. Beneath his tranquil exterior lies a fear of being unable to heal the earth effectively, a burden that challenges his confidence.
Wants & Needs: Wants: To promote the healing power of nature; dreams of restoring natural lands and creating a sanctuary for lost spirits.
- Needs: To let go of the pressure to meet impossibly high expectations and focus on his contributions to the natural world.

Secret or Obstacle: Hides a fear of being unable to heal the earth effectively, feeling pressured to fulfill the boundless potential of his gifts.
Carrying: (Total CP: 31)
- Healing Herbs (8 points): Rare plants used in powerful remedies.
- Scrolls of Earth Magic (7 points): Ancient scripts detailing earth-based spells.
- Charms of Protection (4 points): Talismans that shield him and his allies.
- Staff of the Earth (12 points): A staff that channels the essence of the earth for both offense and restoration.

Kiran Sunward
"Shine bright against the darkness; be a beacon of hope. **10**

Brief: A radiant aasimar mystic who channels divine energy, Kiran serves as a guide for those seeking healing and enlightenment through light-based powers.
Vocation: Light Mystic & Healer
For the Insightful: Possesses a deep intuitive understanding of healing and protective magic, often using it to aid those in need.
Description: Kiran has golden skin, bright white hair, and eyes that shimmer like sunlight. He wears ornate robes adorned with sun motifs and carries a staff shimmering with light. His warm presence comforts and uplifts those around him. Yet, he harbors burdensome memories of past failures, which occasionally cast a shadow over his radiant spirit.
Wants & Needs: Wants: To spread joy and hope in a world veiled in darkness; dreams of uniting individuals through shared experiences and faith.
- Needs: To overcome the weight of past failures and rediscover his boundless optimism.

Secret or Obstacle: Hides his struggle with past failures to save others, burdened by memories that cloud his radiant spirit.
Carrying: (Total CP: 30)
- Staff of Radiance (12 points): A powerful staff that emits soothing and empowering light.
- Healing Potions (10 points): Potions that restore vitality and health.
- Book of Light Magic (5 points): A tome containing sacred spells of healing and protection.
- Elixirs of Hope (3 points): Rare potions that invigorate the spirit.

Necromancers

The concept of a necromancer conjures images of shadowy figures weaving dark magic and communing with the dead in fantasy settings. The role of a necromancer is profoundly influenced by societal views of death, the balance of life and the afterlife, and the moral complexities surrounding the use of their abilities. In some realms, necromancers are feared and reviled as harbingers of doom, while in others, they may be seen as misunderstood scholars or essential guardians against the forces of darkness.

Imagine a world where necromancers are more than mere conduits of death. Some may belong to secretive cults dedicated to understanding the cycle of life through the study of the deceased, while others could be independent practitioners, driven by personal motivations such as revenge, power, or the desire to reclaim lost loved ones. During times of chaos, these masters of the macabre can become both allies and adversaries, wielding their abilities to manipulate the very essence of mortality.

Arcana
- DC 10: Skilled necromancers possess a range of spells that allow them to animate the dead, summon spirits, or drain life from living beings. Their expertise enables them to control lesser undead minions, ensuring they have loyal servants to assist them in their dark pursuits.
- DC 20: Masterful necromancers can command powerful forces that challenge the natural order, using spells to raise powerful undead or unleash devastating curses. Their affinity for shadow magic allows them to tap into lost knowledge and forbidden secrets, making them formidable players in any conflict.

History
- DC 10: Throughout history, necromancers have often been subjects of fear and fascination, their actions driving the narratives of both legend and cautionary tale. Their pursuits can be seen as either grotesque transformations or pivotal moments in the struggle against the encroaching void, leaving a lasting dark legacy.
- DC 15: The motivations behind a necromancer's practice are as varied as their spells. Understanding their histories—whether driven by a thirst for power, the quest for knowledge, or grief over a loved one—provides essential insights into their choices and the paths they walk.

Bribery and Influence
A necromancer's willingness to engage in deals or accept favors is influenced by a complex interplay of ethical considerations and practical interests:
- Motivation: Their primary drives, such as the relentless pursuit of knowledge, the desire for power, or the need to understand loss
- Compensation: The potential for rare artifacts, lost lore, or souls offered in exchange for their expertise or aid
- Goals: Long-term ambitions tied to their understanding of life and death or the desire to rival other powerful magic users
- Consequences: The possible backlash from society, magical authorities, or even rival necromancers for their choices.

Necromancers

Armor Class: 12 (Mage Armor)
Hit Points: 50 (8d8+8)
Speed: 30ft.

STR: 10 (+0) **DEX:** 14 (+2) **CON:** 14 (+2) **INT:** 18 (+4) **WIS:** 12 (+1) **CHAR:** 10 (+0)

Saving Throws: Intelligence +8, Constitution +6

Skills: Arcana +8, Religion +8, Insight +5, Deception +4
Senses: passive Perception 14
Languages: Common, Infernal, and one additional language of choice
Proficiency Bonus: +3
Challenge: 6 (2,300 xp)

Class Features
- Spellcasting: The Necromancer is a spellcaster. Their spellcasting ability is Intelligence (spell save DC 16, +8 to hit with spell attacks).
  - Cantrips: Chill Touch, Minor Illusion, Toll the Dead
  - 1st Level Spells (4 slots): Animate Dead, Inflict Wounds, Ray of Sickness
  - 2nd Level Spells (3 slots): Blindness/Deafness, False Life
  - 3rd Level Spells (3 slots): Vampiric Touch, Fear
  - 4th Level Spells (2 slots): Blight, Greater Invisibility
- Grim Harvest: When the Necromancer reduces a creature to 0 hit points, they regain hit points equal to their Intelligence modifier + the spell's level (if the spell was cast).
- Undead Thralls: The Necromancer can control additional undead creatures beyond the usual limit of animated dead, increasing their effective command over the undead.

Actions
- Multi-attack: The Necromancer can cast one spell and make a melee attack with their dagger.
- Animate Dead: The Necromancer creates one or more undead creatures from fresh corpses. One skeleton or zombie rises under their control.

Reactions
- Dreadful Aspect: When a creature within 30 feet of the Necromancer dies, they can use their reaction to instill fear, forcing creatures within 30 feet to succeed on a Wisdom saving throw or be frightened until the end of their next turn.

Malachai Vexmoor

"Life is fleeting, but power is eternal."

A cunning and ambitious former human necromancer, Malachai is driven by his desire to harness the essence of life and death to achieve immortality.

For the Insightful:
Possesses exceptional knowledge of dark arts and the biology of life forms, allowing him to manipulate life energy.

Description:
Malachai has pale skin and a bald head with piercing gray eyes that seem to carry ancient wisdom. He wears a mask and a cloak adorned with sigils of death, giving him an ominous presence. His demeanor is both charismatic and unsettling, drawing others in with his mysterious allure while instilling a sense of unease. Despite his outward confidence, Malachai harbors a deep fear of failure and death, which drives his obsessive studies.

Wants & Needs:
- **Wants:** To uncover the secret of eternal life while accumulating power over the living and the dead; dreams of creating a necropolis where he reigns supreme.
- **Needs:** To confront his fear of mortality and embrace the limits of his power without letting insecurity cloud his vision.

Secret or Obstacle:
Hides his fear of failure and death, often obsessing over his studies to disguise his deep-seated insecurities.

Carrying: (Total CP: 30)
- **Tome of Eternal Life (10 points):** A compendium of forbidden knowledge about life and death.
- **Staff of the Grave (12 points):** A sinister staff that channels necrotic energy.
- **Alchemical Ingredients (6 points):** Rare components for necromantic rituals.
- **Collection of Ancient Scrolls (2 points):** Texts containing lost secrets of dark magic.

Necromancer Tactics

Necromancers employ a combination of cunning, manipulation, and strategy to achieve their goals. In combat, they often utilize undead minions to create diversions and shield themselves, casting debilitating spells to weaken opponents while their creations do the fighting. With an in-depth understanding of life and death, they can exploit psychological fears, turning allies against one another or instilling dread in their enemies. Outside of direct conflict, necromancers might gather intelligence from the spirits of the deceased, using their insights to gain an upper hand in negotiations or plots.

Necromancer & Scholar

Sylas Grimshadow
"Death is not the end; it is a beginning." **2**

Brief: A brooding half-elf necromancer who believes in the potential of life after death, Sylas uses his abilities to communicate with spirits and reanimate the deceased.
Vocation: Necromancer & Medium
For the Insightful: Possesses the ability to commune with the dead, allowing him to gain insights into the past and understand tragedies.
Description: Sylas has long, wavy black hair and haunting blue eyes. He dresses in flowing black robes that seem to shift like shadows. His calm and somber presence intrigues and intimidates those who encounter him. However, his personal grief over a lost loved one sometimes clouds his judgment, causing him to connect too deeply with the spirits he seeks to help.
Wants & Needs: Wants: To unveil the truths buried with the dead while helping restless spirits find peace; dreams of establishing a sanctuary for lost souls.
- Needs: To find balance in his connections with the living and the dead, ensuring his grief does not overwhelm him.

Secret or Obstacle: Hides his personal grief over a lost loved one, causing him to connect too deeply with the spirits he seeks to help.
Carrying: (Total CP: 28)
- Crystal Orb of Spirits (10 points): A mystical artifact for communicating with spirits.
- Necromancer's Robes (6 points): Enchanted garments that enhance his necromantic abilities.
- Journal of Spirits (7 points): A record of spirit encounters and their wisdom.
- Potions for Spirit Communication (5 points): Elixirs that amplify his ability to commune with the dead.

Elysia Darkwood
"Embrace the shadows to unveil the light." **3**

Brief: A deceptive and morally ambiguous tiefling necromancer, Elysia uses her skills to gain power and manipulate others through fear of death.
Vocation: Dark Arts Practitioner
For the Insightful: Possesses a sharp wit and cleverness, often using her charms and illusions to bend others to her will.
Description: Elysia has deep red skin, elegant curved horns, and long black hair. She often wears dark, seductive attire surrounded by a subtle aura of mystery. Her smile is inviting yet wicked, making her approachable yet dangerous. Despite her confident exterior, she longs for acceptance and fears that her manipulative actions may leave her isolated in the end.
Wants & Needs: Wants: To rise in power by instilling fear and utilizing the undead; dreams of creating a coven of powerful necromancers.
- Needs: To confront her fears of isolation and learn to trust others beyond manipulation.

Secret or Obstacle:
Hides her longing for acceptance and fear that her manipulative actions may leave her isolated in the end.
Carrying: (Total CP: 29)
- Wand of Fear (10 points): A magical wand designed to inspire terror in her foes.
- Cloak of Shadows (8 points): A shroud that enhances her stealth and intimidation.
- Grimoire of Illusions (5 points): A tome filled with spells of deception and misdirection.
- Potion of Control (6 points): A potion that grants her influence over others' actions.

Vespera Nightbloom
"Death is merely a change of perspective." **4**

Brief: An introspective and wise elven necromancer, Vespera believes in understanding the cycle of life and death as an integral part of existence.
Vocation: Philosophical Necromancer & Life Guide
For the Perceptive: Possesses a contemplative attitude, able to help guide others in their acceptance of mortality and afterlife.
Description: Vespera has silvery hair and ethereal green eyes. She dresses in flowing robes adorned with floral patterns that hide her necromantic symbols. Her serene presence calms those around her, often providing comfort. Yet, she struggles with her own fear of the unknown, doubting the faith she offers to others.
Wants & Needs: Wants: To teach others about accepting death and the mysteries of the spirit world; dreams of collecting wisdom from the deceased to help the living.
- Needs: To overcome her fear of the unknown regarding her own death and find peace in her beliefs.

Secret or Obstacle: Hides a fear of the unknown regarding her own death, struggling with the faith that she offers to others.
Carrying: (Total CP: 28)
- Staff of Rebirth (10 points): A magical staff symbolizing renewal and balance.
- Book of Death & Life (6 points): A tome of philosophical insights on mortality.
- Collection of Budding Flowers (7 points): Symbolic blooms used in her rituals.
- Healing Herbs (5 points): Natural remedies for both physical and spiritual ailments.

Tarkhan the Unyielding   *"Strength in death brings power to those unprepared."* 5

Brief: A ruthless and power-hungry orc necromancer, Tarkhan uses his dark arts to control legions of the undead, terrorizing local villages.
Vocation: Conqueror & Necromantic General
For the Perceptive: Possesses considerable strength and knowledge of necromancy, adept at raising the dead to do his bidding.
Description: Tarkhan has a hulking build, a formidable presence, and deep-set amber eyes. He wears dark, spiked armor adorned with bones from defeated foes. His growls command respect, while his unyielding ambition inspires fear. Beneath his menacing demeanor lies a simmering resentment at being underestimated due to his orc heritage, fueling his drive to dominate others.
Wants & Needs: Wants: To build an undead army, dominate the region, and create an empire of monsters ruled through pure terror.
- Needs: To overcome his insecurities about his heritage and find respect through strength, not fear.

Secret or Obstacle: Hides the resentment of being underestimated due to his orc heritage, which pushes him to exert control over others.
Carrying: (Total CP: 31)
- Ledger of the Fallen (5 points): A book chronicling the undead under his control.
- Healing Tinctures (4 points): Potions for rejuvenation after battle.
- Staff of the Necromancer (12 points): A powerful artifact for raising and commanding the dead.
- Dark Armor of Domination (10 points): Spiked armor that enhances his presence and intimidation.

Lorelei Shadowbend   *"Embrace the forgotten; learn from those who came before."* 6

Brief: A charming and enigmatic cholera necromancer, Lorelei believes in learning from the knowledge of the dead.
Vocation: Divination Necromancer & Scholar of the Dead
For the Insightful: Possesses a talent for divination and understanding the cycles of life and death, allowing her to learn secrets from the spirits of the deceased.
Description: Lorelei has pale skin, elegant flowing black hair, and violet eyes that reflect her mysterious nature. She dresses in dark robes adorned with runes, her presence captivating while also instilling a sense of caution. Despite her composed exterior, Lorelei is troubled by anxieties about spirits haunting her, fearing she might disturb the delicate balance of the living and the dead.
Wants & Needs: Wants: To gather knowledge from those who have passed and explore ancient secrets; dreams of creating a library of lost lore.
- Needs: To overcome her fear of the spirits she communes with and ensure she uses her knowledge responsibly.

Secret or Obstacle: Hides her own anxieties about spirits haunting her, often worrying that she might disturb the balance of the living and the dead.
Carrying: (Total CP: 28)
- Spirit Communicator Stone (10 points): A device for contacting the deceased.
- Book of Lost Knowledge (6 points): A collection of forgotten wisdom.
- Ritual Components (5 points): Essential items for necromantic ceremonies.
- Healing Salves (7 points): Remedies to mend both physical and spiritual wounds.

Gideon Blackforge   *"Forge alliances in the darkness; greatness is forged in bones."* 7

Brief: A cursed dwarf necromancer skilled in crafting necromantic artifacts, Gideon uses his talents to create powerful tools for other dark arts practitioners.
Vocation: Necromantic Artificer & Crafter
For the Perceptive: Possesses keen craftsmanship skills, combining magic and machinery to create unique and formidable items for his customers.
Description: Gideon has a weathered face, a thick beard streaked with ghostly white, and tired eyes. He wears practical smithing gear often smudged with soot. His imposing figure belies his cunning and innovative mind. Gideon harbors inner turmoil regarding the darkness that increasingly consumes his craft, fearing he may not escape its grasp.
Wants & Needs: Wants: To gain respect in the underworld of magic while selling artifacts and creating legendary items.
- Needs: To reconcile his craft's darker tendencies and ensure his creations serve a greater purpose.

Secret or Obstacle: Hides inner turmoil regarding the darkness that plagues his craft, worrying he might not escape its grasp.
Carrying: (Total CP: 24)
- Artisan's Tools for Necromancy (10 points): A specialized toolkit for crafting magical artifacts.
- Collection of Necromantic Artifacts (10 points): Unique creations that amplify necromantic power.
- Healing Elixirs (4 points): Potions to restore vitality and clarity.

Asher Nightshade *"Death is merely the beginning of true power."* 8

Brief: A charismatic and cunning human necromancer, Asher uses charm and wit to manipulate others and gather followers for his dark cause.

Vocation: Manipulative Necromancer & Political Player

For the Perceptive: Possesses exceptional abilities to read people and situations, using emotional intelligence to bend others to his will.

Description: Asher has sharp features, long dark hair, and intense gray eyes that seem to dazzle with ambition. He wears stylish dark robes tailored for mobility and disguise. His charming demeanor makes him approachable, concealing his true intentions. Yet, he harbors a constant fear of betrayal, making him overly suspicious of those he manipulates.

Wants & Needs: Wants: To gather followers who will help him create his own faction of powerful necromancers; dreams of establishing a hidden society radicalizing necromantic practices.
- Needs: To overcome his fear of betrayal and learn to trust those who genuinely support him.

Secret or Obstacle: Hides the fear of betrayal from those he's manipulated, causing him to remain suspicious of everyone around him.

Carrying: (Total CP: 30)
- Dagger of Shadows (10 points): A weapon imbued with dark energy for subtle assassinations.
- Charming Robes (8 points): Elegant attire that enhances his charisma.
- Tome of Political Manipulation (6 points): A guide to the dark arts of influence and persuasion.
- Elixirs of Influence (6 points): Potions that amplify his persuasive abilities.

Tahlia Darkwhisper *"Yours is an eternal song, sung by the shadows."* 9

Brief: A mysterious and sensitive dark elf mystic who practices necromancy as a form of art, Tahlia refers to the dead as "symphonies" of eternal stories.

Vocation: Artistic Necromancer

For the Perceptive: Possesses the ability to learn from the dead, drawing wisdom and inspiration for performance art.

Description: Tahlia has long, flowing white hair and ethereal green eyes. She carries herself with elegance, often draped in shadowy attire. Her haunting beauty captivates her audience, highlighting her love for the arts. Despite her confidence, she fears that society may never accept her unique view of the dead as a medium for artistic expression.

Wants & Needs: Wants: To tell the stories of the lost through her art while maintaining her connection with the spirit world; dreams of establishing a theater dedicated to the art of necromancy.
- Needs: To confront societal judgment and embrace her creative vision without fear.

Secret or Obstacle: Hides her fear that society may never accept her unique view of the dead as a form of art.

Carrying: (Total CP: 28)
- Performance Instrument (10 points): A magical instrument that amplifies her ethereal performances.
- Tome of Dark Myth (6 points): A collection of tales and songs derived from the dead.
- Musical Notes of Elysium (7 points): Enchanted sheets of music inspired by the afterlife.
- Communication Stones (5 points): Devices to connect with spirits for inspiration.

Thorne Grimwalker *"To walk among the dead is to know their truths."* 10

Brief: A rugged and battle-hardened orc necromancer known for his fearlessness in wielding dark powers, Thorne uses his skills to travel as a mercenary.

Vocation: Mercenary & Necromancer

For the Insightful: Possesses brutal strength and resilience, able to withstand curses and draw on the power of the undead.

Description: Thorne has a bulky build, deep scars, and fierce green skin. He wears dark armor resonating with unholy symbols and wields a twisted staff topped with a skull. His intimidating presence commands respect and fear. However, he secretly questions whether his path of necromancy could ever lead to redemption rather than chaos.

Wants & Needs: Wants: To grow stronger through necromancy while amassing riches; dreams of leading an army of the undead to prominence across the land.
- Needs: To reconcile his disdain for his chosen path and uncover whether his powers can be used for greater good.

Secret or Obstacle: Hides disdain for the path he chose, questioning whether necromancy could lead to his redemption or choas.

Carrying: (Total CP: 31)
- Staff of Necromancy (12 points): A weapon for commanding the undead.
- Dark Armor of the Fallen (10 points): Protective armor that channels necrotic energy.
- Collection of Battle Tactics (4 points): A manual of strategies for war.
- Healing Decay Potions (5 points): Potions to recover from necrotic injuries.

Nobles

Nobles are the aristocratic elite of a fantasy realm, wielding power, influence, and wealth. Defined by lineage, social standing, and elaborate customs, they play pivotal roles in politics and society. Residing in grand estates or opulent castles, nobles are known for extravagant celebrations, refined attire, and shaping events through decisions and alliances. Beneath their elegance lies a shrewdness, enabling them to navigate court intrigue and ambition with skill. Relationships with adventurers can be both beneficial and dangerous, depending on the motives behind their velvet gloves and gilded invitations.

Adventurers should tread carefully when dealing with nobles, whose world is rife with peril. A cautionary tale speaks of Lady Seraphine, a celebrated figure among nobility, known for her beauty, wit, and relentless ambition. Playing the charming hostess, she secretly manipulated alliances and eliminated rivals, hosting lavish banquets to further her schemes.

One evening, an ambitious adventuring party accepted her invitation, hoping to gain her favor. Unbeknownst to them, Seraphine had darker intentions. After wining and dining them, she flattered them into accepting a seemingly harmless quest.

The mission involved retrieving a cursed artifact—an object of great power she sought for herself. Once the adventurers touched it, the curse ensnared them, leaving them vulnerable and bound to her will. Rather than offering support, Seraphine used them as pawns in her ambitions, while they struggled helplessly against the curse.

This tale warns adventurers of the dangers in dealing with nobility. Their charm often conceals ambition and cunning. Before aligning with a noble, consider their motives, as loyalty can be a double-edged sword. The dazzling masks of high society often hide sharper teeth, and an invitation to grandeur may lead instead to betrayal and despair.

Lord Cedric Ravensworth — *"Power and prestige must be cherished and defended."* 1

Brief: A calculating and ambitious human lord, Cedric is known for his ruthless methods of gaining influence and wealth in the political arena.
Vocation: Political Manipulator & Landowner
For the Insightful: Possesses sharp analytical skills, adept at manipulating both nobles and common folk against each other.
Description: Lord Cedric has piercing hazel eyes, slicked-back dark hair, and a meticulously groomed beard. He wears elegant attire embellished with jewels and embroidered designs representing his noble lineage. His charming smile often belies his true intentions. Behind his polished exterior lies the shadow of his involvement in a dark assassination plot, which continues to haunt him.
Wants & Needs: Wants: To secure his political position and amass greater power through any means necessary; dreams of becoming the Prime Minister of the realm.
- Needs: To confront the consequences of his past actions and maintain the alliances that sustain his rise to power.

Secret or Obstacle: Hides his past involvement in a dark assassination plot, haunted that his actions will catch up with him.
Carrying: (Total CP: 22)
- Genealogy Book (6 points): A detailed record of his noble lineage, used to strengthen alliances.
- Enchanted Signet Ring (10 points): A family heirloom imbued with protective magic.
- Dagger of Deception (6 points): A concealed weapon for critical moments of betrayal.

Duke Alban Frostvale   *"Honor demands sacrifice; strength is born from loyalty."*   2

Brief: A noble and benevolent ice dwarf duke, Alban is the protector of his territory and takes pride in fostering peace among his people.
Vocation: Protector of His Land & Noble Leader
For the Insightful: Possesses considerable physical strength and tactical skills, often leading his forces in defense of his homeland.
Description: Duke Alban is imposing, with a long white beard, icy blue eyes, and armor decorated with frost motifs. He wears a heavy fur cloak, symbolizing his status among the northern tribes. His honorable and calm demeanor earns him the loyalty of his followers. However, he harbors a fear of betrayal within his own court, leading him to focus on securing the loyalty of those closest to him.
Wants & Needs: Wants: To maintain the safety of his people and solidify alliances with neighboring territories; dreams of uniting the northern tribes under his leadership.
- Needs: To address his fears of internal betrayal and build trust with his allies.

Secret or Obstacle: Hides a fear of betrayal from within his own court, focusing on ensuring the loyalty of those close to him.
Carrying: (Total CP: 31)
- Frost-forged Battle Axe (12 points): A powerful weapon imbued with ice magic.
- Noble Family Crest (4 points): A symbol of his authority and heritage.
- Defence Strategy Scrolls (8 points): Plans and tactics for protecting his territory.
- Healing Ice Tinctures (7 points): Remedies crafted for recovery in harsh climates.

Baroness Elara Vargein   *"Power should serve the people; their trust is invaluable."*   3

Brief: A charismatic and generous half-elf baroness, Elara is known for her philanthropic work and desire to uplift her community.
Vocation: Philanthropist & Community Leader
For the Perceptive: Possesses remarkable charm and social acumen, able to inspire loyalty and grace through her words and actions.
Description: Baroness Elara has flowing auburn hair, bright green eyes, and often wears elegant yet practical dresses that signify her noble status. Her warmth attracts crowds, and she is often seen covered in ribbons and flowers during local festivals. Despite her goodwill, she struggles with the nobility's dismissive attitude toward commoners, leaving her feeling isolated in her ideals.
Wants & Needs: Wants: To improve the living conditions of her constituents and create an inclusive community; dreams of establishing an academy for the disadvantaged.
- Needs: To reconcile her ideals with the harsh realities of the nobility's indifference.

Secret or Obstacle: Hides her frustration with the nobility's disposition toward commoners, often feeling isolated in her ideals.
Carrying: (Total CP: 28)
- Ledger of Donations (8 points): A record of contributions to her philanthropic projects.
- Family Crest Ring (5 points): A symbol of her lineage and commitment to her people.
- Plan for Community Projects (6 points): Detailed proposals for improving local infrastructure.
- Healing Charms for the Needy (9 points): Magical items for assisting those in need.

Lord Morven Blackthorn   *"Strength lies in cunning; fear is a powerful weapon."*   4

Brief: A cunning and unscrupulous noble, Morven is known for his involvement in dark dealings and secretive clubs that manipulate the political landscape to his advantage.
Vocation: Manipulative Noble & Power Broker
For the Insightful: Possesses sharp wit and intelligence, often using misdirection and manipulation to achieve his goals.
Description: Lord Morven has slick black hair, a well-groomed goatee, and cold blue eyes that seem to assess everything around him. He dresses in highly fashionable attire, often embellished with silver, and exudes confidence that borders on arrogance. Despite his polished appearance, Morven secretly fears that his dealings with outlaw factions might be exposed, undermining his noble standing.
Wants & Needs: Wants: To control the political landscape of his territory through fear and influence; dreams of expanding his power across the entire kingdom.
- Needs: To balance his ambitions with the risks of his secret dealings coming to light.

Secret or Obstacle: Hides his darker dealings with outlaw factions, fearing discovery that would undermine his noble standing.
Carrying: (Total CP: 29)
- Book of Secrets (8 points): A collection of sensitive information to manipulate others.
- Enchanted Dagger (10 points): A weapon imbued with magical properties for self-defense.
- Charm of Persuasion (4 points): A magical trinket that enhances his ability to influence others.

Sir Hieran Thorne   "Honor binds us; our duty is unwavering."   5

Brief: A noble and valiant knight, Sir Hieran is dedicated to the protection of the innocent and the maintenance of justice within his realm.
Vocation: Knight & Defender of the Realm
For the Insightful: Possesses outstanding martial skills and leadership qualities, often rallying troops to his cause with charisma and honor.
Description: Sir Hieran has a well-built frame, short blonde hair, and keen blue eyes that spark with determination. He wears polished plate armor adorned with his sigil and wields a mighty sword. His strong sense of duty inspires both admiration and loyalty. However, he is haunted by the memory of a past mission where he failed to save a village, driving his fear of failing.
Wants & Needs: Wants: To uphold justice and righteousness throughout the land; dreams of becoming a legendary knight whose deeds are celebrated in history.
- Needs: To overcome his self-doubt and reconcile with his past failures to remain a steadfast leader.

Secret or Obstacle: Hides a fear of failing his duties, haunted by the memory of a past mission where he couldn't save a village from destruction.
Carrying: (Total CP: 30)
- Sword of Justice (12 points): A weapon symbolizing his unyielding commitment to righteousness.
- Ornate Plate Armor (10 points): Intricately designed armor providing exceptional defense and honor.
- Scroll of Oaths (4 points): A declaration of his sworn commitments and ideals.
- Healing Potions (4 points): Essential remedies for battlefield recovery.

Lady Seraphine Goldenleaf   "Beauty and wealth are to be shared."   6

Brief: A radiant and ambitious elven noble, Seraphine is renowned for her cultural gatherings and her desire to influence the arts across the realm.
Vocation: Cultural Influencer & Socialite
For the Perceptive: Possesses exceptional taste in art and music, often using her gatherings to strengthen ties between powerful families.
Description: Lady Seraphine has long golden hair, striking green eyes, and an elegant presence befitting her status. She dresses in colorful gowns adorned with jewels reflecting her family's wealth. Her charm and grace attract admirers, but she secretly fears her lavish lifestyle might create resentment among the less fortunate, forcing her to confront her values.
Wants & Needs: Wants: To expand her influence through the arts and create a lasting legacy; dreams of hosting a legendary festival to unite the nobles of her kingdom.
- Needs: To balance her pursuit of grandeur with genuine concern for the less privileged.

Secret or Obstacle: Hides her fear that her lavish lifestyle may lead to growing resentment from the less fortunate, causing her to question her choices.
Carrying: (Total CP: 24)
- Collection of Unique Artifacts (10 points): Rare and beautiful relics showcased during her events.
- Jewelry of House Goldenleaf (8 points): Family heirlooms symbolizing her lineage and status.
- Invitations to Gatherings (6 points): Personalized scrolls used to attract prominent guests.

Count Roderick Evenfell   "Too much light reveals too many truths."   7

Brief: An enigmatic and secretive noble, harnessing his wealth to live in the shadows, often hosting intrigue-filled gatherings.
Vocation: Shadowy Noble & Political Strategist
For the Insightful: Possesses knowledge of the undercurrents of society, allowing him to manipulate events from the shadows.
Description: Count Roderick has silver hair, a pale complexion, and bright orange eyes that flash with cunning. He wears dark robes adorned with hidden sigils, often appearing more like a ghost than a noble. His whispers are feared among the court. Despite his outward composure, he secretly yearns for genuine trust and companionship, a desire at odds with his morally ambiguous actions.
Wants & Needs: Wants: To control the threads of society from behind the scenes; dreams of expanding his influence without revealing his true motives.
- Needs: To reconcile his desire for trust and respect with the shadows he operates within.

Secret or Obstacle: Hides his desire for true companionship, yearning for trust and respect despite his morally ambiguous actions.
Carrying: (Total CP: 29)
- Book of Secrets (10 points): A detailed record of sensitive information about key figures.
- Enchanted Ring (8 points): A magical ring offering protection and subterfuge.
- Healing Tonics (5 points): Potions to recover from physical and magical ailments.
- Networks of Influence Ledger (6 points): A catalog of his covert alliances and political maneuvers.

Duke Alaric Stormforge   "Strength and vigilance shall defend our legacy." 8

Brief: A proud and dedicated noble wielding both political influence and military strength, Duke Alaric is renowned for his protective nature over his territory.
Vocation: Political Leader & Commander
For the Insightful: Possesses keen instinct and tactical intelligence, often leading troops into battle and guiding his people with foresight.
Description: Duke Alaric is tall and muscular, with short dark hair and brown eyes reflecting fierce loyalty to his people. He wears battle-ready attire adorned with a noble collar and insignias of honor and protection. Despite his steadfast demeanor, Alaric struggles with the overwhelming pressure of living up to the expectations of his family's storied legacy.
Wants & Needs: Wants: To safeguard his territory from outside threats and expand prosperity within his lands; dreams of being remembered as both a wise ruler and a formidable warrior.
- Needs: To overcome self-doubt about his ability to meet the high expectations of his lineage.

Secret or Obstacle: Hides the overwhelming pressure of expectations from his family and kin, worrying he may not measure up to their legacy.
Carrying: (Total CP: 31)
- Family Sword of Governance (12 points): A symbol of his authority and power.
- Signet Pendant of Leadership (8 points): A talisman that commands respect among allies.
- Strategy Scrolls (6 points): Tactical guides for defense and governance.
- Medicinal Supplies for Troops (5 points): Essential remedies for maintaining the strength of his forces.

Lady Amara Windrider   "True power flows with the tides of change." 9

Brief: A shrewd and cunning noblewoman from a coastal city, Amara uses her charm and intellect to navigate the political landscape and maintain influence.
Vocation: Influential Noble & Social Strategist
For the Insightful: Possesses great skills in negotiation and navigating social mechanics, making her an ideal mediator in high-stakes conflicts.
Description: Lady Amara has long, wavy hair the color of a sunset and vibrant green eyes. She often dresses in flowing gowns reflecting the colors of the sea, adorned with seashells and pearls. Her grace and allure captivate the nobility, but she harbors frustration with male-dominated political circles that underestimate her abilities, forcing her to constantly fight for recognition.
Wants & Needs: Wants: To establish her family as the primary voice in coastal trade; dreams of hosting alliances that benefit her city.
- Needs: To overcome resentment toward societal norms and focus on earning recognition through her successes.

Secret or Obstacle: Hides her resentment toward male-dominated political circles that underestimate her capabilities, often fighting for recognition.
Carrying: (Total CP: 21)
- Trade Agreements (10 points): Legal documents securing advantageous deals.
- Family Heirloom Pendant (5 points): A token symbolizing her family's history and influence.
- Directory of Coastal Merchants (6 points): A valuable resource for trade negotiations.

Lord Balin Frostbloom   "Only through sacrifice does true beauty bloom." 10

Brief: A charming and morally dubious noble, Balin is renowned for his lavish banquets and secretive dealings, often benefiting himself at the expense of others.
Vocation: Political Schemer & Socialite
For the Perceptive: Possesses a flair for persuasion and manipulation, allowing him to charm allies into supporting his ventures.
Description: Lord Balin has a well-groomed beard, cold blue eyes, and always wears the latest fashions with pride. His demeanor is both friendly and shrewd, often knowing exactly what to say to achieve his goals. However, his secret dealings threaten to unravel his reputation, forcing him to live in constant fear of exposure.
Wants & Needs: Wants: To climb the ranks of power within the nobility while maintaining a facade of benevolence; dreams of creating a lasting legacy.
- Needs: To navigate his growing web of lies and ensure his manipulations do not lead to personal ruin.

Secret or Obstacle: Hides shady dealings that could unravel his reputation, fearing his manipulations may lead to his downfall.
Carrying: (Total CP: 30)
- Political Treaties (8 points): Agreements forged to expand his influence.
- Lavish Gifts (10 points): Extravagant offerings to secure alliances.
- Wine Collection (12 points): A symbol of luxury and a tool for persuasion during negotiations.

Paladins

Paladins are champions of righteousness and justice in a fantasy realm, embodying honor, virtue, and unwavering devotion. Clad in shining armor and wielding sacred weapons, these holy warriors protect the innocent, uphold the law, and vanquish evil. Drawing power from divine sources, paladins are more than formidable fighters—they are beacons of hope, leaders, and motivators within their communities. Bound by sacred oaths, they act with courage and compassion, battling vile creatures and championing the downtrodden.

Adventurers should approach paladins with respect and caution, as their dedication can lead to intense consequences.

A tale is told of Sir Alaric, a noble paladin revered for his righteous heart and loyalty to the light. One afternoon, as he patrolled a village, he found adventurers arguing over dungeon spoils. Hoping to promote peace, Alaric intervened, but his well-meaning efforts were met with mockery from a defiant rogue. Insulted, Alaric used his divine powers to compel the rogue toward honor and respect. However, the rogue, unable to resist his anger, lashed out, triggering chaos. A rolling barrel of apples knocked over a cart, setting off a chaotic domino effect throughout the village. A festival turned into a frenzy of startled villagers and runaway goods, leaving the once-peaceful scene in disarray. Amid the chaos and laughter of the villagers, Alaric realized his attempt to enforce order had spiraled into amusing turmoil.

This tale reminds adventurers that while paladins are steadfast and stoic, their commitment to justice can lead to unintended outcomes. Provoking them might unleash righteousness—and ridiculous situations. Tread carefully and respect their ideals, for a clash with a paladin could bring as much laughter as it does lessons.

Sir Alaric Stonehelm

"Forge your will with honor." 1

Brief: A noble and steadfast human paladin, Sir Alaric serves as a protector of the weak, championing justice and righteousness with unwavering resolve.
Vocation: Champion of Justice & Protector of the Realm
For the Insightful: Possesses exceptional leadership skills and tactical knowledge, often leading his followers into battle with courage and strategic insight.
Description: Sir Alaric has sandy hair, piercing blue eyes, and shining armor adorned with his order's crest. His commanding presence inspires hope, but he struggles with the weight of responsibility and fears of inadequacy.
Wants & Needs: Wants: To uphold the principles of justice and cleanse the land of evil; dreams of one day establishing a sanctuary for those in need.
- Needs: To overcome his self-doubt and accept that his best efforts may not always save everyone.

Secret or Obstacle: Hides his fears of inadequacy in leading his forces, feeling the weight of his oath as a heavy responsibility.
Carrying: (Total CP: 31)
- Longsword (12 points): A sacred blade symbolizing his unshakable resolve.
- Shield of Honor (5 points): A shield imbued with protective blessings.
- Healing Potions (4 points): Remedies for sustaining himself and his allies.
- Armor of the Radiant (10 points): Gleaming armor infused with divine power.

Paladins

Armor Class: 18 (Plate Armor)
Hit Points: 75 (10d10+20)
Speed: 30ft.

STR: 18 (+4) **DEX:** 10 (+0) **CON:** 16 (+3) **INT:** 10 (+0) **WIS:** 12 (+1) **CHAR:** 16 (+3)

Saving Throws: Wisdom +5, Charisma +7

Skills: Athletics +8, Religion +4, Insight +5, Persuasion +7
Senses: passive Perception 13
Languages: Common and one additional language of choice
Proficiency Bonus: +3
Challenge: 7 (2,900 xp)

Class Features
- **Divine Sense (5/long rest):** The Paladin can sense the presence of celestial, fiend, or undead within 60 feet, as well as the location of consecrated or desecrated areas.
- **Lay on Hands (25 HP pool):** The Paladin has a pool of healing that can be used to restore hit points to themselves or others by using their action; they can heal a total number of hit points equal to their Paladin level times 5.
- **Divine Smite:** When the Paladin hits a target with a melee weapon attack, they can expend a spell slot to deal extra radiant damage equal to 2d8 for a 1st-level spell slot, plus 1d8 for each spell slot level above 1st.
- **Sacred Oath:** The Paladin chooses an oath (e.g., Oath of Devotion, Oath of the Ancients, or Oath of Vengeance) that grants them additional spells and features.

Actions
- **Multiattack:** The Paladin can make two attacks with their weapon.
- **Longsword:** Melee Weapon Attack: +8 to hit, reach 5 ft., one target. Hit: 10 (1d8+4) slashing damage.
- **Javelin:** Ranged Weapon Attack: +8 to hit, range 30/120 ft., one target. Hit: 7 (1d6+4) piercing damage.

Reactions
- **Protection:** When a creature the Paladin can see attacks a target other than themselves within 5 feet, they can use their reaction to impose disadvantage on the attack roll.

Darius Blackthorn   *"True strength is birthed from the shadows."* 2

Brief: A morally ambiguous half-orc paladin, Darius embraces dark powers to achieve his vision of justice, often entwined with revenge.
Vocation: Paladin of Vengeful Justice; Adept in Dark Arts
For the Insightful: Possesses tremendous strength and physical endurance, often using brute force and intimidation to enforce his will.
Description: Darius has rugged features, dark green skin, and piercing yellow eyes. He wears intricately designed black armor adorned with fearsome insignias and wields an intimidating black mace. His fearsome presence draws followers who crave power, though his resentment of traditional paladin morals fuels his pursuit of darker paths.
Wants & Needs: Wants: To purge the land of those who wronged him and establish a dark order loyal to his vision.
- Needs: To balance his vengeful pursuits with the responsibilities of justice, avoiding corruption by his own power.

Secret or Obstacle: Hides his resentment toward traditional paladins, feeling constrained by their strict moral codes.
Carrying: (Total CP: 30)
- Blackened Mace of Retribution (12 points): A weapon that channels his vengeful wrath.
- Heavy Armor of Shadows (10 points): Protective armor that bolsters his dark powers.
- Ritual Tome of Dark Arts (6 points): A guide to forbidden techniques.
- Vials of Healing Tinctures (2 points): Remedies to sustain him during prolonged battles.

Marcus Firebrand   *"Let the flames of righteousness forge steel wills!"* 3

Brief: A passionate and fiery human paladin, Marcus wields elemental fire magic alongside his martial abilities, honing his strength through zeal and determination.
Vocation: Fire Paladin & Crusader
For the Perceptive: Possesses fierce determination and inspiring charisma, often motivating allies with passionate speeches before battle.
Description: Marcus has flame-red hair, freckles, and bright orange eyes that gleam with intensity. His light armor is decorated with flames and symbols of his deity, allowing mobility while igniting passion among his allies. Despite his vibrant energy, he struggles with controlling his temper, fearing it may hinder his focus during critical moments.
Wants & Needs: Wants: To vanquish evil creatures threatening the land and unite hearts through justice and warmth.
- Needs: To control his temper and channel his emotions productively in the heat of battle.

Secret or Obstacle: Hides a volatile temper, needing control over his emotions to stay focused during critical moments.
Carrying: (Total CP: 30)
- Flame-wreathed Sword (12 points): A blade imbued with fire magic.
- Armor of Flame Resistance (10 points): Protective armor shielding against intense heat.
- Amulet of Fire Protection (4 points): Enhances his resistance to flame-based attacks.

Thorne Wintershield   *"Honor the cold as you honor your vow; strike true, strike swift."* 4

Brief: A stoic ice dwarf paladin, Thorne serves as a sentinel of justice in the frigid northern territories, protecting the innocent from dark forces.
Vocation: Frost Paladin & Protector of the Northern Realms
For the Insightful: Possesses great resilience and tactical awareness, skillfully navigating icy landscapes and using them to his advantage.
Description: Thorne has frigid blue skin, snow-white hair, and bright azure eyes. His heavy fur-lined armor shields him from winter's cruelty, and his frost-forged battle axe ensures he stands as an unyielding defender. Thorne is calm and commanding but secretly mourns lost comrades, burdening himself with guilt.
Wants & Needs: Wants: To defend his homeland from winter's dark threats and unite the northern tribes against their enemies.
- Needs: To overcome his grief and realize that leadership requires acceptance of loss.

Secret or Obstacle: Hides grief for lost comrades, feeling personally responsible for their fates in battle.
Carrying: (Total CP: 29)
- Frost-forged Battle Axe (12 points): A weapon that cuts through the harshest frost.
- Winter Armor (10 points): Heavy protection designed for subzero climates.
- Shield of the North (5 points): A defensive relic symbolizing his leadership.
- Healing Salves (2 points): Remedies crafted to endure the extreme cold.

Balthazar Dawnbringer   *"Shine bright against the dark; let courage light the way."* 5

Brief: A revered aasimar paladin, Balthazar embodies the virtues of light and justice, leading by example and inspiring hope in those he encounters.
Vocation: Paladin of Light & Guardian of the Innocent
For the Insightful: Possesses exceptional insight into moral dilemmas, often acting as a mediator between conflicting parties.
Description: Balthazar has radiant skin that seems to glow and long golden hair. He wears glimmering armor adorned with sun motifs and wields a sword of light. His presence exudes warmth and assurance, inspiring those around him. However, he secretly struggles with doubts about his ideals when faced with overwhelming darkness.
Wants & Needs: Wants: To rid the world of darkness and evil while fostering hope; dreams of illuminating the hearts of all who have lost their way.
- Needs: To reaffirm his beliefs and overcome the fear of faltering in his conviction.

Secret or Obstacle: Hides a profound fear of losing faith in his ideals, often questioning his path amidst the darkness.
Carrying: (Total CP: 31)
- Sword of Enlightenment (12 points): A blade imbued with radiant energy to cut through darkness.
- Armor of Luminosity (10 points): Gleaming armor that symbolizes hope and protection.
- Writ of Justice (4 points): Sacred texts outlining his moral convictions.
- Healing Light Elixirs (5 points): Restorative potions to sustain his mission.

Lord Caspian Stormwatcher   *"Stand your ground, for the storm shall not prevail."* 6

Brief: A determined and ruthless noble paladin, Caspian enforces his will with unwavering authority, often crossing moral lines for what he believes to be the greater good.
Vocation: Noble Warlord & Paladin Enforcer
For the Perceptive: Possesses a keen tactical mind and commanding presence, leading troops with unwavering authority.
Description: Caspian has dark hair, sharp features, and piercing storm-gray eyes. His intricately detailed armor crackles with storm energy, and he wields a sword that reflects his unyielding strength. Despite his iron-fisted rule, Caspian fears the growing number of enemies who oppose his methods.
Wants & Needs: Wants: To maintain control over his territories through strict law; dreams of building an empire that adheres to his vision of justice.
- Needs: To find a balance between authority and compassion to prevent alienating his allies.

Secret or Obstacle: Hides a growing list of enemies who oppose his iron-fisted rule, fearing retaliation could threaten his power.
Carrying: (Total CP: 30)
- Storm-forged Sword (12 points): A weapon infused with electrical energy to strike fear into foes.
- Iron-clad Armor (10 points): Durable protection designed for intense battles.
- Writs of Authority (4 points): Documents that cement his rule over his territories.
- Electrum Healing Potions (4 points): Restorative elixirs for himself and his soldiers.

Sir Eldon Ashenvale   *"From the ashes of despair, hope shall rise."* 7

Brief: A reflective and somber paladin, Eldon is known for his commitment to redemption, striving to guide the lost and broken back to the light.
Vocation: Redeemer Paladin & Guide
For the Insightful: Possesses great empathy and understanding, often helping others through their struggles toward redemption.
Description: Eldon has ash-colored hair and soft amber eyes that hold deep compassion. He wears modest but well-crafted armor adorned with symbols of rebirth, wielding a sword symbolizing his journey. His calm presence encourages hope in those he meets, though he carries a sorrow for his past failures to save certain individuals.
Wants & Needs: Wants: To help the lost and broken find their paths to hope; dreams of establishing a sanctuary for those seeking a fresh start.
- Needs: To let go of the guilt from past failures and focus on the lives he has transformed.

Secret or Obstacle: Hides a deep sorrow over his failures to redeem certain individuals, feeling responsible for their downfalls.
Carrying: (Total CP: 29)
- Sword of Redemption (10 points): A blade symbolizing salvation and renewal.
- Robes of Compassion (6 points): Garments that signify his dedication to helping others.
- Journal of Stories (7 points): Chronicles of redemption and guidance.
- Healing Salves (6 points): Remedies for restoring health and hope.

Sir Alden Hawkwing

"Swift justice is justice well served." 8

Brief: A proud and fierce paladin, Alden incorporates speed and agility into his combat style, striking down foes before they can react.
Vocation: Swift Paladin & Avenger
For the Athletic: Possesses incredible reflexes, allowing him to dodge attacks while countering with swift blows.
Description: Sir Alden has short, spiky blonde hair and sharp blue eyes that scan for threats. He wears lightweight, reinforced armor designed for quick movement and wields a slender sword. His quick smile and animated gestures inspire urgency among his allies. Despite his confidence, Alden fears being overwhelmed by the weight of his convictions.
Wants & Needs: Wants: To enact justice quickly and efficiently; dreams of forging an elite order of swift holy warriors.
- Needs: To find balance between speed and wisdom to ensure his actions are just and sustainable.

Secret or Obstacle:
Hides a lingering fear of becoming overwhelmed by the weight of his convictions, struggling to balance speed with wisdom.
Carrying: (Total CP: 28)
- Light Rapier (10 points): A sleek, fast blade designed for precision.
- Agile Armor (6 points): Reinforced lightweight armor that allows optimal movement.
- Guidebook on Combat Speed (7 points): A manual detailing techniques for swift engagement.
- Healing Rations (5 points): Quick restorative supplies for endurance.

Victor Ironbark

"Stronger roots lead to stronger warriors." 9

Brief: A diligent and supportive paladin who believes in the strength of both the land and its people, Victor helps those in need by providing training and protection.
Vocation: Guardian Paladin & Mentor
For the Insightful: Possesses considerable strength and a nurturing instinct that inspires others to grow and become empowered.
Description: Victor has a sturdy frame, medium-length brown hair, and kind eyes that reflect his deep care for others. He wears earth-toned armor embossed with natural patterns, emphasizing his connection to the land. Despite his strong exterior, Victor often feels overwhelmed by the expectations of others.
Wants & Needs: Wants: To foster the growth of aspiring knights and protect the land from threats; dreams of leading a coalition of warriors.
- Needs: To accept his limits and manage the responsibilities placed upon him.

Secret or Obstacle: Hides a fear of not living up to his responsibilities, often feeling overwhelmed by the expectations of others.
Carrying: (Total CP: 29)
- Shield of Resilience (10 points): A defensive tool that reinforces his steadfast nature.
- Robust Armor of Guidance (10 points): Earth-toned armor symbolizing leadership and protection.
- Training Manual (4 points): Instructions for mentoring future knights.
- Healing Salve (5 points): Remedies for aiding both himself and others.

Gideon Darkwylde

"Embrace the shadows; they offer power like no light can." 10

Brief: A diabolical and malevolent paladin, Gideon utilizes dark powers to gain influence, believing the strength of shadows can secure dominion over the light.
Vocation: Dark Paladin & Power Manipulator
For the Perceptive: Used cunning schemes and dark wisdom, using them to manipulate situations while keeping allies on edge.
Description: Gideon has ashen skin, dark hair, and an air of cold authority. He wears black-enchanted armor and wields a wicked curved sword. His daunting presence commands respect through fear and intimidation. However, he hides deep emotional scars from betrayal, leading him to distrust even those he manipulates.
Wants & Needs: Wants: To dominate opponents with dark powers while expanding his reach; dreams of establishing a reign through shadowy might.
- Needs: To reconcile his mistrust with his need for loyalty, learning to balance power and relationships.

Secret or Obstacle: Hides the emotional scars of betrayal, leading him to distrust those around him even as he manipulates them.
Carrying: (Total CP: 26)
- Curved Sword of Shadows (12 points): A weapon imbued with dark, fearsome energy.
- Blackened Plate Armor (10 points): Heavy, enchanted armor offering protection and intimidation.
- Healing Shadows (4 points): Potions that sustain him through his shadow-infused battles.

Pirates

Pirates are the daring scoundrels of the high seas in a fantasy realm, sailing the oceans with reckless abandon and a thirst for adventure. With their weathered ships and ragtag crews, these roguish individuals embody the spirit of freedom, defying the law and living by their own code. Known for their swashbuckling bravado, cunning tactics, and love for treasure, pirates plunder merchant vessels, seek out hidden loot, and carve their legends into the annals of maritime lore.

Their camaraderie runs deep, bound by a shared life of danger, revelry, and the thrill of the chase. While they often evoke images of danger and mystery, the fierce loyalty among pirates can lead to unforgettable alliances forged on the waves.

Imagine a world where pirates are more than simple marauders. Some may belong to notorious crews bound by oaths of loyalty and shared ambitions, while others could be independent captains seeking fortune and fame on their own terms. During times of conflict, these swashbucklers can tip the scales of power, their actions influencing trade routes and the fate of nations as they navigate the turbulent waters of politics and war.

Arcana
- DC 10: Competent pirates often possess a blend of combat skills and seafaring expertise, trained in the use of swords, firearms, and naval tactics. While many focus on physical prowess, some may dabble in basic magical abilities, using charms or enhancements to gain an edge in battles at sea or during boardings.
- DC 20: Masterful pirates might command powerful magical artifacts or spells that affect the tides, summon storms, or provide protection during perilous journeys. Their deep understanding of the ocean may allow them to converse with sea creatures or invoke the favor of maritime deities, making them truly formidable foes on the high seas.

History
- DC 10: Throughout history, pirates have left indelible marks on cultures and nations, their exploits often transforming into legends. Tales of their daring raids, battles with naval forces, and hidden treasures captivate audiences, blurring the lines between heroism and villainy.
- DC 15: The motivations of pirates can be as varied as the seas they sail. Understanding their backstories—whether fueled by a desire for riches, a quest for freedom, or revenge against oppressive regimes—provides essential insight into their demeanor and actions.

Bribery and Influence
A pirate's willingness to engage in deals or accept certain offers is heavily influenced by a variety of motivations and situational factors:
- Motivation: Their primary drives, such as the pursuit of wealth, adventure, or escape from the constraints of society
- Compensation: The treasures, valuable trade secrets, or connections promised in exchange for their help or allegiance
- Opportunity: The potential for acquiring significant gains or leveraging their reputation in negotiations
- Punishments: Expected repercussions for violating pirate codes, engaging in betrayal, or running afoul of powerful enemies at sea.

Pirates

Armor Class: 15 (Leather Armor)
Hit Points: 60 (8d10+16)
Speed: 30ft.

STR: 14 (+2) **DEX:** 18 (+4) **CON:** 14 (+2) **INT:** 10 (+0) **WIS:** 12 (+1) **CHAR:** 16 (+3)

Saving Throws: Dexterity +8, Charisma +7

Skills: Acrobatics +8, Deception +7, Perception +5, Athletics +6, Performance +7
Senses: passive Perception 15
Languages: Common, Thieves' Cant, and one additional language of choice
Proficiency Bonus: +3
Challenge: 5 (1,800 xp)

Class Features
- **Expert Sailor:** The Pirate has proficiency with vehicles (water) and can navigate waterways more easily, gaining advantage on checks related to sailing and navigation.
- **Finesse Fighter:** The Pirate can use their Dexterity modifier for attack and damage rolls when using finesse weapons.
- **Swashbuckler's Duel:** When fighting a creature alone, the Pirate can add their Charisma modifier to their damage rolls against that target.

Actions
- **Multi-attack:** The Pirate can make two attacks with their weapon.
- **Rapier:** Melee Weapon Attack: +8 to hit, reach 5 ft., one target. Hit: 9 (1d8+4) piercing damage.
- **Pistol:** Ranged Weapon Attack: +8 to hit, range 30/120 ft., one target. Hit: 8 (1d10+4) piercing damage.

Bonus Actions
- **Cunning Action:** The Pirate can use a bonus action to Dash, Disengage, or Hide.

Reactions
- **Evasion:** When subjected to an effect that allows a Dexterity saving throw, the Pirate can take no damage on a successful save, and only half damage on a failed save.

Captain Rex "Blackheart" Grimthorne

A notorious and ruthless pirate captain, Grimthorne is feared across the seas for his merciless tactics and reputation for betrayal.

"Fear the storm, for it brings destruction."

For the Insightful:
Possesses sharp instincts and brutal combat skills, often using intimidation to enforce his will over crews and enemies alike.

Description:
Captain Grimthorne is tall and imposing, with long black hair, a weathered face, and sharp, piercing eyes that seem to absorb the light. He wears dark, tattered clothing adorned with bones and trophies from his past conquests. His commanding presence instills both fear and respect, but his paranoia about betrayal from his crew reveals the scars of his ruthless past.

Wants & Needs:
- **Wants:** To amass unimaginable wealth and power while ruling the seas with an iron fist; dreams of becoming the most feared pirate captain in history.
- **Needs:** To address his paranoia and rebuild loyalty among his crew to prevent further mutiny.

Secret or Obstacle:
Hides a vulnerability regarding loyalty and trust, often paranoid about betrayal from his crew due to his past actions.

Carrying: (Total CP: 31)
- **Cutlass of Fear (12 points):** A weapon that exudes menace, striking terror into foes.
- **Blackened Pirate Coat (8 points):** A weathered coat offering protection and intimidation.
- **Map of Lost Treasures (5 points):** A detailed chart leading to hidden riches.
- **Healing Rum (6 points):** A potent brew that restores vigor and morale.

Pirate Tactics

Pirates deploy a cunning combination of audacity and camaraderie to achieve their goals. In combat, they maneuver skillfully on the decks of their ships, using their knowledge of the sea and naval tactics to outwit opponents.

Surprise attacks are their hallmark, striking swiftly and retreating before retaliation. Outside of battle, pirates excel in persuasion and deception—forming temporary truces, negotiating alliances, or charming their way into favorable situations.

Ruthless Pirate Captain

Master Sabin Stormtooth *"Opportunists thrive in chaos."* 2

Brief: A cunning and opportunistic pirate, Sabin waits for the perfect moment to strike, exploiting the misfortunes of others for his gain.
Vocation: Cunning Opportunist & Treasure Seeker
For the Insightful: Possesses incredible cunning and social skills, often pitting enemies against each other while securing hidden treasures.
Description: Sabin is slender, with shaggy brown hair and mischievous gray eyes that flicker with intelligence. He wears slightly tattered but stylish attire, allowing for agility on the deck. His charming smile often conceals his true intentions, hiding a deep fear of failure that stems from his past rejections.
Wants & Needs: Wants: To enrich himself while avoiding confrontations; dreams of owning a fleet of ships.
- Needs: To confront his fear of failure and learn to trust others instead of pushing them away.

Secret or Obstacle: Hides a deep-seated fear of failure, often pushing others away to avoid the pain of rejection.
Carrying: (Total CP: 27)
- Silver Rapier (8 points): A nimble blade perfect for dueling.
- Weathered Pirate Garb (6 points): Stylish attire designed for agility and stealth.
- Vaulting Keys (6 points): Keys used to access hidden compartments and treasure vaults.
- Healing Ointments (7 points): Balms to treat minor wounds and ailments.

First Mate Anders "Ironfist" Thorne *"Loyalty and strength are my code."* 3

Brief: A strong and dependable first mate under Captain Grimthorne, Anders is renowned for his loyalty and fierce fighting skills, often mediating among crew factions.
Vocation: First Mate & Stalwart Defender
For the Insightful: Possesses remarkable strength and combat expertise, providing physical defense for the captain and crew.
Description: Anders is a burly man with short, cropped hair and a long scar running across his cheek. His rugged armor is stained with salt and grime from the sea, reflecting his role as the crew's steadfast protector. Although loyal to Grimthorne, Anders secretly dreams of commanding his own ship one day.
Wants & Needs: Wants: To protect his captain while enforcing loyalty among the crew; dreams of captaining his own ship and breaking free from Grimthorne's shadow.
- Needs: To reconcile his aspirations with his current loyalty, ensuring his ambitions do not lead to betrayal.

Secret or Obstacle: Hides his aspirations of breaking away from Grimthorne, fearing that doing so may require betrayal.
Carrying: (Total CP: 28)
- Heavy Cutlass (10 points): A sturdy blade for close combat.
- Sturdy Armor (8 points): Durable armor offering excellent protection.
- Loyalty Emblem (5 points): A token symbolizing his allegiance to the crew.
- Healing Bandages (5 points): Supplies for treating wounds during battle.

Captain Feran "Crimson" Vargo *"Let the waves carry my legacy."* 4

Brief: A charismatic pirate captain, Feran is known for his charm and love for the sea, focusing on protecting the innocent while seeking adventure and treasures.
Vocation: Charming Pirate Captain & Protector of the Weak
For the Perceptive: Possesses a natural charisma and uncanny intuition that endears him to his crew and locals alike.
Description: Captain Feran has curly red hair, bright green eyes, and a roguish smile that captivates everyone around him. He wears flamboyant pirate attire adorned with luxurious fabrics, exuding charm and bravado. Beneath his charisma, Feran battles lingering fears that his past misdeeds may one day return to haunt him.
Wants & Needs: Wants: To forge a legacy based on heroism while acquiring riches; dreams of finding a legendary treasure that ensures his name is forever remembered.
- Needs: To confront his darker temptations and atone for past misdeeds, ensuring his legacy remains untarnished.

Secret or Obstacle: Hides a fear his past misdeeds may one day catch up with him, constantly battling his darker temptations.
Carrying: (Total CP: 25)
- Rapier (10 points): A blade that reflects his flair and finesse.
- Colorful Pirate Garb (8 points): Vibrant attire that showcases his bold personality.
- Map of Treasures (7 points): A detailed chart marking locations of hidden riches.

Ordan "Two-Scimitar" Velk   *"Death dances with the swift."* 5

Brief: A swift and agile pirate known for his dual-wielding scimitars, Ordan strikes fear into the hearts of enemies with his stunning speed and dexterity.
Vocation: Agile Pirate & Blade Dancer
For the Athletic: Possesses remarkable agility, allowing him to evade attacks and respond quickly in battle.
Description: Ordan has a lean and wiry physique, bright blue eyes, and a well-groomed beard. He wears agile leather armor adorned with trophies from past victories. His playful demeanor masks a deadly focus, but his self-doubt from a past failure lingers, challenging his confidence.
Wants & Needs: Wants: To grow stronger through combat while earning silver and fame; dreams of forming a fellowship of agile fighters.
- Needs: To overcome his self-doubt and prove his worth, rising above his past mistakes.

Secret or Obstacle: Hides his self-doubt stemming from a previous failure, often unsure if he is destined for greatness.
Carrying: (Total CP: 29)
- Twin Scimitars (10 points): Deadly blades perfect for dual-wielding.
- Leather Armor (7 points): Flexible protection that allows swift movement.
- Collection of Combat Techniques (6 points): Manuals detailing advanced fighting styles.
- Healing Accelerants (6 points): Restorative potions for stamina and recovery.

Captain Ewan "Silver Wave" Carrol   *"Maritime laws bend to the waves of fortune."* 6

Brief: A calculating and intelligent pirate captain, Ewan is known for his swift maneuvers and shrewd decision-making on the high seas.
Vocation: Tactical Pirate Strategist
For the Perceptive: Possesses sharp navigation skills, often outsmarting enemy ships in various sea conditions.
Description: Captain Ewan has salt-and-pepper hair, bright blue eyes, and a weathered face from years at sea. He wears practical captain's attire with a weathered tricorn hat, his calm demeanor reflecting his experience. Haunted by memories of lost ships under his command, Ewan strives for redemption through mastery of the sea.
Wants & Needs: Wants: To build a fleet of powerful ships while enhancing his reputation as a master tactician; dreams of exploring uncharted waters.
- Needs: To let go of past failures and trust in his abilities to lead and inspire.

Secret or Obstacle: Hides past failures of lost ships under his command, haunted by the memories that fuel his ambition.
Carrying: (Total CP: 30)
- Captain's Compass (8 points): A reliable tool for precision navigation.
- Longsword (10 points): A sturdy blade symbolizing his command.
- Navigation Scrolls (6 points): Charts for plotting routes through perilous waters.
- Healing Sea Salts (6 points): Remedies to restore vitality on long voyages.

Boden Rivershadow   *"Let no treasure slip through my fingers."* 7

Brief: A cunning and sly pirate trader, Boden strikes deals that often leave others at a disadvantage, showing little mercy in his pursuits.
Vocation: Cunning Trader & Pirate
For the Insightful: Possesses exceptional negotiation skills, able to find profit margins where others see none.
Description: Boden has slicked-back dark hair, sharp facial features, and calculating gray eyes that always seem to size up opportunities. His fine clothing speaks of wealth and success, but behind his elegant presence lies a deep internal conflict about the balance of honor and profit.
Wants & Needs: Wants: To amass wealth through manipulation and trade; dreams of becoming the wealthiest pirate in history.
- Needs: To reconcile his cunning persona with a sense of honor, finding balance between wealth and morality.

Secret or Obstacle: Hides feelings of inadequacy behind his cunning facade, struggling internally with conflicted priorities.
Carrying: (Total CP: 27)
- Ledger of Trade Deals (10 points): Records of his most profitable negotiations.
- Fine Bladed Dagger (8 points): A precise and elegant weapon.
- Healing Ointments (4 points): Restorative salves for recovery.
- Collection of Valuable Goods (5 points): Rare treasures from his many ventures.

Rufus "The Wavebreaker" Penn   *"To shore we sail, in pursuit of fight and revelry."* 8

Brief: A jovial and friendly pirate, Rufus enjoys bringing joy and music to his crew, often viewed as the heart of any celebration on the ship.
Vocation: Jovial Musician & Pirate
For the Perceptive: Possesses a unique ability to rally the crew through music and dance, often leading them into battle with a lighthearted spirit.
Description: Rufus is of average height, with shoulder-length tousled hair and bright, infectious brown eyes. He wears vibrant, colorful attire that reflects his quirky personality. Always ready with his enchanted guitar, Rufus uses his music to inspire joy and unity among his crew. However, he fears that his levity may be overshadowed by the violence of piracy.
Wants & Needs: Wants: To spread joy while sailing the seas, bringing music and laughter to his companions; dreams of becoming a legendary entertainer of the ocean.
- Needs: To confront his fear of losing his crew and find harmony between joy and the realities of piracy.

Secret or Obstacle: Hides the fear of losing his crew in battle, often wrestling with guilt when his levity is overshadowed by violence.
Carrying: (Total CP: 26)
- Enchanted Guitar (10 points): A magical instrument that uplifts spirits.
- Vibrant Pirate Garb (6 points): Clothing that reflects his lively personality.
- Collection of Sea Shanties (5 points): Songs that inspire and motivate his crew.
- Healing Tinctures (5 points): Remedies for minor injuries and ailments.

Captain Sorin Blackwater   *"Darker paths offer greater treasures."* 9

Brief: A sinister and treacherous pirate captain, Sorin delves into the darkest aspects of piracy, often plying morally gray waters.
Vocation: Treacherous Pirate Captain & Terror
For the Perceptive: Possesses tactical brilliance in exploiting fears, often achieving victory through manipulation and intimidation rather than sheer strength.
Description: Captain Sorin has long black hair streaked with gray and cleverly calculated green eyes. He wears dark attire that blends into the shadowy corners of his ship, commanding immediate respect and fear among his crew. Sorin's past is marred by betrayals, which fuel his fears of losing control and facing retribution for his deeds.
Wants & Needs: Wants: To acquire power and wealth through any means necessary; dreams of ruling the seas with an iron fist.
- Needs: To face his complicated past and find balance between terror and control.

Secret or Obstacle: Hides a complicated past marred by betrayals, catalyzing fears of losing control and retribution for his darker deeds.
Carrying: (Total CP: 32)
- Cutlass of Dread (12 points): A weapon that instills fear in foes.
- Black Pirate Coat (10 points): Dark attire that enhances his fearsome presence.
- Log of Hateful Deals (6 points): Records of dark alliances and treacheries.
- Healing Rum (4 points): Restorative brew for recovery.

Yeager Stormchaser   *"Adventure is the greatest prize; the sea is my canvas."* 10

Brief: A benevolent and adventurous pirate, Yeager seeks to explore uncharted territories and discover lost knowledge while treating his crew as family.
Vocation: Explorer & Adventurous Pirate
For the Insightful: Possesses an insatiable curiosity about the world, thriving on new discoveries and challenges.
Description: Yeager has wavy brown hair, bright blue goggles, and an infectious smile. He wears sturdy clothing adorned with trinkets collected during his voyages. His free-spirited nature and enthusiasm are evident, but he secretly fears the dangers his pursuits may bring to his crew.
Wants & Needs: Wants: To chart the unknown and learn from the mysteries of the world; dreams of discovering fabled treasures and forgotten secrets.
- Needs: To overcome his fear of danger and ensure his adventurous spirit does not lead to tragic consequences.

Secret or Obstacle: Hides his fear of the dangers that might befall him and his crew, wondering whether his pursuits could lead to tragedy.
Carrying: (Total CP: 23)
- Explorer's Map (10 points): A chart for navigating uncharted territories.
- Short Sword (5 points): A practical weapon for self-defense.
- Navigational Tools (8 points): Instruments for charting and exploring.

Random City Dwellers

Residents of a city form the vibrant tapestry of life in a fantasy realm, each contributing to the culture and energy of their bustling community. From artisans and merchants to scholars and watchmen, city dwellers reflect a rich mix of backgrounds and stories. Lively streets teem with activity as people forge friendships, run businesses, and navigate urban life. Known for resilience and adaptability, residents pursue prosperity in a world of opportunities and challenges.

Adventurers, however, should be cautious, as not everyone in a city is a friend or ally. A popular tale warns of Eveline, a charismatic bard whose enchanting melodies and flashy tricks captivated marketplace crowds. With her beguiling smile and captivating tales, she became a beloved figure, often collecting gold from her mesmerized audience.

Yet, Eveline's charm concealed her role as leader of the "Flickering Shadows," a cunning thieves' guild. Her performances distracted onlookers while her accomplices deftly picked pockets and stole goods. Many who admired her music later discovered their belongings missing, replaced by the echo of her laughter as she vanished into the crowd.

One unlucky adventurer, drawn in by Eveline's show, offered coins to support her artistry. In the chaos of the performance, he fell victim to her schemes, losing gold and irreplaceable magical trinkets. By the time he realized the betrayal, Eveline and her crew had melted into the shadows.

This tale warns adventurers that city life, though enchanting, is fraught with deception. Not all residents share ideals of honesty; crossing paths with the wrong person can bring unexpected losses. As you navigate bustling streets, remain vigilant, for beneath the charms of urban life may lie darker motives, waiting just a heartbeat away.

Gwenyth Brightleaf — 1
"Nature's remedies hold the power to heal and enchant."

Brief: A spirited Half-Elf herbalist known for her colorful marketplace stall filled with herbal remedies and potions, Gwenyth seeks to brighten the lives of others while perfecting her craft.
Vocation: Herbalist & Potion Maker
For the Insightful: Possesses deep knowledge of local plants, often venturing into nearby forests to gather rare herbs for her unique concoctions.
Description: Gwenyth has long, curly auburn hair, bright green eyes, and a simple yet vibrant dress. Her lively stall is filled with the scents of fresh herbs and flowers, drawing customers with its warmth and charm. Despite her confidence in her craft, Gwenyth often feels overshadowed by more successful tradespeople, which fuels her quiet determination to grow.
Wants & Needs: Wants: To expand her herbal knowledge and gain recognition in the city; dreams of opening a larger apothecary to serve the community.
- Needs: To overcome her lingering self-doubt and embrace her abilities with greater confidence.

Secret or Obstacle: Hides her uncertainty about her skills, often feeling dwarfed by more established tradespeople.
Carrying: (Total CP: 19)
- Herbal Remedies (5 points): Handcrafted cures for common ailments.
- Potion of Healing (5 points): A magical brew for restoring vitality.
- Satchel of Dried Herbs (6 points): A collection of rare ingredients for potion-making.
- Flower-filled Basket (3 points): A fragrant and colorful assortment used to enhance her stall's appeal.

Bran Stonemantle
"Strength and craft shape the heart of a weapon." **2**

Brief: A gruff but skilled Dwarf blacksmith, Bran forges weapons and tools for city guards and adventurers alike, blending craftsmanship with strength.
Vocation: Blacksmith & Weapon Crafter
For the Insightful: Possesses exceptional craftsmanship and physical endurance, dedicating long hours to perfecting his craft.
Description: Bran is shorter and stockier than most dwarves, with a bushy beard and friendly blue eyes. He wears a leather apron over rugged clothes, stained with soot and iron dust. Despite his talent, he worries about the decline of traditional blacksmithing in favor of modern contraptions.
Wants & Needs: Wants: To pass down his trade to future generations and earn the respect of his kin; dreams of forging a legendary weapon.
- Needs: To accept changes in the industry and adapt his craft without losing his heritage.

Secret or Obstacle: Hides his frustration at the decline of traditional craftsmanship, fearing modern inventions may overshadow his art.
Carrying: (Total CP: 20)
- Blacksmith's Hammer (8 points): A sturdy tool for forging weapons.
- Anvil Tools (7 points): Essential instruments for precise craftsmanship.
- Leather Work Gloves (3 points): Protective gear for handling hot metals.
- Collection of Metal Scraps (2 points): Leftovers for creating small projects.

Elara Windwhisper
"Every melody carries a story." **3**

Brief: A young and ambitious bard, Elara performs in taverns and streets, weaving tales of adventure and joy through her music.
Vocation: Bard & Performer
For the Perceptive: Possesses a gift for storytelling and enchanting audiences with melodies that capture life's struggles and triumphs.
Description: Elara has long, wavy hair and striking hazel eyes. She wears colorful outfits adorned with musical notes and carries a lute that enhances her performances. Though admired, she often fears her work will fail to resonate with others.
Wants & Needs: Wants: To grow as a performer and gain recognition in the bardic community; dreams of composing a legendary ballad.
- Needs: To overcome her fear of rejection and trust in her abilities.

Secret or Obstacle: Hides her fear of rejection, often second-guessing her performances.
Carrying: (Total CP: 18)
- Lute (5 points): A well-tuned instrument for her captivating melodies.
- Songbook of Favorites (6 points): A collection of inspiring songs and stories.
- Decorative Belt Pouch (3 points): A practical yet stylish accessory.
- Small Healing Potion (4 points): A remedy for her travels.

Fenwick "Fizz" Glimmergrog
"Science is just magic we can explain." **4**

Brief: A quirky Gnome alchemist known for his eccentric experiments, Fenwick's shop is a chaotic wonderland of potions and gadgets.
Vocation: Alchemist & Inventor
For the Insightful: Possesses a sharp analytical mind that helps him create innovative concoctions, ranging from practical to absurd.
Description: Fenwick is short with wild, curly hair that seems to defy gravity. He wears a stained lab coat filled with pockets for tools and ingredients. While brilliant, Fenwick's overthinking often sabotages his experiments.
Wants & Needs: Wants: To achieve a breakthrough in alchemy that cements his legacy; dreams of becoming the greatest alchemist.
- Needs: To overcome his fear of failure and stop overanalyzing his work.

Secret or Obstacle: Hides his anxiousness about failing in front of peers, leading to self-sabotage.
Carrying: (Total CP: 19)
- Vials of Explosive Powder (5 points): Dangerous yet useful creations.
- Set of Alchemist's Tools (7 points): Essential equipment for experimentation.
- Flask of Healing Potion (3 points): A reliable concoction for emergencies.
- Experiments Notebook (4 points): Notes and diagrams of his work.

Serin Duskveil — 5
"Shadows are my ally; silence is my weapon."

Brief: A skilled rogue and pickpocket, Serin navigates the city's underbelly, retrieving valuable items for a network of thieves.
Vocation: Rogue & Thief
For the Perceptive: Possesses stealth and agility, able to slip between shadows unnoticed by guards.
Description: Serin has deep purple skin, pointed horns, and bright red eyes. She wears dark, form-fitting clothing that allows her to move swiftly and silently. Her charming smile often wins over her targets before she strikes, but she constantly fears betrayal from her allies in the thieves' guild.
Wants & Needs: Wants: To elevate her standing within the thieves' guild and secure greater treasures; dreams of retiring to a comfortable life away from crime.
- Needs: To learn trust and build lasting relationships, ensuring her safety and freedom from her dangerous lifestyle.

Secret or Obstacle: Hides a fear of betrayal from fellow thieves, constantly looking over her shoulder for those who might sell her out.
Carrying: (Total CP: 20)
- Twin Daggers (6 points): Deadly blades perfect for silent takedowns.
- Lockpicking Tools (5 points): Essential equipment for breaking into secure areas.
- Cloak of Shadows (6 points): A dark cloak that enhances her stealth.
- Healing Draught (3 points): A restorative potion for quick recovery.

Gorim Steelbreaker — 6
"Strength keeps the peace; loyalty builds trust."

Brief: A strongman who works as a bouncer for a popular tavern, Gorim uses his imposing figure to protect patrons and maintain order.
Vocation: Bouncer & Guardian
For the Perceptive: Possesses impressive physical strength and a quick temper, making him both respected and feared in the city.
Description: Gorim is tall and heavily muscled, with a prominent brow and rough features. He wears basic clothing under an apron marked by spills. His deep voice commands attention, and his loyalty to the tavern's patrons is unwavering. However, he fears his temper might one day harm his reputation.
Wants & Needs: Wants: To ensure the tavern remains a safe haven for patrons and a hub for community bonds; dreams of being respected as a peacekeeper.
- Needs: To manage his anger and find healthier outlets for his frustrations.

Secret or Obstacle: Hides a struggle with anger management, often fearing that his temper could lead to an incident that harms his reputation.
Carrying: (Total CP: 19)
- Heavy Club (8 points): A sturdy weapon for breaking up brawls.
- Protective Leather Armor (6 points): Ensures his safety in violent encounters.
- Set of Bouncer Tokens (2 points): Symbols of authority within the tavern.
- Healing Ointment (3 points): A salve for minor injuries.

Liora Shadeweaver — 7
"Threads of magic weave elegance into every design."

Brief: A reclusive tailor known for crafting garments that shimmer with magical patterns, blending fashion with spellwork.
Vocation: Tailor & Fashion Designer
For the Insightful: Possesses an incredible talent for design, often charming customers with her unique style.
Description: Liora has long, flowing silver hair and piercing azure eyes. She dresses in flowing robes adorned with floral patterns that subtly conceal her necromantic symbols. Her serene presence reassures customers, though she struggles with self-doubt when faced with rudeness.
Wants & Needs: Wants: To create a line of clothing that blends fashion with magic; dreams of having her designs showcased in high society.
- Needs: To build confidence in her craft and not let negative feedback deter her passion.

Secret or Obstacle: Hides her frustration with the occasional rudeness of customers, which makes her doubt her talent and passion for tailoring.
Carrying: (Total CP: 20)
- Enchanted Needle and Thread (8 points): Magical tools for crafting intricate designs.
- Roll of Fine Fabric (5 points): High-quality material for creating luxurious garments.
- Tailoring Tools (4 points): Precision instruments for detailed craftsmanship.
- Small Mirror (3 points): A tool for final adjustments and fittings.

Alaric Goodbarrel — *"A warm meal and a hearty tale make every traveler a friend."* 8

Brief: A cheerful innkeeper who welcomes travelers to his humble establishment, ensuring everyone feels at home with hearty meals and fine company.
Vocation: Innkeeper & Host
For the Perceptive: Possesses a knack for storytelling, often entertaining patrons with tales on quiet nights.
Description: Alaric has a round face, bright brown eyes, and a perpetually smiling expression. He wears simple but clean clothing with an apron stained from constant work. His tavern is a lively and warm hub for regular patrons. Despite his optimism, Alaric secretly worries about declining patron numbers and the survival of his inn.
Wants & Needs: Wants: To forge friendships with travelers while building his inn's reputation; dreams of hosting a citywide festival to promote local ales.
- Needs: To overcome his fear of losing customers by innovating and expanding his tavern's appeal.

Secret or Obstacle: Hides concerns about declining patronage, fearing that he won't be able to keep his inn afloat.
Carrying: (Total CP: 18)
- Selection of Homemade Ales (6 points): Signature drinks brewed for his patrons.
- Recipe Book (3 points): A collection of traditional and experimental dishes.
- Serving Tray (5 points): Essential for bustling tavern service.
- Healing Brews (4 points): Restorative drinks for weary travelers.

Zorian Clawfoot — *"Every trade tells a story, every trinket has a journey."* 9

Brief: A curious and agile merchant who trades exotic goods, Zorian brings unique wares and vibrant energy to the bustling market.
Vocation: Merchant
For the Insightful: Possesses extraordinary speed and agility, allowing him to navigate crowded markets and react to potential threats.
Description: Zorian has sandy fur with dark spots, vibrant green eyes, and an elegant stature. He wears colorful flowing robes adorned with jewels, his playful demeanor drawing customers to his stall. While his charm entices buyers, he harbors constant skepticism, fearing scams from rival merchants.
Wants & Needs: Wants: To expand his trade network and learn about distant lands and cultures; dreams of becoming the most renowned exotic trader.
- Needs: To build trust with others and overcome his wariness of competitors.

Secret or Obstacle: Hides worries about being scammed by rival merchants, which leads him to distrust those who approach him.
Carrying: (Total CP: 19)
- Collection of Exotic Goods (8 points): Rare treasures from distant lands.
- Merchant's Scale (4 points): A tool to ensure fair trade.
- Pouch of Gems (6 points): Precious stones used for bargaining or trade.
- Healing Salve (1 point): A simple remedy for minor injuries.

Rurik Gravewalker — *"Even the dead deserve peace and respect."* 10

Brief: A mysterious gravekeeper who tends to the city's cemetery, Rurik communicates with spirits while ensuring lost souls are laid to rest.
Vocation: Gravekeeper
For the Perceptive: Possesses unique intuition for understanding the past, aiding him in guiding spirits to their final rest.
Description: Rurik is tall and bulky, with rugged features and dark hair. He wears plain work clothes adorned with symbols of protection, his presence carrying an air of reverence. While he strives to honor the dead, Rurik fears the restless souls he aids may one day turn against him.
Wants & Needs: Wants: To provide peace to the living and honor the dead; dreams of creating a sanctuary for lost souls.
- Needs: To conquer his fear of the restless dead and gain confidence in his calling.

Secret or Obstacle: Hides his fear of betrayal from the souls he helps, worried they may haunt him in return.
Carrying: (Total CP: 20)
- Gravekeeping Tools (8 points): Essential for tending graves and burial sites.
- Holy Symbol (5 points): A sacred charm for protection and guidance.
- Journal of Memories (6 points): Notes documenting the lives and stories of those he has helped.
- Healing Herbs (1 point): Basic remedies for minor ailments.

Talon Emberclaw *"Justice forged in duty, tempered by honor."* **11**

Brief: A fierce guardian of the city, Talon serves as captain of the city guard, tirelessly working to keep the peace and uphold the law.

Vocation: City Guard

For the Insightful: Possesses sharp instincts and strong leadership skills, often motivating his guards to serve the city with honor.

Description: Talon has shimmering bronze scales, sharp golden eyes, and a strong, commanding build. He wears polished armor adorned with the city guard's emblem, instilling respect and loyalty. Despite his steadfast exterior, Talon worries about living up to the legacy of those who served before him.

Wants & Needs: Wants: To protect the citizens and create a legacy where his name is synonymous with justice; dreams of instilling a sense of safety across the city.
- Needs: To overcome feelings of inadequacy and recognize his own contributions to the city's safety.

Secret or Obstacle: Hides feelings of inadequacy, worrying that he may not measure up to the legacies of his predecessors.

Carrying: (Total CP: 28)
- Spear of Command (10 points): A symbol of his leadership and combat prowess.
- Plate Armor (10 points): Durable and protective, featuring the guard's emblem.
- Guard Captain's Badge (4 points): A mark of his authority.
- Healing Potions (4 points): For recovery during critical moments.

Malcolm Blackroot *"Imagination is the key to innovation."* **12**

Brief: A clever inventor and tinkerer, Malcolm creates whimsical gadgets and machines, selling them to adventurers and city folk alike.

Vocation: Inventor & Tinkerer

For the Perceptive: Possesses a creative mind and exceptional problem-solving skills, often fixing issues with a unique twist.

Description: Malcolm has wild brown hair, expressive hazel eyes, and multiple tools strapped to his belt. He wears a stained smock and carries an assortment of gadgets in his pockets. Although brilliant, Malcolm often feels underestimated due to his small stature.

Wants & Needs: Wants: To create breakthroughs that benefit the city; dreams of developing a mechanical marvel that changes everyday life.
- Needs: To assert his capabilities and gain recognition, overcoming the bias against his size.

Secret or Obstacle: Hides frustration at being overlooked, often feeling underestimated by those in his field.

Carrying: (Total CP: 20)
- Toolkit for Inventions (8 points): Essential tools for crafting and repairs.
- Collection of Invention Blueprints (5 points): Plans for his unique creations.
- Small Clockwork Device (4 points): A demonstration of his ingenuity.
- Healing Oil (3 points): A multipurpose remedy for both machines and minor injuries.

Erin Evenstar *"The stars whisper truths if we listen closely."* **13**

Brief: A mysterious fortune teller who runs a small booth in the market, using cards and runes to offer insights into the future.

Vocation: Fortune Teller

For the Insightful: Possesses sharp intuition and an understanding of human emotions, often guiding those in need.

Description: Erin has deep crimson skin, long black hair, and golden eyes that twinkle with mischief. She dresses in flowing robes adorned with mystical symbols, and her booth is filled with incense and candles that create an otherworldly atmosphere. Erin carries the burden of past mistakes, which sometimes haunt her.

Wants & Needs: Wants: To share her gift with others while uncovering her own destiny; dreams of one day reading for important figures in the realm.
- Needs: To regain confidence in her abilities, moving past the fear caused by earlier mistakes.

Secret or Obstacle: Hides her past involving mistaken readings that cost clients dearly, causing her to worry about being trusted again.

Carrying: (Total CP: 18)
- Set of Divination Cards (6 points): Essential for her readings.
- Crystal Ball (8 points): A mystical focus for more intricate visions.
- Incense and Candle Set (3 points): Creates the ambiance of her booth.
- Healing Herb Vials (1 point): A small collection for minor ailments.

Falco Silverbrass   *"Every gem tells a story; I find its worth."* 14

Brief: A skilled merchant specializing in rare metals and gemstones, Falco travels to acquire unique treasures for his clientele.
Vocation: Merchant
For the Perceptive: Possesses an exceptional eye for quality, allowing him to discern real value from mere trinkets.
Description: Falco has a lean physique, sharp facial features, and short blonde hair. He dresses in well-tailored clothes that showcase his wealth and charm, attracting customers with his suave demeanor. Beneath his polished exterior lies a fear of his past dealings with dishonest merchants being uncovered.
Wants & Needs: Wants: To establish a prestigious reputation as a trader of unique valuables; dreams of owning a grand shop to display his rarest findings.
- Needs: To face his past and ensure his integrity while building a trustworthy reputation.

Secret or Obstacle: Hides his past dealings with dishonest merchants, fearing his reputation might be tarnished if discovered.
Carrying: (Total CP: 19)
- Assortment of Gemstones (8 points): Rare and exquisite treasures for trade.
- Scale for Weighing (4 points): Ensures precise valuation of goods.
- Ledger of Transactions (5 points): Records of his business dealings.
- Healing Salve (2 points): A basic remedy for minor ailments.

Kieran Fatekeeper   *"The wisdom of the past lights the path to the future."* 15

Brief: A wise and philosophical librarian, Kieran dedicates his life to preserving forgotten knowledge and ancient texts for future generations.
Vocation: Librarian
For the Perceptive: Possesses a profound understanding of history and magic, able to impart wisdom to those who seek knowledge.
Description: Kieran has long, silver hair and deep green eyes. He wears simple robes with pockets filled with scrolls, exuding a gentle demeanor that invites even the shyest to seek his guidance. Despite his passion, Kieran is disheartened by the townsfolk's lack of curiosity about the treasures of knowledge he safeguards.
Wants & Needs: Wants: To protect ancient knowledge while making it accessible to all; dreams of creating a grand repository of lore for future generations.
- Needs: To overcome his disappointment in others' indifference and find ways to inspire curiosity.

Secret or Obstacle: Hides his frustration with the lack of curiosity from townsfolk, feeling disappointed when his efforts are underappreciated.
Carrying: (Total CP: 20)
- Rare Books Collection (8 points): A selection of invaluable ancient texts.
- Set of Quills and Ink (4 points): Tools for recording knowledge.
- Scroll of Ancient Research (6 points): Contains detailed information about magical history.
- Healing Tea (2 points): A soothing brew to ease tension during long study hours.

Rurik Claystone   *"Strength and grit unearth the city's treasures."* 16

Brief: A grumpy yet skilled Dwarf miner, Rurik spends his days digging for precious resources, deeply connected to the city's economic stability.
Vocation: Miner
For the Insightful: Possesses remarkable strength and endurance, allowing him to work long hours underground.
Description: Rurik is heavily bearded, with rough skin and kind blue eyes. He wears simple miners' clothing, often covered in dirt. While he appears gruff, his strong sense of community drives him to fight for better working conditions for all miners.
Wants & Needs: Wants: To ensure the safety of his work and secure fair wages for miners; dreams of initiating better rights for all workers in the city.
- Needs: To address the city's neglect of its miners and advocate for systemic change.

Secret or Obstacle: Hides his disappointment at how miners are overlooked, feeling a heavy burden of responsibility for his fellow workers.
Carrying: (Total CP: 19)
- Pickaxe (7 points): A sturdy tool essential for mining.
- Miner's Lantern (4 points): Lights the way in dark tunnels.
- Bag of Trade Gems (5 points): Valuables collected from his work.
- Healing Balm (3 points): A salve for minor injuries.

Eldrin Stormblaze *"The flames of passion ignite the hearts of all who see."* 17

Brief: A flamboyant and daring street performer, Eldrin captivates audiences with his fire dances, blending acrobatics and elemental magic to dazzle and entertain.
Vocation: Street Performer
For the Perceptive: Possesses exceptional talent in acrobatics, often incorporating elemental fire into his routines to create awe-inspiring spectacles.
Description: Eldrin has fiery red hair, glowing orange eyes, and a confident stance. He wears loose, flowing attire adorned with bright patterns, his energy contagious to all who watch. While his performances inspire joy, Eldrin harbors a deep fear of injury, worrying that a single misstep could endanger both himself and his audience.
Wants & Needs: Wants: To gain fame as a performer while spreading joy through his artistry; dreams of establishing a renowned circus of fire dancers.
- Needs: To overcome his fears and master his control of fire, ensuring safety for all.

Secret or Obstacle: Hides the fear of injury while performing, concerned that a mistake could have disastrous consequences.
Carrying: (Total CP: 18)
- Fire Dancing Staff (6 points): A tool used to amplify his fiery performances.
- Performer's Outfit (5 points): Bright and flexible attire for movement.
- Collection of Fire-charms (4 points): Magical trinkets that enhance his fire dances.
- Healing Fire Balm (3 points): A remedy for burns or injuries sustained during practice.

Bramble Woodsinger *"Every note carries a spark of happiness."* 18

Brief: A free-spirited bard, Bramble travels the city performing songs and tales, bringing joy and laughter to all he meets.
Vocation: Bard
For the Insightful: Possesses a natural talent for music and storytelling, charming the hearts of all who listen to his lively performances.
Description: Bramble has tousled sandy hair, bright brown eyes, and an infectious smile. He wears colorful attire and carries a well-loved lute that brings warmth to his performances. Despite his cheerful demeanor, Bramble struggles with stage fright, especially in front of large crowds.
Wants & Needs: Wants: To be recognized as a talented bard and inspire others through his music; dreams of performing at the realm's grandest festival.
- Needs: To overcome his stage fright and grow comfortable performing in front of larger audiences.

Secret or Obstacle: Hides a fear of performing for large crowds, battling stage fright despite his otherwise cheerful nature.
Carrying: (Total CP: 19)
- Well-loved Lute (8 points): A trusted instrument for crafting melodies.
- Songbook (5 points): Filled with his favorite compositions.
- Musical Props (4 points): Used to enhance his storytelling.
- Healing Tea (2 points): A calming brew to soothe his nerves before performances.

Cyrus Deepwell *"Every problem is a puzzle waiting to be solved."* 19

Brief: A secretive tinkerer and inventor, Cyrus enjoys creating intricate gadgets and devices to improve daily life in the city.
Vocation: Inventor
For the Perceptive: Possesses a creative mind and exceptional problem-solving skills, often fixing issues with a unique twist.
Description: Cyrus is short with messy brown hair, round spectacles, and twinkling green eyes. He wears a leather apron filled with tools, often seen tinkering with his latest invention in a bright workshop. Though brilliant, Cyrus feels underestimated due to his small stature, which sometimes fuels his determination.
Wants & Needs: Wants: To innovate and create groundbreaking inventions; dreams of developing a mechanical marvel that transforms everyday life.
- Needs: To gain recognition for his work and move past feelings of being overlooked.

Secret or Obstacle: Hides frustration at being underestimated due to his size, often doubting his value among peers.
Carrying: (Total CP: 20)
- Toolkit for Inventions (8 points): Essential for crafting gadgets.
- Invention Blueprints (5 points): Detailed designs for his creations.
- Small Clockwork Device (4 points): A compact invention showcasing his skills.
- Healing Oil (3 points): Multipurpose oil for both mechanical and personal use.

Random Residents of the Slums

Residents of the slums form the resilient undercurrent of life in a fantasy realm, each individual carving out an existence in the shadow of towering cities and opulent districts. From resourceful scavengers and cunning traders to aspiring artisans and hardened laborers, these dwellers embody a tapestry of survival and grit. The narrow, winding streets buzz with quiet determination as people navigate their daily struggles, forming tight-knit communities bound by shared hardship and perseverance. Known for their ingenuity and tenacity, residents of the slums find ways to thrive despite the scarcity of resources, often showcasing a camaraderie unseen in wealthier quarters.

A well-known tale warns of a sharp-witted fence named Marlowe, infamous for brokering deals in the shadowy alleys of the district. Marlowe, with his roguish charm and silver tongue, was known for his uncanny ability to acquire almost anything—for a price. Many unsuspecting adventurers, lured by promises of rare treasures and magical items, sought him out in hopes of striking a bargain.

Yet behind his grin lay a network of schemes. Marlowe's wares were often cursed, stolen, or cleverly rigged to fail when needed most. One ill-fated adventurer, desperate for a magical sword, paid dearly for what was promised to be an enchanted blade. In the heat of battle, the sword shattered on its first swing, leaving the adventurer defenseless and at the mercy of their foes. When they returned to confront Marlowe, he had vanished, leaving only rumors in his wake.

This tale reminds adventurers: while the slums may be a haven for opportunity, they are also rife with deception and danger. Approach with vigilance and respect, for beneath the surface of camaraderie and bargains may lie schemes that could turn the shadows of the slums into a place of peril.

Maris Thornblood — 1
"The love of a mother is a shield against the harshest storms."

Brief: A fierce matriarch of a small family, Maris does everything she can to keep her children safe and fed, often making difficult choices to survive in the unforgiving slums.

Vocation: Survivalist & Caregiver

For the Insightful: Possesses a strong will and relentless determination, adapting daily to the struggles of life in the slums to provide for her family.

Description: Maris has messy brown hair, sunken cheeks, and piercing gray eyes. She wears patched clothing that has seen better days, but her fierce demeanor hides a deep and nurturing care for those she loves. Her tireless efforts to ensure her children's safety reflect her resilience and strength. Maris harbors guilt over the difficult choices she's had to make.

Wants & Needs: Wants: To provide a better life for her children, dreaming of moving to a safer part of the city.
- Needs: To find the strength to forgive herself for the compromises she has made and recognize the love that drives her actions.

Secret or Obstacle: Hides her fears about failing as a mother, often burdened by guilt over the choices she's made to ensure their survival.

Carrying: (Total CP: 14)
- Sewing Kit (4 points): Essential for mending her children's clothes and earning extra income.
- Small Cooking Pot (5 points): Used to prepare meals from meager supplies.
- Herbal Remedies (5 points): Simple concoctions to keep her family healthy.

Jorlan Quickhands
"Quick hands, quick escape, endless survival." **2**

Brief: A nimble pickpocket known for his light fingers, Jorlan survives by taking jobs from clients and stealing from passersby.
Vocation: Rogue & Thief
For the Insightful: Possesses exceptional dexterity and a talent for evading guards, slipping through crowded streets unnoticed.
Description: Jorlan is short with curly blond hair and bright blue eyes. He wears simple clothing that's easy to move in, often paired with a hood to conceal his identity. Despite his cunning nature, he grapples with the emotional scars of being abandoned by his family, which leaves him feeling lonely even in a crowd.
Wants & Needs: Wants: To secure a life free from fear of hunger; dreams of opening a shop to sell honest wares.
- Needs: To confront his feelings of abandonment and find a sense of belonging.

Secret or Obstacle: Hides the reality of being abandoned by his family, leading to feelings of loneliness amid the crowd.
Carrying: (Total CP: 20)
- Set of Lockpicks (6 points): Essential tools for his trade.
- Small Dagger (4 points): A concealed weapon for protection.
- Tattered Cloak (4 points): Worn attire to blend into the crowd.
- Healing Potion (6 points): A remedy for unexpected injuries.

Tobias Grimekeeper
"Every clean street is a small victory." **3**

Brief: A janitor and refuse collector, Tobias works tirelessly to clear the streets, struggling to make ends meet while dreaming of a better life.
Vocation: Sanitation Worker
For the Athletic: Possesses a strong physical build from manual labor, enabling him to endure long hours of hard work.
Description: Tobias has a stout build, a scruffy beard, and deep-set brown eyes. He wears worn-out trousers and a rough shirt, often covered in dirt and grime. Beneath his gruff exterior lies a deep frustration with the neglect shown to the lower classes by the upper city.
Wants & Needs: Wants: To improve his living conditions; dreams of saving enough money to start a small cleaning business.
- Needs: To find hope and motivation, despite feeling overlooked by society.

Secret or Obstacle: Hides bitterness about his situation, resenting how the lower classes are neglected.
Carrying: (Total CP: 18)
- Broom and Dustpan (6 points): Tools for clearing the streets.
- Rubbish Cart (5 points): Used to collect and transport debris.
- Leather Gloves (4 points): Protective wear for his work.
- Healing Balm (3 points): A simple remedy for sore hands.

Rhea Hightide
"Every fish sold brings hope for tomorrow." **4**

Brief: An enterprising fishmonger, Rhea sells whatever her husband catches from the river, striving to provide for her family.
Vocation: Fishmonger
For the Insightful: Possesses adept bargaining skills, often winning over customers with her charm and hospitality.
Description: Rhea has long, flowing hair tied back and warm brown eyes. She wears an apron over simple clothing, often smelling of fresh fish. Her friendly demeanor makes her stall a popular spot in the market. Despite her resilience, she constantly fears losing her business in the competitive slum environment.
Wants & Needs: Wants: To provide enough for her family to escape the slums; dreams of opening a proper fish market to attract customers from across the city.
- Needs: To gain confidence in her trade, overcoming her fears of competition and failure.

Secret or Obstacle: Hides fears of losing her business due to the harsh environment and gossip, constantly seeking the latest information to stay ahead.
Carrying: (Total CP: 19)
- Basket of Fresh Fish (10 points): The main product she sells.
- Weighing Scale (3 points): Ensures fair transactions.
- Fish Filleting Knife (3 points): A tool for preparing fish.
- Small Pouch of Healing Herbs (3 points): Used to soothe minor ailments.

Hadrien Blackforge   *"Through fire and determination, legacies are forged."* 5

Brief: A skilled blacksmith who was once part of the elite, Hadrien now struggles to maintain his shop and reputation in the slums.
Vocation: Blacksmith & Artisan
For the Perceptive: Possesses invaluable expertise in metalwork, able to create exceptional items with minimal resources.
Description: Hadrien is tall and muscular, with graying hair and determined blue eyes. He wears a leather apron over sooty work clothes, emphasizing his dedication to his craft. Despite his skill, he harbors bitterness about being overlooked by the nobility and dreams of reclaiming his former status.
Wants & Needs: Wants: To reclaim his lost status and restore his family's legacy; dreams of crafting a famous weapon that earns him widespread respect.
- Needs: To overcome his frustration and focus on his craft to seize new opportunities.

Secret or Obstacle: Hides frustrations about being overlooked by the nobility, growing increasingly bitter while hoping for a chance to prove himself.
Carrying: (Total CP: 18)
- Simple Blacksmithing Tools (5 points): Essential for forging and repairs.
- Hammer (5 points): A trusted tool for shaping metal.
- Basic Armor Set (6 points): A sample of his craftsmanship.
- Healing Ointment (2 points): For burns or injuries from the forge.

Orlin Springfire   *"A cheeky grin can open the tightest purse strings."* 6

Brief: A street urchin known for his ability to charm passersby into sharing food and coins, Orlin survives using his wit and charisma.
Vocation: Street Urchin
For the Perceptive: Possesses quick thinking and adaptability, able to navigate the streets and play on others' emotions with ease.
Description: Orlin has bright orange hair and glowing red eyes. He dresses in ragged clothing but carries himself with pride. His cheeky grin often earns him sympathy or laughter from strangers. Beneath his confident exterior, he struggles with a fear of abandonment and feelings of loneliness.
Wants & Needs: Wants: To find a place where he belongs; dreams of becoming a successful performer instead of a beggar.
- Needs: To confront his fear of abandonment and embrace his own worth.

Secret or Obstacle: Hides a deep-seated fear of abandonment, often grappling with loneliness despite his upbeat demeanor.
Carrying: (Total CP: 20)
- Tattered Backpack (4 points): Holds his few possessions.
- Street Performer's Props (6 points): Tools for entertaining passersby.
- Few Loose Coins (3 points): Scraped together from his daily efforts.
- Potion of Minor Healing (7 points): A remedy for unexpected injuries.

Hector Ironpaw   *"Quick paws, quick gains."* 7

Brief: A curious and mischievous Catfolk thief, Hector uses his agile body to navigate tight spots in the city, swiping valuables to survive.
Vocation: Thief & Rogue
For the Insightful: Possesses keen senses and lightning-fast reflexes, allowing him to evade capture by city guards.
Description: Hector has sandy fur with dark spots, bright yellow-green eyes, and a playful demeanor. He wears loose clothing for freedom of movement and is always alert for potential marks. While confident in his skills, he often takes unnecessary risks due to his fear of failure.
Wants & Needs: Wants: To gain enough resources to escape the slums and explore the world; dreams of becoming a master thief and adventurer.
- Needs: To overcome his fear of getting caught and balance risk-taking with careful planning.

Secret or Obstacle: Hides a constant worry of being caught by authorities, which often leads him to take reckless chances.
Carrying: (Total CP: 19)
- Set of Lockpicks (6 points): Essential tools for breaking into locks.
- Light Leather Armor (4 points): Offers protection without restricting movement.
- Throwing Daggers (5 points): Handy for defense or quick strikes.
- Bag of Healing Herbs (4 points): A resource for minor injuries.

Viktor Loneshadow *"Each beam and nail builds hope anew."* 8

Brief: A quiet but skilled carpenter, Viktor constructs makeshift homes and shelters for those living in poverty within the slums.
Vocation: Carpenter & Builder
For the Perceptive: Possesses solid woodworking skills and a keen eye for structural integrity, often helping to improve the living conditions around him.
Description: Viktor is tall and burly, with a scruffy beard and dark eyes that reflect his gentle nature. He wears simple work clothes and a leather apron, often dusted with sawdust from his craft. Despite his strength and determination, Viktor struggles with feelings of helplessness in the face of the city's vast wealth disparity.
Wants & Needs: Wants: To provide a safe haven for those suffering in the slums; dreams of starting an initiative to build housing for the homeless.
- Needs: To overcome his sadness about the disparity around him and find ways to inspire change within his community.

Secret or Obstacle: Hides his sadness about feeling powerless against the wealth disparity, constantly reminded of the gap between himself and the city's elite.
Carrying: (Total CP: 18)
- Set of Carpentry Tools (7 points): Essential for crafting sturdy shelters.
- Woodworking Bench (6 points): A portable workspace for his projects.
- Pouch of Nails (3 points): A vital resource for construction.
- Minor Healing Balm (2 points): A remedy for small injuries from his trade.

Felix Greycloak *"The shadows whisper secrets to those who listen."* 9

Brief: A cunning rogue with a knack for gathering information, Felix sells secrets to the highest bidder while flirting with danger.
Vocation: Informant & Rogue
For the Insightful: Possesses swift reflexes and sharp wit, able to navigate social circles and underground deals with ease.
Description: Felix has shoulder-length black hair, faded purple eyes, and an elusive presence. He dresses in muted colors to blend into the shadows, often seen with a sly smile. Although confident, Felix harbors trust issues due to a past betrayal, which leaves him wary of loyalty in any form.
Wants & Needs: Wants: To accumulate wealth through gathered information; dreams of becoming the most well-connected informant in the city.
- Needs: To come to terms with his past betrayal and rebuild his trust in others.

Secret or Obstacle: Hides the details of a betrayal that left him disillusioned about trust, leading him to discount loyalty in his dealings.
Carrying: (Total CP: 20)
- Set of Informant's Tools (6 points): Used to gather and organize sensitive information.
- Simple Dagger (5 points): A weapon for self-defense.
- Notepad of Secrets (6 points): Holds vital information and blackmail material.
- Minor Healing Potion (3 points): A quick remedy for unexpected injuries.

Reddin Mosswood *"Failure is just another way to make them laugh."* 10

Brief: An eccentric tinkerer known for creating whimsical contraptions that often fail hilariously, entertaining the local children.
Vocation: Tinkerer & Inventor
For the Perceptive: Possesses an inventive mind that finds joy in experimentation, often leading to amusing failures that gather crowds.
Description: Reddin has untamed hair, bright blue eyes, and a perpetually smudged face. He wears a patchwork apron filled with odd tools, constantly flailing around in an energetic blur. Beneath his cheerful demeanor, Reddin fears his work won't be taken seriously despite his dreams of creating a masterpiece.
Wants & Needs: Wants: To create a great invention that will amuse and inspire others; dreams of gaining fame and improving lives through his creations.
- Needs: To overcome his feelings of inadequacy and learn to present his ideas confidently.

Secret or Obstacle: Hides fears that nobody takes him seriously, frequently battling self-doubt when sharing his work.
Carrying: (Total CP: 19)
- Jumbled Collection of Gears (7 points): Raw materials for his creations.
- Odd Contraption (5 points): A prototype gadget prone to comical failure.
- Toolkit for Repairs (4 points): Essential tools for maintaining and improving his inventions.
- Healing Nettle Compress (3 points): A natural remedy for minor injuries.

Tobias Driftwood
"Every knot tells a story, every wave holds a secret." **11**

Brief: A once-renowned sailor, Tobias now works as a dockworker. He shares tales of his adventurous past with those who are willing to listen.
Vocation: Dockworker / Former Sailor
For the Insightful: Possesses extensive sailing knowledge, navigating intricate waterways using experience and intuition.
Description: Tobias has sun-kissed skin, a scruffy beard, and fading tattoos from his sailing days. He wears simple dockworker attire, often showing signs of hard labor. Beneath his gruff demeanor lies a longing for one last adventure before retiring from the sea.
Wants & Needs: Wants: To find a crew to return to the seas and fulfill his thirst for adventure; dreams of a last great voyage before settling down.
- Needs: To reconcile with his past mistakes and find closure for the friendships he lost along the way.

Secret or Obstacle: Hides regret over past mistakes during his time at sea, occasionally overwhelmed by the pain of lost friendships.
Carrying: (Total CP: 20)
- Rope and Knots (5 points): Essential for ship maintenance and dockwork.
- Rusty Hook (4 points): A memento of his time at sea, doubling as a tool.
- Sailor's Toolkit (6 points): A collection of tools for repairs and survival.
- Healing Ointment (5 points): A salve for minor injuries.

Darin Stonefist
"Strength protects the weak; loyalty earns respect." **12**

Brief: A tower of muscle and resilience, Darin serves as a bodyguard to various merchants, proving that honor transcends race.
Vocation: Bodyguard & Protector
For the Perceptive: Possesses great physical strength and loyalty to those he protects, ensuring their safety on the streets.
Description: Darin is large and muscular, with a tattooed arm and a half-shaved head. He wears simple leather armor adorned with tokens from the merchants he protects. Despite his fearsome appearance, Darin struggles to distance himself from a dark past as a gang enforcer.
Wants & Needs: Wants: To prove his worth and earn respect in the city; dreams of one day having his own security company.
- Needs: To resist the pull of his past and focus on building a new, honorable life.

Secret or Obstacle: Hides his past as a feared enforcer for a gang, striving to distance himself from that life but fearing it will return.
Carrying: (Total CP: 19)
- Heavy Club (8 points): A weapon for defending his clients.
- Leather Armor (7 points): Sturdy protection during dangerous assignments.
- Protective Amulet (4 points): A charm believed to ward off harm.

Rafferty Knifft
"Every stroke of the brush tells a tale." **13**

Brief: A perceptive street artist who uses his skills to gain attention and small change from passersby with his charming performances.
Vocation: Street Artist
For the Insightful: Possesses remarkable agility and a talent for engaging audiences, grabbing attention through comedic antics.
Description: Rafferty has wild orange hair, sparkling green eyes, and an oversized grin. He wears a colorful outfit covered in paint splatters and always carries a paintbrush. Despite his joyful demeanor, he struggles with self-doubt, fearing his talents may never be recognized.
Wants & Needs: Wants: To share joy and creativity with others; dreams of becoming a renowned artist whose work graces the walls of the city.
- Needs: To overcome his fear of failure and believe in the value of his art.

Secret or Obstacle: Hides his struggles with self-doubt, often fearing his talents will never be recognized.
Carrying: (Total CP: 19)
- Paintbrush (4 points): His primary tool for creating art.
- Canvas (5 points): A surface for his imaginative creations.
- Small Palette of Colors (4 points): Vibrant paints for his work.
- Healing Bandages (6 points): A precaution for accidents while working.

Keller Thornsbristle
"Nurture the soil, and it will nurture the soul." **14**

Brief: A gentle giant who tends to a community garden, Keller provides fresh produce to help feed those in need.
Vocation: Gardener
For the Perceptive: Possesses a nurturing spirit and deep respect for nature, often teaching children about the importance of plants and gardening.
Description: Keller is tall and broad with earthy brown skin and leafy hair. He wears simple clothes and often has dirt under his fingernails. His cheerful disposition draws others seeking help, though he often feels self-conscious about his appearance among city folk.
Wants & Needs: Wants: To maintain the garden and help others access food; dreams of turning the garden into a central community gathering place.
- Needs: To overcome his self-consciousness and embrace his unique appearance.

Secret or Obstacle: Hides a secret longing for acceptance among city folk, often feeling self-conscious about his appearance.
Carrying: (Total CP: 18)
- Gardening Tools (6 points): Essential for tending to his garden.
- Basket of Fresh Produce (7 points): A gift for those in need.
- Herbal Tea Leaves (5 points): A soothing remedy he shares with others.

Alton Bruinheart
"A warm meal and a kind ear heal more than medicine." **15**

Brief: A compassionate healer and bartender at a local tavern, Alton tends to patrons, mixing drinks and providing minor healing when needed.
Vocation: Tavern Keeper
For the Perceptive: Possesses a calming demeanor and a talent for listening, often providing assistance beyond just drinks.
Description: Alton has short, tousled chestnut hair, a warm smile, and brown eyes full of compassion. He wears an apron over simple tavern attire and is often seen bustling about serving patrons. Despite his jovial nature, Alton channels his grief over a lost loved one into helping others.
Wants & Needs: Wants: To help those in need while maintaining his tavern's lively atmosphere; dreams of opening a larger establishment focused on community.
- Needs: To address his own sorrow and find a way to heal himself as he helps others.

Secret or Obstacle: Hides his struggles with the loss of a loved one, often channeling his grief into helping others while inwardly battling sorrow.
Carrying: (Total CP: 20)
- Healing Supplies (8 points): For treating patrons in need.
- Selection of Beers and Ales (5 points): A highlight of his tavern.
- Bartending Tools (4 points): To craft comforting drinks.
- Small First Aid Kit (3 points): Always ready for emergencies.

Gandor Farsight
"The stars whisper wisdom to those who listen." **16**

Brief: A wise and elderly sage who dabbles in divination, Gandor occasionally offers his insights at the city's markets for free.
Vocation: Sage & Diviner
For the Insightful: Possesses powerful foresight abilities, often guiding youths and troubled souls with his advice.
Description: Gandor has long gray hair, deep-set green eyes, and wears flowing robes covered in intricate symbols. His serene presence commands respect and curiosity, though he secretly worries about the weight of his predictions.
Wants & Needs: Wants: To guide others toward fulfilling their potential; dreams of leaving behind ancient wisdom for future generations.
- Needs: To accept that he cannot control the future, even with his foresight.

Secret or Obstacle: Hides his fears of the future becoming grim; he worries that his own foresight might be the cause of undue distress to others.
Carrying: (Total CP: 19)
- Crystal Orb (8 points): Used for his divinations.
- Scrolls of Prophecy (6 points): Records of visions and predictions.
- Elder's Staff (5 points): A symbol of his wisdom and authority.

Eamon Truewatcher *"Justice walks the streets with vigilant eyes."* 17

Brief: A vigilant city guard, Eamon strives to keep the streets safe, patrolling regularly to ensure peace for the struggling folk.
Vocation: City Guard & Protector
For the Perceptive: Possesses excellent observation skills and a strong sense of justice, driving him to work hard for the community.
Description: Eamon has a lean yet muscular build, short dark hair, and serious green eyes. He wears polished guard armor, often seen with a focused and determined expression while patrolling.
Wants & Needs: Wants: To serve and protect the citizens, ensuring their safety while building connections with the people; dreams of rising through the ranks of the guard.
- Needs: To reconcile with his guilt and overcome his feeling of failure from crimes he couldn't prevent.

Secret or Obstacle: Hides a sense of guilt about not being able to prevent certain crimes in the past, often haunted by the feeling of failure.
Carrying: (Total CP: 20)
- Guard Shield (10 points): A sturdy defense against any threat.
- Short Sword (4 points): A weapon for close combat.
- Guard Badge (2 points): Symbolizing his commitment to justice.
- Basic Healing Potions (4 points): Essential for emergencies.

Asher Wildfoot *"Every step is a new story waiting to be told."* 18

Brief: A carefree wanderer who sells trinkets and oddities from his travels, Asher enjoys sharing tales of his adventures with anyone who will listen.
Vocation: Wanderer & Merchant
For the Insightful: Possesses exceptional agility and storytelling skills, captivating audiences with his tales of adventure.
Description: Asher has sleek fur with dark stripes, striking amber eyes, and a constantly energetic demeanor. He wears eclectic attire reflecting his travels and carries various trinkets in pouches.
Wants & Needs: Wants: To continue exploring and sharing stories of his experiences; dreams of writing a book about the wonders he's witnessed.
- Needs: To overcome his feelings of loneliness and find a true sense of belonging.

Secret or Obstacle: Hides the reality of his loneliness, often feeling out of place despite his cheerful exterior, struggling to fit in with those around him.
Carrying: (Total CP: 19)
- Assorted Trinkets (7 points): Collected from his travels.
- Stories and Baubles Collection (6 points): A curated assortment of tales and treasures.
- Traveler's Pack (4 points): Packed with essentials for his journey.
- Healing Tea (2 points): A calming brew for moments of rest.

Garrick Foxtail *"Every child deserves a chance to dream."* 19

Brief: A small but wise teacher who runs a school for children in the slums, Garrick devotes his life to educating those who cannot afford proper schooling.
Vocation: Teacher & Educator
For the Perceptive: Possesses a natural talent for teaching, always finding innovative methods to make learning fun and engaging.
Description: Garrick has spiky silver hair and lively blue eyes filled with joy. He wears simple yet colorful clothes, often hastily dressed amid his busy schedule. His warm presence inspires hope in the young minds he nurtures.
Wants & Needs: Wants: To provide a safe space for education and nurture young minds; dreams of opening a larger school that can help even more children.
- Needs: To build his confidence and trust in his abilities as a teacher, easing his fear of failure.

Secret or Obstacle: Hides his fears about failing his students, constantly anxious about letting down the curious young souls who look up to him.
Carrying: (Total CP: 20)
- Stack of Books (7 points): Knowledge and stories to share.
- Quill and Ink Set (5 points): For writing lessons and notes.
- Bag of Educational Games (5 points): Tools to make learning engaging.
- Small Healing Ointment (3 points): For tending to minor scrapes and injuries.

Random Village Residents

Villagers are the heart of a fantasy realm, embodying community, tradition, and resilience. Living in close-knit hamlets or rural settlements, they engage in trades like farming, crafting, fishing, and trading. Relying on one another for support, villagers form strong bonds that shape their lives. Rich in folklore and customs, they pass down ancestral stories and celebrate seasonal festivals, creating stability amid the turbulence of the wider world.

Adventurers should tread carefully, as not all villagers have pure intentions. A cautionary tale warns of Old Greta, a revered homesteader known for her knowledge of herbs and healing. Villagers trusted her remedies and kind demeanor, but beneath her gentle exterior lay a dark secret. Whispers spread of villagers who disappeared after seeking her help. Greta, as it turned out, practiced dark magic, harvesting the life essence of her visitors to prolong her own existence.

One evening, adventurers seeking a legendary elixir visited Greta's cottage. Welcomed warmly, they listened as she spun tales and brewed enticing potions. But as the elixir simmered, they grew weak, realizing too late they were not guests, but sacrifices for her unholy craft.

They fought to escape, but one by one, fell victim to her dark arts, leaving only echoes of their laughter behind.

This tale warns adventurers that while villagers may appear humble, their kindness can conceal sinister motives. Not every resident is trustworthy, and crossing paths with the wrong one can lead to disaster. As you explore villages, stay alert and trust your instincts; the greatest dangers may not come from the outside world, but from within the village itself.

Elowen Brightwood

"Nature's remedies mend both body and soul." 1

Brief: A skilled herbalist, Elowen uses her extensive knowledge of plants to craft remedies and potions, supporting the health and well-being of her village community.

Vocation: Herbalist & Healer

For the Insightful: Possesses an instinctive connection with nature, enabling her to heal others and nurture her garden with exceptional care.

Description: Elowen has long chestnut hair, vibrant green eyes, and a serene presence. She wears simple earth-toned clothes adorned with flowers and herbs, exuding a natural charm that mirrors her deep bond with the land.

Wants & Needs: Wants: To share her herbal knowledge with the community and establish a school of healing to teach others her methods.
- Needs: To overcome her self-doubt and earn the trust of villagers, ensuring her remedies are seen as valuable and effective.

Secret or Obstacle: Hides her fear of the villagers doubting her abilities, often wondering if they will trust her remedies over more traditional methods.

Carrying: (Total CP: 17)
- Herbal Remedies (5 points): A selection of potent blends to treat common ailments.
- Potions of Healing (7 points): Crafted elixirs for swift recovery.
- Field Guide to Plants (5 points): A well-worn book filled with botanical knowledge.

Brom Stoutheart *"Through fire and steel, I forge our future."* 2

Brief: A steadfast blacksmith known for crafting weapons and tools that arm the village against danger, Brom's forge is a cornerstone of the community's survival.
Vocation: Master Blacksmith
For the Insightful: His unmatched strength and intricate craftsmanship produce creations that seem imbued with a spark of magic.
Description: Brom is short and burly, with a thick beard streaked with gray and eyes as bright as molten steel. He wears an apron smudged with soot, his powerful hands etched with years of labor at the forge. Though stoic and grounded, he secretly dreams of crafting a weapon worthy of legend, one that will endure long after he's gone.
Wants & Needs: Wants: To pass on his knowledge and create a legendary weapon that will cement his legacy.
- Needs: To find an apprentice willing to carry on his craft and ensure his trade survives.

Secret or Obstacle:
Hides a deep sadness over his son's disinterest in smithing, fearing the trade he cherishes will die with him.
Carrying: (Total CP: 18)
- Forgehammer of the Ages (6 points): A heavy, rune-carved tool said to hum with latent power.
- Anvil of Eternal Flame (5 points): A portable anvil enchanted to remain ever-warm, aiding in crafting on the go.
- Ember-forged Armor (6 points): An intricate chestplate, its surface shimmering like live coals, offering both protection and pride.
- Flask of Soothefire (1 point): A warm, glowing potion that soothes burns and invigorates the spirit.

Thalia Riverbend *"Raise a glass and a smile; life tastes better together."* 3

Brief: A warm and welcoming alewife, Thalia brews the village's signature ales, bringing a sense of joy and camaraderie to her tavern.
Vocation: Alewife & Brewer
For the Perceptive: Possesses a deep understanding of brewing techniques, crafting ales with flavors as rich as her laughter.
Description: Thalia has wavy auburn hair and bright blue eyes that sparkle like fresh spring water. She wears a simple yet elegant dress with an apron always dusted in flour or hops. Her hearty laugh and keen sense of hospitality make her tavern a second home for many villagers. Beneath her warm demeanor lies an unwavering determination to preserve her family's brewing traditions.
Wants & Needs: Wants: To innovate her brewing methods and win recognition at regional competitions.
- Needs: To secure resources for her brewery's growth while preserving the charm of her tavern.

Secret or Obstacle: Fears that the rising competition in neighboring villages might overshadow her beloved ale, leaving her struggling to keep the business afloat.
Carrying: (Total CP: 19)
- Barrels of Golden Froth (8 points): Aged oak casks containing her signature ale, said to bring luck with each sip.
- Brewer's Charm Pendant (5 points): A necklace adorned with a small hop leaf, rumored to ensure perfect fermentation.
- Recipe Book of Forgotten Brews (4 points): An ancient tome filled with rare recipes and brewing secrets passed down through generations.
- Herbal Draught (2 points): A potent brew infused with local herbs to heal fatigue and bolster spirits.

Finnigan Lowtide *"The sea's bounty provides for all who respect her."* 4

Brief: A cheerful fisherman, Finnigan is beloved for his hearty tales and abundant catches, providing fresh fish to the village with pride.
Vocation: Fisherman
For the Insightful: Possesses an intuitive understanding of tides and weather patterns, rarely returning empty-handed.
Description: Finnigan is short and stocky, with sun-kissed skin and a wide smile that brightens even the stormiest of days. He wears salt-stained clothing and a hat adorned with colorful fishing lures. His jovial nature and knack for storytelling make him a beloved figure at village gatherings. Beneath his carefree exterior lies concern for the future of the waters he calls home.
Wants & Needs: Wants: To teach the next generation the art of sustainable fishing.
- Needs: To protect the local fishing grounds from overuse and preserve the village's livelihood.

Secret or Obstacle: Hides his growing worry that dwindling fish stocks may signal trouble for the village, burdening him with a sense of helplessness.
Carrying: (Total CP: 20)
- Rod of Tidal Whispers (5 points): A finely carved fishing rod said to hum with the rhythm of the ocean.
- Basket of Endless Catch (9 points): A magical basket that keeps fish fresh and plentiful, even on the longest journeys.
- Sailor's Net of Luck (3 points): A net woven with seaweed charms, believed to attract fish to its user.
- Healing Salt Tonic (3 points): A briny potion that soothes wounds and invigorates weary limbs.

Galen Windrunner *"Speed is not just a gift—it's a responsibility."* 5

Brief: A swift and agile elf who delivers vital news and messages across the region, Galen is renowned for his unmatched speed and dedication.
Vocation: Messenger & Courier
For the Athletic: Possesses extraordinary reflexes and agility, allowing him to navigate dangerous paths with ease while maintaining impeccable delivery times.
Description: Galen has long silver hair that flows like wind in motion, vibrant green eyes, and a lean, muscular frame honed by years of running through forests and fields. He wears light, weather-resistant clothing and is rarely seen without his satchel of letters strapped securely to his side. Though outwardly calm, Galen harbors a fierce determination to protect the connections he builds with his deliveries, carrying the weight of every message as though it were his own.
Wants & Needs: Wants: To strengthen the bonds between distant communities through his work as a courier.
- Needs: To overcome the political tensions of neighboring settlements that threaten his role as a neutral messenger.

Secret or Obstacle: Hides a deep worry about strained relationships between elven realms, fearing the impact of failure on his village's reputation.
Carrying: (Total CP: 19)
- Satchel of Windborne Letters (5 points): An enchanted bag that ensures letters remain protected, even in the harshest storms.
- Blade of the Swift (5 points): A sleek elven shortsword designed for speed and precision in combat.
- Map of the Endless Paths (4 points): A magical map that reveals shortcuts and hidden routes only to its bearer.
- Healing Elixirs of the Fleet (5 points): A potion infused with energy-restoring herbs, perfect for regaining stamin.

Ilias Blackthorn *"The forest whispers secrets; I am but its humble student."* 6

Brief: An accomplished herbalist and half-orc who forages potent herbs to heal the sick, earning the trust of villagers despite his rugged demeanor.
Vocation: Herbalist & Healer
For the Perceptive: Possesses keen survival instincts and an unmatched ability to identify and cultivate rare plants in the wilderness.
Description: Ilias stands tall and broad-shouldered, his green skin speckled with scars from years of foraging through dense woods. His rugged appearance belies his gentle nature and precise touch when handling delicate herbs. He wears practical clothing adorned with leather patches, often stained with soil and sap. Though he seldom speaks of his past, his eyes reveal a yearning for belonging in a village that sees him as an outsider.
Wants & Needs: Wants: To establish a healing sanctuary that ensures no one in his village suffers without care.
- Needs: To overcome the deep-seated prejudice he feels from others and prove his worth beyond his heritage.

Secret or Obstacle: Struggles with doubts about his place in a community that judges him by his appearance.
Carrying: (Total CP: 19)
- Satchel of Herbal Mysteries (3 points): A weathered bag that carries enchanted compartments for preserving herbs.
- Mortar & Pestle of Verdant Alchemy (4 points): Crafted from rare stone, it enhances the potency of his remedies.
- Tonic of the Verdant Grove (5 points): A healing potion that accelerates recovery and soothes pain instantly.
- Enchanted Pouch of Herb Whispers (8 points): Contains rare ingredients that sing faintly when touched, guiding him to create life-saving mixtures.

Roderick Stonewall *"A home's foundation is trust, and trust is built with care."* 7

Brief: A grizzled carpenter known for his precise craftsmanship, Roderick builds homes that stand firm against time and storms.
Vocation: Carpenter
For the Insightful: Holds a deep understanding of structural integrity and design, ensuring the safety and beauty of his creations.
Description: Roderick is a stout man with a sturdy build, his gray hair peppered with wood shavings and his calloused hands evidence of decades at the workbench. He dresses in durable work clothes, often smelling faintly of sawdust and pine. His serious expression rarely softens, yet his passion for his craft is unmistakable in the precision of every beam he cuts. He dreams of mentoring an apprentice to pass on his legacy, though his quiet demeanor hides his inner longing for recognition.
Wants & Needs: Wants: To train an apprentice who can carry on his legacy of impeccable craftsmanship.
- Needs: To overcome the frustration he feels from being underappreciated by villagers who take his hard work for granted.

Secret or Obstacle: Hides his disappointment in his community's lack of gratitude for his dedication, often questioning the purpose of his work.
Carrying: (Total CP: 19)
- Hammer of Unyielding Resolve (8 points): A carpenter's hammer imbued with runes that ensure every strike is precise.
- Blueprints of the Stonewall Method (5 points): A collection of Roderick's personal designs, renowned for their durability.
- Bundle of Cured Timber (4 points): Lumber enchanted to resist rot and withstand harsh weather conditions.
- Balm of Craftsman's Rest (2 points): A salve that soothes aching muscles after a long day of labor.

Samuel Brightforge *"Every spark holds the promise of something extraordinary."* 8

Brief: A lively and chatty metalworker, Samuel crafts intricate decorative items, blending artistry with traditional blacksmithing skills.
Vocation: Metalworker & Artisan
For the Perceptive: Possesses exceptional creativity and a knack for combining function with beauty, making his works treasured in the village.
Description: Barrel-chested and sturdy, Samuel is a dwarf with a hearty laugh and lively gray eyes that light up when discussing his craft. His apron is perpetually dusted with filings, and his hands bear the calluses of a true artisan. Known for his good humor and passion, he often showcases his creations at village gatherings, hoping to bring a bit of artistry into the everyday lives of others.
Wants & Needs: Wants: To create stunning masterpieces that tell stories, dreaming of seeing his works in renowned galleries.
- Needs: To overcome self-doubt about his relevance, yearning for validation beyond the village's borders.

Secret or Obstacle: Fears stagnation and obscurity, worrying that his work might never be recognized outside his small community.
Carrying: (Total CP: 20)
- Set of Rune-Engraving Tools (8 points): Enables the crafting of decorative designs imbued with minor enchantments.
- Glimmering Ingots (6 points): Precious metals that shimmer with a mystical glow.
- Ornamental Trinket Samples (4 points): A selection of Samuel's finest work, meant to inspire commissions.
- Tonic of Artisan's Relief (2 points): A potion that soothes aching hands after a long day at the forge.

Tobias Everbrook *"A warm meal and a hearty laugh—life's simplest joys."* 9

Brief: A jovial halfling tavern owner who prides himself on creating a welcoming space for stories, music, and camaraderie.
Vocation: Tavern Owner
For the Insightful: Possesses an innate ability to connect with others, fostering a sense of community through his social acumen and hospitality.
Description: Tobias is a round-faced, rosy-cheeked halfling with an ever-present wide smile. He dons colorful vests and a well-worn apron, always bustling about with a tray or a tankard in hand. Though he appears carefree, he carries the weight of running the village's central hub with pride, hiding his worries behind his infectious humor.
Wants & Needs: Wants: To ensure his tavern remains the beating heart of the village while expanding its renown.
- Needs: To manage the mounting financial pressures that threaten his livelihood without letting it affect his patrons.

Secret or Obstacle: Hides his financial struggles from the villagers, fearing the loss of their respect and trust if his debts were revealed.
Carrying: (Total CP: 19)
- Cask of Everbrook's Finest (6 points): A signature brew that's said to warm both body and soul.
- Recipe Scrolls of Tavern Treats (5 points): Handwritten notes containing generations-old recipes.
- Hearty Cookware Set (4 points): Trusted pots and pans used for preparing Tobias's renowned meals.
- Bottle of Liquid Cheer (4 points): A magical drink mix that uplifts spirits, even on the darkest days.

Quinlan Foxfire *"Let the flames dance, and with them, the hearts of the crowd."* 10

Brief: A flamboyant Fire Genasi street performer who captivates audiences with fiery acrobatics and spellbinding displays.
Vocation: Street Performer
For the Perceptive: Displays extraordinary agility and a flair for performance, weaving fire magic into his routines to enchant even the most skeptical onlookers.
Description: Quinlan's fiery red hair flickers like embers in the wind, and his golden eyes burn with mischief and charm. Dressed in brightly colored, fire-motif attire, he leaps and twirls through village squares, leaving trails of sparks that elicit gasps from the crowd. Beneath his confident exterior, Quinlan longs for a sense of belonging, seeking both recognition and camaraderie among his peers.
Wants & Needs: Wants: To inspire awe and wonder in every audience, dreaming of founding a grand circus of performers.
- Needs: To overcome his insecurities about being accepted for who he truly is, beyond his dazzling performances.

Secret or Obstacle: Hides his fear of letting his flames burn out, metaphorically and literally, constantly striving to prove himself.
Carrying: (Total CP: 20)
- Flame-Touched Staff of Elegance (8 points): A mesmerizing prop that channels Quinlan's fire magic for dazzling displays.
- Performance Kit of Endless Wonder (5 points): Contains tools for juggling, acrobatics, and minor illusions.
- Cloak of Ember Veils (4 points): An enchanted garment that leaves fiery trails when he moves.
- Elixir of Smoldering Confidence (3 points): A potion that temporarily boosts his charisma and theatrical flair.

Kian Brightsmoke *"Innovation lights the path to progress."* 11

Brief: A clever and resourceful tinkerer, Kian creates ingenious gadgets to aid his village, infusing practical tools with fantastical charm.
Vocation: Tinkerer & Inventor
For the Insightful: Kian's sharp intellect allows him to transform mundane items into creative tools, earning him both admiration and skepticism.
Description: Kian is a wiry half-elf with messy black hair and bright hazel eyes that shimmer with curiosity. He wears a patched leather apron adorned with tinkering tools and pockets brimming with small gears and components. His passion for improving village life drives him to tinker late into the night, guided by a spark of inspiration few can match.
Wants & Needs: Wants: Kian dreams of creating a groundbreaking invention that will earn him a place in history.
- Needs: He must overcome his self-doubt and prove that his ingenuity is more than just youthful ambition.

Secret or Obstacle: Kian struggles with being overlooked due to his age and size, often feeling he must constantly prove his worth to the more experienced craftsmen in the village.
Carrying (Total CP: 19):
- Tinkering Tools (6 points): A compact kit of gears, pliers, and precision tools.
- Collection of Gadgetry (7 points): A satchel of creations like a clockwork lantern and an automaton bird.
- Notepad of Designs (4 points): A worn book filled with imaginative blueprints.
- Healing Oil (2 points): A golden vial that quickly mends wounds.

Hector Hollowbranch *"The forest speaks to those who listen."* 12

Brief: A serene and watchful ranger, Hector protects the village and its borders, ensuring harmony between the wild and the community.
Vocation: Ranger & Protector
For the Perceptive: Hector's deep bond with nature enables him to track, hunt, and defend the village with effortless precision.
Description: Hector is a tall, broad-shouldered wood elf with long brown hair adorned with feathers and beads. His emerald-green eyes seem to glint with the wisdom of centuries, and his leather armor is intricately decorated with leaf patterns. Beneath his calm exterior lies a fierce determination to preserve the balance of nature and shield the village from unseen dangers.
Wants & Needs: Wants: Hector dreams of creating a sanctuary where villagers can learn to live in harmony with nature.
- Needs: He must reconcile his desire to protect the village with his love for the untamed wild, finding a balance between his two worlds.

Secret or Obstacle: Hector sometimes feels the pang of isolation, wondering if his dedication to the wild keeps him from fully connecting with the people he protects.
Carrying (Total CP: 20):
- Bow and Quiver of Arrows (8 points): A finely crafted bow with enchanted raven-feathered arrows.
- Survival Kit (6 points): A pouch filled with dried herbs, a bone knife, and a silver whistle.
- Nature's Tome (4 points): A book with detailed knowledge of plants and animals.
- Minor Healing Herbs (2 points): A bundle of fragrant leaves that soothe wounds

Finn Silverleaf *"Every arrow tells a story."* 13

Brief: A skilled hunter and archer, Finn provides for the village while safeguarding the delicate balance of the wild.
Vocation: Hunter & Archer
For the Insightful: Finn's unmatched marksmanship and stealth ensure that no prey escapes his gaze.
Description: Finn is a lithe elf with golden hair tied back with a leather cord, his blue eyes sharp and attentive. His supple leather armor is adorned with carved leaf patterns that reflect his deep respect for the wild. With every movement, he exudes quiet confidence, his keen senses honed by years of hunting.
Wants & Needs: Wants: Finn wishes to pass his knowledge to younger villagers, teaching them sustainable hunting practices to preserve the wild.
- Needs: Must confront his lingering grief over the loss of a trusted hunting companion, finding peace to focus on the present.

Secret or Obstacle: Finn's grief often manifests as hesitation in crucial moments, a shadow he must overcome to remain the skilled protector the village needs.
Carrying (Total CP: 19):
- Longbow (8 points): An enchanted bow that never misses its mark.
- Quiver of Arrows (4 points): Arrows with tips that glow faintly in darkness.
- Survival Gear (4 points): A satchel with rations, a flask, and a crystal to detect safe water.
- Healing Balm (3 points): A jar of salve made from rare forest herbs.

Zeke Farglow *"Cultivate the land, and the future will flourish."* 14

Brief: An energetic farmer who dedicates his life to tending crops and livestock, Zeke is optimistic about the future and well-loved by his neighbors.
Vocation: Farmer & Cultivator
For the Perceptive: Possesses extraordinary work ethic and problem-solving skills to cultivate the land effectively.
Description: Zeke has short brown hair, a sun-kissed complexion, and an infectious smile. He wears work clothes, often patched but functional, with dirt from his daily labor. His dedication to his farm reflects his strong connection to the community and nature.
Wants & Needs: Wants: To cultivate the best crops in the region while ensuring fair prices for his produce; dreams of one day expanding his farm into a thriving business.
- Needs: To secure proper resources and support from the local village to safeguard his harvest during challenging seasons.

Secret or Obstacle: Hides his worries about failing due to poor harvests, often doubting whether he can manage his farm properly in hard times.
Carrying (Total CP: 20):
- Farming Tools (8 points): Well-worn tools designed for efficient tilling and planting.
- Seed Packs (6 points): Carefully preserved seeds for seasonal crops.
- Harvest Basket (4 points): Sturdy and hand-woven, perfect for carrying fresh produce.
- Healing Salves (2 points): Simple herbal ointments to treat minor injuries from farm work.

Cedric Dreamweaver *"Every tale spun preserves a piece of us."* 15

Brief: A compassionate storyteller and bard, Cedric entertains villagers with tales from long ago, preserving their culture through performances.
Vocation: Bard & Storyteller
For the Perceptive: Possesses a gift for engaging narrations, often rallying spirits during tough times with uplifting tales.
Description: Cedric has medium-length brown hair, a welcoming smile, and lively eyes. He dresses in simple, colorful clothing and carries a well-worn lute, ready for storytelling at a moment's notice. His performances bridge the gap between past and present, keeping tradition alive.
Wants & Needs: Wants: To keep his village's history alive; dreams of compiling a grand storybook that preserves traditions for future generations.
- Needs: To find a way to inspire the younger generation to value the lessons within his tales.

Secret or Obstacle: Hides his disappointment in not being recognized for his contributions, often feeling overshadowed by others with grander ambitions.
Carrying (Total CP: 19):
- Well-loved Lute (7 points): A finely crafted instrument worn smooth from years of use.
- Collection of Tales and Songs (6 points): A weathered book brimming with cultural lore.
- Performance Props (4 points): Colorful trinkets to captivate audiences.
- Healing Elixirs (2 points): Mild remedies for soothing a performer's throat or minor ailments.

Ronan Dustfall *"Shape the world, and it will reflect your vision."* 16

Brief: An ambitious craftsman who creates unique pottery and ceramics infused with magic, often selling them at local markets.
Vocation: Potter & Craftsman
For the Insightful: Possesses a keen understanding of both fire elementals and clay, enabling him to produce magical yet functional pieces.
Description: Ronan has flickering red-orange hair, deep amber eyes, and a warm smile. He wears simple, charcoal-stained clothes and has his arms covered in creative tattoos reflecting his craft. His creations carry an air of enchantment, inspiring awe in those who see them.
Wants & Needs: Wants: To create works that inspire others; dreams of one day opening a school for aspiring craftsmen to learn the art of enchanted pottery.
- Needs: To gain recognition and a steady supply of magical resources to enhance his creations further.

Secret or Obstacle: Hides struggles to gain recognition in a crowded market, doubting whether his art is truly valued or unique.
Carrying (Total CP: 20):
- Set of Pottery Tools (8 points): Forged from enchanted metals for perfect shaping.
- Collection of Clay (5 points): Magical clay that responds to his elemental magic.
- Bags of Enchantment Dust (4 points): Used to infuse his creations with minor magical properties.
- Healing Clay (3 points): A soothing mixture used for burns and scrapes from the kiln.

Thorne Windstrider   *"The wild holds no secrets for those who listen."* 17

Brief: A resourceful scout for the village, Thorne is known for his ability to navigate through the wild without getting lost.
Vocation: Scout & Tracker
For the Perceptive: Possesses exceptional tracking skills, able to scout for threats or guide villagers through dangerous terrains.
Description: Thorne has messy brown hair, bright green eyes, and a mischievous grin. He dresses in lightweight clothing designed for movement, often covered in leaves and twigs from the forests. His swift movements and sharp instincts make him a trusted protector of the village's borders.
Wants & Needs: Wants: To ensure the safety of his village from outside dangers; dreams of establishing a scouting academy for future adventurers.
- Needs: To acquire better resources and training to strengthen his skills against potential threats.

Secret or Obstacle: Hides his anxiety over feeling unprepared for threats that may endanger his loved ones, constantly feeling the weight of responsibility.
Carrying (Total CP: 19):
- Leather Armor (7 points): Light yet durable, designed for agility in the wilderness.
- Set of Tracking Tools (5 points): Essential instruments for identifying trails and hidden signs.
- Short Bow (4 points): A finely crafted weapon for silent precision.
- Healing Kit (3 points): Basic supplies to treat injuries in the wild.

Hugo Emberstone   *"A hearty laugh and a full pint cure all woes."* 18

Brief: A jolly and hearty pub owner, Hugo loves entertaining guests with stories and good ale, always up for a laugh and a hearty meal.
Vocation: Innkeeper & Brewmaster
For the Perceptive: Possesses a talent for creating exquisite brews and hearty meals that keep patrons returning for more.
Description: Hugo has a thick beard, twinkling blue eyes, and a constant, boisterous laugh. He wears an apron over well-fitted clothing with a few pawed handprints from customers—a sign of his popularity. His cheerful demeanor makes his tavern a warm and lively hub of the village.
Wants & Needs: Wants: To keep his pub lively and welcoming; dreams of expanding his business into a larger tavern that draws in travelers.
- Needs: To secure funding and the trust of patrons to support his ambitions of growth.

Secret or Obstacle: Hides his worries about the financial stability of his tavern, often battling fears that he could lose his cherished memories.
Carrying (Total CP: 20):
- Selection of Local Ales (10 points): Brewed with a secret recipe loved by villagers.
- Cooking Utensils (4 points): Well-used tools for hearty meals.
- Regulars' Loyalty Cards (3 points): A sign of his close relationship with patrons.
- Healing Brew (3 points): A restorative drink that soothes and warms.

Kendric Brightforge   *"Every strike of the hammer shapes more than just metal."* 19

Brief: A proud apprentice blacksmith following in his father's footsteps, Kendric strives to learn the trade while proving himself worthy.
Vocation: Apprentice Blacksmith
For the Perceptive: Possesses strong physical prowess and growing skills in metallurgy, eager to master the art of blacksmithing.
Description: Kendric has tousled brown hair, determined hazel eyes, and a muscled build. He wears a stained leather apron over a simple shirt. His dedication is evident in his hard work, with every crafted piece reflecting his determination to uphold his family's legacy.
Wants & Needs: Wants: To forge his path and become a respected blacksmith; dreams of creating a masterpiece that honors his father's legacy.
- Needs: To overcome his doubts and find his unique style in crafting to stand out as a blacksmith.

Secret or Obstacle: Hides his self-doubt regarding his skills and often feels overshadowed by the accomplishments of his father.
Carrying (Total CP: 18):
- Basic Blacksmithing Tools (7 points): A set of sturdy tools essential for forging.
- Anvil Hammer (5 points): Passed down from his father, heavy and reliable.
- Leather Gloves (3 points): Protective gear worn during intense heat.
- Healing Salve (3 points): A balm for burns and small cuts from the forge.

Rangers

The concept of a Ranger evokes images of skilled hunters, guardians of nature, and wanderers adept in survival in fantasy settings. The role of a ranger is shaped by their bond with the natural world, their mastery of wilderness skills, and the balance they strike between civilization and the wild.

In some realms, rangers are celebrated as protectors of the land, revered for their abilities to track, hunt, and maintain harmony within nature. In others, they may be viewed as solitary figures or outcasts, navigating the margins of society.

Imagine a world where rangers are more than mere hunters. Some may belong to ancient orders dedicated to preserving the wild, while others could be independent explorers, setting out to discover uncharted lands or uncover hidden secrets. During times of unrest, these resilient individuals can become crucial allies, using their expertise to lead others safely through treacherous terrain and to strike back against those who threaten nature's balance.

Arcana
- DC 10: Competent rangers possess an assortment of skills related to survival, tracking, and combat. They are proficient with ranged weapons and often utilize spells that enhance their abilities or commune with nature, such as healing or animal friendship spells that align them with their environment.
- DC 20: Master rangers may command powerful spells that summon nature's fury or allow them to blend seamlessly into their surroundings. They might invoke the aid of animal companions, command elements of nature, or create protective wards, strengthening their connection to the wilderness and augmenting their combat effectiveness.

History
- DC 10: Throughout history, rangers have played a vital role in safeguarding realms from encroaching dangers, their stories entwined with tales of heroism and adventure. Their journeys often serve as moral allegories about respecting nature and the consequences of disrupting the delicate balance of the world.
- DC 15: The motivations of rangers can be diverse, ranging from a deep-seated respect for nature and a personal code of conduct to personal quests driven by vengeance or seeking justice. Understanding these motivations provides essential insight into their actions and relationships with allies and foes.

Bribery And Influence:
A ranger's willingness to engage in shady dealings or accept offers is influenced by various principles and practical considerations:
- Motivation: Their primary drives, such as the desire to protect the wild, seek retribution for wrongdoings, or gain knowledge of the world
- Compensation: The rare resources, magical items, or alliances offered in exchange for their skills or expertise
- Consequences: The possible repercussions on their standing in the community and the natural world following their choices

Rangers

Armor Class: 16 (Hide Armor)
Hit Points: 75 (10d10+20)
Speed: 30ft.

STR: 14 (+2) **DEX:** 18 (+4) **CON:** 14 (+2) **INT:** 10 (+0) **WIS:** 16 (+3) **CHAR:** 10 (+0)

Saving Throws: Strength +5, Dexterity +8

Skills: Athletics +6, Stealth +8, Survival +7, Perception +7, Animal Handling +7
Senses: passive Perception 17
Languages: Common, Elvish, and one additional language of choice
Proficiency Bonus: +3
Challenge: 6 (2,300 xp)

Class Features

- Favored Enemy: The Ranger has experience tracking and hunting specific creatures, gaining advantage on Survival checks to track them and Intelligence checks to recall information about them.
- Natural Explorer: The Ranger excels in a specific terrain (such as forest or mountains), gaining bonuses on initiative rolls, and the ability to navigate and forage in that terrain without difficulty.
- Spellcasting: The Ranger is a spellcaster, using Wisdom as their spellcasting ability (spell save DC 15, +7 to hit with spell attacks).
    - 1st Level Spells (4 slots): Hunter's Mark, Goodberry
    - 2nd Level Spells (3 slots): Pass Without Trace, Barkskin
    - 3rd Level Spells (3 slots): Conjure Animals, Lightning Arrow

Actions

- Multi-attack: The Ranger can make two attacks with their weapon.
- Longbow: Ranged Weapon Attack: +8 to hit, range 150/600 ft., one target. Hit: 10 (1d8+4) piercing damage.
- Shortsword: Melee Weapon Attack: +6 to hit, reach 5 ft., one target. Hit: 7 (1d6+4) slashing damage.

Reactions

- Uncanny Dodge: When the Ranger is hit by an attack, they can use their reaction to halve the damage taken.

Lucian Galeheart

"Adventure beckons; I'm always ready to answer the call."

A dashing and suave ranger known for his charm and good looks, Lucian offers his services as a guide for free, driven solely by a thirst for adventure and exploration.

For the Insightful:

Possesses exceptional charisma and keen instincts, able to navigate both people and terrain effortlessly. His social skills make him a favored companion among villagers and travelers.

Description:

Lucian has striking features, with tousled dark hair, a chiseled jawline, and captivating brown eyes that sparkle with mischief. He dresses in functional fitted clothing, often blending style with practicality. His confident stride and warm smile attract attention wherever he goes. A born wanderer, Lucian's presence often inspires those around him to embrace the thrill of the unknown.

Wants & Needs:

- Wants: To experience the thrill of adventure and to discover hidden places in the wild; dreams of writing an adventurous memoir about his journeys.
- Needs: To balance his thirst for adventure with his desire for meaningful connections.

Secret or Obstacle:

Hides his fear of becoming too comfortable or settling down, often battling the inner conflict of wanting companionship while craving freedom.

Carrying (Total CP: 19):

- Elegant Sword (8 points): A finely forged blade with an ornate hilt, a symbol of his polished demeanor.
- Throwing Knives (4 points): Balanced and razor-sharp, perfect for quick and precise attacks.
- Traveler's Cloak (4 points): A sturdy yet stylish cloak that offers protection from the elements.
- Collection of Healing Elixirs (3 points): Small vials of restorative potions, useful for quick recovery in the wild.

Ranger Tactics

Rangers employ a combination of stealth, strategy, and survival skills to achieve their objectives. In combat, they often utilize hit-and-run tactics, striking from a distance before vanishing into the underbrush, using their knowledge of terrain to navigate and control engagements. They are adept at setting traps, using the environment to their advantage, and coordinating with animal companions to execute complex maneuvers. Beyond combat, their skills in navigation and tracking allow them to lead others through tough landscapes and uncover hidden paths, acting as scouts for their allies.

Ranger & Adventure Guide

Thalion Greenbark *"Nature speaks, and I listen."* 2

Brief: A skilled Elf archer and hunter, Thalion roams the forests protecting nature and its creatures, ensuring the balance between civilization and wilderness.
Vocation: Ranger & Protector of Nature
For the Insightful: Possesses exceptional marksmanship and an innate understanding of animal behavior.
Description: Thalion has long silver hair, piercing green eyes, and an elegant stature. He dresses in earth-toned leathers adorned with leaves, allowing him to blend seamlessly into nature. His calm demeanor reflects a deep connection to the wild, earning the trust of creatures and villagers alike.
Wants & Needs: Wants: To protect the natural world and maintain harmony; dreams of fostering a deeper understanding between villagers and forest dwellers.
- Needs: To inspire others to value and preserve the environment as much as he does.

Secret or Obstacle: Hides his disappointment with the lack of appreciation for wilderness; often feels isolated from those who do not see its value.
Carrying (Total CP: 20):
- Longbow (8 points): A beautifully crafted bow imbued with elven artistry, precise and powerful.
- Quiver of Arrows (4 points): A set of arrows fletched with feathers for swift and silent shots.
- Herbal Brooch (4 points): A charm made from enchanted herbs to ward off harm in the wild.
- Small Healing Potion (4 points): A vial of natural remedies to mend wounds and restore vitality.

Gavin Swiftfoot *"Speed and stealth are my greatest allies."* 3

Brief: A light-hearted Halfling ranger with a knack for stealth and speed, Gavin scouts for raiding parties and alerts his village to impending danger.
Vocation: Ranger & Scout
For the Athletic: Possesses heightened agility and reflexes, able to traverse difficult terrain with ease.
Description: Gavin has tousled brown hair, bright hazel eyes, and a cheerful demeanor. He wears light leathers that allow for ease of movement and carries a backpack filled with supplies. Despite his lighthearted nature, he is fiercely devoted to his duties and his people.
Wants & Needs: Wants: To keep his village safe while spreading laughter and camaraderie; dreams of forming a task force of scouts to improve security.
- Needs: To trust in his abilities and encourage others to work together.

Secret or Obstacle: Hides his struggles with self-doubt, often questioning whether he is truly the protector he believes himself to be.
Carrying (Total CP: 19):
- Shortbow (5 points): A compact and swift bow designed for quick and accurate shots.
- Quiver of Specialized Arrows (4 points): Arrows tailored for piercing or stunning specific targets.
- Stealthy Cloak (6 points): A dark, lightweight cloak that aids in concealment.
- Healing Rations (4 points): Dried herbs and tonics stored for quick rejuvenation during scouting missions.

Dorian Nightshade *"From the shadows, I shall strike."* 4

Brief: A brooding Human ranger who patrols the shadowy edges of the forest, Dorian specializes in tracking rogue creatures and dangerous beasts.
Vocation: Ranger & Beast Hunter
For the Perceptive: Possesses remarkable tracking skills and a keen sense of direction in the dark wilderness.
Description: Dorian has raven-black hair, dark eyes that glimmer in the shadows, and a tall, lean build. He wears dark leather armor, blending into the night as he stalks through the woods. His serious demeanor and sharp gaze exude an air of mystery and determination.
Wants & Needs: Wants: To rid the forest of dangerous creatures that threaten the village; dreams of finding and uniting the scattered ranger forces of the region.
- Needs: To confront his inner demons and overcome the regrets of his past.

Secret or Obstacle: Hides his past mistakes in hunting, often blame-ridden and haunted by regrets despite his skills.
Carrying (Total CP: 20):
- Darkwood Bow (9 points): A sleek bow made from rare enchanted wood, ideal for precision strikes.
- Night Vision Glasses (4 points): A pair of enchanted lenses to see clearly in total darkness.
- Hunting Daggers (4 points): Razor-sharp blades designed for close combat with wild beasts.
- Healing Salve (3 points): A potent blend of herbs to treat injuries sustained in the field.

Finnian Riversong
"Let the rivers guide our paths." **5**

Brief: A charismatic Half-Elf ranger with a love for the waterways, Finnian guides travelers through rivers and lakes while safeguarding the aquatic creatures.
Vocation: Ranger & Aquatic Guardian
For the Perceptive: Possesses expert knowledge of river currents and aquatic ecosystems, often calming dangers with his skills.
Description: Finnian has tousled sandy hair, bright blue eyes, and an agile build. He wears light clothing suitable for water travel, adorned with symbols of water. His upbeat personality captivates companions.
Wants & Needs: Wants: To ensure clean rivers and lakes; dreams of establishing a guardian group dedicated to protecting aquatic life.
- Needs: To overcome his lingering doubts about his ability to protect those he guides.

Secret or Obstacle: Hides his vulnerability regarding losing a close friend to an accident in the river, continuously feels the weight of that loss.
Carrying (Total CP: 19):
- Canoe Paddle (5 points): A sleek paddle carved with aquatic motifs, light but sturdy.
- Sling and Stones (6 points): A reliable weapon for quick, ranged defense.
- Driftwood Staff (5 points): A sturdy staff made from enchanted driftwood, resonating with water magic.
- Minor Healing Ointment (3 points): A soothing balm made from river herbs for treating minor wounds.

Ronan Stormwatcher
"Let the storm rise; I will meet it with fire." **6**

Brief: A Fire Genasi and a fierce defender of the coastal villages, Ronan uses his elemental powers to protect the land from sea invaders and dangerous storms.
Vocation: Ranger & Elemental Guardian
For the Perceptive: Possesses powerful elemental abilities, harnessing flames to defend and protect against threats.
Description: Ronan has fiery hair that dances like flames, amber eyes that reflect his fierce spirit, and a strong athletic build. He dons a flame-patterned cloak and minimal combat gear.
Wants & Needs: Wants: To protect his coastal homeland and the villagers; dreams of becoming a fabled elemental guardian whose tales are sung.
- Needs: To learn to channel his powers effectively during tense situations.

Secret or Obstacle: Hides his struggle with controlling his fire abilities during emotional moments, fearing that it may one day cause harm.
Carrying (Total CP: 20):
- Flame-imbued Staff (10 points): A staff that glows with fiery runes, capable of conjuring controlled flames.
- Light Armor (6 points): Flame-resistant attire that allows ease of movement.
- Essence of Fire (2 points): A magical vial that enhances his elemental powers when consumed.
- Minor Healing Potion (2 points): A restorative potion to mend light injuries.

Kethan Wildgrove
"Nature unifies us; let us respect her balance." **7**

Brief: A wise Elf ranger who acts as a mediator between the natural world and the villagers, often negotiating for resources and understanding.
Vocation: Ranger & Environmental Mediator
For the Insightful: Possesses an intricate understanding of flora and fauna, able to live harmoniously while educating others on nature's values.
Description: Kethan has long chestnut hair, deep green eyes, and an elegant tattoo running down his arm. He wears clothing made from natural fibers that help him blend into the forest.
Wants & Needs: Wants: To foster a love for nature among villagers; dreams of creating a cooperative garden that sustains both!
- Needs: To balance his relationships between villagers and the wild creatures he protects.

Secret or Obstacle: Hides his internal conflict about whether he can bridge the gap between two worlds, often feeling an outsider in both.
Carrying (Total CP: 19):
- Longbow (8 points): A finely crafted bow etched with symbols of growth and renewal.
- Quiver of Special Arrows (5 points): Arrows designed with herbal infusions for non-lethal shots.
- Herbalist's Kit (4 points): A compact collection of tools for preparing salves and remedies.
- Healing Salve (2 points): A quick-acting balm for injuries sustained in the wild.

Brom Riverwatch
"A river's strength lies in its flow." **8**

Brief: A determined Dwarf ranger who behaves as the village sentinel, ensuring the local rivers remain pristine and safe.
Vocation: Waterway Ranger & Guardian
For the Perceptive: Possesses keen observation skills, often spotting dangers lurking in the waters or along the banks.
Description: Brom is stout with a thick beard, short hair, and bright blue eyes. He wears practical clothing suited for both water exploration and forest stealth.
Wants & Needs: Wants: To protect the waterways and educate villagers about their importance; dreams of inspiring youth to become stewards of nature.
- Needs: To forgive himself for past mistakes and trust his instincts when making decisions.

Secret or Obstacle: Hides his guilt from past environmental mistakes when he overfished, believing he failed in his responsibility to the river.
Carrying (Total CP: 20):
- Fishing Rod (5 points): A sturdy rod designed for both sustenance and survival.
- Sword (5 points): A reliable blade crafted to handle both river beasts and forest dangers.
- Small Net (6 points): A versatile net used for capturing fish or small game.
- Healing Potions (4 points): Handy elixirs brewed from local river herbs.

Tobias Starroot
"Each trail tells a story; let me help you hear it." **9**

Brief: A charismatic Half-Elf ranger and guide, Tobias leads travelers through the wilderness, sharing stories of the land along the way.
Vocation: Ranger & Guide
For the Perceptive: Possesses strong wilderness navigation skills, helping those unfamiliar with the terrain find safe paths.
Description: Tobias has curly blond hair, bright green eyes, and a boyish grin. He dresses in lightweight clothing suitable for travel and is decorated with nature-themed patches.
Wants & Needs: Wants: To share knowledge about the land and foster appreciation for the outdoors; dreams of one day charting lost trails and creating a guidebook.
- Needs: To overcome his fear of getting lost and strengthen his confidence when leading larger groups.

Secret or Obstacle: Hides his fear of the wilderness because of an early childhood experience, feeling insecure when leading larger groups.
Carrying (Total CP: 19):
- Map of Local Trails (6 points): Hand-drawn maps marked with safe paths and landmarks.
- Short Bow (5 points): A lightweight bow, perfect for a traveling ranger.
- Traveler's Pack (6 points): A durable pack containing essentials for long journeys.
- Healing Balm (3 points): A soothing salve for minor wounds, made from wild herbs.

Rico Stonewalker
"To guard is to care; to care is to protect." **10**

Brief: A dedicated Human ranger who watches over the transitions between village and wild, often seen with his trusty hound.
Vocation: Ranger & Animal Protector
For the Insightful: Possesses great strength and loyalty, ensuring the safety of his home and the people living within it.
Description: Rico is tall and burly with a tattooed arm, dark hair, and a serious expression. He wears rugged clothing suited for protection in the wild.
Wants & Needs: Wants: To ensure the safety of his village from wild creatures; dreams of starting a fellowship of animal guardians to protect the land.
- Needs: To find courage in confronting larger threats to the village while trusting his bond with nature.

Secret or Obstacle: Hides his fear of the dangers that may arise from wild animals; he often doubts whether he can maintain safety for the villagers.
Carrying (Total CP: 20):
- Well-loved Longbow (8 points): A bow that has seen many years of faithful use, etched with protective symbols.
- Leather Armor (6 points): Reinforced for defense without compromising agility.
- Tracking Collar for Dog (3 points): A leather collar with a carved emblem, symbolizing his bond with his hound.
- Healing Kit (3 points): A compact kit for treating injuries, stocked with herbs and bandages.

Rogues

The word Rogue conjures images of shadowy operatives, cunning strategists, and silver-tongued manipulators who dance between hero and scoundrel in fantasy realms. Rogues are masters of stealth, deception, and adaptability, slipping through society's cracks to seize opportunities others overlook. Celebrated as daring heroes in some tales and reviled as ruthless outlaws in others, their exploits inspire awe and fear alike.

Rogues are shaped by their worlds: from secretive guilds ruling urban underworlds to lone adventurers surviving through wits and guile. Some wield their talents as spies and saboteurs, shaping the fates of kingdoms with a stolen letter or whispered word. Others thrive as adventurers, bypassing traps, unlocking forbidden vaults, and outsmarting foes with ingenuity and charm.
Far from mere thieves, rogues often follow their own code—loyal to a crew, cause, or moral compass as sharp as their blades. In a realm of rigid laws and boundless magic, rogues are the wild cards, wielding clever audacity to tip the scales of fate and remind all that destiny can be rewritten in the shadows.

Arcana
- DC 10: Competent rogues possess a range of skills related to stealth, acrobatics, and cunning tactics. They often make use of tools for lockpicking and trap disarming, and they can be adept at using deception and persuasion to manipulate situations to their advantage.
- DC 20: Master rogues may attain powerful abilities that enhance their agility, allow them to blend into their surroundings, or execute devastating sneak attacks. Some may even dabble in magical artifacts or minor spells that complement their skills, such as illusions or enchantments that help them avoid detection.

History
- DC 10: Throughout history, rogues have often been pivotal figures in both legend and lore, their tales a mixture of morality, adventure, and intrigue. Their exploits might cover everything from daring escapes to clever schemes that led to significant political shifts or treasure discoveries.
- DC 15: The motivations of rogues can be as varied as their skills and backgrounds. Understanding their histories—whether driven by ambition, revenge, survival, or the thrill of the chase—provides valuable insight into their headspace and decisions.

Bribery And Influence:
A rogue's willingness to engage in deals or accept bribes is influenced by a complex web of ethical considerations and individual motives:
- Motivation: Their primary drives, such as the pursuit of wealth, freedom, thrill, or revenge
- Compensation: The tangible rewards or resources offered in exchange for their services, skills, or discretion
- Allegiances: Loyalty to rogue guilds, crime syndicates, or personal codes of conduct
- Opportunity: The potential for lucrative ventures or advantageous partnerships that align with their goals
- Punishments: Potential repercussions for dishonoring contracts, betraying allies, or failing to uphold the code of their guild or community

Rogues

Armor Class: 15 (Leather Armor)
Hit Points: 50 (8d8+8)
Speed: 30ft.

STR: 10 (+0) **DEX:** 18 (+4) **CON:** 14 (+2) **INT:** 12 (+1) **WIS:** 10 (+0) **CHAR:** 14 (+2)

Saving Throws: Dexterity +8, Intelligence +5

Skills: Acrobatics +8, Stealth +8, Investigation +5, Deception +6, Sleight of Hand +8
Senses: passive Perception 14
Languages: Common and two additional languages of choice
Proficiency Bonus: +3
Challenge: 5 (1,800 xp)

Class Features
- Sneak Attack (3d6): Once per turn, the Rogue deals an extra 3d6 damage to a target if they have advantage on the attack roll or if another enemy of the target is within 5 feet of it and isn't incapacitated.
- Thieves' Cant: The Rogue can communicate in a secret mix of dialects and symbols understood by other rogues.
- Cunning Action: The Rogue can use their bonus action to take the Dash, Disengage, or Hide action.
- Uncanny Dodge: When an attacker that the Rogue can see hits them with an attack, they can use their reaction to halve the damage.

Actions
- Multi-attack: The Rogue can make one attack with a weapon and use their Sneak Attack feature if conditions are met.
- Rapier: Melee Weapon Attack: +8 to hit, reach 5 ft., one target. Hit: 9 (1d8+4) piercing damage, plus 3d6 Sneak Attack damage if applicable.
- Shortbow: Ranged Weapon Attack: +8 to hit, range 80/320 ft., one target. Hit: 8 (1d6+4) piercing damage, plus 3d6 Sneak Attack damage if applicable.

Reactions
- Evasion: When subjected to an effect that allows a Dexterity saving throw, the Rogue takes no damage on a successful save, and only half damage on a failed save.

Jasper "Jet" Blackmoor — *"Every treasure has a story."* 1

A notoriously dashing, suave, and charming scoundrel known for his exquisite taste in expensive items; Jasper pulls off heists for fun rather than need.

For the Insightful:
Possesses keen negotiation skills, allowing him to talk his way through most situations while pulling off daring escapes.

Description:
Jasper has striking features, with tousled dark hair, a chiseled bearded jawline, and captivating brown eyes that sparkle with mischief. He dresses in fine armor that allows him to mix among the wealthiest, often hiding tools within the seams of his clothes.

Wants & Needs:
- **Wants:** To enjoy life's luxuries without the burden of responsibility; dreams of pulling off the biggest heist the city has ever seen.
- **Needs:** To find purpose in his actions and balance his thirst for thrills with a deeper sense of fulfillment.

Secret or Obstacle:
Hides his fear of being bored with life's offerings, struggling to find excitement without risking everything.

Carrying (Total CP: 19):
- **Fine Dagger (6 points):** A sleek, polished blade with an ornate hilt, perfect for swift, silent strikes.
- **Revitalizing Elixir (4 points):** A sparkling drink said to restore energy and confidence in moments of need.
- **Collection of Elegant Masks (5 points):** Disguises crafted with artistry, ideal for blending into high-society gatherings.
- **Minor Healing Potion (4 points):** A quick remedy for injuries, carried discreetly in a small crystal vial.

Rogue Tactics
Rogues employ a clever mix of subterfuge, agility, and strategic thinking to achieve their aims. In combat, they excel at hit-and-run tactics, striking swiftly from the shadows to incapacitate foes before retreating back into cover. Their expertise allows them to exploit vulnerabilities in their opponents, often striking where it hurts most. Outside of combat, their skills in stealth and deception allow them to gather intelligence, pick locks, and forge documents, making them invaluable for information gathering and planning heists or escapes.

Rogue & Scoundrel

Kellan Shadowstep   *"Fortune favors the bold; darkness is my friend."* 2

Brief: A Half-Elf master thief known for his daring exploits and charm, Kellan thrives in the shadows, pulling off impossible heists with wit and skill.
Vocation: Master Thief
For the Athletic: Possesses exceptional agility and stealth, allowing him to navigate locked doors and guarded areas with ease.
Description: Kellan has tousled brown hair, captivating green eyes, and an easy smile that disarms even the most suspicious onlookers. He wears dark leather clothing adorned with hidden pockets for tools and treasures. Beneath his calm demeanor lies a longing for recognition as a legend among thieves.
Wants and Needs:
- Wants: To gather treasures and stories from his escapades; dreams of becoming a legend whose exploits are sung by bards.
- Needs: To maintain his network of allies and connections for a steady stream of heist opportunities.

Secret or Obstacle: Hides a fear of getting caught during a heist, which could lead to dangerous enemies and ruin his reputation.
Carrying (Total CP: 20):
- Set of Lockpicks (6 points): A finely crafted toolkit capable of opening even the most intricate locks.
- Dagger of Silence (8 points): A sleek blade that strikes without a whisper, leaving no trace of its wielder.
- Cloak of Shadows (5 points): An enchanted mantle that melts the wearer into the surrounding darkness.
- Minor Healing Potion (1 point): A quick draught to close wounds in the heat of danger.

Dorian "The Viper" Arkwright   *"Life is fleeting; make the most of every strike."* 3

Brief: A cold and calculating assassin, Dorian eliminates targets with precision and efficiency, making him a sought-after killer for hire.
Vocation: Assassin & Contract Killer
For the Insightful: Possesses a sharp intellect and unparalleled cunning to devise foolproof assassination plans.
Description:
Dorian has short black hair, piercing gray eyes, and a wiry build that exudes silent lethality. His form-fitting dark attire is adorned with subtle weaponry, enabling swift and silent kills. Haunted by the lives he's taken, he struggles with the moral weight of his actions.
Wants and Needs:
- Wants: To secure his position as the top assassin in the city; dreams of leaving the life of murder behind for simplicity.
- Needs: To suppress the guilt and doubts that accompany his profession, which could otherwise cloud his judgment.

Secret or Obstacle: Hides his guilt over the lives he has taken, battling inner demons about the morality of his actions.
Carrying (Total CP: 20):
- Twin Daggers (8 points): Razor-sharp blades honed to slice through armor and flesh with deadly precision.
- Poison Vials (4 points): A collection of deadly toxins brewed for swift, silent kills.
- Silent Step Boots (5 points): Lightweight, enchanted footwear that muffles every footfall.
- Minor Healing Potion (3 points): A restorative liquid to ease pain and heal wounds quickly.

Sylra Nightveil   *"When the truth is a coin, I'll always pick the side that shines."* 4

Brief: A cunning and charismatic rogue, using lies and charm to manipulate and pull off daring cons with masterful precision.
Vocation: Deceptive Con Artist
For the Perceptive: Possesses extraordinary persuasive skills, allowing her to navigate dangerous situations with ease.
Description: Sylra has sleek black hair, glowing violet eyes, and an enigmatic aura that captivates her targets. She dresses in flamboyant attire, adorned with jewelry that serves as tools for deception. Beneath her polished exterior lies a fear of becoming ensnared in the very webs she spins.
Wants and Needs:
- Wants: To gather wealth and influence, dreams of running an underground network that pulls the strings of the elite.
- Needs: To build trust among her allies to execute her schemes while evading suspicion.

Secret or Obstacle: Hides a fear of getting too deeply involved in dangerous games, worrying that her schemes may one day catch up to her.
Carrying (Total CP: 19):
- Set of Disguises (8 points): An assortment of costumes and accessories to transform her appearance at will.
- Dagger of Deception (6 points): A jeweled blade that distracts foes with its dazzling glow.
- Charm Bracelet (4 points): A magical adornment that subtly influences those she interacts with.
- Minor Healing Potion (1 point): A small yet potent elixir for patching up injuries mid-scheme.

Jax Thornspear *"Quick hands and a sharper mind; that's how we thrive."* 5

Brief: A nimble Halfling pickpocket renowned for his deft fingers and quick wit, Jax thrives in bustling markets, swiping valuables from unsuspecting bystanders.
Vocation: Pickpocket & Street Rogue
For the Perceptive: Possesses extraordinary dexterity, allowing him to slip unnoticed into crowded spaces and evade capture with ease.
Description: Jax has curly reddish-brown hair, sparkling blue eyes, and a mischievous grin that hints at his daring nature. His loose-fitting clothes, adorned with concealed pockets, allow him to move freely and keep his tools hidden. Despite his roguish tendencies, his upbeat personality often makes him unexpectedly charming.
Wants and Needs:
Wants to live a life of excitement and gather treasures; dreams of orchestrating a legendary heist that cements his name in infamy.
Secret or Obstacle: Fears the consequences of failure, constantly haunted by the possibility of imprisonment and disgrace.
Carrying (Total CP: 20):
- Set of Lockpicks (5 points): Sleek and worn tools, crafted for precision and silence.
- Slick Dagger (3 points): A finely balanced blade with a subtle curve for swift strikes.
- Coin Purse (8 points): Heavy with coins, jingling softly with every step.
- Healing Brew (4 points): A small vial of herbal tincture, known to mend wounds quickly.

Viktor Darkshade *"Knowledge is power; let me be the key."* 6

Brief: A cunning Human rogue who thrives in the shadows, Viktor is an expert at extracting secrets and information from the most dangerous territories.
Vocation: Spy & Information Broker
For the Perceptive: Exhibits unparalleled stealth and a keen insight into the motives of others, leveraging these skills to outmaneuver foes and gain the upper hand.
Description: Viktor's tousled dark hair and piercing blue eyes give him an air of quiet intensity, while his lean frame moves with calculated grace. His dark, nondescript clothing helps him blend seamlessly into the shadows, allowing him to vanish from sight when needed. Beneath his calm exterior lies a mind constantly assessing every detail.
Wants and Needs: Wants to uncover secrets that could shift the balance of power; dreams of becoming the most revered spy among the elite.
Secret or Obstacle: Lives in fear of exposure, knowing that revealing his sources could cost him not only his life but also the lives of those he protects.
Carrying (Total CP: 20):
- Grappling Hook (5 points): A lightweight tool with reinforced rope, ideal for scaling walls.
- Collection of Disguises (5 points): An assortment of clothing and accessories to assume different identities.
- Lockpicking Tools (4 points): Compact yet reliable instruments for bypassing locks.
- Minor Healing Potion (6 points): A faintly glowing red liquid, warm to the touch and potent in effect.

Bramble Lightfoot *"Jest and laugh; beneath it all lies the art of deception."* 7

Brief: A charismatic Tabaxi street performer whose charm and agility are matched only by his skill in lifting valuables unnoticed.
Vocation: Rogue & Performer
For the Insightful: Possesses an innate ability to read people, discerning the perfect moment to switch from entertainer to thief.
Description: Bramble's patterned fur glimmers with subtle stripes under the sun, and his amber eyes twinkle with playful mischief. His colorful attire is adorned with dangling trinkets and charms, giving him the appearance of a jovial performer. Yet, beneath his cheerful demeanor lies a mind ever-calculating opportunities for profit.
Wants and Needs: Wants to craft an unforgettable legacy as a performer while amassing wealth; dreams of performing for audiences in distant, exotic lands.
Secret or Obstacle:
Struggles to balance his double life, fearing his reputation as a thief could overshadow his talents and lead to ruin.
Carrying (Total CP: 19):
- Juggling Balls (5 points): Weighted spheres imbued with faint glowing patterns, captivating onlookers.
- Set of Thieving Tools (5 points): Ingeniously designed instruments that fold neatly into his belt pouch.
- Fancy Dagger (4 points): A ceremonial blade with a jeweled hilt, both flashy and functional.
- Small Healing Potion (5 points): A delicately crafted vial, its liquid swirling with golden light.

Valen Shadowcaster   *"Magic and mischief dance together in the night."* 8

Brief: A darkly handsome Half-Orc rogue with skills in illusion magic, Valen uses tricks and illusions to distract and confuse his victims before taking what he wants.
Vocation: Rogue & Illusionist
For the Perceptive: Possesses both magical talent for deception and the physical skills necessary to execute daring thefts.
Description: Valen has an athletic build, deep green skin, and long black hair with striking features. He dresses in dark outfits with subtle magical insignia, enabling him to blend into the shadows. His commanding presence often masks a keen intellect and an unrelenting ambition to rise above his station.
Wants and Needs:
- Wants: To master his illusions while achieving fame in thievery.
- Needs: To pull off legendary heists that involve elaborate swindles.

Secret or Obstacle:
Hides his ambition from others, fearing they may see him as only a lowly thief rather than an ingenious artist.
Carrying (Total CP: 20):
- Set of Illusion Cards (8 points) - A deck enchanted to cast minor distractions and confusions.
- Dagger of Tricks (6 points) - A blade that emits a burst of magical smoke when drawn.
- Cloak of Shadows (4 points) - Allows the wearer to meld into dim light or darkness.
- Minor Healing Potion (2 points) - A vial of shimmering green liquid that mends minor wounds.

Kordel Steelshade   *"Shadows reveal the truth, if you dare to look."* 9

Brief: A surly male Dwarf rogue known for infiltrating criminal organizations, Kordel seeks justice for the wronged while dodging the very people he targets.
Vocation: Rogue & Vigilante
For the Perceptive: Possesses comprehensive knowledge of the criminal underworld, using it to navigate and dismantle illicit operations.
Description: Kordel has a thick, braided beard, fierce blue eyes, and a stocky frame. He wears rugged leather armor that reflects his tough lifestyle, often covered with a hood. Despite his gruff demeanor, his resolve to rid his homeland of corruption is unwavering, making him a force to be reckoned with.
Wants and Needs:
- Wants: To rid his homeland of unscrupulous crime.
- Needs: To unite the rogue factions against the true evildoers in power.

Secret or Obstacle:
Hides a past of criminal ties that still haunt him, dealing with occasional repercussions for previous misdeeds.
Carrying (Total CP: 19):
- Short Bow (5 points) - A compact and silent weapon favored for quick engagements.
- Set of Thieving Tools (7 points) - A kit of lockpicks and pry bars crafted for precision.
- Heavy Dagger (4 points) - A robust blade with a serrated edge for maximum damage.
- Healing Draught (3 points) - A strong herbal concoction that restores vitality.

Celestia Duskveil   *"Charm is the veil behind which shadows linger."* 10

Brief: A beautiful and enigmatic Tiefling rogue, excels at charming her targets before making her move to steal their belongings.
Vocation: Rogue & Enchantress
For the Insightful: Possesses sharp instincts for reading emotions, often using her wit and beauty to delight her victims before stealing from them.
Description: Celestia has deep red skin, alluring green eyes, and luxurious black hair. She wears elegant dresses adorned with subtle enchantments for allure and stealth. Her beguiling presence often leaves those she encounters spellbound, concealing a cunning mind always calculating her next move.
Wants and Needs:
- Wants: To master the art of persuasion while amassing wealth and influence.
- Needs: To unearth long-forgotten powerful treasures.

Secret or Obstacle: Hides her loneliness underneath her charm, feeling a lack of true connections beneath the mask she wears.
Carrying (Total CP: 20):
- Enchanted Dagger (9 points) - A beautifully engraved blade that hums with latent magic.
- Con Artist's Toolkit (6 points) - A collection of forged documents and disguises.
- Cloak of Enchantment (3 points) - Renders the wearer harder to notice in a crowd.
- Minor Healing Potion (2 points) - A bright red elixir that heals minor injuries.

Scouts

Scouts are the agile eyes of the wilderness, serving as vital guides and informants for adventurers and military forces alike. Masters of stealth, tracking, and navigation, they traverse treacherous terrains and interpret the signs of the wild with unmatched skill. Whether patrolling forests, mountains, or plains, scouts gather crucial intelligence, scouting ahead to assess threats, locate resources, and chart safe paths. With keen instincts and versatile abilities, they bridge the gap between civilization and the untamed, ever-ready for unexpected encounters. Yet adventurers should be wary, for not all scouts operate with noble intentions. A cautionary tale speaks of Fenwick, a once-renowned scout whose talents were unmatched.

Enamored by whispers of ancient artifacts hidden in treacherous ruins, Fenwick's ambition led him to consort with unsavory figures promising wealth and influence.

One day, he discovered a ruin deep in a cursed forest, its treasures protected by arcane traps and fierce guardians. Instead of reporting his find, Fenwick plotted to claim the artifacts for himself. Spinning tales of grandeur, he recruited adventurers to help, intending to exploit their skills while keeping the spoils.

As they delved into the ruins, the party realized too late that Fenwick's knowledge was flawed. He had failed to warn of the warding spells and deadly guardians. When the wards were triggered, destructive magic erupted, scattering the group and leaving them vulnerable to traps and monstrous foes. Amid the chaos, Fenwick vanished, abandoning the adventurers to their fate.

This tale reminds adventurers that while scouts often provide invaluable guidance, trust must be earned. The wrong tracker can lead to treachery and disaster. As you traverse the wilds, trust your instincts and remain cautious —what seems like a helpful guide may lead you straight into peril.

Kael Thornstep

"The wild whispers; I carry its message." 1

Brief: A skilled and dependable scout, Kael is known for his ability to navigate treacherous terrains and interpret the language of the wild. His sharp instincts and quick thinking make him a trusted guide and ally in dangerous lands.

Vocation: Scout & Wilderness Navigator

For the Insightful: Possesses an extraordinary talent to track creatures, locate hidden paths, and sense danger.

Description: Kael is lean and athletic, with a sun-weathered complexion and keen green eyes that seem to catch every detail. His short, unkempt auburn hair and confident stance give him a rugged yet approachable aura. Kael wears muted forest-toned clothing, blending seamlessly with his surroundings, and his quiet demeanor exudes a sense of calm reliability.

Wants and Needs:
- Want: To chart unexplored regions and leave behind detailed maps that ensure the safety of future travelers.
- Need: To overcome his lingering doubts about his abilities after a past mission that ended in disaster.

Secret or Obstacle: Hides the guilt of losing a former scouting party due to his own miscalculated judgment, which still haunts him during quiet moments.

Carrying (Total CP: 16):
- Well-worn Compass (5 points): A battered but reliable tool that has guided him through countless adventures.
- Sturdy Shortbow (7 points): A lightweight weapon with engravings of the trees he holds dear.
- Healing Herbs (4 points): A small pouch of medicinal plants he gathers along his travels.

Erynn Silverwind
"Every breeze carries a warning; I listen to them all." **2**

Brief: A swift and resourceful scout, Erynn is renowned for her ability to move silently and read the winds for subtle changes in weather and danger. Her knowledge of the skies makes her an asset in both navigation and survival.
Vocation: Scout & Sky-Watcher
For the Insightful: Excels in interpreting wind patterns and weather shifts, providing early warnings of storms or natural disasters.
Description: Erynn is a lithe Elf with silvery hair that cascades like a flowing stream and piercing blue eyes that seem to see beyond the horizon. Her movements are fluid and graceful, often compared to the gentle breeze she so carefully studies. She dresses in light, airy garments of pale blues and grays that reflect her bond with the skies, and her soft voice belies her fierce determination to protect those under her watch.
Wants and Needs:
- Want: To discover a long-lost valley said to hold the secrets of controlling weather.
- Need: To trust others more deeply, as her independence often isolates her.

Secret or Obstacle: Carries the burden of her clan's expectations to unlock and preserve ancient Elven weather magic.
Carrying (Total CP: 20):
- Windreader's Pendant (6 points): A magical charm that hums when danger approaches.
- Lightweight Cloak (4 points): Woven with enchanted thread to keep her warm in storms.
- Traveler's Notebook (5 points): Filled with notes on weather signs and personal sketches.
- Skyroot Bow (5 points): A flexible bow carved from wood said to bend with the wind.

Thorne Raventrail
"A shadow moves unseen; a shadow strikes unmissed." **3**

Brief: A cunning and shadowy scout, Thorne specializes in nighttime operations, slipping through enemy lines and relaying critical intelligence with precision.
Vocation: Scout & Night Prowler
For the Insightful: Has exceptional vision in low light and can blend into shadows so effectively he seems to vanish.
Description: Thorne is a wiry Human with raven-black hair, pale skin, and sharp gray eyes that gleam in the moonlight. He wears dark leather armor that muffles sound and is adorned with subtle patches of charcoal gray. His quiet demeanor is often mistaken for aloofness, but his every action is deliberate and calculated. Haunted by a betrayal in his past, Thorne's loyalty is hard-earned but unshakable.
Wants and Needs:
- Want: To infiltrate the ranks of a powerful enemy and dismantle them from within.
- Need: To forgive himself for failing to prevent a comrade's capture during a mission.

Secret or Obstacle: Fears his reliance on shadows and subterfuge might erode his sense of honor.
Carrying (Total CP: 20):
- Shadowglass Dagger (8 points): A blade forged to reflect no light, perfect for silent strikes.
- Nightveil Cloak (6 points): Enchanted to mask his presence in darkness.
- Signal Whistle (2 points): Emits a barely audible tone heard only by his allies.
- Tracking Powder (4 points): A fine dust used to mark trails that glow faintly in the dark.

Lyra Dawnstride
"First light brings new paths; I find them all." **4**

Brief: A hopeful and energetic scout, Lyra thrives in the open plains, using her speed and optimism to guide others to safety.
Vocation: Scout & Pathfinder
For the Insightful: Possesses an unerring sense of direction, even in unfamiliar territory, always finding the quickest route.
Description: Lyra is a Half-Elf with golden hair that shines like the rising sun and warm hazel eyes full of curiosity. She wears light traveling clothes with a distinct pattern of rolling hills, always ready to dart across the terrain. Her boundless enthusiasm masks a deep fear of losing those she cares about, driving her to push beyond her limits.
Wants and Needs:
- Want: To map every inch of the plains and uncover ancient routes used by her ancestors.
- Need: To confront her fear of failure, stemming from a childhood accident where she got lost.

Secret or Obstacle: Keeps a hidden journal of regrets, chronicling every mistake she has made as a scout.
Carrying (Total CP: 20):
- Sunlit Compass (6 points): Shines softly, pointing toward the safest path.
- Grassweave Satchel (4 points): Durable and lightweight for carrying supplies.
- Plainswalker's Shoes (6 points): Designed to move swiftly across uneven ground.
- Herb Kit (4 points): A bundle of healing plants collected during her travels.

Jory Flintfoot
"Every stone tells a story; I've walked them all." **5**

Brief: A grizzled veteran of mountain scouting, Jory has spent decades navigating treacherous cliffs and icy peaks, guiding others through danger.
Vocation: Scout & Mountain Guide
For the Insightful: Expert in identifying safe routes through hazardous mountain paths, often spotting danger before it strikes.
Description: Jory is a stocky Dwarf with a braided gray beard and piercing brown eyes. His sturdy frame is wrapped in thick, weatherproof garments lined with fur. His blunt manner often disguises his deep care for those he guides, and his laugh is as hearty as the echoes of the mountains he calls home.
Wants and Needs:
- Want: To retire peacefully in a hidden valley he has yet to find.
- Need: To pass his vast knowledge to a worthy apprentice before age catches up with him.

Secret or Obstacle: Haunted by the memory of a climbing party he couldn't save during an avalanche.
Carrying (Total CP: 20):
- Climber's Pick (7 points): A durable tool that doubles as a weapon.
- Farsight Goggles (5 points): Enhances vision for spotting distant trails.
- Heatstone (4 points): A magical stone that provides warmth during freezing nights.
- Emergency Rope (4 points): Woven from enchanted fibers for strength and lightness.

Tess Willowglade
"The forest whispers secrets; I am its voice." **6**

Brief: A tranquil and intuitive scout, Tess specializes in forested regions, navigating dense woods and uncovering hidden dangers with an almost supernatural connection to nature.
Vocation: Scout & Forest Seer
For the Insightful: Has an uncanny ability to communicate with forest creatures, often gaining their guidance or warnings.
Description: Tess is a serene Human with soft brown hair adorned with small braids and mossy-green eyes that seem to glow faintly in the shade. She wears forest-hued leather armor, decorated with leaves and vines, blending seamlessly with her surroundings. Her calm demeanor and quiet wisdom make her a trusted guide, though she keeps a personal sadness hidden behind her peaceful exterior.
Wants and Needs:
- Want: To safeguard an ancient forest said to hold magical relics.
- Need: To reconcile her isolationist tendencies and accept help from others.

Secret or Obstacle: Struggles with guilt over an irreversible decision that led to a forest clearing being destroyed.
Carrying (Total CP: 20):
- Whisperwood Staff (7 points): A slender staff attuned to the sounds of the forest.
- Camouflaging Cloak (6 points): Changes its shades to match the surrounding foliage.
- Herbal Pouch (3 points): Contains rare forest remedies and poisons.
- Tracker's Knife (4 points): A versatile blade crafted for carving, cutting, and self-defense.

Rowan Emberwatch
"Through fire and ash, I'll lead the way." **7**

Brief: A daring scout with a flair for danger, Rowan braves volcanic landscapes and scorched terrains, guiding adventurers through perilous environments others wouldn't dare approach.
Vocation: Scout & Ash Explorer
For the Insightful: Excels in reading seismic activity and locating safe paths through unstable ground.
Description: Rowan is a rugged Fire Genasi with fiery orange hair that flickers like embers and glowing red eyes. His ash-streaked clothing is reinforced against heat, and he moves with a confident stride, unfazed by the heat or fumes around him. Though he projects a tough exterior, Rowan harbors a deep compassion for the people he protects from the fire's wrath.
Wants and Needs:
- Want: To uncover a rumored forge hidden beneath a dormant volcano.
- Need: To prove he is more than his fiery origins, often misunderstood by those he aids.

Secret or Obstacle: Fears losing control of his elemental fire during moments of heightened emotion.
Carrying (Total CP: 20):
- Flameproof Boots (7 points): Enchanted to withstand molten surfaces.
- Smoke Compass (6 points): Functions even in dense volcanic haze.
- Cooling Flask (3 points): Keeps water chilled in extreme heat.
- Embercarved Blade (4 points): A weapon forged from volcanic rock, sharp and durable.

Silas Thornveil — "What's hidden will be found, no matter how deep the shadows." 8

Brief: A mysterious scout who thrives in caves and underground caverns, Silas is a master of navigating dark, treacherous depths to uncover secrets lost to time.
Vocation: Scout & Cave Explorer
For the Insightful: Exceptional at mapping underground networks and detecting unstable structures.
Description: Silas is a pale Half-Orc with gray-green skin, black hair tied into a knot, and eyes that shine faintly in the dark. His clothing is rugged and functional, with straps holding tools for climbing and excavation. Reserved and analytical, Silas speaks sparingly, preferring to let his actions guide the way. Despite his stoic demeanor, he is fiercely protective of his allies.
Wants and Needs:
- Want: To uncover a lost Dwarven kingdom rumored to lie beneath the earth.
- Need: To overcome his fear of narrow spaces, a remnant of a childhood accident.

Secret or Obstacle: Carries guilt over losing a friend during a cave collapse, which still haunts his every descent.
Carrying (Total CP: 20):
- Glowstone Lantern (6 points): Emits steady light in pitch-dark caves.
- Sturdy Rope (4 points): Essential for climbing and crossing chasms.
- Rock Chisel (5 points): Used for clearing pathways or extracting rare minerals.
- Cavewalker Boots (5 points): Designed to grip slippery or uneven surfaces.

Alina Froststep — "The cold reveals all; I walk where others freeze." 9

Brief: An unyielding scout of frozen landscapes, Alina is renowned for her ability to traverse icy terrain and endure brutal cold to bring back invaluable intelligence.
Vocation: Scout & Arctic Guide
For the Insightful: Can identify weak points in ice and snow, ensuring safe travel across frozen regions.
Description: Alina is a Human with frostbitten scars on her pale skin, silver hair tied in a tight braid, and steely blue eyes. She wears thick, fur-lined armor with layers of white and gray to blend into snowy backdrops. Her quiet, measured tone reflects her resilience, though she often hides her exhaustion to inspire confidence in her companions.
Wants and Needs:
- Want: To map an uncharted glacier said to hide an ancient temple.
- Need: To face her fear of avalanches, a danger that took her mentor's life.

Secret or Obstacle: Keeps her frostbitten hand hidden, ashamed of her vulnerability in the cold.
Carrying (Total CP: 20):
- Icepick Axe (7 points): Useful for climbing and defense.
- Snowshade Goggles (5 points): Protects against snow blindness.
- Warming Stone (4 points): Radiates gentle heat in freezing temperatures.
- Frozen Map Case (4 points): Keeps her charts and maps intact in icy conditions.

Milo Bramblethorn — "Small feet leave no trail; I'll lead you unseen." 10

Brief: A jovial scout who excels in weaving through thick brush and undergrowth, Milo is a trusted guide for those venturing into dense jungles and hidden paths.
Vocation: Scout & Jungle Tracker
For the Insightful: Skilled at identifying edible plants and hidden dangers in lush, overgrown areas.
Description: Milo is a cheerful Halfling with curly auburn hair, bright green eyes, and a sun-tanned complexion. His leather armor is adorned with leaves and feathers, blending into the jungle effortlessly. Though his lighthearted jokes bring levity to tense situations, Milo is deadly serious when it comes to ensuring the safety of his charges.
Wants and Needs:
- Want: To uncover a legendary golden flower said to cure any illness.
- Need: To overcome his self-doubt, stemming from being underestimated due to his size.

Secret or Obstacle: Keeps a hidden stash of rare jungle artifacts, which he feels guilty for taking without permission.
Carrying (Total CP: 20):
- Featherlight Net (6 points): For capturing small creatures or blocking paths.
- Jungle Machete (5 points): Used for clearing thick undergrowth.
- Beast Repellent (4 points): A pungent mixture that keeps predators at bay.
- Leafwoven Satchel (5 points): Holds survival tools and collected plants.

Shaman

Shamans are the spiritual guides and healers of a fantasy realm, acting as intermediaries between the physical world and the spirits of nature. Drawing upon ancient traditions, they harness the power of elements, earth, and ancestral spirits to provide guidance, healing, and protection. Often found in secluded groves, mountaintops, or tribal encampments, shamans possess a deep understanding of the natural world. They communicate with spirits through rituals, dance, and sacred objects, weaving magic into their practices for both spiritual enlightenment and physical healing.

However, adventurers should be cautious, as not all shamans use their spiritual connections for good.

A cautionary tale speaks of Grothak, a once-revered orc shaman known for his healing and wisdom. Over time, Grothak became obsessed with the power of ancient spirits and sought the aid of a dark entity promising immense strength in exchange for a terrible sacrifice.

In his desperation, Grothak lured villagers under the guise of offering healing, using their life force to satisfy the spirit's insatiable hunger. When a group of adventurers approached seeking aid, they unknowingly walked into his trap. Instead of guidance, they found themselves trapped in a ritual to drain their vitality, their strength fading with each passing moment.

As Grothak closed in to fulfill his pact, the adventurers fought back, disrupting the ritual and escaping into the wilderness. The malevolent spirit, furious at being denied, sought vengeance. Grothak, forever bound to the dark entity, became a twisted figure of power, shunned by the very people he once protected.

This chilling tale reminds adventurers that while shamans may appear benevolent, their connections to the spirit world can harbor malevolence. Crossing paths with the wrong shaman can lead to disastrous consequences. As you seek guidance from those who commune with spirits, tread carefully and remain vigilant —what seems like an innocent encounter may transform into a dark path, altering your fate forever.

Kaelu Windsong

"The spirits whisper, and I listen." [1]

Brief: A mysterious and wise shaman, Kaelu serves as a bridge between her people and the unseen forces of the natural world. She uses her abilities to heal the wounded, ward off evil, and uncover the truths hidden in the winds.

Vocation: Spiritweaver & Healer

For the Perceptive: Possesses an ability to sense spiritual energy, through shifts in nature and voices of ancestral spirits.

Description: Kaelu is an enigmatic figure with long, silver-streaked hair adorned with feathers and beads, her eyes glowing faintly with an otherworldly light. Her staff, gnarled and crowned with a cluster of glowing crystals, serves as both a conduit for her magic and a symbol of her spiritual authority. Often surrounded by an ethereal mist, Kaelu's presence inspires reverence and curiosity in equal measure.

Wants and Needs:
- Want: To guide her people toward harmony with nature and the spirits, preserving ancient traditions.
- Need: To confront the darker aspects of her power, learning to balance her connection to the spiritual realm.

Secret or Obstacle: Hides a growing fear of a dark spirit that has begun to shadow her dreams, threatening to corrupt her.

Carrying (Total CP: 20):
- Spiritbound Staff (8 points): A gnarled wooden staff with glowing crystals, humming faintly with magical energy.
- Dreamcatcher of Voices (6 points): A delicate web of thread and beads that captures whispers of ancestral spirits.
- Satchel of Sacred Herbs (4 points): A small pouch containing herbs for rituals, healing, and banishment spells.
- Vial of Moonlit Water (2 points): A rare elixir gathered under a full moon, said to enhance spiritual clarity.

Orin Duskthorn   *"The balance of life lies in the shadows of the unseen."* 2

Brief: A reclusive shaman who walks the fine line between light and dark, Orin wields the spirits of twilight to guide and protect his people, though his methods often evoke fear.
Vocation: Twilight Spiritcaller
For the Perceptive: Channels the duality of light and shadow to manipulate spiritual energies, often crafting protective wards and illusions.
Description: Orin is a wiry figure with ash-gray hair braided with animal bones and dark feathers. His piercing violet eyes seem to see into the soul, and his flowing black-and-indigo robes shimmer faintly like twilight. He carries a crescent-shaped blade adorned with glowing runes, and his skin is marked with intricate tattoos that shift in faint patterns when he performs rituals. Though quiet, Orin exudes an aura of power that demands respect.
Wants and Needs:
- Want: To protect his homeland by maintaining the delicate balance of spiritual energies.
- Need: To confront his fear of losing control over the darker spirits he calls upon.

Secret or Obstacle: Hides a tragic past where his rituals inadvertently caused harm, leaving him haunted by the memory of those he could not save.
Carrying (Total CP: 20):
- Crescent Blade of Twilight (8 points): A crescent-shaped weapon imbued with protective and shadow-manipulating runes.
- Warding Totem (6 points): A carved wooden idol that deflects harmful spirits.
- Ritual Ink (4 points): A vial of magical ink used to create protective tattoos or sigils.
- Pouch of Ashen Herbs (2 points): Sacred herbs that enhance his connection to the spirit realm.

Aela Stormveil   *"The winds carry the wisdom of the ages; listen closely."* 3

Brief: A wandering shaman who listens to the winds for guidance, Aela is known for her mastery of elemental air magic and her unerring intuition in times of crisis.
Vocation: Skyseer & Elementalist
For the Perceptive: Uses the currents of the wind to perceive distant events and foresee dangers, often whispering answers carried by unseen breezes.
Description: Aela is a striking woman with flowing white hair that seems to float as if caught in a perpetual breeze. Her sky-blue robes are lined with silver threads that shimmer like lightning, and her voice carries an airy, melodic quality. She wields a staff shaped like a lightning bolt and wears an amulet carved from stormglass, which glows faintly during her rituals. Her presence is serene yet electric, like the calm before a storm.
Wants and Needs:
- Want: To guide her people through the chaos of life by interpreting the will of the winds.
- Need: To overcome her fear of the destructive side of her powers, which could harm those she seeks to protect.

Secret or Obstacle: Hides the truth that a powerful storm spirit has marked her as its chosen conduit, binding her fate to its.
Carrying (Total CP: 20):
- Stormglass Staff (8 points): A staff crafted from crystalline shards that channel wind and lightning magic.
- Pendant of Whispering Winds (6 points): An amulet that amplifies her ability to hear distant voices and events.
- Satchel of Skyroot (4 points): Rare wood that aids in calming storms.
- Bottle of Lightning Essence (2 points): A volatile elixir containing pure storm energy.

Korruk Ironroot   *"The strength of the earth is in its roots—and its people."* 4

Brief: A stout and grounded shaman, drawing upon the resilience of the earth to protect his people and strengthen their spirits.
Vocation: Earthwarden & Protector
For the Perceptive: Commands the power of stones to shield allies and stop foes, his magic as unyielding as the mountains.
Description: Korruk is a towering half-orc with a braided beard streaked with clay and stone dust. His green-gray skin is etched with earthy symbols, and he wears armor adorned with moss and crystals. He carries a massive stone hammer engraved with runes, and his booming laughter resonates like an earthquake. Though gruff, his wisdom runs deep, and his protective nature earns him the trust of many.
Wants and Needs:
- Want: To preserve his people's traditions and protect their lands from encroaching forces.
- Need: To reconcile his connection to the destructive potential of the earth, learning restraint in his power.

Secret or Obstacle: Fears that his growing strength will one day shatter the balance he has worked so hard to maintain.
Carrying (Total CP: 20):
- Runestone Hammer (8 points): A massive stone hammer engraved with protective runes.
- Gem of Earthen Resonance (6 points): A crystal that allows him to communicate with the earth.
- Bag of Fertile Soil (4 points): Earth imbued with life-giving energy.
- Clay Jug of Mountain Water (2 points): A simple vessel containing water with restorative properties.

Kael Frostveil — *"The cold reveals truths hidden in the warmth of comfort."* 5

Brief: A stoic shaman who draws upon the power of frost, Kael uses ice to protect, preserve, and punish those who threaten the natural order.
Vocation: Frostcaller & Winter Guardian
For the Perceptive: Commands the icy winds and snow to create barriers, trap foes, and preserve life.
Description: Kael is a pale-skinned human with short white hair and icy blue eyes that seem to pierce through lies. He wears furs lined with frost, and his staff resembles a shard of jagged ice. His voice is cold and calculated, and his presence feels like a chill on a winter morning.
Wants and Needs:
- Want: To ensure the balance of the seasons remains unbroken.
- Need: To confront his fear of losing himself to the endless stillness of winter.

Secret or Obstacle: Carries the burden of an ancient frost spirit that tempts him toward destructive ends.
Carrying (Total CP: 38):
- Iceheart Staff (12 points): A staff imbued with the ability to summon snowstorms and protective frost barriers.
- Cloak of Endless Winter (10 points): A fur-lined cloak that keeps the wearer warm and enhances frost magic in harsh environments.
- Shard of Eternal Ice (8 points): A shimmering crystal that strengthens cold-based spells and traps.
- Flask of Glacial Essence (8 points): A frosty elixir that preserves vitality and slows aging.

Esryn Willowshade — *"The whispers of the trees hold endless wisdom."* 6

Brief: A gentle shaman who communes with the spirits of the forest, Esryn uses her magic to heal and nurture all living things.
Vocation: Forest Guardian & Lifebinder
For the Perceptive: Harnesses the energy of ancient trees to mend wounds and restore vitality.
Description: Esryn is a delicate half-elf with moss-green hair and soft hazel eyes. She wears robes adorned with leaves and vines, and her wooden staff is carved with intricate floral patterns. Her gentle demeanor radiates calm, and the faint scent of blossoms always surrounds her.
Wants and Needs:
- Want: To protect her forest home from exploitation.
- Need: To find the courage to leave her sanctuary when others need her help.

Secret or Obstacle: Feels an overwhelming guilt for failing to save a sacred grove that was destroyed.
Carrying (Total CP: 26):
- Lifebloom Staff (10 points): A gnarled staff that channels the healing energies of ancient trees.
- Amulet of Verdant Spirit (6 points): A charm that amplifies plant magic and protects against poison.
- Pouch of Enchanted Seeds (6 points): Seeds that sprout into barriers or healing plants when planted.
- Flask of Forest Dew (4 points): A rejuvenating drink that restores vitality and soothes ailments.

Darokk Bonebinder — *"The spirits of the fallen still have their purpose."* 7

Brief: A fearsome orc shaman who communes with ancestral spirits, Darokk channels their strength for protection and vengeance.
Vocation: Ancestral Guardian & Spirit Warrior
For the Perceptive: Summons ancestral spirits to shield allies and exact vengeance upon foes.
Description: Darokk is a towering orc with braided black hair and a necklace made of bones. His green skin is scarred with runic patterns, and his deep-set eyes burn with intensity. He carries a massive totem staff adorned with skulls and talismans, and his guttural chants seem to resonate with the very earth. Though intimidating, his loyalty to his tribe is unwavering.
Wants and Needs:
- Want: To avenge the fallen of his tribe and ensure their spirits find peace.
- Need: To confront the hatred that binds some spirits, preventing them from moving on.

Secret or Obstacle: Carries the spirit of a vengeful ancestor who sometimes takes control, threatening his will.
Carrying (Total CP: 45):
- Totem of Ancestral Wrath (15 points): A massive totem that summons vengeful ancestral spirits to fight alongside him.
- Spiritbind Necklace (12 points): A bone necklace that anchors powerful spirits to his call.
- Ash of the Fallen (10 points): Sacred ash used in rituals to empower spirits and provide protection.
- Jug of Spirit Mead (8 points): A ceremonial brew that strengthens spiritual bonds and grants clarity of vision.

Lyrien Starshadow
"The stars whisper truths to those who listen." **8**

Brief: A celestial shaman who draws power from the constellations, Lyrien guides her people with wisdom written in the stars.
Vocation: Celestial Seer & Dreamweaver
For the Perceptive: Reads the movements of the stars to foresee events and empower her magic with celestial energy.
Description: Lyrien is a tall and graceful elf with hair as dark as the night sky, speckled with silver strands that shimmer like starlight. Her robes are embroidered with constellations, and she carries a silver staff tipped with a glowing star-shaped crystal. Her voice has a melodic, ethereal quality, and her gaze carries the weight of timeless knowledge.
Wants and Needs:
- Want: To unite her people under the guidance of the stars.
- Need: To overcome her fear of misinterpreting celestial signs, leading her people astray.

Secret or Obstacle: Hides the knowledge of an ominous prophecy she discovered but is unsure how to prevent.
Carrying (Total CP: 32):
- Starcrystal Staff (12 points): A staff that channels celestial energy for spells and rituals.
- Tome of Starlore (10 points): A thick tome filled with ancient star charts and celestial prophecies.
- Moondust Vial (6 points): A shimmering dust that enhances ritual magic.
- Celestial Pendant (4 points): A silver necklace that heightens her connection to the stars.

Zephyra Windsong
"The wind carries whispers of the past and future alike." **9**

Brief: A free-spirited shaman who communes with the winds, Zephyra channels their boundless energy to guide, protect, and scatter her foes.
Vocation: Windcaller & Elemental Dancer
For the Perceptive: Harnesses the winds to disorient enemies, shield allies, and carry messages over great distances.
Description: Zephyra is a lithe human with wild, wind-tousled hair that shifts from silver to pale blue. Her flowing robes ripple as if caught in an unseen breeze, and her silver bracelets chime softly with every movement. Her energetic presence is infectious, though her piercing gray eyes suggest she sees far beyond the horizon.
Wants and Needs:
- Want: To ensure the winds of change bring prosperity to her people.
- Need: To overcome her reluctance to settle, fearing she might lose her freedom.

Secret or Obstacle: Hides the truth that a cursed storm she once unleashed wiped out a village, and she carries guilt for its aftermath.
Carrying (Total CP: 28):
- Galeheart Staff (10 points): A sleek staff that channels the winds into protective barriers and offensive gales.
- Windchime Amulet (8 points): A delicate charm that allows her to commune with elemental spirits of the air.
- Featherlight Cloak (6 points): A cloak that enhances her agility and allows her to leap great distances.
- Elixir of Soothing Breezes (4 points): A cooling potion that calms and heals those who drink it.

Mokru Stonehand
"The earth remembers what we forget." **10**

Brief: A steadfast shaman who draws strength from the earth, Mokru channels its resilience and wisdom to protect and heal.
Vocation: Earthkeeper & Tribal Protector
For the Perceptive: Commands the power of stone and soil to fortify allies, heal the wounded, and strike down threats.
Description: Mokru is a towering half-orc with skin the color of rich soil and hands as calloused as ancient stone. He wears a cloak adorned with beads and carvings that resemble mountains, and his thick staff is embedded with raw crystals. Though his demeanor is gruff, his deep brown eyes reveal a profound connection to the world beneath his feet.
Wants and Needs:
- Want: To restore sacred lands desecrated by invaders.
- Need: To let go of his anger toward those who harmed his homeland, lest it consume him.

Secret or Obstacle: Hides his fear that the spirits of the earth are beginning to fade, leaving him powerless to protect his tribe.
Carrying (Total CP: 36):
- Cragstaff (12 points): A heavy staff capable of summoning stone barriers and quakes.
- Earthstone Talisman (10 points): A pendant that enhances his connection to the land, amplifying his magic.
- Bag of Spirit Pebbles (8 points): A pouch of enchanted stones that create traps or explode on impact.
- Flask of Earthen Essence (6 points): A thick, muddy liquid that restores stamina and strengthens the drinker's resolve.

Smiths

Smiths are the master craftsmen of a fantasy realm, forging everything from weapons and armor to intricate tools and delicate jewelry. Found in bustling towns and remote villages, these artisans harness fire and metal to create their masterpieces, pouring sweat and creativity into their work. With a sharp eye for detail and dedication to their craft, Smiths are vital pillars of their communities, providing essential goods for adventurers, soldiers, and everyday folk. Their forges echo with clanging metal and the scent of smoke, breathing life into raw materials.

However, adventurers should approach certain Smiths with caution, as their eccentric personalities can lead to humorous outcomes. A popular tale tells of Braggart the Bold, a boisterous Smith known for grandiose claims about the magical powers of his creations. While celebrated for his craftsmanship, Braggart's outrageous stories often overshadowed his skill.

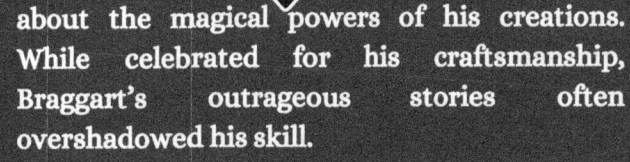

One day, a group of adventurers visited his forge to purchase weapons for an impending quest. Braggart enthusiastically pitched his latest creation—an ornate sword—boasting it could "slice through anything, even the fabric of reality!" Skeptical but amused, the adventurers purchased the sword, eager to test its supposed powers.

Their chance came when they encountered a stubborn vine blocking their path. Remembering the Smith's claims, they swung the sword, only for it to get hilariously stuck, sending the wielder tumbling into the dirt. The fine blade proved durable but lacked the miraculous powers Braggart had promised. The adventurers' laughter echoed through the woods as they recounted the tale back in town.

This lighthearted story reminds adventurers that while Smiths are skilled artisans, their exaggerated claims can spark unexpected hilarity. When seeking the perfect item for your quest, take a Smith's boasts with a grain of salt —and a good sense of humor. For what seems like a magical artifact might become the source of your next great (and amusing) misadventure!

Barik Ironflame
"The forge speaks to me, and I answer with steel." 1

Brief: A legendary smith with an eccentric flair, crafting weapons and armor that rival the quality of even the most renowned forges. Known for his fiery passion and quirky personality, his creations come with hidden, whimsical features.
Vocation: Master Blacksmith
For the Insightful: Possesses unparalleled expertise enabling him to imbue his creations with unique magical properties.
Description: Barik is a burly dwarf with a soot-streaked face, braided auburn hair, and piercing amber eyes that gleam like molten metal. His hands are rough from years of wielding hammers, yet his craftsmanship exudes precision and finesse. He has a knack for weaving humor into his creations, sometimes adding surprises like a sword that whistles when swung.
Wants and Needs:
- Want: To create a legendary masterpiece that will cement his name in history.
- Need: To reconcile with his estranged apprentice, whose betrayal haunts him.

Secret or Obstacle: Hides his fear of stagnation, dreading the idea that he may have already crafted his greatest work.
Carrying (Total CP: 43):
- Enchanted Hammer (12 points): A massive forge hammer imbued with runes of strength and precision.
- Heatproof Apron (8 points): A durable leather apron resistant to flames and magical sparks.
- Blueprint Collection (10 points): A portfolio of detailed designs for weapons, tools, and experimental constructs.
- Runic Tongs (6 points): Forged from rare metals, these tongs channel elemental energy for precision work.
- Flask of Forgefire (7 points): Container of magical flame that never extinguishes, used for igniting forges anywhere.

Thalina Emberforge
"The fire tests both steel and soul." **2**

Brief: A disciplined and thoughtful smith, Thalina creates armor and tools that blend practicality with artistic elegance, often sought after by both warriors and nobles.
Vocation: Armorer & Artisan
For the Insightful: Has the ability to infuse metals with protective enchantments, making her creations durable and magical.
Description: Thalina is a tall, muscular human with bronze-toned skin and dark hair tied back in a tight braid. Her piercing green eyes convey focus and determination. Always adorned with a utility belt of tools, she exudes an air of professionalism, rarely seen without soot on her hands. Her forge is tidy and well-organized, adorned with intricate wall carvings that reflect her ancestral traditions. Despite her disciplined exterior, Thalina has a soft spot for children, often crafting small trinkets for them in her spare time.
Wants and Needs:
- Want: To craft an impenetrable suit of armor that becomes the stuff of legends.
- Need: To balance her obsession with perfection and allow herself to make mistakes.

Secret or Obstacle: Hides a secret rivalry with her brother, a fellow smith, whose shadow she feels she can never escape.
Carrying (Total CP: 38):
- Runed Anvil Pendant (8 points): A miniature enchanted anvil she wears as a necklace for inspiration.
- Precision Hammer (17 points): A lightweight tool designed for detailed work on intricate armor designs.
- Toolkit of Miniature Engraving Tools (8 points): A set of fine instruments for carving detailed patterns and runes.
- Pouch of Rare Alloys (5 points): Small quantities of magical metals reserved for special commissions.

Grimdak Coalborn
"Steel doesn't lie—it reveals your worth." **3**

Brief: A gruff yet fiercely skilled smith, Grimdak specializes in forging brutal weapons for battle-hardened warriors, often adding fearsome flourishes to his work.
Vocation: Weapon Master
For the Perceptive: Known for his acute sense of balance and weight, Grimdak crafts weapons that feel like extensions of their wielders.
Description: Grimdak is a stout orc with charcoal-gray skin and a tangled mane of black hair streaked with ash. His tusks are chipped, and his hands are as calloused as the steel he works. Despite his gruff demeanor, he has a deep respect for warriors and often listens intently to their tales before crafting their weapons. His forge is a chaotic blend of raw materials and half-finished creations, reflecting his spontaneous and instinct-driven process.
Wants and Needs:
- Want: To forge a weapon powerful enough to be named a relic of war.
- Need: To overcome his temper, which often leads to destructive outbursts in the forge.

Secret or Obstacle: Hides guilt over a weapon he once forged that caused the death of an innocent.
Carrying (Total CP: 42):
- Skull-Emblazoned Warhammer (14 points): A fearsome hammer adorned with a carved handle depicting an ancient battle.
- Molten Forge Pendant (8 points): A talisman that keeps his forge's flames burning longer.
- Battle-Tested Apron (10 points): Sturdy leather armor reinforced with steel plates, useful in both the forge and combat.
- Twin Steel Tongs (10 points): Heavy-duty tools for shaping large, brutal weapons.

Liora Firespark
"Every spark tells a story." **4**

Brief: A vibrant and creative smith, Liora is renowned for her intricate jewelry and ceremonial weapons, coveted by all.
Vocation: Jewelcrafter & Enchanter
For the Insightful: Combines precious gems and metals, channeling latent magic to create beautiful yet powerful objects.
Description: Liora is a petite gnome with fiery red hair that glows faintly under the forge's light, her bright amber eyes constantly darting with curiosity. She moves with quick, precise gestures, her forge filled with an array of colorful gems and shimmering metals. A whimsical individual, Liora often hums old songs while she works, her pieces inspired by the stories of her clients. Despite her cheerful exterior, she is fiercely protective of her work and refuses to sell to those she deems unworthy.
Wants and Needs:
- Want: To craft a jeweled crown worthy of a queen.
- Need: To learn to let go of her creations and accept that they are no longer hers once sold.

Secret or Obstacle: Hides the fact that some of her gems are stolen, fearing that her past will catch up to her.
Carrying (Total CP: 31):
- Enchanted Gemsetter (10 points): A tool that channels magic into gemstones during crafting.
- Luminous Tiara (8 points): A radiant piece she created for inspiration, glowing faintly in the dark.
- Bag of Raw Crystals (7 points): A collection of uncut gems infused with latent energy.
- Miniature Forge Toolkit (6 points): A portable set of tools designed for precision work on delicate pieces.

Bram Ironhide
"Strength may win battles, but skill wins wars." **5**

Brief: An elder blacksmith revered for his battle-ready armor and weapons, Bram has dedicated his life to arming those who defend the innocent.
Vocation: Legendary Armorsmith
For the Insightful: Possesses unparalleled knowledge of ancient forging techniques, producing armor imbued with elemental resilience.
Description: Bram is a weathered dwarf with a silver beard braided with small steel rings, each one a mark of a masterpiece he has created. His forge, nestled deep within a mountain, glows with an otherworldly light from enchanted flames. Despite his gruff exterior, Bram carries a deep sense of duty, often working tirelessly to perfect his craft for those he deems worthy.
Wants and Needs:
- Want: To craft a suit of armor that can withstand any force in the world.
- Need: To mentor a successor who can carry on his legacy and ancient techniques.

Secret or Obstacle: Hides the secret that his forge is fueled by a cursed flame that could one day consume him if not controlled.
Carrying (Total CP: 44):
- Stormforged Gauntlet (12 points): A reinforced glove that channels lightning into strikes.
- Rune-Etched Smithing Hammer (10 points): A hammer that imbues protective runes into metal during forging.
- Fireproof Forge Cloak (8 points): A heavy, enchanted garment resistant to both heat and magical flames.
- Box of Ancient Templates (8 points): Detailed designs of forgotten armor styles.
- Flask of Forgebrew (6 points): A potent dwarven ale said to boost stamina during long hours at the forge.

Zara Goldflame
"A blade should be as sharp as its wielder's mind." **6**

Brief: An innovative smith specializing in lightweight, elegant weapons, Zara's creations are prized by adventurers who value speed and finesse.
Vocation: Bladesmith & Innovator
For the Perceptive: Masters the art of forging alloyed blades that are both lighter and stronger than traditional weapons.
Description: Zara is a tall, wiry half-elf with sun-kissed skin and bright, calculating eyes. She wears simple yet practical attire, adorned with a belt filled with crafting tools. Her forge is meticulously clean, reflecting her precise and methodical nature. Zara often tests her creations herself, wielding blades with a grace that rivals professional duelists.
Wants and Needs:
- Want: To craft a blade so sharp it can cut through magic itself.
- Need: To overcome her need for perfection, which often delays her work.

Secret or Obstacle: Fears her reliance on experimental techniques will one day fail her, tarnishing her reputation.
Carrying (Total CP: 39):
- Feathersteel Rapier (12 points): An ultra-light blade designed for speed and precision.
- Set of Precision Tongs (8 points): Tools crafted for holding delicate alloys during forging.
- Moltensteel Flask (7 points): A container of liquid metal that can be shaped on the go.
- Protective Smithing Visor (8 points): An enchanted mask that shields her eyes from magical sparks.
- Pouch of Alchemical Compounds (4 points): Special powders for enhancing the properties of her blades.

Orik Flintstrike
"Metal bends to my will, but I am no master of my own fate." **7**

Brief: A fiery-tempered smith known for forging brutal and unorthodox weapons, his creations are often as unpredictable as him.
Vocation: Experimental Weaponcrafter
For the Insightful: Excels in crafting unconventional weapons that blend creativity with devastating effectiveness.
Description: Orik is a burly orc with ash-gray skin and a prominent scar running down one arm from a forging accident. His forge is a chaotic mess of half-finished weapons, failed experiments, and scraps of metal. Despite his short temper, Orik has an infectious passion for his craft and thrives on creating one-of-a-kind designs that challenge conventional ideas of warfare.
Wants and Needs:
- Want: To craft a weapon capable of single-handedly turning the tide of a war.
- Need: To find balance in his chaotic life and avoid the destructive habits that jeopardize his work.

Secret or Obstacle: Hides his frustration over being dismissed by more traditional smiths, leading him to question his self-worth.
Carrying (Total CP: 41):
- Chainblade (12 points): A flexible weapon that can be used as a whip or a sword.
- Explosive Smithing Mallet (10 points): A hammer that releases bursts of kinetic energy on impact.
- Heatproof Gauntlets (8 points): Gloves that allow him to handle molten materials directly.
- Bag of Experimental Prototypes (7 points): Small-scale models of weapons he's testing.
- Flask of Cooling Elixir (4 points): A potion that rapidly cools hot metals or overheated skin.

Lira Emberforge — 8
"The fire whispers its secrets; I only listen."

Brief: A reclusive smith whose work incorporates intricate elemental designs, Lira crafts weapons and tools that channel the power of fire.

Vocation: Elemental Smith

For the Insightful: Possesses a rare ability to infuse her creations with elemental magic, drawing from the energy of natural flames.

Description: Lira is a petite fire genasi with glowing ember-like hair that seems to flicker with every movement. Her forge is carved into the side of a volcanic cliff, using natural magma as its heat source. Lira is quiet and reserved but deeply passionate about her craft, finding solace and inspiration in the crackling of fire.

Wants and Needs:
- Want: To create a weapon that can tame the wildest inferno.
- Need: To overcome her fear of losing control over the fire magic she wields.

Secret or Obstacle: Hides her past failure that resulted in a devastating fire, fearing her creations might one day cause harm again.

Carrying (Total CP: 37):
- Inferno Blade (12 points): A sword that ignites with flames when unsheathed.
- Embersteel Tongs (8 points): Tools enchanted to withstand extreme heat.
- Flame-etched Anvil (9 points): A portable anvil that channels fire magic into metal.
- Flask of Smoldering Ash (8 points): Ash that enhances the heat of any forge or spell.

Grint Ironmaul — 9
"A true smith shapes metal and minds alike."

Brief: A jovial smith known for his massive warhammers and hearty laugh, Grint is a beloved figure in his community, often serving as both craftsman and mentor.

Vocation: Master Hammerwright

For the Insightful: Excels in creating balanced, devastating hammers that can crush both armor and stone with ease.

Description: Grint is a towering human with a barrel chest, a broad grin, and arms like tree trunks. His forge, located in a bustling village square, is a hub of activity where apprentices gather to learn. Despite his intimidating stature, Grint is kind-hearted and patient, always eager to share his knowledge and stories with anyone willing to listen.

Wants and Needs:
- Want: To craft a hammer worthy of a king's champion.
- Need: To ensure his apprentices surpass his skill and carry his legacy forward.

Secret or Obstacle: Struggles with his health after years of heavy labor, though he hides it to avoid worrying his apprentices.

Carrying (Total CP: 42):
- Titan's Maul (15 points): A massive warhammer capable of shattering stone.
- Runed Forge Gloves (8 points): Gloves that enhance grip strength and reduce strain.
- Bag of Tempering Powders (10 points): Special compounds that toughen metals during forging.
- Portable Forge Kit (9 points): A compact, foldable forge he uses for field repairs.

Theda Steelweaver — 10
"Elegance is strength in disguise."

Brief: A refined smith specializing in intricate chainmail and jewelry, Theda's creations are as beautiful as they are functional.

Vocation: Chainmail Artisan

For the Perceptive: Possesses an unmatched ability to weave delicate yet unbreakable chainmail, blending artistry with protection.

Description: Theda is a slender elf with platinum hair tied into an elaborate braid, often adorned with her own delicate jewelry. Her forge is an immaculate studio filled with fine tools and shimmering threads of metal. Theda's demeanor is calm and composed, with an eye for beauty in all things, and she often takes on commissions for noble families.

Wants and Needs:
- Want: To create a masterpiece that will endure through the ages.
- Need: To earn the respect of her peers, who often dismiss her work as decorative rather than practical.

Secret or Obstacle: Hides her struggles to secure rare materials, sometimes resorting to deals with dubious merchants.

Carrying (Total CP: 39):
- Moonlight Chainmail (14 points): An exquisite set of chainmail that is both lightweight and nearly indestructible.
- Filigree Smithing Tools (9 points): Precision instruments for crafting fine details.
- Bag of Enchanted Links (10 points): Pre-forged chainmail links imbued with protective magic.
- Silver-threaded Apron (6 points): A garment that deflects sparks and light projectiles.

Sorcerers

A Sorcerer evokes images of innate magic, raw power, and a deep connection to the arcane in fantasy settings. Unlike wizards who study tomes or clerics who pray to divine entities, sorcerers embody magic itself, their abilities flowing from within as naturally as breathing. Their role is shaped by the source of their magic, whether a mysterious ancestral lineage, a cosmic event, or a rare twist of fate. Societal perceptions of sorcerers vary widely; in some realms, they are revered as powerful figures destined for greatness, while in others, they are feared or shunned for the unpredictability of their arcane gifts.

Imagine a world where sorcerers are more than mere magic users. Some claim bloodlines tied to ancient beings, channeling the power of dragons, fiends, or celestial entities. Others may have been touched by extraordinary circumstances—exposure to volatile ley lines, forgotten relics, or even divine intervention. These origins make every sorcerer unique, their magic deeply personal and often tied to their identity. During times of upheaval, sorcerers can be pivotal figures, reshaping battlefields, bending the tides of fate, or even challenging the very fabric of reality.

Arcana
- DC 10: Competent sorcerers harness a variety of spells derived from their magical lineage or innate abilities, including elemental magic, enchantments, and protective wards. They can tap into their magical reserves to cast spells on the fly, often improvising creatively to meet the challenges they face.
- DC 20: Master sorcerers may channel powerful magic that can bend reality itself, casting spells that summon creatures from other planes or unleash devastating bursts of energy. Their intimate knowledge of their own source of power allows them to manipulate it with precision and finesse, creating extraordinary feats of magic.

History
- DC 10: Throughout history, sorcerers have often played pivotal roles in shaping the destinies of empires and civilizations. Legendary sorcerers become the subjects of myths and folktales, their wondrous acts of magic inspiring awe and reverence or fear and caution.
- DC 15: The motivations of sorcerers can vary widely, from a quest for knowledge and mastery over their abilities, to personal quests for revenge against those who wronged them, or the desire to fulfill a destiny foretold by prophecy. Understanding these motivations clarifies their actions within the narrative.

Bribery And Influence:
A sorcerer's response to offers of favors or enticements is influenced by their unique perspectives and motivations:
- Motivation: Their primary drives, whether for power, knowledge, acceptance, or a sense of duty to their magical heritage
- Compensation: The artifacts, knowledge, or connections promised in exchange for their assistance or allegiance
- Consequences: The possible ramifications of their choices within society, especially penalties for using their powers unwisely or engaging in actions that violate the norms established for sorcerers

Sorcerers

Armor Class: 12 (Mage Armor)
Hit Points: 40 (8d6+8)
Speed: 30ft.

STR: 8 (-1) **DEX:** 14 (+2) **CON:** 14 (+2) **INT:** 10 (+0) **WIS:** 12 (+1) **CHAR:** 18 (+4)

Saving Throws: Constitution +6, Charisma +8

Skills: Arcana +4, Persuasion +8, Deception +8, Insight +5
Senses: passive Perception 15
Languages: Common, Draconic, and one additional language of choice
Proficiency Bonus: +3
Challenge: 5 (1,800 xp)

Class Features
- Spellcasting: The Sorcerer is a spellcaster. Their spellcasting ability is Charisma (spell save DC 16, +8 to hit with spell attacks).
  - Cantrips: Fire Bolt, Sorcerous Whispers, Minor Illusion
  - 1st Level Spells (4 slots): Magic Missile, Shield, Disguise Self
  - 2nd Level Spells (3 slots): Misty Step, Hold Person
  - 3rd Level Spells (3 slots): Fireball, Counterspell
  - 4th Level Spells (2 slots): Greater Invisibility, Ice Storm
- Sorcery Points: The Sorcerer has a pool of sorcery points (equal to their Sorcerer level) that they can use to convert into spell slots, or vice versa, allowing them greater flexibility in spellcasting.

Actions
- Multi-attack: The Sorcerer can cast one spell and make one melee attack with a dagger.
- Dagger: Melee Weapon Attack: +6 to hit, reach 5 ft., one target. Hit: 5 (1d4+4) piercing damage.
- Fireball: The target must make a DC 16 Dexterity saving throw. On a failed save, the target takes 28 (6d6) fire damage, or half as much on a successful save.

Bonus Actions
- Metamagic - Quickened Spell: As a bonus action, the Sorcerer can cast a spell using a spell slot of 1st level or higher as a bonus action instead of its normal casting time.

Reactions
- Shield: When the Sorcerer is hit by an attack, they can use a reaction to cast Shield, increasing their AC by 5 until the start of their next turn.

Aethra Starborn

"The stars whisper my name, and their power answers my call." 1

A Aetherial magic courses through Aethra's veins, a gift bestowed by a celestial event that marked her birth beneath a rare convergence of stars.

For the Insightful:
Possesses a unique connection to cosmic forces, granting her unparalleled skill in manipulating light and gravitational magic.

Description:
Aethra has silvery hair that glimmers faintly, like moonlight, and eyes speckled with star-like patterns. Her voice carries an otherworldly resonance, and her ethereal presence often leaves others in awe or trepidation. Her movements are graceful, as if guided by unseen celestial rhythms.

Wants and Needs:
- **Want:** To understand the full extent of her celestial powers and the reason behind her cosmic destiny.
- **Need:** To balance the overwhelming influx of celestial magic threatening to consume her mortal form.

Secret or Obstacle: Fears that her celestial connection might sever her humanity, leaving her a mere vessel for the stars.

Carrying (Total CP: 38):
- **Orb of Starlight (10 points):** A shimmering sphere that pulses with cosmic energy, illuminating the darkest corners with a gentle silver glow.
- **Veil of Moonlit Silk (8 points):** A flowing garment that seems to absorb the light of the stars, concealing the wearer from prying eyes.
- **Gravitational Shard Pendant (12 points):** A crystal fragment that warps gravity around it, allowing its wielder to move unnaturally.
- **Vial of Astral Essence (8 points):** A small flask containing glowing, swirling starlight said to rejuvenate both body and mind.

Sorcerer Tactics

Sorcerers employ a mix of bold strategies, improvisation, and creative spellcasting to achieve their goals. In combat, they often rely on powerful area-of-effect spells that can turn the tide of battle, using their innate magic to disrupt enemy formations and bolster their allies. With a keen understanding of their own strengths, they often position themselves where they can influence the battle while remaining relatively safe from direct conflict. Outside the heat of battle, they utilize their formidable charisma and magical insight to negotiate, gather information, and form alliances with powerful figures.

Celestial Sorcerer

Tharion Firebrand *"The flame within burns brighter than any forge."* 2

Brief: Descended from an ancient fire dragon, Tharion's fiery magic fuels his defiance and determination. His power, deeply tied to his emotions, has made him both a prodigy and a danger, as he struggles to control the roaring inferno within.

Vocation: Draconic Sorcerer

For the Insightful: Wields powerful flame-based spells, resistant to heat and capable of summoning draconic aspects in battle.

Description: Tharion's crimson hair shimmers like embers, and his eyes blaze with golden intensity. His fiery temper often matches his elemental magic, but his charisma can either ignite camaraderie or spark chaos. Scales fleck his arms, hinting at his draconic heritage.

Wants and Needs:
- Want: To uncover the truth about his draconic lineage and prove himself worthy of the power within.
- Need: To temper his impulsive nature and avoid losing control of his destructive flames.

Secret or Obstacle: Haunted by dreams of a dragon's roar, he fears becoming the very beast that cursed his bloodline.

Carrying (Total CP: 34):
- Flameforged Rod (10 points): A staff carved from volcanic rock, crowned with a gem that flickers like a living flame.
- Cloak of Emberweave (8 points): A cloak that shimmers with fiery hues, offering both warmth and resistance to heat.
- Draconic Claw Amulet (10 points): A polished claw encased in obsidian, granting the wearer bursts of raw, destructive energy.
- Phoenix Feather Charm (6 points): A crimson feather that radiates heat, capable of reigniting small flames with a touch.

Kael Shadowvein *"The shadows bend to my will; darkness is my ally."* 3

Brief: Born under a lunar eclipse, Kael channels the enigmatic power of shadow magic to weave illusions and ensnare enemies. His mastery over the void grants him both strength and isolation, as others fear the unknown depths of his sorcery. Despite his aloof nature, Kael possesses a cunning mind and an unyielding resolve.

Vocation: Shadow Sorcerer

For the Insightful: Adept at manipulating shadows to create illusions and traps, while blending into darkness to avoid detection.

Description: Kael's raven-black hair falls in unruly waves, framing his sharp features and pale complexion. His piercing gray eyes seem to reflect the void itself, and his calm, measured demeanor often unsettles those around him. A faint aura of chilling darkness surrounds him, leaving a haunting impression.

Wants and Needs:
- Want: To unlock the full potential of shadow magic and uncover the ancient texts of his dark ancestry.
- Need: To connect with others and resist the temptation of total solitude, which could consume him.

Secret or Obstacle: Fears the shadows will one day overpower his will, turning him into a vessel of darkness.

Carrying (Total CP: 38):
- Veilbound Grimoire (12 points): A leather-bound tome that absorbs light, inscribed with runes visible only in darkness.
- Voidglass Pendant (10 points): A translucent black gem that vibrates faintly with shadow energy, granting him the ability to phase through walls momentarily.
- Mantle of Midnight (8 points): A shimmering cloak that blends into the shadows, rendering its wearer invisible in low light.
- Stiletto of Silent Echoes (8 points): A sleek black blade that emits no sound, designed for precise and silent strikes.

Sylra Willowshade *"The whispers of the forest guide me"* 4

Brief: Gifted by an ancient dryad, Sylra's magic stems from her deep bond with the natural world, blending life and arcane energy. Her spells bloom with vitality, protecting allies and smiting foes with the fury of nature.

Vocation: Nature Sorcerer

For the Insightful: Specializes in earth-based spells and healing magic, drawing on the natural world to empower her abilities.

Description: Sylra's emerald-green eyes seem to glow with an otherworldly light, and her cascading auburn hair is entwined with vines and blossoms. Her skin carries a faint shimmer, as though kissed by moonlight, and her voice holds a calming melody that soothes even the fiercest hearts.

Wants and Needs:
- Want: To ensure the safety of her forest and the creatures that inhabit it, preserving the balance of nature.
- Need: To overcome her hesitation to wield destructive magic, as it clashes with her nurturing instincts.

Secret or Obstacle: Haunted by visions of a blighted forest, she fears her power may someday become the cause of its ruin.

Carrying (Total CP: 31):
- Heartwood Staff (12 points): A gnarled wooden staff adorned with glowing runes, said to channel the will of the forest spirits.
- Bloomstone Amulet (10 points): A crystal embedded with seeds that sprout protective vines when danger is near.
- Spiritbound Lantern (9 points): An enchanted lantern that glows with ethereal green light, revealing hidden paths.

Ardyn Emberfall
"Through fire, I rise; through ashes, I endure." **5**

Brief: Ardyn's fiery magic mirrors the volcanic eruption that scarred his homeland and awakened his arcane abilities. His temper flares as unpredictably as his flames, but beneath his fiery exterior lies a protective heart. Determined to control his volatile power, Ardyn strives to prevent destruction while harnessing it for the greater good.

Vocation: Flame Sorcerer
For the Insightful: Commands explosive fire magic capable of devastating foes and shielding allies with walls of searing flames.
Description: Ardyn's fiery red hair blazes like a living flame, and his amber eyes shimmer with sparks of intensity. His scarred but resolute features reflect the trials he has endured, and his molten aura warms those around him—both literally and metaphorically.

Wants and Needs:
- Want: To master his elemental fury and become a beacon of hope for those displaced by the destruction he once caused.
- Need: To trust others and seek guidance, rather than isolating himself in fear of hurting those he cares for.

Secret or Obstacle: Haunted by the memory of losing control and harming innocents, he doubts his ability to ever fully harness his power.

Carrying (Total CP: 37):
- Inferno Gauntlets (12 points): Gloves that channel his fire magic into concentrated blasts, searing enemies with precision.
- Ashen Cloak (10 points): A dark, fireproof cloak that shimmers with embers and protects the wearer from heat-based attacks.
- Volcanic Crystal Shard (8 points): A jagged piece of obsidian that amplifies destructive spells at the cost of their stability.
- Flameborn Amulet (7 points): A pendant that glows with an inner fire, granting Ardyn enhanced resistance to cold.

Mira Eclipsedawn
"The stars whisper secrets only I can hear." **6**

Brief: Mira's magic draws from the mysterious energy of the cosmos, allowing her to bend time and space in subtle, awe-inspiring ways. Born under a rare celestial alignment, carries the wisdom of the stars but finds herself disconnected from earthly concerns.

Vocation: Cosmic Sorcerer
For the Insightful: Harnesses celestial energy to manipulate gravity, create portals, and unleash bursts of radiant starlight.
Description: Mira's deep indigo hair flows like the night sky, flecked with silvery strands resembling stardust. Her luminous violet eyes seem to peer into other realms, and her calm demeanor exudes an aura of infinite patience.

Wants and Needs:
- Want: To unravel the secrets of the universe and understand her role within its grand design.
- Need: To remain grounded and forge meaningful connections, resisting the temptation to drift into the arcane unknown.

Secret or Obstacle: The stars have warned her of a catastrophic event tied to her power, leaving her to wrestle with whether she should act or let fate take its course.

Carrying (Total CP: 43):
- Celestial Orb (12 points): A crystalline sphere filled with swirling constellations, used to scry and summon radiant light.
- Starglow Robes (10 points): Elegant robes that shimmer like the Milky Way, granting protection against mind-altering effects.
- Ethereal Compass (9 points): A faintly glowing magical device that points to the nearest source of arcane energy.
- Gravity-Warping Bracers (12 points): Bracelets etched with celestial runes, enabling Mira to reduce her weight and leap great distances.

Theros Grimshard
"In darkness, there is strength; in silence, there is power." **7**

Brief: An orphan raised in the shadow of a cursed fortress, Theros discovered his powers in a moment of despair, calling upon the forbidden energy of the void. His dark magic, though powerful, isolates him from others, making him a reluctant hero.

Vocation: Void Sorcerer
For the Insightful: Wields destructive void energy, capable of erasing enemies and disrupting magical barriers with ease.
Description: Theros has jet-black hair and piercing eyes that seem to shimmer with dark energy. His gaunt features and somber expression reflect his haunted past, and his every movement exudes a calculated precision. The faint hum of void energy accompanies his presence, unsettling those nearby.

Wants and Needs:
- Want: To lift the curse that binds him to the void, granting him freedom from its consuming influence.
- Need: To overcome his fear of forming bonds with others, believing that his power makes him a danger to those he cares for.

Secret or Obstacle: Theros fears that the void's power will one day devour his soul, leaving only emptiness behind.

Carrying (Total CP: 34):
- Voidcaller's Staff (14 points): A staff carved from darkwood, topped with a glowing obsidian orb that channels void magic.
- Shadowveil Cloak (12 points): A flowing black cloak that muffles sound and allows him to fade into the shadows.
- Fatebound Journal (8 points): A tattered journal filled with cryptic entries and void-rune translations, vital to understanding his curse.

Lyssara Windspire
"The winds whisper my name, and through them, I soar." **8**

Brief: Lyssara's magic is tied to the tempestuous power of the wind, granting her unmatched speed and the ability to shape the air itself. Born during a fierce storm atop a mountain peak, her connection to the skies is as unyielding as it is exhilarating. Her free-spirited nature hides a deep sense of responsibility to protect those below.

Vocation: Tempest Sorcerer

For the Insightful: Commands wind-based magic, creating barriers of swirling air and unleashing devastating gusts to scatter foes.

Description: Lyssara's hair flows like silver strands caught in a constant breeze, and her bright blue eyes shimmer with the energy of storm clouds. Her lithe frame seems to dance with the currents, and her presence carries an electrifying charge, as if the air itself responds to her emotions.

Wants and Needs:
- Want: To master the storms within her, becoming a symbol of strength and freedom for her mountain-dwelling kin.
- Need: To temper her recklessness and embrace the value of grounding herself in relationships and responsibilities.

Secret or Obstacle: Lyssara fears losing control during a storm, as her magic grows unstable when emotions run high.

Carrying (Total CP: 36):
- Windcaller Gauntlets (12 points): Lightweight gloves that amplify her ability to shape air into precise gusts.
- Featherlight Cloak (8 points): A shimmering, sky-blue cloak that allows her to glide gracefully from great heights.
- Stormglass Pendant (10 points): A pendant that stores residual storm energy, releasing bolts of lightning when activated.
- Skyborne Boots (6 points): Boots infused with air magic, enabling her to sprint effortlessly across uneven terrain.

Kaelen Duskmire
"Shadows shield the secrets of the soul." **9**

Brief: Kaelen draws his power from the twilight realms, mastering shadow magic to manipulate light and dark alike. His brooding demeanor belies a heart dedicated to justice, as he uses his arcane talents to uncover hidden truths and protect the downtrodden. Each spell cast is a step toward reclaiming his fractured past.

Vocation: Shadow Sorcerer

For the Insightful: Wields shadow magic to obscure vision, craft illusions, and strike from the darkness with eerie precision.

Description: Kaelen's ashen-gray hair falls in loose waves, framing piercing violet eyes that seem to glow faintly in dim light. His voice carries a quiet intensity, and his dark, layered clothing allows him to vanish seamlessly into the night. His aura hums with an unsettling quiet, as though the shadows themselves bow to his will.

Wants and Needs:
- Want: To dismantle a shadowy organization that once enslaved him, freeing others from its grip.
- Need: To let go of his obsession with vengeance and embrace trust in those willing to stand beside him.

Secret or Obstacle: The power of the shadows whispers temptations of corruption, testing his moral compass with every spell.

Carrying (Total CP: 42):
- Umbral Staff (12 points): A staff tipped with an obsidian crescent that enhances his ability to control shadows.
- Twilight Cloak (10 points): A midnight-black cloak that blends perfectly with darkness, rendering him almost invisible.
- Moonlit Compass (8 points): A mystical device that reveals hidden paths and secret chambers under moonlight.
- Nightbane Amulet (12 points): A talisman that strengthens his resistance to light-based attacks while boosting shadow magic.

Elara Starfire
"I am the light that pierces the void, the spark that ignites hope." **10**

Brief: Elara's magic radiates the brilliance of the stars, her power fueled by a cosmic connection to the heavens. Her commanding presence and unwavering resolve make her an inspiring figure, as she wields starlight to illuminate the darkest of nights. She views her gift as both a blessing and a responsibility.

Vocation: Starfire Sorcerer

For the Insightful: Harnesses the energy of stars, casting beams of light that heal allies and sear enemies with celestial fire.

Description: Elara's golden hair shimmers as though kissed by sunlight, and her silver eyes glow with the brilliance of distant galaxies. Her regal bearing is softened by her warm smile, and her movements leave faint trails of light, as if the stars themselves.

Wants and Needs:
- Want: To restore balance to a realm plunged into darkness, becoming a beacon of hope for all who suffer.
- Need: To accept her own vulnerabilities and share the burden of her quest with others.

Secret or Obstacle: A prophecy tells she'll die in blaze of glory, leaving her grappling with fear of sacrificing herself for her cause.

Carrying (Total CP: 45):
- Starlight Scepter (15 points): A radiant scepter that channels her power into focused beams of light.
- Celestial Mantle (12 points): A shimmering white robe that glows faintly in the dark, granting resistance to shadow magic.
- Eclipse Pendant (10 points): A pendant etched with lunar and solar symbols, enhancing both her healing and offensive spells.
- Nova Stone (8 points): A crystalline artifact that stores cosmic energy, releasing bursts of radiant power when activated.

Spies

Spies are the unseen operatives of a fantasy realm, moving through the shadows to gather intelligence and manipulate events from behind the scenes. Masters of stealth, deception, and subterfuge, these cunning figures thrive in the art of disguise, seamlessly blending into various factions and communities. Whether working for kingdoms, mercenary guilds, or secret cabals, spies wield their sharp wits and keen senses to uncover secrets and shift the balance of power. Their lives, however, are perilous, as a single misstep can lead to betrayal and ruin.

Adventurers should tread carefully when dealing with spies, for their motives often serve no cause but their own. A dark tale is told of Elias, a once-renowned spy whose charm and cunning made him a master manipulator. Once a nobleman, Elias turned to espionage to gain power, weaving a web of intrigue and betrayal that elevated his standing but eroded his honor.

One fateful night, Elias orchestrated an elaborate plot to eliminate a rival lord. But the plan backfired, exposing his duplicity to those he had betrayed. Outmaneuvered and abandoned by his network, Elias was captured and dragged into the shadows he once ruled.

Tavern whispers tell of his imprisonment in a hidden dungeon, his fate sealed as a grim warning of the cost of treachery.

Some say his former allies, seeking to send a brutal message, cursed him with a magical shackle that severed his connection to the webs he once spun. Others claim he haunts the dungeons he was cast into, murmuring fragmented secrets of those who wronged him, forever yearning for vengeance he can never achieve.

This tale reminds adventurers to tread lightly in the realm of spies. While their secrets and knowledge may seem tempting, their world is rife with danger and deceit. Trust sparingly, for crossing paths with the wrong spy can pull you into a spiral of treachery, where the choices made in the dark might haunt you forever.

Zara Nightshade

"Secrets are my currency, and silence is my weapon." 1

Brief: A resourceful spy known for her unmatched skill in deception and subterfuge, Zara manipulates people and events with calculated precision. Her charm and sharp instincts have earned her a reputation as a shadow no one can escape.

Vocation: Spy & Master Manipulator

For the Perceptive: Possesses a sharp intellect and the ability to read people's intentions, enabling her to anticipate threats and opportunities with uncanny accuracy.

Description: Zara is a slender woman with raven-black hair that falls in loose waves, and piercing violet eyes that seem to see right through a person. She often dresses in understated yet elegant attire, blending into both courts and common gatherings, and her quiet confidence exudes danger and allure.

Wants and Needs:
- Wants: To uncover secrets that could topple the most powerful factions; dreams of ruling from the shadows.
- Needs: To secure alliances that shield her from the consequences of her schemes, ensuring her survival.

Secret or Obstacle: Hides a deep sense of isolation, fearing that her life of lies will leave her without anyone she can truly trust.

Carrying (Total CP: 24):
- Shadow-Weave Cloak (8 points): A dark, lightweight cloak that seems to merge with the surrounding shadows.
- Inscribed Dagger (6 points): A blade etched with faint runes, gifted by a mysterious benefactor.
- Ciphered Journal (5 points): A locked book containing encrypted notes about her targets.
- Whispering Stone (5 points): A small enchanted stone used for discreet communication.

Aric Thornveil

"Trust is a commodity, and I am its broker." 2

Brief: Aric is a shrewd and calculating spy known for infiltrating noble circles and unraveling political conspiracies. With a silver tongue and a knack for uncovering hidden truths, he has brought down entire houses with nothing but whispered rumors.

Vocation: Spy & Court Infiltrator

For the Perceptive: Possesses an uncanny ability to blend into any social environment, gaining trust while discreetly extracting information.

Description: Aric is a tall, lithe man with short, neatly combed auburn hair and sharp green eyes that constantly assess his surroundings. His refined attire and subtle charm allow him to move undetected through noble courts, while his smooth voice hides his ruthless intentions.

Wants and Needs:
- Wants: To expose secrets that could destabilize rival kingdoms, ensuring his employer's dominance.
- Needs: To keep his own past hidden, protecting himself from the consequences of his actions.

Secret or Obstacle Hides his fear of being unmasked, knowing that exposure would mean losing everything he has worked for.

Carrying (Total CP: 27):
- Noble's Signet Ring (8 points): A forged ring used to gain access to restricted areas.
- Poisoned Hairpin (6 points): A small, discreet weapon coated with a lethal toxin.
- False Documents (7 points): Papers crafted to provide him with multiple identities.
- Silent Boots (6 points): Footwear enchanted to suppress sound entirely.

Selene Vervain

"The truth is rarely pure, and never simple." 3

Brief: A cunning and mysterious spy, Selene specializes in extracting valuable secrets from unwilling informants. Her alluring demeanor hides a mind as sharp as the daggers she keeps concealed.

Vocation: Spy & Seductress

For the Perceptive: Excels at reading emotions and exploiting vulnerabilities, turning even the most guarded into unwitting allies.

Description: Selene has flowing midnight-black hair and piercing blue eyes that seem to pierce through lies. Her elegant yet practical clothing enhances her graceful movements, and her soft-spoken voice hides an unwavering determination.

Wants and Needs:
- Wants: To dismantle the corrupt powers ruling from the shadows; dreams of creating a more just society through manipulation.
- Needs: To build a network of loyal allies, ensuring she has protection when her enemies retaliate.

Secret or Obstacle: Hides a deep sense of guilt for betraying those who once trusted her, questioning the morality of her methods.

Carrying (Total CP: 25):
- Shadow-Silk Gloves (6 points): Gloves enchanted to leave no fingerprints.
- Venom Vial Necklace (5 points): A small container of potent poison disguised as jewelry.
- Listening Charm (7 points): A trinket that amplifies sounds from nearby rooms.
- Disguise Kit (7 points): Tools for altering her appearance with ease.

Kael Dravenmark

"In darkness, I see opportunity." 4

Brief: Kael is a rogue operative who thrives in chaos, using manipulation and sabotage to tilt the scales of power. With his ruthless pragmatism and unmatched stealth, he is both feared and respected in the underworld.

Vocation: Spy & Saboteur

For the Perceptive: Possesses exceptional knowledge of traps and sabotage, making him a master of creating distractions and diversions.

Description: Kael has a rugged, weathered appearance, with short black hair streaked with silver and calculating gray eyes. His dark, practical attire is designed for stealth, and his calm, measured demeanor contrasts with the danger he carries within.

Wants and Needs:
- Wants: To dismantle oppressive regimes from within, becoming a silent force of rebellion.
- Needs: To overcome his internal struggles, regaining the humanity he sacrifices for his missions.

Secret or Obstacle: Hides his growing weariness of the endless deceit, fearing he may one day lose his sense of self entirely.

Carrying (Total CP: 24):
- Explosive Orbs (10 points): Compact devices capable of creating loud, blinding distractions.
- Grappling Hook (8 points): A sturdy, enchanted tool for scaling walls and cliffs.
- Spyglass of Secrets (6 points): A magical device that reveals hidden pathways and compartments.

Lira Nightshade — *"Even shadows bow to those who command them."* 5

Brief: Lira is a shadowy spy with an affinity for infiltrating the most fortified places, leaving no trace of her presence. Her enigmatic demeanor hides a past steeped in betrayal and survival.
Vocation: Spy & Shadow Dancer
For the Perceptive: Possesses the supernatural ability to meld into shadows, moving unseen through even the most guarded corridors.
Description: Lira is a slender woman with short silver hair and sharp violet eyes that gleam with an otherworldly light. She wears lightweight dark leathers that shimmer faintly like flowing shadows, enhancing her ethereal presence.
Wants and Needs:
- Wants: To uncover the truth about the betrayal that shaped her life, seeking both vengeance and closure.
- Needs: To find a purpose beyond survival, mending the trust she has lost in herself and others.

Secret or Obstacle: Hides her growing attachment to her targets, struggling to separate her missions from her humanity.
Carrying (Total CP: 32):
- Cloak of Wraiths (10 points): A magical cloak that turns her nearly invisible in darkness.
- Shadow Dagger (8 points): A blade that disappears into shadow when thrown.
- Whisper Stone (6 points): A magical stone that allows silent communication across distances.
- Night Elixir (8 points): A potion that heightens her vision in complete darkness.

Gideon Vex — *"Information is power, and I hold the key."* 6

Brief: Gideon is a brilliant and calculating spy who specializes in uncovering secrets through subterfuge and manipulation. With his disarming charm, he makes allies of enemies and enemies of allies.
Vocation: Spy & Master Manipulator
For the Perceptive: Excels at planting misinformation and influencing others, creating webs of lies that serve his goals.
Description: Gideon is a tall man with neatly styled dark hair and ice-blue eyes that betray his cunning nature. He dresses in sharp, unassuming attire that allows him to blend seamlessly into any environment, always carrying a wry smile.
Wants and Needs:
- Wants: To expose and control the hidden puppet masters of the world, securing his place as the ultimate power broker.
- Needs: To maintain the delicate balance of his double life, ensuring he never becomes too entangled in his own deceptions.

Secret or Obstacle:
Hides his crippling fear of exposure, knowing that even a single misstep could unravel his entire operation.
Carrying (Total CP: 28):
- Amulet of Whispers (8 points): An enchanted amulet that amplifies overheard conversations.
- Forged Documents (6 points): Perfectly crafted papers granting him access to restricted areas.
- Smoke Locket (6 points): A device that releases a calming haze to confuse pursuers.
- Discerning Lens (8 points): A small glass that reveals hidden messages and magical runes.

Seraph Tindrel — *"I weave secrets like a spider weaves its web."* 7

Brief: Seraph is a meticulous and patient spy who gathers intelligence through careful observation and subtle intervention. Her methods are slow but reliable, leaving no stone unturned.
Vocation: Spy & Web Weaver
For the Perceptive: Possesses unparalleled patience and observational skills, uncovering truths hidden in the smallest of details.
Description: Seraph has an elegant presence, with long auburn hair often tied back and calm green eyes that miss nothing. She dresses in modest, practical clothing that helps her blend into common surroundings, her demeanor unassuming yet commanding.
Wants and Needs:
- Wants: To dismantle corrupt systems piece by piece, ensuring lasting change.
- Needs: To reconcile her need for justice with the morally gray actions she takes to achieve it.

Secret or Obstacle: Hides her fear of becoming too invested in her missions, knowing attachment could compromise her.
Carrying (Total CP: 29):
- Silk Thread Gloves (7 points): Enchanted gloves that allow her to manipulate small mechanisms and locks with ease.
- Marking Ink (6 points): A magical ink that can only be seen under moonlight.
- Listening Cuffs (8 points): Small enchanted devices that amplify distant sounds.
- Tracker's Compass (8 points): A compass that always points toward her target.

Cael Duskwatch
"A secret is only as safe as its keeper." **8**

Brief: Cael is a shadowy figure who thrives in secrecy, known for his ability to extract vital information from even the most fortified strongholds. His calculated demeanor hides a relentless drive for perfection.

Vocation: Spy & Silent Observer

For the Perceptive: Expert in deciphering encrypted messages and bypassing magical wards, allowing him to gain access to even the most secure areas.

Description: Cael is of average height, with ash-gray hair and piercing amber eyes that seem to see through lies. He wears a fitted black coat adorned with hidden pockets and carries himself with the silent confidence of one who knows no obstacle is insurmountable.

Wants and Needs:
- Wants: To uncover the ultimate truth behind a vast network of lies that has plagued his homeland.
- Needs: To master his emotional vulnerabilities, ensuring they do not compromise his missions.

Secret or Obstacle: Hides his growing disillusionment with the morality of his work, questioning whether the ends truly justify the means.

Carrying (Total CP: 35):
- Phantom Blade (12 points): A sword enchanted to leave no trace of its cuts.
- Invisibility Pouch (8 points): A small bag that conceals its contents from magical detection.
- Cipher Ring (10 points): A tool for quickly decrypting encoded messages.
- Spectral Key (5 points): A key that adapts to fit any lock, mundane or magical.

Seline Frostveil
"Trust is a currency I'll gladly steal." **9**

Brief: Seline is a charismatic spy who infiltrates circles of power with her charm and cunning, weaving lies and truths so intricately that even she sometimes forgets the difference.

Vocation: Spy & Social Manipulator

For the Perceptive: Possesses unmatched skill in reading people, using subtle cues to predict their actions and exploit their weaknesses.

Description: Seline is a striking woman with frost-white hair and sapphire-blue eyes that seem to captivate anyone who meets her gaze. She dresses in elegant, flowing garments that conceal her array of tools, her every movement calculated to draw attention or deflect it as needed.

Wants and Needs:
- Wants: To climb the social ladder and command respect from those who once dismissed her.
- Needs: To maintain her moral compass amidst the treachery she navigates daily.

Secret or Obstacle: Hides her guilt over betraying those who grow close to her, fearing the day her dual life might collapse.

Carrying (Total CP: 30):
- Glamour Cloak (10 points): A shimmering cloak that shifts colors to match its surroundings.
- Hypnotic Pendant (8 points): A jewel that subtly influences those who gaze into it.
- Glass Quill (7 points): A writing tool that leaves invisible ink only readable by its owner.
- Locket of Secrets (5 points): A trinket that magically records whispered conversations.

Rylan Thornstride
"The truth often lies buried beneath a thousand falsehoods." **10**

Brief: Rylan is a resourceful spy who specializes in uncovering long-forgotten secrets, using his knack for disguise and sharp intellect to infiltrate ancient ruins and forbidden libraries.

Vocation: Spy & Relic Seeker

For the Perceptive: Master of ancient languages and arcane traps, he retrieves valuable artifacts and hidden knowledge with unparalleled precision.

Description: Rylan is a wiry man with tousled chestnut hair and pale green eyes that burn with curiosity. He dresses in simple traveler's garb, blending seamlessly into crowds and carrying an air of quiet intrigue.

Wants and Needs:
- Wants: To piece together the fragmented history of a lost civilization and reveal its secrets to the world.
- Needs: To avoid drawing the attention of powerful factions that would misuse the knowledge he uncovers.

Secret or Obstacle: Hides a cursed artifact in his possession, its whispers urging him toward increasingly reckless endeavors.

Carrying (Total CP: 33):
- Relic Hunter's Satchel (10 points): A bag enchanted to safely hold fragile artifacts.
- Shifting Mask (8 points): A mask that changes its appearance to match any identity.
- Thief's Lantern (9 points): A light source that reveals hidden passages and magical traps.
- Binding Cord (6 points): A rope imbued with magic that binds even spectral entities.

Alara Shadowthorn
"A whispered word can topple empires." **11**

Brief: Alara is a cunning spy who specializes in manipulating political intrigue, weaving chaos through secrets and lies. Her sharp mind and seductive charm make her a formidable player in the game of power.
Vocation: Spy & Political Saboteur
For the Perceptive: Gifted at forging alliances and sowing dissent, Alara has a knack for turning rivals into pawns in her intricate schemes.
Description: Alara has flowing raven-black hair, piercing emerald eyes, and an air of mystery that draws others toward her. She wears sleek, dark attire that combines elegance with practicality, her movements as graceful as her words are sharp.
Wants and Needs:
- Wants: To dismantle a corrupt ruling council and replace it with her vision of a fairer system.
- Needs: To reconcile her growing attachment to those she manipulates, which threatens her focus.

Secret or Obstacle: Hides a traumatic past tied to the ruling council she seeks to overthrow, a truth that fuels her ambition but also blinds her to unintended consequences.
Carrying (Total CP: 36):
- Whispering Quill (10 points): A pen that records conversations even when not in use.
- Spider's Silk Gloves (9 points): Delicate gloves that enhance her dexterity for picking locks or planting evidence.
- Veil of Forgetting (8 points): A scarf that clouds the memories of those who see her pass.
- Poisoned Dagger (9 points): A blade laced with a toxin that induces temporary paralysis.

Dorian Nightspear
"In shadows, I find clarity; in darkness, I find purpose." **12**

Brief: Dorian is a brooding spy who thrives in the most perilous of missions, using his deadly precision and unmatched patience to eliminate threats before they emerge.
Vocation: Spy & Silent Assassin
For the Perceptive: Skilled at blending into the darkest corners, Dorian uses his unparalleled stealth and focus to infiltrate enemy strongholds undetected.
Description: Dorian is a tall, gaunt figure with ashen hair and storm-gray eyes that seem to pierce through deceit. He wears a dark, hooded cloak that flows like liquid shadow, masking his presence in even the faintest light.
Wants and Needs:
- Wants: To uncover the identities of a secret cabal threatening his homeland.
- Needs: To balance his unyielding drive for vengeance with the humanity he fears losing.

Secret or Obstacle: Hides a deep fear of failure, haunted by a mission gone wrong that cost the lives of those who trusted him.
Carrying (Total CP: 40):
- Shadowstep Boots (12 points): Enchanted boots that silence his movements completely.
- Raven's Eye Amulet (10 points): A charm that allows him to see through magical illusions.
- Assassin's Toolkit (9 points): A compact set of tools for breaking locks and neutralizing traps.
- Night's Fang Blade (9 points): A curved dagger that absorbs light, rendering it nearly invisible.

Eryndis Thornveil
"A sharp mind is a spy's deadliest weapon." **13**

Brief: Eryndis is a master strategist who specializes in gathering information through subtle manipulation, playing long games to ensure her goals are achieved without direct confrontation.
Vocation: Spy & Master Strategist
For the Perceptive: Exceptional at interpreting subtle changes in behavior, Eryndis uses her observations to predict and control events with meticulous precision.
Description: Eryndis is a slender woman with silver-streaked auburn hair and soft hazel eyes that belie her calculating mind. Her attire is a mix of muted greens and browns, helping her blend seamlessly into urban and wilderness settings alike.
Wants and Needs:
- Wants: To prevent a rising conflict between two rival nations by dismantling their web of deceit.
- Needs: To resist the temptation to manipulate allies for personal gain, ensuring her methods remain just.

Secret or Obstacle: Hides her growing paranoia, constantly fearing that her own plans may one day be turned against her.
Carrying (Total CP: 38):
- Veil of Whispers (12 points): A cloak that muffles sounds around her, ensuring conversations remain private.
- Arcane Lens (10 points): A magical monocle that reveals hidden details, from invisible ink to concealed compartments.
- Silent Blade (9 points): A knife enchanted to cut through materials without making a sound.
- Thoughtstone (7 points): A small crystal that allows brief telepathic communication with trusted allies.

Kaelen Vipershadow
"The truth is a weapon, and I wield it with precision." **14**

Brief: Kaelen is a charismatic spy who infiltrates high society, charming his way into exclusive circles to uncover secrets that can turn the tide of power. His silver tongue and daring escapades are as legendary as his ability to vanish without a trace.
Vocation: Spy & Infiltrator
For the Perceptive: Kaelen possesses an uncanny ability to read people's intentions, allowing him to adapt his approach and turn enemies into allies.
Description: Kaelen is a striking man with jet-black hair tied in a sleek ponytail and sapphire eyes that gleam with mischief. He wears a tailored midnight-blue coat with hidden pockets for his tools, exuding confidence and allure wherever he goes.
Wants and Needs:
- Wants: To expose and dismantle a secret society pulling the strings of the kingdom's nobility.
- Needs: To reconcile his growing guilt over betraying those he befriends during his missions.

Secret or Obstacle:
Hides a personal vendetta against the secret society, which clouds his judgment and risks compromising his mission.
Carrying (Total CP: 42):
- Shadowed Ring (12 points): A ring that cloaks him in magical shadows when activated.
- Hidden Blade Gauntlet (10 points): A discreet weapon concealed within his sleeve for quick defense.
- Lure's Pendant (8 points): An enchanted necklace that subtly influences those nearby to trust him.
- Spy's Toolkit (12 points): A refined set of tools, including lockpicks, coded parchments, and false credentials.

Lyra Nightveil
"Every secret has a price, and I never leave unpaid debts." **15**

Brief: Lyra is a deadly yet elegant spy who thrives in chaos, using distraction and cunning to extract information and escape unscathed. Her enigmatic demeanor ensures that no one truly knows where her loyalties lie.
Vocation: Spy & Master of Deception
For the Perceptive: Lyra excels in creating diversions and using disguise to slip past even the most vigilant of guards, her quick thinking unmatched in dire situations.
Description: Lyra has wavy auburn hair that cascades down her shoulders, with smoky gray eyes that seem to pierce through deception. She wears a flowing crimson cloak with intricate embroidery, designed to conceal hidden compartments for her tools and weapons.
Wants and Needs:
- Wants: To gain leverage over a ruthless merchant guild that threatens to destabilize her homeland's economy.
- Needs: To overcome her reluctance to trust anyone, as her paranoia isolates her from potential allies.

Secret or Obstacle:
Hides a dangerous double life as a spy for opposing factions, walking a tightrope that could collapse with one misstep.
Carrying (Total CP: 40):
- Mirage Cloak (12 points): A magical garment that shifts in appearance, aiding her disguises.
- Ember Dagger (10 points): A blade that glows faintly, capable of igniting flammable materials.
- Smoke Orb (9 points): A small orb that releases a cloud of smoke, perfect for quick escapes.
- Cipher Book (9 points): A journal containing encoded messages, used to communicate with her handlers.

"In whispered halls and unseen sight, a spy moves swift as fading light. Truth and lie, a tangled thread —trust not the path where they have led."

– Corin Veilsong, Shadowbard of the Silent Court

Theives

Thieves are the shadowy rogues of a fantasy realm, masters of stealth, agility, and cunning. Operating from the shadows, they tread the thin line between law and crime, thriving on deception and trickery. Whether part of a sprawling guild or working alone, thieves rely on wits and skill to pilfer treasures, uncover secrets, and vanish without a trace. Their lives are a dance of danger and reward, filled with thrilling heists and the constant risk of capture. Some see them as daring antiheroes, while others regard them as threats to the safety and order of their communities.

Adventurers, however, should beware, for not all thieves adhere to a code of honor. A chilling tale tells of Jarek the Betrayer, a master thief infamous for his ruthless schemes.

Jarek, born into hardship, turned to crime to survive, quickly gaining notoriety for his audacious heists. With a façade of generosity, he recruited others into his schemes, only to lead them into traps that served his ambitions.

In his most infamous act, Jarek assembled a crew to steal a mythical artifact from the ruler of a prosperous city, promising wealth and glory. But treachery was his true intent. As the crew infiltrated the castle, Jarek sealed their escape, abandoning them to the guards while he fled with the artifact. Yet, his triumph turned to ruin. The artifact was cursed, unleashing chaos that warped reality around him. Trapped in a nightmarish dimension, Jarek relived the betrayal of his crew for eternity, their cries haunting him in a twisted realm of his own making.

This tale serves as a grim reminder to adventurers: thieves, for all their charm and resourcefulness, often mask darker intentions. Greed and treachery lead to ruin, and even the most cunning rogue may find themselves ensnared by their own deceit. Trust cautiously, for a thief's shadow may lead not to treasure, but to a fate far darker than gold or glory.

Ronan "Shadowstep" Daggerfall — *"In the silence of the night, I find my treasures."* 1

Brief: A cunning and elusive rogue, "Shadowstep" is a name whispered in awe and fear among the criminal underworld. An enigmatic loner, known for his uncanny ability to infiltrate the most secure locations and escape without a trace.
Vocation: Master Thief & Infiltrator
For the Insightful: Possesses an exceptional ability to quickly identifying hidden passages, traps, and vulnerabilities in a target's security.
Description: Ronan has jet-black hair that falls in sharp layers around his angular face, and piercing silver eyes that seem to see into the shadows themselves. His lithe frame and quick movements make him almost impossible to catch, while his demeanor blends charm with an unsettling edge. Dressed in dark, form-fitting clothing adorned with faintly glowing runes for enhanced stealth, he is the epitome of a professional thief.
Wants and Needs:
- Wants: To pull off the ultimate heist that will make his name legendary and untouchable.
- Needs: To confront the lingering guilt and fear stemming from a betrayed ally.

Secret or Obstacle: Hides a fear of betrayal, stemming from a past where a trusted partner sold him out to the authorities.
Carrying (Total CP: 21):
- Nightpiercer Dagger (7 points): A sleek, enchanted blade that absorbs light, rendering it nearly invisible in the dark.
- Shadowmantle Cloak (8 points): A magical cloak that muffles sound and bends light, helping him vanish from sight.
- Smoke Vials (6 points): Small glass vials that release a thick, obscuring fog when shattered, perfect for quick getaways.

Selene Velara   *"The richest treasures are those never meant to be found."* 2

Brief: Selene "Whisperfang" Velara is a shadowy thief known for her graceful movements and the audacity to steal from nobles in plain sight. Her exploits are whispered about in taverns, her name a byword for elegance and danger.
Vocation: Phantom Thief & Acrobat
For the Insightful: Possesses an uncanny sense of timing and balance, enabling her to traverse perilous environments and avoid even the most intricate traps.
Description: Selene's emerald eyes gleam with cunning, framed by raven-black hair tied into a sleek braid. Her lean, athletic frame is draped in dark silks, which shift like shadows as she moves. An intricate tattoo of a crescent moon graces her collarbone, a signature she leaves behind in her escapades. Though calm and composed, her past as an orphan fuels her ambition to amass wealth and security, all while hiding the loneliness that gnaws at her.
Wants and Needs:
- Wants: To uncover and claim a legendary artifact said to grant eternal freedom and fortune.
- Needs: To let go of her obsession with wealth and find a purpose beyond material gain.

Secret or Obstacle: Hides her vulnerability to guilt, often second-guessing her actions when her thefts harm innocent lives.
Carrying (Total CP: 32):
- Dagger of Echoes (9 points): A lightweight blade that creates distracting whispers in the dark.
- Shadowgrip Boots (8 points): Boots that enhance her ability to climb and move silently on any surface.
- Grappling Cord (7 points): A magical cord that anchors itself to any surface when thrown.
- Phantom Smoke Bombs (8 points): Tiny bombs that emit a silent, shadowy haze, obscuring her movements completely.

Kaelen "Locke" Fenriver   *"A locked door isn't a barrier—it's an invitation."* 3

Brief: Kaelen "Locke" Fenriver is a charming rogue with an unparalleled knack for picking locks and cracking vaults. He thrives on challenges, viewing each heist as a puzzle to solve with ingenuity and flair.
Vocation: Vault Cracker & Charmer
For the Insightful: Exceptional at deciphering mechanical systems and magical wards, often creating tools to bypass even the most complex defenses.
Description: Kaelen's tousled brown hair and mischievous grin give him a roguish charm, complemented by his sharp wit and quick tongue. His deep blue eyes glint with excitement whenever a challenge arises. He dresses in a patchwork of functional leather armor, adorned with hidden pockets for tools and trinkets. Despite his jovial demeanor, Kaelen harbors a secret fear of being caught and imprisoned, which drives his meticulous planning.
Wants and Needs:
- Wants: To solve the "Vault of Eternity," a fabled uncrackable safe rumored to hold untold riches.
- Needs: To realize his worth lies not in proving himself, but in building connections with those he trusts.

Secret or Obstacle: Hides his deep-rooted anxiety about his reliance on luck, fearing that one day, his fortune will run out.
Carrying (Total CP: 25):
- Clockwork Lockpicks (9 points): An advanced set of enchanted lockpicks that can adapt to complex mechanisms.
- Illusionary Cloak (6 points): A short cloak that creates a shimmering mirage to misdirect pursuers.
- Pocket Escape Kit (5 points): A small pouch containing smoke pellets, caltrops, and a collapsible grappling hook.
- Silent Step Gloves (5 points): Gloves that mask any sound when handling objects.

Nessa Elowen   *"The world's wealth belongs to those bold enough to take it."* 4

Brief: Nessa "Silverthread" Elowen is a daring thief whose finesse with sleight of hand and charm earns her invitations to the very banquets she intends to rob. Her reputation precedes her as a master of deception and misdirection.
Vocation: Gentleman Thief & Illusionist
For the Insightful: Adept at sleight of hand and creating distractions, she can manipulate both objects and people with ease.
Description: Nessa's platinum-blonde hair and pale blue eyes give her an almost ethereal appearance, while her honeyed voice disarms even the most guarded. She wears fine clothing tailored for stealth, with hidden compartments and shimmering threads of illusionary enchantments. Though confident in her skills, she carries the weight of her estranged family's shame, fueling her need to prove herself in her own unconventional way.
Wants and Needs:
- Wants: To steal a priceless artifact from a royal treasury to cement her legacy.
- Needs: To confront her family and resolve the wounds left by their rejection.

Secret or Obstacle: Hides a deep fear of losing her charisma and charm, she believes are her only weapons in a harsh world.
Carrying (Total CP: 21):
- Veil of Glamour (8 points): A scarf imbued with magic to briefly alter her appearance.
- Thorned Dagger (7 points): A blade laced with a mild paralytic poison, useful for incapacitating foes.
- Decoy Orb (6 points): A small enchanted sphere that creates illusory duplicates of her to distract enemies.

Davin "Shadewhisper" Vex   *"A shadow knows no bounds, and neither do I."*   5

Brief: Davin "Shadewhisper" Vex is a master infiltrator, known for slipping into the most secure locations and leaving no trace of his presence. His reputation is built on precision and the thrill of the impossible heist.

Vocation: Silent Infiltrator & Saboteur

For the Insightful: Excels in exploiting weaknesses in defenses, from creaky floorboards to magical wards, ensuring a silent and efficient heist.

Description: Davin's wiry frame is clad in muted, dark fabrics, blending seamlessly into the shadows. His silver hair is tied back, while his sharp gray eyes are ever watchful, calculating every move. A scar along his jaw hints at a dangerous past, yet his calm demeanor and subtle smirk reveal his confidence. While Davin's actions are driven by a need for independence, his past as a betrayed guild member leaves him hesitant to trust others.

Wants and Needs:
- Wants: To steal a legendary artifact that is said to make the wielder truly invisible.
- Needs: To rebuild his sense of trust and find allies who will not betray him.

Secret or Obstacle: Hides a growing fear of his reputation, knowing that one mistake could topple the image he has worked so hard to maintain.

Carrying (Total CP: 30):
- Shadowstep Boots (10 points): Enchanted footwear that silences all footsteps, even on noisy terrain.
- Ghostblade (7 points): A blade that leaves no wounds, instead weakening the target's strength.
- Lockbreaker Vial (6 points): A potent liquid that dissolves locks within seconds.
- Cloak of Fading (7 points): A shimmering cloak that briefly turns its wearer invisible.

Lyra "Flicker" Merris   *"A quick hand and a quicker smile can open any door."*   6

Brief: Lyra "Flicker" Merris is a charming thief whose wit and speed make her a force to be reckoned with. Her knack for improvisation has saved her from countless sticky situations, earning her the nickname "Flicker" among her peers.

Vocation: Quick-Handed Trickster

For the Insightful: Her agile reflexes and uncanny ability to read people allow her to anticipate and exploit weaknesses before her targets even realize it.

Description: Lyra's auburn hair is often tied into a loose braid, with strands framing her freckled face. Her hazel eyes sparkle with mischief, reflecting her playful personality. She dresses in snug, lightweight leathers, perfect for quick escapes and acrobatics. Though her carefree demeanor hides it well, Lyra is deeply driven by the desire to prove herself after a troubled upbringing.

Wants and Needs:
- Wants: To break into a noble's vault rumored to contain a map to hidden treasures.
- Needs: To confront her past and mend the broken relationships she left behind.

Secret or Obstacle: Hides her fear of being outmatched, doubting her abilities whenever facing seasoned rivals.

Carrying (Total CP: 27):
- Glimmering Dagger (8 points): A blade that distracts opponents with a dazzling flash of light.
- Larcenist's Gloves (6 points): Special gloves that enhance grip and dexterity for quick pickpocketing.
- Pocket Dust Bomb (5 points): A small pouch that bursts into a cloud of blinding dust when thrown.
- Whispering Cloak (8 points): A cloak that muffles sounds and aids in silent movements.

Taren "Cinders" Grath   *"If it's locked, it's mine."*   7

Brief: Taren "Cinders" Grath is a bold and fiery thief whose daring escapades often leave chaos in their wake. His unorthodox methods prioritize speed over subtlety, making him infamous among those he robs.

Vocation: Flame-Touched Burglar

For the Insightful: Specializes in using fire-based tools and tactics to bypass barriers and create diversions, relying on his quick thinking to escape.

Description: Taren is a rugged man with short-cropped black hair and fiery amber eyes that seem to burn with determination. His leather armor is adorned with singed patches, a testament to his fiery exploits. Despite his reckless tendencies, Taren is surprisingly meticulous when planning his heists, driven by a desire to leave a lasting legacy.

Wants and Needs:
- Wants: To claim a hidden stash of magical gemstones said to amplify elemental magic.
- Needs: To learn patience and restraint, realizing that his brashness often puts himself and others in danger.

Secret or Obstacle: Hides his fear of failure, pushing himself to extremes to ensure he doesn't fall short of his ambitions.

Carrying (Total CP: 24):
- Inferno Pickaxe (10 points): A tool that can burn through locks and barriers.
- Molten Cloak (8 points): A cloak resistant to fire, allowing Taren to safely handle his fiery tools.
- Ember Ring (8 points): A ring that generates a controlled flame, used for precision tasks.

Nyssa Vale — "A shadow doesn't steal; it simply reclaims what was never truly yours." 8

Brief: Nyssa "Whisperfang" Vale is a renowned thief whose silence in the dark is as deadly as her blade. Known for her feline grace and enigmatic demeanor, she is a legend among her peers.

Vocation: Silent Shadow & Infiltrator

For the Insightful: Possesses an unmatched ability to move silently, slipping through even the most heavily guarded spaces undetected.

Description: Nyssa is a sleek and agile figure, her dark gray leathers blending seamlessly into the night. Her piercing green eyes seem to see through any façade, and her raven-black hair is always tied back to avoid distraction. Her calm, collected exterior hides a fiercely independent spirit that thrives on freedom.

Wants and Needs:
- Wants: To infiltrate the grand vault of a corrupt noble to redistribute their ill-gotten wealth.
- Needs: To overcome her tendency to isolate herself and learn to rely on others.

Secret or Obstacle:
Hides a haunting memory of a failed heist that cost the life of her closest friend, fueling her distrust.

Carrying (Total CP: 29):
- Phantom Blade (9 points): A dagger that strikes without a sound, making it ideal for stealth takedowns.
- Ebonshroud Cloak (8 points): A cloak that seems to absorb light, rendering Nyssa nearly invisible in darkness.
- Vial of Smokewrap (6 points): A potion that allows her to temporarily blend into shadows.
- Whisper Boots (6 points): Enchanted footwear that nullifies all sound of movement.

Kieran Alen — "Every coin has a story, and I'll be the one to write its ending." 9

Brief: Kieran "Coinshade" Alen is a charming rogue with a talent for sleight of hand and misdirection. His tongue is as sharp as his blade, making him a natural at charming marks before relieving them of their valuables.

Vocation: Cunning Grifter & Pickpocket

For the Insightful: Masters the art of distraction, using his charisma and sleight of hand to disarm, deceive, and outwit targets.

Description: Kieran is a tall and lean figure, his chestnut hair often tousled and his mischievous blue eyes gleaming with confidence. He dresses in simple, well-worn clothing that belies his finesse, with hidden compartments for stashing stolen goods. Though his words often win the room, Kieran's heart carries the weight of a life spent dodging the law.

Wants and Needs:
- Wants: To secure enough wealth to buy freedom for his imprisoned family.
- Needs: To curb his risk-taking nature, as it frequently lands him in dangerous situations.

Secret or Obstacle:
Hides the guilt of having abandoned his family during their greatest time of need.

Carrying (Total CP: 32):
- Gilded Coin Dagger (10 points): A weapon disguised as an ornate coin, perfect for quick and subtle strikes.
- Shadowlight Satchel (8 points): A magical bag that can hide its contents from detection spells.
- Trickster's Deck (7 points): A set of enchanted cards used for distractions or illusions.
- Vanishing Powder (7 points): A fine dust that blinds and confuses opponents when thrown.

Arden Fenwick — "Reflections reveal more than truth—they show where to strike." 10

Brief: Arden "Glassblade" Fenwick is an eccentric thief who uses mirrors and illusions to outsmart his foes. Known for his theatrical flair, he turns every heist into a performance.

Vocation: Illusionist Thief & Tactician

For the Insightful: Crafts clever diversions using light and reflections, ensuring his escapes are as dazzling as they are effective.

Description: Arden is a wiry man with sandy blond hair and sharp hazel eyes that sparkle with mischief. His dark, fitted clothing is interwoven with shards of mirrored fabric that catch and redirect light in dazzling patterns. Despite his flamboyant exterior, Arden is deeply thoughtful, often planning every move well in advance.

Wants and Needs:
- Wants: To steal the Mirror of Eternity, a fabled artifact said to reveal the past, present, and future.
- Needs: To balance his thirst for fame with the dangers it attracts, learning when to work discreetly.

Secret or Obstacle:
Hides the truth of his lineage, fearing that the noble family he abandoned will one day catch up to him.

Carrying (Total CP: 27):
- Shimmerblade (10 points): A glass-like dagger that refracts light to create disorienting illusions.
- Prism Cloak (9 points): A cloak that bends light, allowing Arden to blend into his surroundings.
- Pocket Mirror Trap (8 points): A small enchanted mirror that captures and redirects magic.

Riven "Nightcoil" Draven   *"A silent hand in the dark rewrites the fate of the unwary."* 11

Brief: Riven "Nightcoil" Draven is a cold and calculating thief known for his precision and unrelenting focus on high-risk heists. His reputation is built on his ability to execute flawless plans, leaving no trace behind.

Vocation: Master Planner & Silent Intruder

For the Insightful: Possesses an exceptional ability to read security measures, devising intricate plans to bypass them with surgical precision.

Description: Riven is a tall, slender figure with sharp cheekbones and piercing gray eyes that seem to scrutinize every detail. He wears dark, fitted attire made from enchanted silk, granting him unmatched stealth. Despite his calm demeanor, his unwavering focus masks a deeply hidden thirst for vengeance against those who wronged him.

Wants and Needs:
- Wants: To amass enough wealth to retire in anonymity, far from the chaos of his past.
- Needs: To confront his deep-seated need for revenge, which often clouds his judgment.

Secret or Obstacle:
Hides his involvement in a failed heist that left an innocent bystander injured, a mistake that haunts him daily.

Carrying (Total CP: 28):
- Ghoststep Boots (8 points): Enchanted footwear that muffle all sound, even on the loudest surfaces.
- Shadowlock Picks (7 points): Lockpicks imbued with magic to bypass even the most intricate locks.
- Nightshade Cloak (7 points): A cloak that absorbs light, making the wearer nearly invisible in darkness.
- Whisper Dagger (6 points): A blade enchanted to pierce silently, leaving no trace of its strike.

Mila "Flicker" Thistledown   *"What's yours was always destined to be mine."* 12

Brief: Mila "Flicker" Thistledown is a quick-witted thief with a knack for sleight of hand and charm. Her bright personality belies her sharp instincts and unmatched dexterity.

Vocation: Charming Pickpocket & Fast-Talker

For the Insightful: Excels at disarming targets through charm and misdirection, leaving them clueless as she vanishes with their valuables.

Description: Mila is a petite woman with curly auburn hair and vibrant hazel eyes that twinkle with mischief. Her brightly colored attire is adorned with subtle pockets for stashing stolen goods, and her light-hearted demeanor often earns her trust she doesn't deserve. Beneath her jovial exterior lies a deep-seated determination to prove herself in a world that underestimates her.

Wants and Needs:
- Wants: To perfect her craft and outshine every thief in the guild.
- Needs: To overcome her insecurities and believe in her worth beyond her skillset.

Secret or Obstacle: Hides a fear of being caught and abandoned by her guild, stemming from a past failure she barely escaped.

Carrying (Total CP: 26):
- Glitterdust Vial (6 points): A shimmering powder that blinds and confuses pursuers.
- Quickfingers Gloves (7 points): Thin gloves that enhance her dexterity for sleight of hand.
- Vanishing Cape (7 points): A cape that creates a momentary illusion of the wearer disappearing.
- Featherlight Dagger (6 points): A lightweight blade ideal for quick strikes or last-minute escapes.

Talon "Ravencut" Morrek   *"A blade in the dark is worth a thousand warnings."* 13

Brief: Talon "Ravencut" Morrek is a brooding thief who specializes in daring heists and quick escapes. His stoic nature hides a sharp intellect and an even sharper blade.

Vocation: Stealthy Duelist & Escape Artist

For the Insightful: Skilled in using his surroundings to outmaneuver opponents, often turns the tides of danger into opportunities.

Description: Talon is a rugged man with short-cropped black hair and deep-set blue eyes that reflect his no-nonsense attitude. He wears a worn leather jacket adorned with small steel studs, each representing a successful heist. His stoicism hides a burning desire to challenge himself with increasingly dangerous jobs, pushing his limits to the edge.

Wants and Needs:
- Wants: To steal the legendary Crown of Shadows, a treasure said to bring power to its holder.
- Needs: To temper his reckless ambition, which often endangers himself and his allies.

Secret or Obstacle: Hides his fear of aging and becoming obsolete, which drives his relentless pursuit of glory.

Carrying (Total CP: 24):
- Ravensteel Blade (10 points): A lightweight sword that hums with dark energy, striking true in the dimmest light.
- Silentstep Greaves (8 points): Boots that make running and climbing completely soundless.
- Pocket Smoke Bombs (6 points): Small orbs that release thick smoke, ideal for quick escapes.

Erynn "Shadowlace" Valara   *"Every lock is a riddle, and every riddle has a solution."*   14

Brief: Erynn "Shadowlace" Valara is a meticulous thief renowned for her ability to infiltrate heavily guarded areas without a whisper of detection. Her intricate plans and calm demeanor make her an invaluable asset to any heist.

Vocation: Silent Infiltrator & Trap Expert

For the Insightful: Masterfully disables traps and deciphers the most complex security systems, making even the most fortified vaults accessible.

Description: Erynn is a wiry, graceful woman with silver hair tied into a tight braid and pale blue eyes that seem to see through walls. She dresses in dark, flexible clothing woven with faintly glowing runes that enhance her agility. Though methodical and composed, she secretly battles feelings of inadequacy, driving her to outdo even her most daring feats.

Wants and Needs:
- Wants: To complete the ultimate heist that will cement her name in legend.
- Needs: To learn to trust others and share the burdens of her dangerous lifestyle.

Secret or Obstacle:
Hides a personal vendetta against a powerful guildmaster who betrayed her, fueling her relentless drive for perfection.

Carrying (Total CP: 34):
- Runespun Cloak (10 points): A cloak etched with magic that dampens sound and enhances flexibility.
- Trapwright's Toolkit (8 points): Compact tools capable of dismantling the most intricate traps.
- Obsidian Dagger (6 points): A blade forged from enchanted stone, cutting silently through any material.
- Phantom Dust Pouches (10 points): Small bags containing powder that obscures vision and muffles sound.

Kassian Thorn   *"The wind carries my whispers, and none can catch its secrets."*   15

Brief: Kassian "Driftblade" Thorn is a roguish thief known for his unparalleled speed and mastery of evasion, darting through crowds and scaling walls as if defying gravity itself. His carefree demeanor hides a deeply strategic mind.

Vocation: Swiftblade & Escape Artist

For the Insightful: Excels at weaving through combat and narrow spaces, outpacing pursuers and making even daring escapes look effortless.

Description: Kassian is a lean, wiry figure with short-cropped auburn hair and sharp green eyes filled with mischief. His sleeveless leather armor is reinforced with lightweight metal plating, designed for mobility. While his confidence often charms his allies, it also leads him to take reckless risks, pushing his luck further than most would dare.

Wants and Needs:
- Wants: To uncover a legendary lost artifact said to grant unmatched agility.
- Needs: To curb his overconfidence, which often lands him in precarious situations.

Secret or Obstacle:
Hides the trauma of losing a childhood friend during a failed escape, a memory that fuels his determination to never be caught.

Carrying (Total CP: 32):
- Windborne Boots (10 points): Enchanted footwear that allows him to run faster and leap farther than any normal human.
- Flicker Dagger (8 points): A blade that blurs when swung, making it difficult for opponents to anticipate his attacks.
- Whispering Grapple (7 points): A magical grappling hook that silently latches onto any surface.
- Veilstone Shard (7 points): A small, enchanted crystal that emits a thin mist to obscure his movements.

"With silent step and shadowed grace, a thief slips through the darkest place. Quick of hand and sharp of eye, they'll leave you none the wiser why."

– Lira Swiftfinger, Balladeer of the Gilded Alley

Town Cryers

Town criers are the heralds of the fantasy realm, their booming voices carrying news and proclamations to the bustling streets. Clad in vibrant attire and brimming with confidence, these figures announce everything from market bargains to royal decrees, serving as the vital link between townsfolk and the greater world. With their knack for drama and commanding presence, town criers are both entertainers and informants, wielding the power to sway public opinion with their words. Loved by some and feared by others, their influence over the crowd is undeniable.

Adventurers should approach town criers with caution, as their power can just as easily destroy as inform. A cautionary tale speaks of Bartholomew Bluster, a jovial town crier famed for his booming voice and flair for gossip. Beloved by many, Bartholomew's penchant for embellishment often concealed a vindictive streak toward those who slighted him.

When Elira, a brash adventurer, dismissed his proclamations as mere theatrics, Bartholomew seized the chance for revenge. With dramatic flair, he declared her a "dangerous rogue," turning the townsfolk against her. Whispers of her supposed misdeeds followed her everywhere, and her once-warm welcome became cold suspicion.

Desperate to clear her name, Elira confronted Bartholomew, but he laughed, twisting the knife further by accusing her of plotting to steal the town's prized harvest. Bartholomew's influence left Elira a pariah, her reputation ruined by a single, vengeful voice.

This tale reminds adventurers of the power town criers wield. While they may seem harmless, their words can shape perceptions and destroy reputations. Tread carefully, for the feathers of their plume may conceal claws of ruin, spreading rumors like wildfire and leaving you at the mercy of the crowd's judgment.

Reginald "Echo" Whitmere

"My voice carries the weight of truth." 1

Brief: A charismatic and flamboyant town crier, Reginald "Echo" Whitmere is the heartbeat of the marketplace, his voice weaving tales of hope, despair, and intrigue. With his booming announcements, he draws the attention of crowds, carefully balancing truth with flair to stir emotions and shape opinions.

Vocation: Town Crier & Crowd Influencer

For the Insightful: Possesses an uncanny ability to read the mood of the crowd, tailoring his words to inspire hope, provoke outrage, or calm unrest as needed.

Description: Reginald is a striking figure with a tall, lean frame, wrapped in vibrant, flowing garments adorned with golden trim and intricate embroidery. His sapphire-blue eyes gleam with intelligence, and his shoulder-length silver hair adds to his air of authority. He carries himself with theatrical grace, his every movement calculated to captivate.

Wants and Needs:
- Want: To gain fame as the most celebrated town crier in the realm, ensuring his name echoes through history.
- Need: To reconcile the moral burden of manipulating public opinion for both good and ill.

Secret or Obstacle: Hides a deep connection to a covert resistance group, using his platform to subtly spread their messages while risking exposure and imprisonment.

Carrying (Total CP: 14):
- Enchanted Bell (8 points): An ornate bell that amplifies his voice, ensuring it carries over even the rowdiest crowds.
- Scroll of Announcements (6 points): A mix of royal proclamations, market updates, and his own coded messages.

Darian "Thunderbell" Grayshade   *"When the bell tolls, the truth resounds."* 2

Brief: Darian "Thunderbell" Grayshade is a commanding town crier whose deep, resonant voice can silence even the rowdiest marketplace. Known for his no-nonsense delivery and striking presence, he is both respected and feared for his unwavering dedication to the truth.
Vocation: Town Crier & Herald of Justice
For the Insightful: Possesses an unmatched ability to project his voice, ensuring every word is heard clearly across vast crowds, no matter the conditions.
Description: Darian is a tall, broad-shouldered man with a grizzled appearance, his salt-and-pepper hair and piercing gray eyes giving him an air of authority. He wears a heavy black coat with brass buttons and a wide-brimmed hat adorned with feathers. Despite his stern demeanor, Darian has a deep love for his city and its people, which drives his pursuit of fairness and clarity.
Wants and Needs:
- Want: To ensure every citizen is informed and empowered by truth, leaving no room for manipulation.
- Need: To find balance, as his rigid adherence to justice often alienates those he seeks to protect.

Secret or Obstacle: Hides a past where he unknowingly spread misinformation, a mistake that led to a public riot and fuels his obsession with accuracy.
Carrying (Total CP: 30):
- Bronze Bell of Echoes (12 points): A bell that reverberates with a magical hum, amplifying his words across entire districts.
- Scroll of Edicts (10 points): A finely crafted scroll case containing decrees and speeches written in his bold hand.
- Heavy Boots of Stability (8 points): Durable boots that keep him grounded, even in chaotic crowds or uneven terrain.

Felix "Quicktongue" Brightwell   *"The news waits for no one, and neither do I!"* 3

Brief: Felix "Quicktongue" Brightwell is a sprightly town crier known for his rapid delivery of announcements and knack for uncovering the latest gossip before anyone else. His energy and enthusiasm make him a beloved figure in the community.
Vocation: Town Crier & Gossipmonger
For the Insightful: Possesses an uncanny ability to gather information from various sources, piecing together rumors and facts with surprising accuracy.
Description: Felix is a wiry man with a mischievous smile, his bright hazel eyes always scanning for the next big scoop. He wears a patchwork vest and breeches, adorned with small trinkets and charms collected from grateful townsfolk. Despite his carefree nature, Felix is deeply loyal to his city, using his platform to uplift the voices of the overlooked and oppressed.
Wants and Needs:
- Want: To become the most trusted source of information in the region, ensuring no story goes untold.
- Need: To learn the value of discretion, as his eagerness for the next big story often leads to unintended harm.

Secret or Obstacle: Hides his guilt over a story he once shared that led to the exile of an innocent family, a mistake he silently works to rectify.
Carrying (Total CP: 28):
- Lightweight Brass Bell (8 points): A small but resonant bell perfect for quick announcements and swift movement.
- Pocket Notebook (6 points): A leather-bound book filled with shorthand notes and contact details of informants.
- Map of City Secrets (8 points): A detailed map marking hidden alleys, rooftops, and other vantage points.
- Bottle of Energizing Elixir (6 points): A drink that keeps him sharp and alert during long hours of work.

Garrick Helmsworth   *"Every proclamation is a promise; every word, a bond."* 4

Brief: Garrick "Iron Voice" Helmsworth is a steadfast town crier who delivers news with a tone of absolute authority, his booming voice carrying both weight and sincerity. He is known for his unshakable demeanor and a reputation for reliability.
Vocation: Town Crier & Voice of the People
For the Insightful: Possesses a natural gravitas that commands respect, ensuring even the most defiant listeners are compelled to heed his words.
Description: Garrick is a towering figure with a powerful build, his chiseled features framed by a neatly trimmed black beard. He wears a simple yet dignified uniform of dark blue with silver accents, along with a sash bearing the crest of his town. Though his exterior is imposing, Garrick is a kind-hearted man who values honesty above all else, often going out of his way to aid those in need.
Wants and Needs:
- Want: To maintain the trust of his community, ensuring they always have a voice through him.
- Need: To reconcile his duty with his personal feelings, as he sometimes struggles to deliver news he disagrees with.

Secret or Obstacle: Hides a forbidden romance with a rival town's crier, a relationship that could undermine his reputation.
Carrying (Total CP: 22):
- Steel Bell of Command (12 points): A sturdy bell with an authoritative tone that silences even the noisiest crowds.
- Ledger of Proclamations (10 points): A meticulously kept record of every announcement he's ever made, symbolizing his commitment.

Tiberius Merriweather   *"Words are my weapon, and the crowd is my battleground."*   5

Brief: Tiberius "Silver Tongue" Merriweather is a flamboyant town crier who captivates audiences with his lyrical delivery and sharp wit. His announcements are as much performance as they are proclamations, making him a favorite among townsfolk.
Vocation: Town Crier & Performer
For the Insightful: Possesses an unparalleled gift for turning even the dullest news into an engaging story, often leaving his listeners enchanted and inspired.
Description: Tiberius is a lean man with silver-streaked hair and an elegantly styled mustache, his sharp blue eyes twinkling with charm. He dresses in finely tailored outfits adorned with embroidered patterns and vibrant colors, carrying an air of sophistication. Though he thrives in the spotlight, Tiberius secretly yearns for a quiet life away from his public persona.
Wants and Needs:
- Want: To become a renowned storyteller whose name is remembered for generations.
- Need: To find someone who sees beyond his charisma and appreciates him for who he truly is.

Secret or Obstacle: Hides self-doubt, fearing that his fame is a fleeting illusion rather than a testament to his talent.
Carrying (Total CP: 40):
- Golden Bell of Melody (15 points): A bell that rings with a harmonious chime, turning his announcements into musical performances.
- Scroll of Riddles (10 points): A collection of witty phrases and humorous riddles used to entertain the crowd.
- Feathered Plume Hat (10 points): A lavish hat that adds flair to his persona and draws attention wherever he goes.
- Potion of Clarity (5 points): A brew that sharpens his mind and helps him craft impeccable speeches.

Bramwell "Iron Will" Stoneward   *"A cities strength lies in the voice of its people."*   6

Brief: Bramwell "Iron Will" Stoneward is a steadfast and no-nonsense town crier, known for his unwavering dedication to delivering the truth. His booming voice and commanding presence leave no room for doubt.
Vocation: Town Crier & Guardian of Truth
For the Insightful: Possesses an unyielding moral compass, ensuring that every word he delivers is rooted in honesty and justice.
Description: Bramwell is a broad-shouldered man with a weathered face and steel-gray eyes that seem to pierce through falsehoods. He wears a practical leather doublet and sturdy boots, accented by a simple silver pin denoting his official role. Though often stoic, Bramwell harbors a deep love for his community, frequently assisting with disputes and offering guidance to those in need.
Wants and Needs:
- Want: To foster a sense of unity among the townsfolk, creating a community built on trust and understanding.
- Need: To reconcile with his estranged family, whose trust he lost due to his relentless pursuit of the truth.

Secret or Obstacle: Hides the guilt of a secret he was forced to keep, a burden that conflicts with his commitment to transparency.
Carrying (Total CP: 37):
- Iron Bell of Resonance (12 points): A sturdy bell that projects his voice with an authoritative, unshakable tone.
- Civic Charter Scroll (10 points): A scroll detailing the laws and decrees of the city, always on hand to settle disputes.
- Weatherproof Cloak (10 points): A durable cloak that shields him from the elements during long hours in the streets.
- Pouch of Herbal Lozenges (5 points): A mix of herbs that soothes his throat and keeps his voice strong.

Elenora "Bright Voice" Fairwind   *"In every word lies the power to inspire greatness."*   7

Brief: Elenora "Bright Voice" Fairwind is a radiant and eloquent town crier whose warm presence and uplifting messages bring hope to her listeners. She is admired for her ability to transform the most challenging news into an opportunity for resilience.
Vocation: Town Crier & Inspirational Orator
For the Insightful: Possesses a profound empathy that allows her to tailor her announcements to the emotional needs of her audience, fostering hope even in dark times.
Description: Elenora is a graceful woman with chestnut hair tied in a loose braid and kind hazel eyes that seem to shine with compassion. She wears a flowing green cloak embroidered with silver vines, her polished boots and leather satchel hinting at her tireless dedication. Though she appears serene, Elenora has endured great personal loss, which fuels her mission to uplift others.
Wants and Needs:
- Want: To inspire her community to face challenges with courage and determination.
- Need: To find personal peace and healing from the tragedies that shaped her path.

Secret or Obstacle: Hides the lingering grief of losing her family in a past tragedy, a pain that often surfaces when she's alone.
Carrying (Total CP: 36):
- Silver Bell of Harmony (14 points): A beautiful bell that emits a soothing chime, calming even the most anxious crowds.
- Journal of Reflections (10 points): A leather-bound book filled with inspiring quotes and notes from her travels.
- Ornate Sash of Station (12 points): A ceremonial sash that marks her as an official representative of the town.

Alaric Morland
"The truth may be bitter, but I'll serve it with a golden spoon." **8**

Brief: A well-spoken and elegant town crier, Alaric "Silver Tongue" Morland is known for his ability to spin even the darkest news into a palatable tale. His charismatic demeanor draws crowds, but his true gift lies in the subtle manipulation of audiences.
Vocation: Town Crier & Diplomatic Voice
For the Insightful: Possesses exceptional rhetorical skills, weaving words with a finesse that calms riots or ignites movements with a mere change in tone.
Description: Alaric stands tall with a poised and regal air, his dark, wavy hair always impeccably groomed and his green eyes radiating intelligence. His attire is a blend of practicality and elegance, featuring a finely tailored doublet with silver embroidery and a long crimson cloak. Beneath his polished exterior, Alaric harbors a history of betrayal, using his craft to rebuild trust in himself and the world.
Wants and Needs:
- Want: To earn the trust and respect of even the most skeptical crowds, securing his legacy as a voice of reason.
- Need: To overcome the lingering doubt in his own integrity after once being used as a pawn in a political conspiracy.

Secret or Obstacle: Hides his involvement in delivering a false proclamation that led to a rebellion, a past mistake that haunts him despite his efforts to make amends.
Carrying (Total CP: 28):
- Silver-Plated Bell (10 points): A bell that emits a harmonious tone, calming crowds even before he speaks.
- Proclamation Scrolls (8 points): Rolled parchments that include official decrees, coded messages, and inspiring speeches.
- Embroidered Gloves (6 points): Gloves enchanted to stay pristine, symbolizing his untarnished public image.
- Potion of Clarity (4 points): A concoction that sharpens his focus, ensuring flawless delivery of important messages.

Merrick "Echoheart" Talbain
"The louder the roar, the deeper the truth strikes." **9**

Brief: A passionate and fearless town crier, Merrick "Echoheart" Talbain delivers news with fiery conviction, unafraid to call out corruption or injustice. His booming voice and heartfelt words resonate with both nobles and commoners alike.
Vocation: Town Crier & Advocate of Justice
For the Insightful: Possesses a magnetic presence that stirs hearts and inspires action, often swaying the tide of public opinion toward righteous causes.
Description: Merrick is a burly man with a booming voice to match his stature, his thick auburn beard and windswept hair adding to his rugged charm. He wears a weathered leather coat adorned with badges representing the towns he's served. Beneath his commanding exterior lies a deep empathy for the downtrodden, fueling his unwavering resolve to bring their voices to light.
Wants and Needs:
- Want: To expose corruption and bring justice to his homeland through the power of his words.
- Need: To learn restraint, understanding that some battles are better fought with strategy rather than volume.

Secret or Obstacle: Hides a secret alliance with a rebel faction, risking his position to ensure their cause is heard without implicating himself.
Carrying (Total CP: 32):
- Iron Bell of Thunder (12 points): A heavy bell that amplifies his voice to startling levels, demanding attention.
- Rebel's Codebook (8 points): A leather-bound journal filled with encoded messages and contact information for allies.
- Heavy Cloak of Resilience (8 points): A thick cloak that protects him from harsh weather during outdoor proclamations.
- Herbal Voice Tonic (4 points): A restorative potion that ensures his voice remains strong despite hours of shouting.

Quentin "Songspire" Delmont
"Words carry weight, but a melody carries souls." **10**

Brief: Quentin "Songspire" Delmont is a melodious town crier who delivers news with a flair for song, turning mundane announcements into captivating performances. His unique approach has earned him fame and admiration far and wide.
Vocation: Town Crier & Musical Messenger
For the Insightful: Possesses an unparalleled talent for combining music with speech, captivating audiences.
Description: Quentin has an enchanting aura, with golden-blond hair tied back neatly and sparkling blue eyes that exude warmth. His colorful attire features flowing scarves and embroidered patterns resembling musical notes. Though his confidence shines on stage, Quentin struggles with self-doubt, fearing that his art may one day fail to inspire.
Wants and Needs:
- Want: To spread joy and inspiration through his musical announcements, leaving a lasting cultural impact.
- Need: To overcome his fear of irrelevance, understanding that his worth isn't tied solely to public admiration.

Secret or Obstacle: Hides a debilitating fear of losing his voice, which he believes would strip him of his identity and purpose.
Carrying (Total CP: 24):
- Golden Chime Rod (8 points): A slender rod that emits a magical chime, harmonizing with his voice to amplify its reach.
- Lute of Resonance (6 points): A lute used to accompany his sung proclamations, adding a layer of charm to his delivery.
- Scarf of Enchantment (6 points): A vibrant scarf that subtly enhances his stage presence, drawing all eyes to him.
- Vial of Honeyed Elixir (4 points): A soothing potion that ensures his voice remains sweet and clear during long performances.

Warriors

Warriors are the steadfast defenders and fearless champions of a fantasy realm, embodying strength, honor, and mastery in battle. Trained from diverse backgrounds—noble knights, rugged mercenaries, and fierce tribal champions—these formidable fighters wield weapons and armor with unparalleled skill. Standing at the forefront of conflicts, warriors face monsters, invading armies, and threats to their people with unwavering courage, earning respect as leaders in times of peril.

Yet, adventurers should tread carefully when dealing with certain warriors, as their reputations can be both inspiring and intimidating. A well-known tale recounts the half-orc Drogath the Unyielding, famed for his unmatched battle prowess and fierce loyalty.

With rippling muscles and a commanding presence, Drogath was a figure of awe, revered for his strength but known to grant his loyalty only to those he deemed worthy.

One day, a group of adventurers sought Drogath's aid in defending a village from raiders. True to his code, he refused to fight until they proved their mettle. Tasked with confronting the raiders themselves, the adventurers accepted his challenge, venturing into the hideout. There, they discovered the raiders' disorganization and outmaneuvered them with clever tactics and teamwork. Victorious, they returned to Drogath, bearing the spoils of their success.

Impressed by their courage and ingenuity, Drogath joined their cause. Together, they became an unstoppable force, defending the village and forging a bond of trust that carried them through countless battles.

This tale reminds adventurers that while warriors like Drogath may seem imposing, proving your valor can turn a daunting encounter into an unbreakable alliance. Strength tempered by loyalty is a shield against any foe, and those who earn the respect of a warrior may find a stalwart ally who stands beside them in the face of any peril.

Darius Ironstride

"Stand firm, and the storm shall break upon your shield." 1

Brief: Darius Ironstride is a battle-hardened warrior, renowned for his unmatched resilience and unyielding loyalty to his comrades. A former soldier turned wandering protector, he now dedicates his life to defending the defenseless.

Vocation: Warrior & Shieldbearer

For the Insightful: Possesses an uncanny ability to read the flow of battle, anticipating enemy movements and using his shield not only as a defense but as a powerful weapon to turn the tide.

Description: Darius is a towering figure with a weathered face, his steely gray eyes reflecting countless battles fought. His broad shoulders and muscular frame are clad in dented yet meticulously maintained plate armor adorned with faintly glowing runes of protection. A tattered red cloak drapes from his shoulders, a reminder of the kingdom he once served.

Wants and Needs:
- Want: To rebuild his honor and become a symbol of hope for those who have lost faith in heroes.
- Need: To confront the memories of his fallen comrades, finding peace with the choices that led to their sacrifice.

Secret or Obstacle: Hides the shame of a moment of hesitation in his past that cost the lives of his closest allies.

Carrying (Total CP: 43):
- Shield of Unyielding Aegis (20 points): A massive shield etched with runes that glows faintly when absorbing damage.
- Longsword (15 points): A finely balanced blade, honed to perfection, with a hilt wrapped in worn leather.
- Pendant of the Fallen (8 points): A silver chain bearing a token from each of his lost comrades, serving as a constant reminder of his purpose.

Kaelen Vyrn   "The weight of my blade is nothing compared to the burden of my duty." 2

Brief: Kaelen Vyrn is a stoic warrior whose unwavering resolve has earned him the moniker "Ironheart." Hailing from a remote mountain village, he wields his blade to defend those who cannot defend themselves, seeing every battle as a test of his endurance and principles.
Vocation: Mountain Defender
For the Insightful: Possesses an unmatched endurance that allows him to withstand extended skirmishes, shrugging off exhaustion while continuing to protect his allies.
Description: Kaelen is a broad-shouldered man with short, raven-black hair and piercing blue eyes that seem to see through to a person's soul. He carries himself with quiet dignity, his presence exuding calm even in the heat of battle. A wolf's tooth talisman hangs from his neck, a symbol of his village's guardian spirit.
Wants and Needs:
- Want: To forge a legacy that will inspire future generations of his village to rise against oppression.
- Need: To reconcile with his own doubts, often questioning whether his strength alone is enough to bring lasting peace.

Secret or Obstacle: Hides the fact that his family's ancestral blade, which he wields, is cursed to bring tragedy to its bearer.
Carrying (Total CP: 44):
- Ancestral Blade of Vyrn (20 points): Forged with an unbreakable alloy, its edge shimmers with an otherworldly hue.
- Steelbound Plate Armor (15 points): Heavy armor reinforced with rare mountain metals, providing extra protection.
- Wolf's Tooth Talisman (5 points): A charm said to ward off evil spirits, though its magic remains unproven.
- Mountainforged Canteen (4 points): A sturdy vessel filled with invigorating spring water from his homeland.

Eryk "Stormbreaker" Thorne   "The storm rages, but my fury burns brighter." 3

Brief: Eryk Thorne is a fearless warrior known for his explosive temper and ferocious combat style, which earned him the title "Stormbreaker." A mercenary by trade, he walks the fine line between hero and rogue, often choosing coin over cause.
Vocation: Mercenary Champion
For the Perceptive: Excels in high-pressure combat, harnessing his rage into devastatingly precise strikes that can dismantle even the strongest foes.
Description: Eryk's fiery red hair is as untamed as his personality, with a beard singed at the tips from countless close calls. His bronze chest plate bears the sigil of a thunderstorm, and his boots are lined with iron to crush those who stand in his path. His smirk, though charming, carries an edge of danger, hinting at his unpredictable nature.
Wants and Needs:
- Want: To amass wealth and renown, dreaming of one day establishing his own mercenary guild.
- Need: To find purpose beyond the chaos of battle, seeking something to fight for other than gold.

Secret or Obstacle: Fears the day his reckless tactics will fail, leaving him vulnerable and costing him everything.
Carrying (Total CP: 38):
- Thunderclap Axe (18 points): A massive axe engraved with runes that crackle faintly with electricity when swung.
- Bronze Chestplate of Defiance (10 points): A sturdy piece of armor designed to intimidate opponents while deflecting heavy blows.
- Pouch of Smoke Bombs (6 points): Small, quick-release bombs used for strategic escapes or creating diversions.
- Stormborn Cloak (4 points): A lightweight cape enchanted to resist wind and rain, keeping him agile in all weather.

Garrik Stonewarden   "A fortress is as strong as its foundation—I am that foundation." 4

Brief: Garrik Stonewarden is a towering, stoic warrior who serves as the shield of his comrades, willing to endure any hardship to ensure their survival. Known for his impenetrable defense, he is the first to stand and the last to fall in any battle.
Vocation: Shieldbearer of the Realm
For the Insightful: Specializes in creating defensive strategies, using his environment and shield to control the battlefield.
Description: Garrik has a rugged appearance, with a thick brown beard and weathered skin from years spent in the elements. His massive shield is nearly as tall as he is, etched with protective glyphs that glow faintly in the heat of combat. His deep voice carries the weight of authority, and his calm demeanor inspires confidence in his allies.
Wants and Needs:
- Want: To create a safe haven for war-weary adventurers, dreaming of a peaceful life after the fight.
- Need: To overcome his survivor's guilt, believing he could have done more in battles long past.

Secret or Obstacle: Carries the burden of knowing his shield's magic siphons a portion of his life force with each use.
Carrying (Total CP: 50):
- Runed Tower Shield (25 points): A colossal shield imbued with ancient glyphs that can absorb and redirect attacks.
- Warden's Halberd (15 points): A versatile weapon with a wickedly sharp blade, ideal for both defense and offense.
- Stonering Gauntlets (6 points): Heavy gloves reinforced with enchanted stone, granting him a crushing grip.
- Stonewarden's Flask (4 points): A durable flask filled with a hearty brew to restore his strength in dire moments.

Aldara "Blade of the Dawn" Selwyn   *"Every sunrise is a promise of victory."*   5

Brief: Aldara Selwyn is a noble knight whose valor and grace on the battlefield have earned her the title "Blade of the Dawn." A beacon of hope for her comrades, she fights with a radiant determination, embodying the ideals of chivalry and sacrifice.

Vocation: Knight of the Radiant Order

For the Insightful: Harnesses an unparalleled sense of timing in combat, striking when the odds seem bleakest to turn the tide of battle.

Description: Aldara is a striking figure clad in gleaming silver armor that catches the light of the sun, symbolizing her unyielding resolve. Her long, golden hair is often braided into a crown, and her emerald-green eyes shine with an unshakable will. Her sword, always at her side, seems to hum faintly when drawn, as if resonating with her unwavering spirit.

Wants and Needs:
- Want: To protect her homeland and ensure its prosperity, dreaming of a future without war.
- Need: To prove her worth to herself, often haunted by self-doubt despite her outward confidence.

Secret or Obstacle:
Hides the secret that her blade, gifted by her order, is slowly draining her vitality to power its radiant glow.

Carrying (Total CP: 42):
- Sunforged Longsword (20 points): A blade enchanted to shine with the brilliance of the sun, blinding foes and bolstering allies.
- Dawnshard Armor (15 points): A suit of armor imbued with protective runes that reflect light, dazzling attackers.
- Pendant of Morninglight (5 points): A charm said to grant courage to those who carry it, though its true power is unknown.
- Vial of Sacred Water (2 points): A small flask containing holy water, used for blessings or healing minor wounds.

Thorne "Ironhide" Drakhar   *"Hit me if you can—but know I'll hit back twice as hard."*   6

Brief: Thorne Drakhar is a battle-hardened warrior renowned for his unbreakable defense and devastating counterattacks. A former gladiator, he thrives in the chaos of combat, turning even the fiercest blows against his enemies.

Vocation: Champion of the Arena

For the Perceptive: Uses his imposing presence and mastery of feints to manipulate enemies into making fatal mistakes.

Description: Thorne is a towering figure with scars crisscrossing his sun-darkened skin, each a testament to his countless victories. His armor is pieced together from salvaged gladiator gear, reinforced with iron plates that glint menacingly in the light. His gravelly voice and piercing gaze command respect, even from his fiercest rivals.

Wants and Needs:
- Want: To establish a training school for aspiring warriors, ensuring his knowledge lives on.
- Need: To overcome his lingering anger toward the nobles who exploited him as a gladiator.

Secret or Obstacle:
Keeps hidden a crippling injury from his gladiator days, which could resurface at any moment in battle.

Carrying (Total CP: 46):
- Gladiator's Maul (18 points): A massive hammer capable of shattering shields and breaking through armor with ease.
- Ironhide Breastplate (15 points): A heavy, scarred chestplate that has withstood countless battles.
- Arena Champion's Belt (8 points): A trophy from his days as a gladiator, said to grant resilience to its wearer.
- Battle Ointment (5 points): A thick salve used to quickly numb pain and seal wounds.

Saryna "Stormcall" Velkor   *"The storm bends to no one—but with me, it strikes true."*   7

Brief: Saryna Velkor is a fierce tribal warrior who commands the elements of the storm, her presence electrifying both friend and foe. Her ferocity in battle is matched only by her devotion to her people, whom she will protect at any cost.

Vocation: Stormbound Protector

For the Insightful: Channels her connection to the elements to augment her strikes, unleashing lightning-fast attacks that leave her enemies reeling.

Description: Saryna's wild, silver-streaked hair seems to crackle with static, framing her sharp, stormy-blue eyes. Her leather armor is adorned with feathers and beads, each symbolizing a victory or a lost comrade. Her voice carries the weight of thunder, commanding attention and respect wherever she goes.

Wants and Needs:
- Want: To unite her fractured tribe and lead them to prosperity, ensuring their survival in a harsh world.
- Need: To master her volatile powers, which often manifest unpredictably in moments of anger.

Secret or Obstacle: Fears that her storm magic will one day consume her, leaving her a danger to those she loves.

Carrying (Total CP: 48):
- Stormcaller's Spear (20 points): A sleek, enchanted spear that crackles with electricity when wielded in battle.
- Thunderhide Armor (15 points): Lightweight leather infused with elemental magic, granting agility and lightning resistance.
- Totem of the Sky (8 points): A carved wooden relic that strengthens her bond with the storm.

Garrick "Stonebreaker" Flint

"The earth endures, and so do I." 8

Brief: Garrick Flint is a rugged mountain warrior whose strength is matched only by his steadfast loyalty. Known for his near-unbreakable resolve, he wields a colossal warhammer to crush any who threaten his homeland.

Vocation: Mountain Guardian

For the Insightful: Harnesses immense physical power and endurance, capable of turning the most desperate battles in his favor.

Description: Garrick is a burly man with a thick, gray-streaked beard and a face weathered by years of harsh mountain winds. His armor is forged from dark iron, etched with runes of protection passed down by his ancestors. He carries himself with the calm authority of one who has faced countless battles and emerged victorious.

Wants and Needs:
- Want: To preserve the ancient traditions of his mountain clan, ensuring their legacy is not forgotten.
- Need: To find peace in a world that often demands violence, balancing his role as protector with his desire for harmony.

Secret or Obstacle: Hides his guilt over a past failure to protect his village, a memory that haunts him every time he takes up his hammer.

Carrying (Total CP: 43):
- Earthshaker Warhammer (20 points): A massive weapon capable of splitting stone, imbued with magic to amplify its force.
- Runed Iron Plate (15 points): Heavy armor inscribed with protective enchantments that grant him increased resistance to damage.
- Clan Emblem Pendant (5 points): A worn silver medallion representing his oath to defend his people.
- Mountain Salve (3 points): A herbal remedy for pain and exhaustion, made from rare mountain herbs.

Dorian Calder

"A blade in hand, a cause in heart—that's all a warrior needs." 9

Brief: Dorian "The Crimson Fang" Calder is a fiery mercenary with a flair for the dramatic, known for his unparalleled skill with twin swords. Though he fights for coin, his charisma and cunning make him a natural leader on the battlefield.

Vocation: Mercenary Duelist

For the Perceptive: Excels in dual-weapon combat, using speed and precision to overwhelm opponents before they can react.

Description: Dorian is a lean but muscular man with a sharp jawline and a roguish smirk, his auburn hair often tied back in a loose ponytail. His leather armor is intricately stitched, balancing mobility and protection, while his twin swords gleam with an ominous red hue. His piercing green eyes are always scanning for opportunity, both in battle and beyond.

Wants and Needs:
- Want: To earn enough wealth and reputation to retire as a free man, away from the chaos of war.
- Need: To reconcile with his estranged family, whose approval he silently craves despite his mercenary lifestyle.

Secret or Obstacle: Keeps hidden a cursed blade among his twin swords, which grants him power but whispers dark thoughts into his mind.

Carrying (Total CP: 46):
- Twin Blades of Embersteel (18 points): Razor-sharp swords enchanted to ignite with flame upon striking a foe.
- Shadowleather Jerkin (15 points): A lightweight armor crafted for speed, imbued with minor stealth-enhancing magic.
- Coin Purse of Plunder (8 points): A pouch jingling with ill-gotten gains, a reminder of his mercenary ways.
- Elixir of the Fox (5 points): A potion that temporarily enhances agility and reflexes.

Kael Ironwood

"Nature's wrath has a protector, and its name is Kael." 10

Brief: Kael "Warden of the Wild" Ironwood is a wandering warrior whose bond with nature fuels his strength. Fiercely protective of the wild, he wields a greatsword forged from meteorite iron, channeling the fury of the elements into every strike.

Vocation: Wilderness Protector

For the Insightful: Masters elemental combat, using the power of wind and earth to augment his strikes and defend against foes.

Description: Kael has long, dark hair streaked with silver, his piercing amber eyes reflecting the storms he's weathered. His armor is a patchwork of natural materials—wood, bone, and steel—blended seamlessly to offer protection and mobility. His voice carries the weight of a lone guardian, a man shaped by his solitary battles against the encroaching dangers of civilization.

Wants and Needs:
- Want: To safeguard the untouched wilderness from exploitation, ensuring its survival for generations.
- Need: To find a community where he belongs, as years of solitude have left him yearning for connection.

Secret or Obstacle: Carries the burden of a curse tied to his sword, demanding blood each time it's drawn.

Carrying (Total CP: 47):
- Stormcleave Greatsword (25 points): A massive blade forged from meteorite iron, imbued with the fury of wind and thunder.
- Ironbark Pauldrons (15 points): Shoulder armor made from enchanted wood, providing surprising resilience against attacks.
- Spirit Totem Necklace (7 points): A charm carved from animal bone, said to connect the wearer to nature's spirits.

Witches

Witches are enigmatic spellcasters, their magic deeply rooted in nature and ancient mysticism. These practitioners harness the elements, herbal lore, and arcane rituals to cast spells, brew potions, and commune with spirits. Often dwelling on the fringes of society—in shadowed woods, remote cottages, or hidden among bustling towns—they inspire both reverence and fear. Witches' abilities to heal, curse, or divine futures grant them a dual reputation: allies to some, harbingers of dread to others.

Adventurers must tread carefully when dealing with witches, for their power can be both wondrous and fearsome. A chilling tale tells of Morwenna the Maleficent, once a healer renowned for her herbal craft, who became infamous for her descent into darker magics. Driven by vengeance, she turned to curses and manipulation, weaving misfortune into the lives of those who crossed her. Crops failed, livestock perished, and villagers dared not speak her name for fear of invoking her wrath.

When a group of brash adventurers sought her aid, dismissing her as a fraud, they demanded spells of great power. Morwenna, unfazed, offered them a potion promising glory. Unbeknownst to them, the elixir carried a curse, amplifying their greed. Consumed by an insatiable hunger for power, the adventurers betrayed one another, descending into chaos. Their quest for dominance unraveled their bonds, revealing the witch's mastery not of brute force, but of desires turned against their wielders.

As the adventurers succumbed to the curse, Morwenna's laughter echoed through the forest, a chilling reminder of the peril in underestimating a witch's power. Broken and aimless, they became shadows of their former selves, forever chasing the strength they lost. This tale serves as a dire warning: while witches may offer great magic and wisdom, their darker inclinations can unleash devastation. Approach with respect and caution, for the wrong witch may entangle you in a web of curses, leaving you haunted by the very desires you sought to fulfill.

Selene Thornweaver — 1
"Nature's wisdom is my power, and the forest is my ally."

Brief: A reclusive enchantress who resides deep within a secluded forest, Selene is both revered and feared for her mastery of natural magic and ancient rituals. Her spells are said to weave life and death together, protecting her domain while striking fear into trespassers.

Vocation: Forest Witch & Spirit Guide

For the Insightful: Possesses an unparalleled connection to nature's spirits, allowing her to channel their energy into powerful enchantments and protective wards.

Description: Selene's appearance is as mysterious as her craft; she has long, silver-streaked hair adorned with wildflowers, eyes that glimmer like moonlit pools, and a serene yet unnerving presence. Whispers of her tragic past—when she lost her family to war and turned to the forest for solace—shape her compassion for outcasts and her mistrust of outsiders.

Wants and Needs:
- Want: To preserve the balance between the natural world and encroaching civilization, protecting her sacred forest.
- Need: To reconcile her loneliness by forming bonds of trust, even with those outside her woodland sanctuary.

Secret or Obstacle: Hides the burden of a cursed spirit bound to her soul, which tempts her to embrace darker magic.

Carrying (Total CP: 27):
- An Enchanted Herbal Satchel (8 points), filled with rare plants that emit soothing or toxic aromas.
- A Witch's Moonstone Amulet (10 points) that amplifies her connection to lunar energy.
- A Tome of Forgotten Rituals (9 points), bound in bark and etched with glowing runes.

Morrigan Duskbloom
"The line between curse and cure is a path I walk alone." **2**

Brief: A cunning herbalist and spellcaster, Morrigan thrives in her isolated marshland home, offering aid to those brave enough to seek her. Whispers of her powerful potions and enigmatic demeanor spread across the realm, attracting both desperate allies and vengeful foes.
Vocation: Swamp Witch & Potion Crafter
For the Insightful: Known for her unparalleled ability to brew potions that heal the gravest wounds or deliver the deadliest poisons, using the swamp's flora and fauna.
Description: Morrigan has raven-black hair streaked with silvery strands, often adorned with swamp lilies and moss. Her deep green eyes shimmer with wisdom, and her sharp features are both alluring and intimidating. Draped in a cloak woven from reeds and enchanted spider silk, she exudes an aura of primal strength.
Wants and Needs:
- Want: To perfect a potion capable of reversing death, a personal obsession born from losing her sister.
- Need: To overcome her growing detachment from humanity, which threatens her ability to form meaningful connections.

Secret or Obstacle: Hides the lingering pain of a magical scar left by her former master, which weakens her powers.
Carrying (Total CP: 30):
- Swamp-Born Cauldron (10 points): A portable cauldron that absorbs magic from the earth around it.
- Bottled Moonlight (8 points): A rare ingredient capable of breaking any curse.
- Pouch of Venomous Roots (7 points): Deadly plants used in her most lethal concoctions.
- Lantern of Wisps (5 points): A glowing lantern that guides travelers through dark waters.

Elyra Ashenveil
"The ashes of the past fuel the flames of my magic." **3**

Brief: An enigmatic fire witch who wields the power of destruction and renewal, Elyra is both feared and admired. Her magic, born from the ashes of her burned homeland, burns fiercely to protect what remains.
Vocation: Fire Witch & Pyromancer
For the Insightful: Draws power from fire and ash, using destructive flames to annihilate foes or cleanse corruption from the land.
Description: Elyra's fiery red hair crackles with embers, and her golden eyes seem to smolder with unspoken power. Her skin bears faint burn marks, a reminder of the devastation she once endured. Clad in robes resembling flickering flames, she carries herself with a quiet, unrelenting determination. She holds a deep grief for the family she lost but channels it into unwavering protection for those in need.
Wants and Needs:
- Want: To rebuild her homeland, using her magic to restore its once-thriving forests.
- Need: To overcome her fear of losing control over her destructive powers, which often hold her back.

Secret or Obstacle: Hides the truth about her magic's origins—a pact with a fiery spirit that could one day claim her life.
Carrying (Total CP: 38):
- Ashbound Cloak (10 points): A magical cloak that protects her from extreme heat and flames.
- Phoenix Feather Amulet (9 points): A talisman that boosts her fire magic and grants a spark of regeneration.
- Charcoal Grimoire (8 points): A fireproof tome containing her most devastating spells.
- Obsidian Wand (6 points): A short wand with the ability to channel flames into precise strikes.
- Flask of Ember Elixir (5 points): A fiery potion that enhances her stamina and magical output.

Naida Frostglow
"The cold reveals truth, and I am its herald." **4**

Brief: A mysterious frost witch from the northern reaches, Naida is known for her icy demeanor and unyielding resolve. Her magic brings both life-saving protection and bone-chilling retribution.
Vocation: Ice Witch & Winter Seer
For the Insightful: Can summon blizzards and freezing winds, freezing her enemies in their tracks or preserving life in suspended animation.
Description: Naida's pale blue hair flows like a frozen river, and her crystalline eyes pierce into the souls of those who meet her gaze. Once a healer of a northen tribe, she now roams the frozen wastes, offering aid and justice as the spirits guide her.
Wants and Needs:
- Want: To uncover the truth behind the destruction of her tribe, seeking justice for those lost.
- Need: To let go of her past grief, allowing herself to embrace the possibility of new bonds.

Secret or Obstacle: Hides a frost-bound curse placed upon her by a rival sorcerer, growing stronger with every life she saves.
Carrying (Total CP: 31):
- Icy Diadem (12 points): A crown that grants her command over ice and snowstorms.
- Winter's Grimoire (10 points): A magical book that contains ancient frost spells and enchantments.
- Cryoshard Staff (9 points): A tall staff made of enchanted ice that never melts, amplifying her power.

Thyra Nightshade

"From shadows and whispers, the truth takes root." **5**

Brief: A reclusive forest witch who thrives in the darkest corners of the woods, Thyra's magic bends shadows and flora to her will. Her knowledge of poisonous plants and obscure rituals makes her both feared and sought after.

Vocation: Forest Witch & Shadowbinder

For the Insightful: Masters shadow magic intertwined with botanical lore, crafting poisons and antidotes with equal precision.

Description: Thyra has long, ebony hair braided with vines, and her piercing violet eyes seem to glow in the dark. Her flowing robes are adorned with living moss and bioluminescent fungi, blending her into the eerie glow of her forest home. Once a healer for a betrayed noble family, she now lives in exile, guarding her secrets from those who might exploit them.

Wants and Needs:
- Want: To perfect a ritual that could purify corrupted lands, restoring balance to the forests.
- Need: To forgive herself for abandoning the noble family she once served, a guilt that haunts her.

Secret or Obstacle:
Hides a pact with shadow spirits who constantly demand tributes, threatening to consume her if she falters.

Carrying (Total CP: 39):
- Shadowwoven Cloak (10 points): A magical cloak that allows her to vanish into darkness.
- Vial of Nightbloom Essence (9 points): A rare elixir distilled from a deadly flower, used for powerful spells.
- Runed Staff of Obscurity (8 points): A twisted wooden staff that channels shadow magic.
- Pouch of Whispering Seeds (7 points): Seeds that sprout rapidly into shadowy vines on command.
- Moonlit Lantern (5 points): A faintly glowing lantern used to summon spirits during her rituals.

Isolde Frostvine

"The frost preserves what the fire seeks to destroy." **6**

Brief: A stoic yet compassionate ice witch, Isolde wanders the tundras, preserving the lives of those who brave the cold. Her magic is both a shield and a sword, embodying the beauty and danger of winter.

Vocation: Ice Witch & Winter Protector

For the Insightful: Harnesses frost to create barriers of ice and life-preserving enchantments, keeping her allies safe in the harshest conditions.

Description: Isolde has pale, icy-blue skin and hair that cascades like frozen silk. Her piercing silver eyes seem to reflect the northern lights, and her breath always carries a frosty mist. She wears robes adorned with intricate snowflake patterns and lined with enchanted fur. A tragic loss in her youth drives her to protect others from a similar fate, though her stoicism hides the warmth of her heart.

Wants and Needs:
- Want: To create an eternal sanctuary where the harshness of winter can be tamed for those in need.
- Need: To trust others to help shoulder her burden of protecting the vulnerable.

Secret or Obstacle: Hides the sorrow of an ancient frost spirit bound to her, whispering doubts and threatening to consume her.

Carrying (Total CP: 37):
- Glacierheart Amulet (12 points): A crystalline pendant that amplifies her frost magic.
- Aurora Staff (10 points): A staff that summons icy winds and the light of the northern skies.
- Frostwoven Cloak (9 points): A magical cloak that shields her from even the fiercest blizzards.
- Icicle Dagger (6 points): A blade of solid ice that never melts, used in both combat and rituals.

Marla Emberthorn

"Fire burns brighter when fueled by purpose." **7**

Brief: A passionate fire witch with a talent for destructive and creative magic, Marla's flames ignite both hope and fear. Her fiery personality mirrors the unpredictable nature of her spells.

Vocation: Fire Witch & Flame Artist

For the Insightful: Specializes in flame-based magic that can destroy her enemies or forge tools of wonder.

Description: Marla's fiery red hair crackles with embers, and her amber eyes seem to blaze with intensity. She wears an asymmetrical robe, singed at the edges, with intricate flame motifs embroidered in gold. Her hands bear burn scars from her early experiments with fire magic. A former circus performer, she uses her magic to awe audiences.

Wants and Needs:
- Want: To master a legendary flame spell that could create everlasting warmth for her people.
- Need: To temper her recklessness, which often endangers those around her.

Secret or Obstacle: Hides a cursed flame that burns within her, threatening to consume her entirely if she loses control.

Carrying (Total CP: 37):
- Flamelash Whip (12 points): A magical whip of fire that extends and contracts at will.
- Blazing Circlet (10 points): A crown that enhances her fire magic while shielding her from heat.
- Phoenix-Feather Robes (9 points): Enchanted garments that allow her to absorb and redirect flames.
- Jar of Eternal Embers (6 points): A mystical jar containing embers that never die, used in rituals.

Lysara Moondrake
"The moon whispers secrets only the wise dare to hear." **8**

Brief: A mystic moon witch who draws her power from lunar cycles, Lysara's magic flows with the rhythm of the celestial bodies. Her spells often blur the line between enchantment and prophecy, guiding lost souls to their destinies.

Vocation: Moon Witch & Lunar Oracle

For the Insightful: Harnesses moonlight to weave powerful enchantments and divinations, using her magic to reveal hidden truths and protect the vulnerable.

Description: Lysara has shimmering silver hair that cascades like moonbeams, and her pale skin glows faintly in the dark. Her robes are adorned with crescent moons and constellations that seem to move when touched by light. Her serene demeanor belies a tragic past, where her prophecies were misunderstood, leading to a village's downfall.

Wants and Needs:
- Want: To create a sanctuary for those seeking wisdom and peace under the guidance of the moon.
- Need: To forgive herself for past mistakes and trust her visions once more.

Secret or Obstacle:
Hides her growing connection to an ancient lunar entity that demands greater sacrifices with each spell she casts.

Carrying (Total CP: 38):
- Lunar Scepter (12 points): A silver staff tipped with a glowing moonstone, amplifying her connection to the moon.
- Veil of Starlight (10 points): A shimmering cloak that allows her to fade into moonlit shadows.
- Moonlit Orb (8 points): A crystal ball that reflects the phases of the moon, aiding her in divination.
- Silver-Tipped Arrows (8 points): Enchanted projectiles imbued with lunar energy, meant for protection.

Thalena Briarhollow
"Even the fiercest thorn hides a bloom within." **9**

Brief: A mysterious hedge witch who thrives in dense, overgrown forests, Thalena's magic entwines the beauty and danger of wild flora. Her spells often combine herbal wisdom with unpredictable elemental surges.

Vocation: Hedge Witch & Keeper of the Wilds

For the Insightful: Commands the wild growth of plants, using her powers to entangle foes, heal wounds, and nurture the forest.

Description: Thalena's auburn hair is woven with small twigs, moss, and flowers, giving her an unkempt but enchanting appearance. Her green eyes seem to reflect the heart of the forest, and her earthy-toned garb is layered with pockets filled with herbs and seeds. She once protected an enchanted grove from poachers, earning both the forest spirits' favor and a deep scar across her cheek.

Wants and Needs:
- Want: To restore a dying grove that serves as a sacred refuge for endangered creatures.
- Need: To overcome her distrust of outsiders, whose greed she has witnessed too many times.

Secret or Obstacle: Hides a cursed seed planted in her heart by a jealous rival, which slowly drains her life force.

Carrying (Total CP: 39):
- Staff of Blossoms (11 points): A wooden staff that sprouts flowers and vines, responding to her emotions.
- Thornweave Cloak (9 points): A protective garment of brambles that ensnares attackers.
- Satchel of Enchanted Seeds (8 points): Magical seeds that grow into traps or barriers in seconds.
- Potion of Verdant Renewal (7 points): A brew that heals wounds and restores vitality.
- Herbalist's Kit (4 points): Tools for crafting salves and potions on the go.

Erynn Duskwind
"With the breeze comes whispers of the forgotten." **10**

Brief: A nomadic wind witch who roams the open plains, Erynn channels the power of the winds to cast spells of freedom and fury. Her magic is as unpredictable as a storm, making her both a savior and a danger to those she aids.

Vocation: Wind Witch & Stormcaller

For the Insightful: Manipulates air currents to create protective barriers, launch devastating gusts, and summon storms.

Description: Erynn's ash-blonde hair constantly seems to move, as if stirred by an unseen breeze, and her sharp blue eyes gleam with restless energy. Her flowing robes ripple like the wind, embroidered with streaks of silver resembling lightning. She wears a necklace made of storm glass, said to hold the essence of captured lightning. Haunted by an incident where she accidentally unleashed a tornado, she travels to atone for the destruction caused.

Wants and Needs:
- Want: To harness her chaotic storm magic into a focused tool for justice.
- Need: To find a permanent home where she can feel grounded and escape her guilt.

Secret or Obstacle: Hides her fear of losing control, as her magic grows stronger and harder to contain with each passing year.

Carrying (Total CP: 30):
- Stormglass Pendant (12 points): A charm that amplifies her control over storms but demands a mental toll.
- Windswept Cloak (10 points): A billowing cloak that grants her flight in short bursts.
- Bottled Tempest (8 points): A glass vial containing a captured storm, unleashed in emergencies.

Isolde Blackthorn "Even in the darkest woods, life stirs beneath the shadow." 11

Brief: A reclusive forest witch feared by nearby villagers, Isolde uses her knowledge of deadly plants and arcane rituals to safeguard her home. Her presence commands both respect and apprehension, as she decides who may tread within her domain.

Vocation: Forest Witch & Keeper of Secrets

For the Insightful: Uses her affinity for poisonous plants and dark magic to protect her home and those who seek her aid, blending danger and healing in equal measure.

Description: Isolde's raven-black hair is streaked with white, tied back with vines that bloom with nightshade flowers. Her dark, piercing eyes seem to watch the soul, and her pale skin is decorated with runic tattoos glowing faintly green. She carries an eerie calm, her voice soft yet commanding, born of decades spent in isolation after being betrayed by those she once called family.

Wants and Needs:
- Want: To preserve the ancient forest she calls home from encroaching settlers and hunters.
- Need: To reconnect with others and let go of her self-imposed exile.

Secret or Obstacle: Hides her fear of losing control over the dark powers she has cultivated, which grow stronger with each ritual.

Carrying (Total CP: 38):
- Nightshade Staff (12 points): A gnarled branch imbued with venomous magic, amplifying her poison-based spells.
- Cloak of Whispering Shadows (10 points): A cloak that allows her to blend into the forest's darkness, becoming nearly invisible.
- Grimoire of Toxic Spells (9 points): A leather-bound tome containing rare incantations involving poisons and hexes.
- Vial of Eternal Night (7 points): A potion that temporarily blinds her enemies while shielding her in darkness.

Cerridwen Greenspire "The earth speaks to those who listen; let me teach you its language." 12

Brief: A gentle herbal witch and healer, Cerridwen travels between villages to aid the sick and spread wisdom about living harmoniously with nature. Her kindness is matched only by her unyielding resolve to protect the natural world.

Vocation: Herbal Witch & Nature's Healer

For the Insightful: Harnesses the earth's energy and her encyclopedic knowledge of herbs to brew powerful healing potions and protective wards.

Description: Cerridwen's hair is the color of autumn leaves, falling in soft waves around her freckled face. Her warm green eyes radiate a sense of comfort, and her simple linen dress is adorned with belts and pouches brimming with dried herbs. Despite her serene exterior, she carries the weight of guilt from failing to save her sister, a tragedy that pushed her to master her craft.

Wants and Needs:
- Want: To create a sanctuary for endangered plants and animals where nature can thrive undisturbed.
- Need: To forgive herself for past failures and find confidence in her abilities.

Secret or Obstacle: Hides that she once unintentionally cursed a village's crops while experimenting with forbidden spells.

Carrying (Total CP: 34):
- Herbalist's Satchel (10 points): A bag containing rare herbs and seeds, each with unique magical properties.
- Earthbound Staff (9 points): A wooden staff that strengthens her connection to the land and its energies.
- Pouch of Warding Stones (8 points): Smooth stones etched with sigils, used to protect homes from curses and hexes.
- Healing Balm of the Ancients (7 points): A salve that cures nearly any ailment, made from a long-lost recipe.

Maelira Duskrune "The stars and shadows weave a fate no mortal can escape." 13

Brief: A mysterious star witch who specializes in divination and weaving illusions, Maelira's predictions are as dazzling as they are unsettling. She is sought after for her prophetic visions, though her cryptic words often leave more questions than answers.

Vocation: Star Witch & Weaver of Fate

For the Insightful: Channels celestial magic and manipulates starlight to craft illusions, read destinies, and mislead foes.

Description: Maelira's platinum hair seems to shimmer like starlight, and her violet eyes glitter with an otherworldly glow. Her flowing robes are dyed midnight blue, embroidered with constellations that shift and sparkle under the moon. A tragic event in her youth, where her predictions failed to save her village from a devastating attack, fuels her obsessive drive to perfect her craft.

Wants and Needs:
- Want: To unlock the secrets of the stars and rewrite her own fate.
- Need: To trust others and accept help in her quest for redemption.

Secret or Obstacle: Hides her dependence on an ancient star spirit, whose demands grow more dangerous with each prophecy.

Carrying (Total CP: 39):
- Celestial Orb (12 points): A glowing sphere that captures starlight, used for her most powerful spells.
- Mantle of the Cosmos (10 points): A cloak that projects shifting illusions of the night sky, confounding her enemies.
- Runic Star Charts (9 points): Intricate maps that allow her to navigate the heavens and tap into cosmic energy.
- Vial of Stardust (8 points): A sparkling powder that blinds foes and creates dazzling illusions.

Lyssandra Nightshade — 14
"In the still of the forest, whispers of ancient power awaken."

Brief: A reclusive shadow witch, Lyssandra uses her mastery over twilight magic to shield the innocent and curse the corrupt. Her presence is both mysterious and commanding, leaving an indelible impression on those who dare to approach her secluded domain.

Vocation: Shadow Witch & Twilight Protector

For the Insightful: Manipulates shadows and moonlight, creating powerful illusions and imbuing her spells with the silent strength of the night.

Description: Lyssandra's long, flowing hair glimmers like silver under the moonlight, framing a face with piercing, dark eyes that seem to see into the soul. Her intricate robes shimmer with shifting patterns of light and shadow, and the soft chiming of charms attached to her belt echoes as she moves.

Wants and Needs:
- Want: To uncover the secrets of the ancient moon goddess and restore balance to her cursed forest.
- Need: To find peace with her past failures and embrace her role as a protector.

Secret or Obstacle: Hides her fear of losing herself to the shadows she wields.

Carrying (Total CP: 40):
- Twilight Scepter (12 points): A staff crafted from blackened wood, tipped with a crescent moon that glows faintly in the dark.
- Cloak of Moonlit Veil (10 points): A shimmering garment that allows her to vanish into shadows at will.
- Pouch of Lunar Dust (8 points): A sparkling powder that blinds enemies and reveals hidden paths under moonlight.
- Rune of Eternal Night (7 points): A stone etched with ancient glyphs, enabling her to cast protective wards.
- Bottle of Midnight Elixir (3 points): A potent concoction that restores her magical energy during battle.

Eryndra Thornwild — 15
"The roots of the earth hold secrets only the brave dare to seek."

Brief: A fierce hedge witch with a reputation for brewing powerful elixirs, Eryndra combines primal magic and cunning wit to overcome her foes. Her deep bond with the wilderness makes her a formidable ally and an unpredictable adversary.

Vocation: Hedge Witch & Brewmaster of the Wilds

For the Insightful: Masters the art of alchemy and druidic magic, crafting potions from rare ingredients and unleashing the forces of nature in combat.

Description: Eryndra's auburn hair is wild and adorned with feathers, beads, and twigs, giving her the appearance of a walking forest. Her amber eyes are sharp and calculating, and her earthy garb is reinforced with moss and bark, blending her seamlessly into her surroundings. She is fiercely independent, driven by a desire to protect her land from encroachment after her ancestral home was ravaged by greedy settlers.

Wants and Needs:
- Want: To restore her homeland to its former glory, free from the scars of human greed.
- Need: To open her heart to allies who share her goal, rather than shouldering the burden alone.

Secret or Obstacle: Hides the fact that she made a pact with a forest spirit, whose increasing demands may one day force her to betray her morals.

Carrying (Total CP: 46):
- Thornwood Staff (14 points): A gnarled staff covered in sharp thorns, which channels both defensive and offensive magic.
- Potion of Verdant Fury (10 points): A vial containing a potion that transforms her into a living embodiment of the forest, covered in vines and thorns.
- Satchel of Foraged Wonders (9 points): A collection of rare herbs and fungi, used for brewing her most potent elixirs.
- Chime of Wild Spirits (8 points): A small bell that summons minor forest spirits to her aid.
- Barkskin Talisman (5 points): An amulet that hardens her skin, making her nearly impervious to physical harm.

"Beware the witches' whispered rhyme, for words may twist like creeping vines. A gift they give, a curse they bind, their secrets kept in shadowed minds."

— Elowen Nightwhisper, Bard of the Midnight Grove

Witch Hunters

Witch hunters are the relentless enforcers of a fantasy realm, guardians against the threats of dark magic and malevolent sorcery. Skilled in tracking practitioners of forbidden magics and supernatural beings, these individuals wield arcane knowledge, religious zeal, and specialized weapons. Operating on the fringes of legality, their righteous pursuit often blurs the line between justice and fanaticism, making them both feared and respected within their communities.

Adventurers should tread cautiously around witch hunters, for their fervor can lead to catastrophic outcomes. A chilling tale speaks of Seraphina, a striking half-elf witch hunter whose beauty masked an unyielding determination to cleanse the world of dark magic.

Her charm won allies, but her zeal revealed a darker side, one willing to act without question or mercy.

One fateful night, Seraphina pursued rumors of a witch deep in the forest, accused of causing deadly accidents in a nearby village. In a secluded glade, she found a frightened young healer who pleaded her innocence. Blinded by zeal, Seraphina dismissed her protests and struck her down. Too late, the truth was revealed: the healer was a guardian spirit of the forest, and her death unleashed an ancient curse. Chaos erupted as storms raged and nature withered, leaving Seraphina hunted by the very forces she sought to destroy.

Branded a harbinger of doom by those she once protected, Seraphina's legend became a warning.

Her tale serves as a grim reminder to adventurers: while witch hunters may pursue noble goals, their unchecked zeal can bring ruin. Beware their fervor, for the line between hunter and hunted is thin, and their actions may draw you into a web of vengeance, where justice twists into shadow.

Alaric Ironbrand
"The light shall pierce the shadow, no matter how deep it runs." 1

Brief: A grim and resolute witch hunter who is renowned for his unyielding dedication to purging the world of dark magic. Haunted by a past encounter with a coven that claimed his family.

Vocation: Witch Hunter & Arcane Tracker

For the Perceptive" Possesses an uncanny ability to detect residual traces of magic and track supernatural entities.

Description: A towering figure with rugged features, piercing gray eyes, and a streak of silver in his dark, shoulder-length hair—a testament to years spent confronting otherworldly horrors. He wears reinforced leather armor etched with warding runes, paired with a long, tattered cloak that obscures his weaponry.

Wants and Needs:
- Want: Eliminate all dark magic from the realm, dreaming of a future where no family endures the loss he suffered.
- Need: To reconcile his faith with his growing doubt, learning compassion for those caught between light and shadow.

Secret or Obstacle:

Hides his guilt over a young girl he once condemned, later discovering she was innocent. This memory haunts him, often manifesting as vivid nightmares that shake his resolve.

Carrying (Total CP: 26):
- Runed Crossbow (10 points): A weapon infused with light-based enchantments to sear magical beings.
- Silvered Longsword (9 points): A finely crafted blade, its edges imbued with holy water to cut through dark magic.
- Holy Relic Amulet (7 points): A charm said to shield the wearer from curses and hexes.

Elyria Shadowthorn — *"Evil hides in plain sight, but so do I."* 2

Brief: A cunning and resourceful witch hunter, Elyria uses her wits and guile to outsmart witches who hide among society. Raised by a secretive order dedicated to rooting out magical corruption, she operates in the shadows.
Vocation: Witch Hunter & Infiltrator
For the Perceptive: Possesses an unrivaled ability to blend seamlessly into any environment, using keen observation to uncover hidden practitioners of dark magic.
Description: Elyria is a slender figure with sharp features, piercing emerald eyes, and long black hair tied back in a braid adorned with charms of protection. She wears dark leather armor designed for silent movement, with hidden compartments for vials and daggers. Elyria wrestles with the moral complexities of her work, especially when innocents become collateral.
Wants and Needs:
- Want: To dismantle every dark coven from within, dreaming of a world where the innocent can thrive without fear.
- Need: To trust others, learning to rely on allies rather than shouldering the burden of justice alone.

Secret or Obstacle: Hides a personal connection to a powerful witch she cannot bring herself to hunt—her estranged sister, who may yet be redeemable.
Carrying (Total CP: 26):
- Shadowpiercer Dagger (8 points): A blackened blade enchanted to dispel magical wards upon contact.
- Lockbreaker's Toolkit (7 points): Tools designed to bypass arcane and mundane locks alike.
- Witchbane Grenades (6 points): Small glass orbs filled with anti-magic powder that disrupt spellcasting.
- Cloak of Silence (5 points): A lightweight garment that muffles sound and hides her in the dark.

Gareth Hollowsteel — *"With every strike, I avenge those who cannot fight for themselves."* 3

Brief: A stoic and disciplined warrior-turned-witch hunter, channeling his grief into a relentless crusade against the dark forces that claimed his homeland. His unshakable resolve and unmatched combat prowess make him a fearsome opponent of evil.
Vocation: Witch Hunter & Heavy Blade Specialist
For the Perceptive: Possesses extraordinary strength and a deep understanding of combat techniques to counteract magic.
Description: Gareth is a towering figure clad in heavy plate armor adorned with faintly glowing holy runes. His steel-gray eyes reflect a lifetime of hardship, while his grizzled beard and scarred hands tell the story of countless battles. At his side is a massive greatsword etched with symbols of protection. Despite his intimidating exterior, Gareth is a man of quiet compassion, offering guidance and protection to those who have been victimized by dark magic.
Wants and Needs:
- Want: To restore his fallen village's honor by eradicating the witches responsible for its destruction.
- Need: To accept that vengeance alone cannot heal the wounds of his past, finding solace in building a new future.

Secret or Obstacle: Hides growing reliance on enchanted weapons, fears they may corrupt him as much as the magic he fights.
Carrying (Total CP: 45):
- Runeforged Greatsword (15 points): A massive blade blessed to cut through magical barriers and dark entities.
- Holy Lantern (10 points): A light source that reveals hidden magical traces and wards off spirits.
- Witchward Gauntlets (8 points): Heavy gloves that protect the wearer from curses and hexes when in direct contact.
- Alchemist's Belt (7 points): A bandolier holding vials of anti-venom, purifying elixirs, and flammable oil.
- Reinforced Healing Tonic (5 points): A potent mixture to recover from even the gravest injuries.

Maelis Dawnspire — *"Justice is my creed, and fire is my language."* 4

Brief: A zealous and charismatic witch hunter, Maelis is as much a symbol of hope as she is a weapon of divine wrath. Blessed with the ability to conjure holy flames, she uses her fiery power to cleanse corruption and rally others to her cause.
Vocation: Witch Hunter & Holy Fire Conduit
For the Perceptive: Possesses a natural connection to holy fire, enabling her to summon flames that both purify and destroy.
Description: Maelis is a striking woman with short, fiery red hair and golden eyes that seem to flicker with embers. Her staff, crowned with a blazing crystal, serves as both weapon and beacon.
Wants and Needs:
- Want: To unite scattered witch-hunting factions into a singular force of justice, ensuring no soul suffers under dark magic.
- Need: To temper her burning passion with patience, learning that mercy can be as powerful as wrath.

Secret or Obstacle: Hides the truth about her powers' origin: a deal made with an ancient spirit of fire, with unknown motives.
Carrying (Total CP: 35):
- Blazing Staff of Purity (12 points): A long staff crowned with a holy crystal that channels her fire magic.
- Purification Medallion (10 points): A pendant that amplifies her protective spells and wards against possession.
- Flameforged Boots (8 points): Sturdy footwear enchanted to grant immunity to fire and scorching heat.
- Spellbound Satchel (5 points): A bag containing sacred texts, ritual candles, and binding scrolls.

Ravik Ironbrand   *"The line between hunter and hunted is razor-thin."*   5

Brief: A hardened and pragmatic witch hunter, Ravik is a lone wanderer who thrives in the harshest environments. With an unshakable resolve and years of survival experience, he specializes in tracking and eliminating witches who prey on remote communities.

Vocation: Witch Hunter & Survivalist Tracker

For the Perceptive: Possesses unparalleled tracking skills and a deep understanding of wilderness survival, enabling him to pursue targets across any terrain.

Description: A grizzled man with sun-weathered skin, piercing gray eyes, and a mane of unkempt brown hair streaked with silver. His patched leather armor is adorned with trophies from his hunts—bone charms, dried herbs, and strange trinkets. Despite his rugged demeanor, Ravik carries a quiet sense of justice, determined to protect those who cannot protect themselves.

Wants and Needs:
- Want: To rid the untamed lands of witch covens that prey on isolated communities.
- Need: To reconcile with the guilt of past hunts where innocent lives were lost, finding peace in his mission.

Secret or Obstacle: Hides a curse inflicted upon him by a witch's dying breath, slowly eroding his health and his ability to fight.

Carrying (Total CP: 42):
- Ironwood Crossbow (12 points): A sturdy weapon imbued with enchantments to pierce magical shields.
- Tracker's Journal (10 points): A well-worn tome filled with notes on various witches and their weaknesses.
- Witchbane Bolts (8 points): Specially crafted projectiles designed to disrupt spellcasting on impact.
- Hunter's Cloak (7 points): A weather-resistant garment that conceals him in the wilderness.
- Elixir of Endurance (5 points): A potion that grants temporary resistance to fatigue and physical pain.

Ilyana Frostveil   *"Truth burns brighter than any flame—it exposes, cleanses, and purges."*   6

Brief: Ilyana is an icy and unrelenting witch hunter whose stoic demeanor masks a passionate hatred for dark magic. Trained by a secluded monastery, she uses her unique blend of holy magic and martial skill to unearth and destroy evil.

Vocation: Witch Hunter & Frostbound Purifier

For the Perceptive: Possesses the rare ability to channel frost magic into her weapons, breaking through magical defenses.

Description: Ilyana is a pale-skinned woman with silvery hair braided down her back, her ice-blue eyes glowing faintly with arcane power. She dons a silver-trimmed coat reinforced with frost-forged steel, exuding a chill that unsettles even her allies. Despite her frosty exterior, Ilyana's conviction drives her to protect the innocent, though she is often misunderstood for her unyielding methods.

Wants and Needs:
- Want: To uncover and destroy a hidden network of witches spreading corruption across the land.
- Need: To balance her pursuit of justice with compassion, learning to value mercy alongside discipline.

Secret or Obstacle: Hides a painful secret: her magic originates from an ancient pact made by her ancestors, which demands a terrible price over generations.

Carrying (Total CP: 36):
- Frostbound Blade (12 points): A longsword that radiates icy energy, capable of shattering magical constructs.
- Wardbreaker Pendant (9 points): A charm that disrupts protective enchantments in her vicinity.
- Cryoshard Elixirs (8 points): Potions that amplify her frost magic temporarily while protecting her from heat-based spells.
- Sealed Tome of Frost (7 points): An ancient book containing rituals and spells tied to her unique abilities.

Darin Blackthorn   *"Magic can twist the mind, but a steel heart remains unbroken."*   7

Brief: A stoic and disciplined witch hunter, Darin employs a meticulous approach to his hunts, wielding a combination of logic and brute force. Once a military officer, he now channels his tactical expertise into the war against dark sorcery.

Vocation: Witch Hunter & Tactical Enforcer

For the Perceptive: Possesses an analytical mind and exceptional combat strategy, allowing him to outwit and overpower foes.

Description: Darin is a broad-shouldered man with dark hair tied back in a short ponytail and a heavy beard streaked with gray. His weathered armor is adorned with intricate engravings of shields and swords, symbols of his military past. Beneath his stern exterior lies a man haunted by the loss of his comrades to a dark sorceress years ago, fueling his tireless quest.

Wants and Needs:
- Want: To build a united force capable of eradicating witchcraft from the realm.
- Need: To confront the trauma of his past and forgive himself for the lives he couldn't save.

Secret or Obstacle: Hides a reliance on forbidden anti-magic techniques, fearing they may cost him the soul he seeks to protect.

Carrying (Total CP: 40):
- Runed Warhammer (15 points): A weapon designed to break magical barriers and physical defenses alike.
- Tactical Map Kit (10 points): A set of enchanted maps that reveal magical activity within a radius.
- Holy Flame Grenades (8 points): Explosive devices that burn away corruption and purify cursed areas.
- Iron Resolve Amulet (7 points): A charm that bolsters his resistance to mental manipulation and fear-based magic.

Erynn Duskbane — "The shadows conceal many evils, but I am the light that exposes them." 8

Brief: Erynn is a fierce and unwavering witch hunter, trained in secret by an ancient order dedicated to purging dark magic. Known for her methodical precision and sharp instincts, earning her a fearsome reputation in both criminal and magical circles.
Vocation: Witch Hunter & Shadow Purger
For the Perceptive: Possesses an uncanny ability to sense magical auras and trace lingering spells, making her a relentless tracker of witches.
Description: Erynn has piercing amber eyes that seem to see through lies and a cascade of dark hair tied in a warrior's braid. She wears a long leather coat reinforced with silver-threaded plating, and her utility belt brims with specialized tools for banishing and disrupting magic. Calm and deliberate, she has a no-nonsense demeanor that can be intimidating, though she is fiercely protective of innocents. Her dedication stems from a tragic event in her youth, when a witch's curse devastated her village.
Wants and Needs:
- Want: To dismantle a powerful coven that has evaded capture for decades.
- Need: To find peace from her past, learning to see herself as more than a weapon for revenge.

Secret or Obstacle: Hides her growing dependency on a charm imbued with suppressed magic, which enhances her powers but risks corrupting her.
Carrying (Total CP: 38):
- Silveredge Rapier (12 points): A blade forged with enchanted silver to disrupt dark energies with every strike.
- Censer of Purging Mist (9 points): A device that releases a thick, enchanted fog that neutralizes magic within its radius.
- Runed Shackles (10 points): Heavy restraints imbued with anti-magic glyphs to detain captured witches.
- Hunter's Focus Elixirs (7 points): Potions that heighten her reflexes and resistance to magical fatigue.

Thalin Ironspire — "Steel cuts deeper when guided by conviction." 9

Brief: A stalwart and principled witch hunter, Thalin is a former blacksmith who turned his craft into a weapon against dark magic after his family was destroyed by a sorcerer. His unyielding faith and physical strength make him a formidable adversary.
Vocation: Witch Hunter & Forgemaster Avenger
For the Perceptive: Possesses unmatched strength and endurance, along with the skill to craft improvised anti-magic weapons in the heat of battle.
Description: Thalin is a towering man with a broad frame, his arms crisscrossed with scars from years of combat and forge work. His fiery red hair and beard, streaked with ash, give him the appearance of a living ember. He wears a customized set of plate armor etched with protective runes, and his hammer swings with the force of a mountain. Though gruff and stoic, Thalin has a compassionate side, particularly toward those affected by magical curses.
Wants and Needs:
- Want: To forge a weapon powerful enough to destroy any sorcerer or magical construct.
- Need: To rebuild the community he lost, finding purpose beyond vengeance.

Secret or Obstacle: Hides a fractured relationship with his faith, doubting whether his path truly honors his family's memory.
Carrying (Total CP: 44):
- Rune-etched Warhammer (15 points): A massive weapon imbued with glyphs that disrupt and shatter magical barriers.
- Anvil of Containment (10 points): A portable enchanted device used to suppress and seal magical artifacts.
- Forged Flame Grenades (12 points): Explosive orbs that unleash searing flames capable of neutralizing magical constructs.
- Blacksmith's Toolkit (7 points): A compact set of tools for emergency repairs and improvised creations.

Kaida Stormveil — "Lightning strikes swift and true—so must we." 10

Brief: Kaida is a cunning and agile witch hunter who harnesses the power of storms to track and combat magical threats. A former thief turned crusader, she combines precision and unpredictability in her relentless pursuit of justice.
Vocation: Witch Hunter & Stormbringer Stalker
For the Perceptive: Possesses a unique connection to storm magic, allowing her to channel lightning for swift attacks.
Description: Kaida is a lithe and nimble figure with striking silver hair that crackles faintly with static and storm-gray eyes that shimmer when she channels her powers. Once a street urchin who relied on her wits and agility to survive, Kaida now channels her skills into protecting those who cannot protect themselves.
Wants and Needs:
- Want: To bring down a network of corrupt nobles secretly funding dark magical experiments.
- Need: To forgive herself for her criminal past, embracing the responsibility of her new path.

Secret or Obstacle: Hides that her storm magic grows unstable when she's under emotional duress, endangering all around her.
Carrying (Total CP: 40):
- Stormlash Whip (12 points): A weapon that crackles with lightning, allowing her to disarm or incapacitate foes.
- Tempest Compass (10 points): An enchanted device that guides her toward magical disturbances.
- Stormcaller Amulet (10 points): A pendant that enhances her control over lightning magic, though at a cost to her stamina.
- Thunderstep Boots (8 points): Footwear enchanted for incredible speed and silent movement, perfect for ambushes.

Wizards

Wizards are the scholarly spellcasters of a fantasy realm, wielding arcane magic through rigorous study and ancient tomes. Devoted to the pursuit of knowledge, they master the intricate weave of the cosmos, uncovering secrets that shape the world. Found in lofty towers, hidden libraries, or magical academies, wizards command immense power, their spells ranging from minor illusions to reality-altering transformations. Their unending quest for understanding often leads them to realms of wonder and danger, making them central figures in many adventures.

Adventurers should approach wizards with humor and caution, as their eccentricities can yield both enlightenment and chaos. A humorous tale tells of Wizzlefump the Wondrous, an eccentric wizard famous for his bizarre experiments and outlandish charms. With his wild hair, mismatched robes, and tower cluttered with oddities, Wizzlefump was beloved by townsfolk for his wisdom—but they never knew quite what to expect.

One afternoon, eager adventurers sought Wizzlefump for magical enhancements to aid their quest. Delighted by their request, he promised fantastic potions—but only if they completed a silly challenge. Tasked with bringing him the most ridiculous items they could find, the adventurers returned with treasures such as a squeaky rubber chicken and a jar of pickled eyeballs.

Cackling with glee, Wizzlefump brewed his potions, but when the adventurers drank them, hilarity ensued. One was turned into a singing frog, another sprouted chicken wings, and another grew bright orange polka dots. Instead of unmatched power, they became the town's laughingstock, croaking ballads and flapping about in absurdity.

This tale serves as a lighthearted reminder: while wizards can be sources of incredible magic and lore, whimsical ones like Wizzlefump may lead you to unexpected hilarity. Embrace the adventure with laughter, for what begins as a quest for power may leave you singing odes to potatoes in the form of a frog!

Alaric Thistlewick

"The pursuit of knowledge is the purest form of magic." **1**

Brief: A brilliant yet eccentric male wizard, is renowned for his obsessive curiosity and unyielding dedication to the arcane arts. His penchant for experimental magic often results in unintended, yet surprisingly creative, consequences.

Vocation: Master of Experimental Arcana

For the Insightful: Possesses an unparalleled ability to devise new spells by combining forgotten techniques with unorthodox materials, pushing the boundaries of traditional magic.

Description: A wiry man with wild, silver-streaked hair that seems to have a mind of its own. His vivid green eyes gleam with an intensity that can be both unnerving and inspiring. Clad in a patchwork of robes adorned with arcane symbols and ink stains, he exudes an aura of chaotic brilliance. Though his absent-minded demeanor often leads to humorous misunderstandings, his undeniable intellect and mastery of magic make him an invaluable ally.

Wants and Needs:
- Want: To uncover a groundbreaking magical discovery that will earn him recognition in the annals of arcane history.
- Need: To learn to balance his relentless pursuit of knowledge with the wisdom to foresee the potential consequences.

Secret or Obstacle: Hides the guilt of a failed experiment that caused a magical catastrophe.

Carrying (Total CP: 28):
- Spellbook (10 points): Brimming with half-finished spells and personal annotations that reflect his unorthodox methods.
- Wand of Convergence (8 points): A unique wand capable of channeling magical sources at once with unpredictable effects.
- Bag of Mystic Components (10 points): Filled with rare herbs, stones, and magical reagents gathered from his journeys.

Magnus Spellwright *"Knowledge is the fire that lights the darkness."* 2

Brief: A towering figure in the magical community, is a male wizard known for his unshakable discipline and scholarly pursuits. His meticulous study of the arcane has led him to unlock secrets long thought lost, earning him both admiration and fear.
Vocation: Scholar of Forbidden Tomes
For the Insightful: Possesses the unique ability to decipher forbidden spells without succumbing to their corrupting influence.
Description: Magnus is a broad-shouldered man with a commanding presence, his piercing blue eyes framed by silver-rimmed spectacles. His thick, dark hair is streaked with gray, and his long, elegant robes are adorned with subtle, glowing runes that shift with his movements. A solemn demeanor surrounds him, though a glimmer of wit occasionally breaks through when he engages in intellectual debates.
Wants and Needs:
- Want: To compile the ultimate tome of magical knowledge, chronicling the forgotten and forbidden for future generations.
- Need: To confront his fears of the darker side of magic and the temptations it presents.

Secret or Obstacle: Hides a cursed scar on his arm that flares with pain when he uses forbidden magic, a reminder of a past ritual gone awry.
Carrying (Total CP: 40):
- Grimoire of Lost Shadows (15 points): A heavy tome filled with forbidden spells, locked with an intricate magical seal.
- Staff of Ethereal Wards (10 points): A sturdy staff adorned with a crystal that projects powerful protective barriers.
- Runed Gauntlet of Control (8 points): Allows precise manipulation of unstable magical forces.
- Elixir of Clarity (7 points): A shimmering potion that sharpens the mind and aids in deciphering complex spells.

Cedric Starfall *"The stars guide those who dare to dream."* 3

Brief: An enigmatic male wizard, is a celestial mage who draws his power from the stars and the vastness of the cosmos. His dreamy demeanor and profound wisdom make him both a guide and an enigma to those who meet him.
Vocation: Celestial Sage
For the Insightful: Possesses the ability to harness the constellations' magic, weaving their light into potent spells that inspire awe and wonder.
Description: Cedric has a tall, slender frame, his silver hair flowing like moonlight against his deep blue robes embroidered with constellations. His violet eyes seem to hold the vastness of the night sky, and his voice carries a melodic cadence that soothes even the most troubled minds. Often gazing upward, Cedric speaks in cryptic yet insightful riddles, leaving those around him pondering their deeper meaning.
Wants and Needs:
- Want: To uncover the lost constellations that hold secrets to ancient magic.
- Need: To ground himself in the present, learning to connect with others beyond his celestial musings.

Secret or Obstacle: Hides the sorrow of a past failure when a misinterpreted celestial omen led to devastating consequences.
Carrying (Total CP: 38):
- Astrolabe of Foresight (12 points): A gilded device used to interpret celestial movements and predict future events.
- Starbound Robes (10 points): Enchanted robes that shimmer with starlight and enhance his cosmic spells.
- Wand of Stellar Embers (8 points): A slender wand tipped with a fragment of a fallen star, radiating cosmic energy.
- Scrolls of Celestial Wisdom (8 points): Ancient parchment inscribed with spells drawn from the heavens.

Thalos Ironmind *"Strength of will is the mightiest of spells."* 4

Brief: A rugged male wizard, combines the brute force of a warrior with the intellect of a spellcaster. Known for his resilience and practical approach to magic, he often channels elemental forces to devastating effect.
Vocation: Elemental Battlemage
For the Insightful: Possesses unmatched control over elemental energies, bending fire, earth, water, and air to his command with explosive precision.
Description: Thalos is a stocky, broad-chested man with a square jaw and fiery red hair tied back in a warrior's braid. His robes are reinforced with leather and steel, designed for battle as much as study, and his hands bear the callouses of both a craftsman and a mage.
Wants and Needs:
- Want: To master a long-lost elemental spell capable of reshaping entire landscapes.
- Need: To temper his impulsive nature and learn patience in his pursuit of power.

Secret or Obstacle: Hides a deep fear of losing control over the elemental forces he wields, knows the destruction it could bring.
Carrying (Total CP: 37):
- Runed Battle Staff (15 points): A hefty staff reinforced with steel and etched with runes, perfect for both casting and combat.
- Elemental Orb of Fury (12 points): A volatile artifact containing raw elemental energy, usable in dire situations.
- Armor of Flame and Frost (10 points): A set of magically enhanced armor granting resistance to both extreme heat and cold.

Orin Spellweaver
"Magic is a tapestry, and I am but a thread in its eternal design." **5**

Brief: A male wizard renowned for his intricate spellcraft, weaving enchantments that rival the beauty of nature itself. His gentle demeanor masks an unwavering dedication to understanding the finer nuances of arcane magic.

Vocation: Master Enchanter

For the Insightful: Possesses a rare talent for crafting enduring enchantments, imbuing everyday objects with extraordinary magical properties.

Description: Orin is a wiry, middle-aged man with short, silver-streaked auburn hair and a soft voice that carries the weight of wisdom. His robes are delicately embroidered with glowing geometric patterns that pulse faintly as he casts spells. Despite his calm and humble nature, Orin is haunted by a past experiment that went awry, driving his obsession with precision and control.

Wants and Needs:
- Want: To create a self-sustaining enchantment capable of protecting an entire city.
- Need: To overcome his self-doubt, which stems from a magical failure that once endangered those he cared for.

Secret or Obstacle: Hides the guilt of an old rival's downfall, fearing that his success indirectly caused their ruin.

Carrying (Total CP: 36):
- Wand of Filigree Arcana (10 points): A slender wand intricately carved to amplify enchantments with precision.
- Spellbinding Amulet (8 points): A shimmering pendant that stabilizes unstable magical flows.
- Satchel of Enchanter's Tools (10 points): A collection of fine chisels, inks, and enchanted thread for crafting magical objects.
- Journal of Arcane Blueprints (8 points): A thick, leather-bound book filled with complex enchantment designs.

Edran Stormrune
"The storm bends to my will, as must all things." **6**

Brief: A fierce male wizard who channels the raw, untamed power of storms to crush his foes and defend his allies. His imposing presence and booming voice make him as intimidating as the tempests he commands.

Vocation: Tempest Conjurer

For the Insightful: Harnesses the primal forces of thunder and lightning, summoning storms that can level entire battlefields.

Description: Edran is a tall, muscular man with wild, ash-gray hair that crackles faintly with static. His storm-gray robes are adorned with jagged lightning motifs, and his hands bear scorch marks from years of channeling raw energy. Despite his fierce exterior, he has a protective heart, often risking his safety to shield others from harm.

Wants and Needs:
- Want: To master a legendary storm spell capable of vanquishing any foe in a single strike.
- Need: To maintain control over his emotions, as his power grows dangerously unstable when he is enraged.

Secret or Obstacle: Hides the fact that his powers come at a cost—every storm he summons drains a fraction of his life force.

Carrying (Total CP: 42):
- Thunderstrike Staff (15 points): A massive staff tipped with a crystal that hums with unspent lightning.
- Gauntlets of the Maelstrom (10 points): Enchanted gloves that allow him to direct storms with precision.
- Orb of Weathered Fury (10 points): A spherical artifact that stores the energy of past storms for future use.
- Scrolls of Stormbinding (7 points): Weathered parchments containing spells to summon and control tempests.

Veyrin Duskshade
"True power lies not in light or shadow, but inbetween." **7**

Brief: A wizard who walks the delicate line between light and darkness, mastering magic that intertwines both realms. His enigmatic presence often leaves others unsure whether to trust or fear him.

Vocation: Twilight Arcanist

For the Insightful: Draws power from the twilight hours, weaving spells that blend radiant light and deep shadow for unparalleled versatility.

Description: Veyrin is a lithe figure with jet-black hair streaked with silver, his pale skin contrasting sharply with his dark, flowing robes. His piercing gray eyes seem to shift between light and dark, reflecting his inner struggle to maintain balance. Though often aloof, he carries an air of quiet wisdom that attracts those seeking guidance.

Wants and Needs:
- Want: To uncover the secrets of twilight magic and unlock its ultimate potential.
- Need: To confront the growing darkness within himself, which threatens to consume his light.

Secret or Obstacle: Hides a cursed talisman that binds him to the very shadows he seeks to control, whispering dark temptations.

Carrying (Total CP: 28):
- Staff of Dusklight (12 points): A slender staff that glows faintly with both radiant and shadowy magic.
- Talisman of Shadow's Grasp (8 points): A cursed artifact that enhances his power at the cost of his soul's purity.
- Tome of Luminous Shades (8 points): A worn book filled with spells that fuse light and shadow.

Eldrin Frostveil — *"The frost whispers secrets the fire will never know."* 8

Brief: A Eldrin Frostveil is a male wizard with an affinity for ice and snow, weaving frost into spells that are as beautiful as they are deadly. His calm demeanor belies the cold precision with which he wields his magic.

Vocation: Frost Mage

For the Insightful: Harnesses the chilling power of frost to immobilize foes and protect allies, shaping the battlefield with icy constructs.

Description: Eldrin is a tall, lean figure with icy-blue eyes and frost-kissed silver hair that falls in soft waves. His robes shimmer like freshly fallen snow, and a faint chill surrounds him at all times. Despite his frosty exterior, he has a warm heart and often uses his magic to preserve rather than destroy.

Wants and Needs:
- Want: To master the legendary spell "Winter's Heart," which can freeze entire armies in their tracks.
- Need: To let go of his obsession with perfection, as his pursuit of flawless magic blinds him to the beauty of imperfection.

Secret or Obstacle: Hides the painful memory of accidentally freezing an ally in battle, a mistake that haunts his every spell.

Carrying (Total CP: 40):
- Frostbound Staff (12 points): A staff encrusted with icy crystals, capable of summoning snowstorms.
- Cloak of Perpetual Winter (10 points): A heavy cloak that protects him from heat and enhances frost-based spells.
- Gloves of Glacial Precision (8 points): Enchanted gloves that allow for precise manipulation of frost magic.
- Tome of Eternal Frost (10 points): A book bound in ice, containing ancient frost spells and secrets.

Tharion Spellbrand — *"Knowledge is power, but wisdom is the true key to greatness."* 9

Brief: Tharion Spellbrand is a male wizard known for his scholarly pursuits, with an insatiable curiosity that drives him to uncover the universe's arcane mysteries. His deep intellect makes him a master of intricate spellcraft and magical theory.

Vocation: Arcane Scholar

For the Insightful: Specializes in decoding ancient texts and unraveling complex spells, often revealing secrets long forgotten by mortal minds.

Description: Tharion is a middle-aged man with neatly combed chestnut hair and piercing blue eyes framed by wire-rimmed spectacles. His robes are adorned with glowing runes, a testament to his relentless pursuit of arcane knowledge. Despite his brilliance, his single-mindedness often alienates him from others.

Wants and Needs:
- Want: To uncover the lost spells of an ancient civilization and immortalize their wisdom.
- Need: To find balance between his scholarly pursuits and the relationships he neglects in the process.

Secret or Obstacle: Hides a forbidden spell he accidentally discovered, fearing it could bring ruin if it falls into the wrong hands.

Carrying (Total CP: 42):
- Staff of Runes (10 points): A carved staff inscribed with glowing runes that amplify spell precision.
- Codex of Forgotten Spells (12 points): A massive tome containing powerful spells from an extinct language.
- Scrying Crystal (10 points): A perfectly cut gem that reveals hidden magical auras and veiled truths.
- Inkpot of Endless Knowledge (10 points): A magical inkpot that replenishes itself and is used for inscribing spell scrolls.

Kaelen Ironflame — *"Steel and fire are tools; magic bends them to my will."* 10

Brief: Kaelen Ironflame is a male wizard who blends his blacksmithing roots with fiery arcane magic, forging enchanted weapons that rival the strength of dragons. His unorthodox methods make him a visionary in his craft.

Vocation: Runeforger

For the Insightful: Combines the power of fire magic with the precision of runecrafting, creating enchanted weapons and armor.

Description: Kaelen is a broad-shouldered man with fiery red hair tied back in a loose braid and a rugged appearance that reflects his blacksmithing background. His robes are singed and patched, a testament to his fiery experiments. Though brash and stubborn, his loyalty to his friends is as unyielding as the steel he forges.

Wants and Needs:
- Want: To forge a weapon capable of slaying a mythical dragon.
- Need: To temper his recklessness, as his bold experiments often lead to catastrophic failures.

Secret or Obstacle: Hides his fear that his creations might fall into the wrong hands, turning his gifts into tools of destruction.

Carrying (Total CP: 38):
- Forgeheart Staff (15 points): A heavy staff with a molten core, channeling fire magic into devastating attacks.
- Runesmith's Hammer (12 points): A hammer used to inscribe runes onto metal with precision and power.
- Runic Forging Manual (11 points): A charred book containing the secrets of combining smithing with arcane runes.

Alaric Voidweaver — 11
"The stars are not just lights—they are doorways to infinity."

Brief: Alaric Voidweaver is a male wizard who studies the mysteries of the cosmos, channeling celestial energy into his spells to warp space and time. His fascination with the heavens fuels his relentless quest for enlightenment.

Vocation: Celestial Arcanist

For the Insightful: Harnesses cosmic magic to manipulate gravity and summon celestial phenomena, creating dazzling and destructive effects.

Description: Alaric is a wiry man with jet-black hair streaked with silver, resembling starlight. His robes are dark and embroidered with shimmering constellations that seem to move. His piercing gray eyes shine with an otherworldly intensity, often unsettling those who meet his gaze. Despite his aloof demeanor, he carries empathy for the mortal struggles he observes.

Wants and Needs:
- Want: To unlock the secrets of an ancient star-bound relic rumored to grant cosmic omniscience.
- Need: To reconcile his detachment from earthly concerns, as his celestial focus often blinds him to the needs of those around him.

Secret or Obstacle: Fears that his meddling with cosmic forces may one day open a portal to something humanity is not ready to face.

Carrying (Total CP: 46):
- Astrolabe Staff (15 points): A gilded staff topped with an enchanted model of a star system that projects gravitational waves.
- Celestial Tome (12 points): A book that glows faintly, containing spells of cosmic manipulation and prophecy.
- Orbiting Stones (9 points): Floating enchanted stones that deflect attacks and channel his spells.
- Stargazer's Lens (10 points): A crystal monocle that reveals hidden constellations and celestial alignments.

Darion Emberglow — 12
"Fire brings destruction, but also warmth—it's all about how you wield it."

Brief: A wizard who wields fire magic with passionate precision, believing that fire is both a weapon and a tool for creation. His fiery nature is matched by his fervent loyalty to his companions.

Vocation: Pyromancer

For the Insightful: Specializes in flame-based spells, conjuring infernos that scorch enemies or forge protective barriers of fire.

Description: Darion is a muscular man with short, flame-colored hair and ember-like freckles dotting his tanned skin. His robes are accented with fiery orange and red patterns, constantly smoldering at the edges but never burning through. His confident smile and booming laugh make him as warm as the flames he commands.

Wants and Needs:
- Want: To craft a spell that can reignite dying volcanoes, restoring life to barren lands.
- Need: To control his impulsiveness, as his fiery temper often lands him in trouble.

Secret or Obstacle: Carries guilt over a fire spell gone wrong in his youth, which devastated a village and left him scarred emotionally.

Carrying (Total CP: 38):
- Blazewrought Staff (12 points): A staff tipped with a molten crystal, channeling intense heat for devastating fire spells.
- Phoenix Charm (8 points): A pendant that revives its wearer once in a fiery burst if they fall in battle.
- Cloak of Embers (10 points): A fireproof cloak that trails harmless sparks, protecting him from flame damage.
- Ignition Scrolls (8 points): A collection of pre-inscribed fire spells for emergencies.

Faelric Runeveil — 13
"Runes are the language of creation; let me teach you to speak it."

Brief: A wizard who combines traditional spellcasting with intricate rune magic, carving arcane symbols that unleash powerful effects. His meticulous nature ensures that his runes are as elegant as they are effective.

Vocation: Runic Sage

For the Insightful: Masters the art of inscribing runes on surfaces to create traps, enchantments, and powerful wards.

Description: Faelric is a middle-aged man with salt-and-pepper hair, neatly trimmed, and sharp blue eyes that exude intelligence. His robes are adorned with glowing runes that shift and rearrange themselves as he moves. A steady and calm presence, he often speaks in measured tones, emphasizing thoughtfulness in every word.

Wants and Needs:
- Want: To compile a definitive guide to all rune magic, preserving the knowledge for future generations.
- Need: To break free from his reliance on logic, learning to trust his instincts in unpredictable situations.

Secret or Obstacle: Fears that his runes, if deciphered by others, could be weaponized in ways he cannot control.

Carrying (Total CP: 44):
- Runic Etcher's Staff (12 points): A staff tipped with a sharp point for carving runes into any material.
- Glyphstone Codex (14 points): A tome containing hundreds of runes, glowing faintly with stored energy.
- Sigil-Carving Kit (8 points): A set of tools designed for precise rune crafting on various surfaces.
- Amulet of Arcane Balance (10 points): An enchanted amulet that stabilizes volatile magical effects.

Eldrin Mistcloak 14
"Magic is a dance, and I am its choreographer."

Brief: Eldrin Mistcloak is a male wizard whose mastery of illusion magic weaves reality and fantasy into a seamless tapestry, confounding foes and delighting allies. Known for his theatrical flair, he uses his talents to inspire awe and manipulate perceptions.

Vocation: Illusionist

For the Insightful: Specializes in conjuring vivid illusions that deceive the senses and mislead enemies, as well as creating phantasmal constructs to aid in battle.

Description: Eldrin is a tall, wiry man with silvery hair that falls to his shoulders and pale blue eyes that glimmer with mischief. His flowing robes shimmer like mist in the sunlight, constantly shifting and blending with his surroundings. Eldrin carries an air of playful arrogance, speaking in riddles and often punctuating his words with dramatic gestures.

Wants and Needs:
- Want: To craft the ultimate illusion spell, one so real it could rewrite memories.
- Need: To learn the value of truth, as his reliance on deception often alienates those closest to him.

Secret or Obstacle: Fears that his illusions may one day trap him in a world where he can no longer discern reality from fantasy.

Carrying (Total CP: 42):
- Mirrorbound Staff (12 points): A staff capped with an enchanted mirror that amplifies and refracts his illusions.
- Cloak of Shifting Veils (10 points): A cloak that renders him nearly invisible when he moves.
- Deck of Phantasms (8 points): A magical deck of cards that conjure realistic illusions when thrown.
- Gleamstone Orb (12 points): A crystal orb that projects dazzling lights to disorient enemies and enhance his spells.

Thalric Ironflare 15
"Steel bends to strength; magic bends to will."

Brief: Thalric Ironflare is a male wizard who merges arcane mastery with smithing prowess, forging enchanted weapons and armor that hum with magical energy. His unique blend of magic and metallurgy sets him apart as both a craftsman and a combatant.

Vocation: Arcane Smith

For the Insightful: Excels in enchanting equipment, using fire and lightning magic to imbue weapons with destructive power or fortify armor with protective wards.

Description: Thalric is a broad-shouldered man with a mane of fiery red hair and a thick beard streaked with ash. His leather apron is etched with runic symbols, and his hands are calloused from years of wielding both hammer and spell. Despite his gruff exterior, his deep voice carries a warmth that inspires trust among those who work alongside him.

Wants and Needs:
- Want: To create a legendary weapon that will be remembered for generations.
- Need: To overcome his fear of losing control over his creations, as he knows the destruction they could cause in the wrong hands.

Secret or Obstacle: Harbors guilt over an enchanted blade he once forged, which was used in a war to devastating effect.

Carrying (Total CP: 48):
- Forgehammer of Embers (15 points): A massive hammer that channels fire magic to shape both steel and enemies.
- Runed Gauntlets (12 points): Gauntlets that enhance his spellcasting and protect him from magical feedback.
- Tome of Arcane Crafting (10 points): A heavy book filled with instructions for enchanting weapons and armor.
- Flask of Liquid Flame (11 points): A volatile potion that can be used as a weapon or to fuel his forge in emergencies.

"In cloaks of stars and runes they dwell, wizards weave both light and hell. Their minds are deep, their hands are flame; tread lightly near, lest you be claimed."

– Thalen Fireweaver, Sage of the Arcane Veil

"Oh, list to my song of a tome most divine,
With characters plenty for quests to ignite.
From heroes to villains, their stories entwine,
To aid clever GMs in weaving the night.
A blacksmith who whispers of blades cursed with woe,
A princess disguised, her kingdom at stake.
An innkeeper sly, with tales she won't show,
Each name in the tome, a tale to awake.
Five hundred and one, a feast for the mind,
With quirks and ambitions, with secrets untold.
This book is a treasure for those who would find,
Adventures unbounded, more precious than gold.
So wield it with glee, this tome in your hand,
Let quests be emboldened, let stories expand.
"

– Cedric Quillsong, Bard of the Eternal Ballad

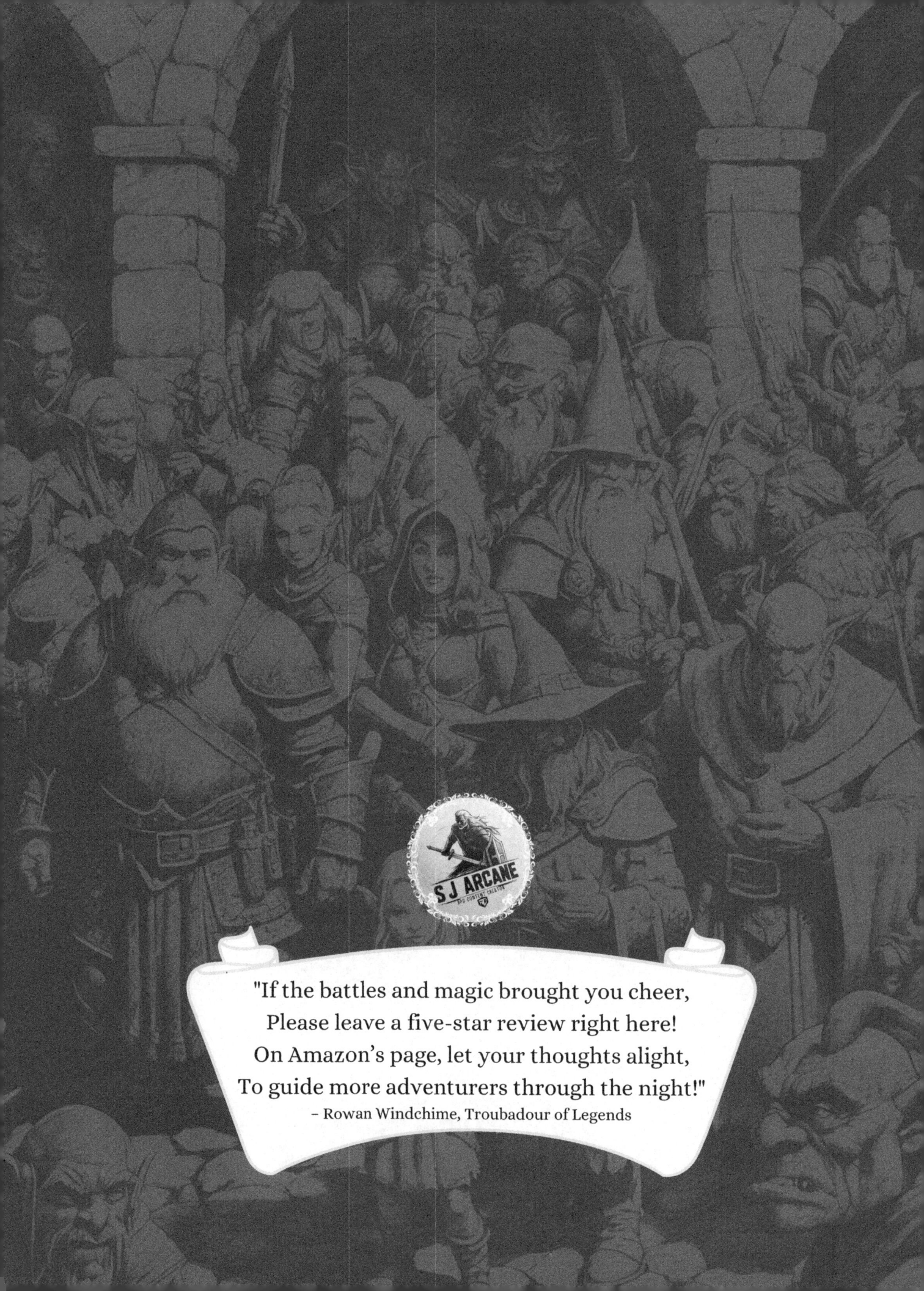

"If the battles and magic brought you cheer,
Please leave a five-star review right here!
On Amazon's page, let your thoughts alight,
To guide more adventurers through the night!"
– Rowan Windchime, Troubadour of Legends

Made in the USA
Columbia, SC
10 February 2025